THE FORENSIC FILES of BATMAN ™

ALSO AVAILABLE

THE SCIENCE OF SUPERMAN
by Mark Wolverton

COMING SOON

GREEN LANTERN: SLEEPERS, BOOK 1
by Christopher J. Priest and Mike Baron

THE FORENSIC FILES of BATMAN™

THE WORLD'S GREATEST DETECTIVE

DOUG MOENCH

BATMAN CREATED BY

BOB KANE

ibooks

NEW YORK
WWW.IBOOKS.NET

An Original Publication of ibooks, inc.

An ibooks, inc. Book

Distributed by Simon & Schuster, Inc.
1230 Avenue of the Americas, New York, NY 10020

ibooks, inc.
24 West 25th Street
New York, NY 10010

The ibooks World Wide Web site address is:
http://www.ibooks.net

The DC Comics World Wide Web site address is:
www.dccomics.com

ISBN 0-7434-8732-x

First ibooks, inc. printing June 2004
10 9 8 7 6 5 4 3 2 1

Edited by Howard Zimmerman
Jacket illustration by Alex Ross
Jacket design by Georg Brewer/DC Comics
Interior design by Dean Motter

Printed in the U.S.A.

Contents

For Winnie, Gil, Pam,
Debra, and Derek

Acknowledgments

If every manuscript is written alone, no book comes into being without the unsung efforts of an entire team behind the scenes. Time to sing.

First gratitude goes to Byron Preiss for the wisdom of his upfront choice. (And you don't look so mangy either.) Howard Zimmerman proved immediately receptive to the author's every left-field notion and backed them all. The fearless Commander then edited the manuscript with both perspicacity and restraint. Several helpful suggestions and only one donnybrook. Wow.

Perpetually overworked Charlie Kochman nevertheless found time for the best pep talk an author could receive—and then went over the manuscript one more time on behalf of DC Comics. John Nee, of DC's licensing department, helpfully opened the way. And Steve Korte kept the way open. As a mere glance at the cover makes evident, Alex Ross painted his little brush off to put our best face forward. Georg Brewer integrated that painting with all the other necessary elements to create an impressive cover design. Whereupon Dean Motter slipped inside to provide the nifty interior design. And, as in any endeavor involving the Batman, gratitude must go to Bob Kane and Bill Finger. Without them, the Dark Knight Detective would not exist, leaving many a baffling and bizarre crime unsolved.

Thanks also to a great good friend Julie Schwartz, the legendary editor who wisely gave the Batman a redefining boost just when times demanded.

Put it all together and here we are. Thanks to all.

Doug Moench
February 2004

KEY TO FORENSICS ICONS

Note: Each casefile has been coded with icons specific to the evidence in the case for quick visual reference. This forensic evidence represents the information available to the Batman at the beginning of each investigation or as later determined.

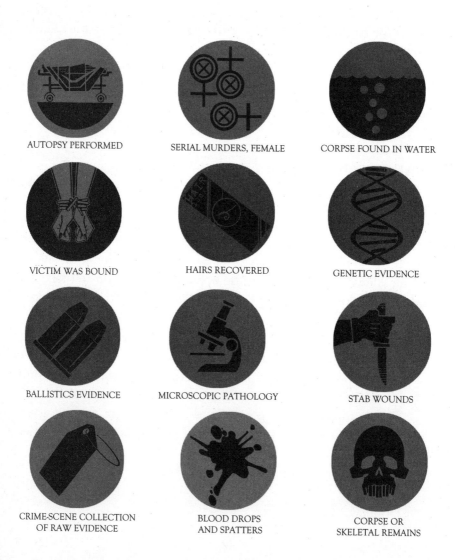

AUTOPSY PERFORMED

SERIAL MURDERS, FEMALE

CORPSE FOUND IN WATER

VICTIM WAS BOUND

HAIRS RECOVERED

GENETIC EVIDENCE

BALLISTICS EVIDENCE

MICROSCOPIC PATHOLOGY

STAB WOUNDS

CRIME-SCENE COLLECTION
OF RAW EVIDENCE

BLOOD DROPS
AND SPATTERS

CORPSE OR
SKELETAL REMAINS

POWDER BURNS

FINGERPRINT EVIDENCE

CAT BURGLER

EXPLOSIVE DEVICE USED

VICTIM HANGED

CRIME SCENE SET AFIRE

EVIDENCE OF ARSON

BLUNT TRAUMA

HANDGUN USED

DENTAL PATHOLOGY

ENTAMOLOGICAL EVIDENCE:
INSECT INFESTATION
OF CORPSE

THE FORENSIC FILES OF BATMAN

"When a man dies, a world passes away."

-Heraclitus

Prologue: Secret Files

Alfred,

You were right.

The close call after last night's Arkham Asylum debacle, as you tried to stress in no uncertain terms, was indeed an object lesson in mortality. No one, not even the Batman, lives forever. Consider this note, therefore, to be a covert clause in Bruce Wayne's last will and testament.

I have been compiling secret accounts of the Bat's more important or interesting experiences to date. Begun more or less as diary entries, including some written as a youth struggling to reach an uncertain future, these writings were originally meant for private and personal use only.

Once our collaborative enterprise actually began, however, I realized a larger potential. The entries became more detailed even as they evolved into "subjective casefiles" containing certain insights, all with value for the future. Should the Batman survive long enough to retire, I will decide the fate of these files personally. The vague intent is to somehow share them, perhaps in sanitized form with a crime historian, or even as they stand, with a "successor" if one ever comes to exist. The latter chance, of course, is probably remote. And yet, other than mortality, who knows what the future may hold or how this ongoing mission will end?

Should it terminate abruptly, on the other hand, I'm afraid the care and ultimate dispensation of these documents falls to you. Feel free to add any of your own insights that may have value.

Some of the passages are admittedly melodramatic, but they were written while the experiences were fresh and impressions vivid. It felt *important to convey both. Threaded through all the subjective blood and thunder, more important, the accounts convey useful information about criminology in general, as well as detailed data regarding specific forensics tools and techniques. These aspects illustrate the importance of the smallest clue and slightest trace of evidence. Placed within their context of actual cases, they further show how unknown murderers were identified and apprehended. In certain cases, they even demonstrate how additional deaths were prevented.*

This is what it's all about, obviously—the whole point of our shared mission. And last night aside, old friend, we've done fairly well thus far. If anyone eventually benefits from our experience, if just one future victim is spared, all the better.

You can find the material in the south cavern wall's evidence storage, third vault drawer from the left, bottom row. If and when our secret no longer matters, feel free to share some or all of these accounts, notes, and casefiles at your discretion and with whomever you deem most appropriate.

As things stand right now into the foreseeable future, my own obvious choice would be Police Commissioner James Gordon.

Thank you,
B.W.

Introduction: Crime Most Foul

From the Private Files of Bruce Wayne

MURDER is the ultimate arrogance, the one crime transcending all others by monstrously erasing its victim. It is also the foul deed that forever altered my future, shaped my sole reason for living. Having felt its effect and feeling it still, I know it to be permanent. I cannot escape murder, and I can never forget its horror. Murder will never leave my mind. I loathe this ultimate evil, and I must always remember why.

I am both the sole survivor and the third victim of a horrific double killing. It happened when I was still a child, just a child, but the blood remains more vivid than the broken glass strewn across the carpet of this room. I can still see that blood flowing from the two people I loved and needed most, spilling into the filth of that alley, the fabric of precious life fouled and forever lost. And I can still hear the fatal gunshots, awful explosions cracking the night without warning to destroy my world.

The shock of those sounds haunts my mind and their finality obsesses my soul. Once fired, I knew even as a child, those gunshots could never be silenced. They continue to echo through my waking mind and invade my sleep with nightmares that will never end. They are the harsh, ugly sounds that marked a terrible turning point, slamming the door on every bright tomorrow to lock me in a darkness with no dawn. They are the sounds of hell, transforming hope into tragedy by dashing life into death.

One moment I was whole and secure in the company of my parents, a child deeply loved and loving, and the next moment I stood shattered and alone. Instantly helpless, I was unable to stop the blood. I could do nothing to turn back the clock and make things right. I could only scream as I watched my mother die, watched my father die, and I could only scream some more as their killer ran free through the night.

He came out of nowhere, a figure of dark menace stepping from deep shadows with a black gun heavy in his hand. The first bullet struck my father as he attempted to protect his wife and son. I remember the spit of bright fire. Then another, and my mother fell too. Somehow the man with the gun was gone, back into the shadows, back to nowhere, leaving me all alone and completely broken. Screaming and screaming again over the two bodies bleeding and dying in the filth where they had fallen.

There was no one to pursue their killer, and his crime of murder was never solved. I don't know which is worse—what he did or the fact that he escaped it, perhaps to murder again. His freedom became the prison of my mind and soul.

I was the sole survivor of that night, and yet the death of my parents also took me, erasing whatever I might have become had they lived to see me reach that point. In a very real sense, then, I died along with them. And yet, although I hardly knew it at the time, I was also reborn, my shockingly altered life lurched onto a new track of vital purpose and pounding urgency.

Murder most foul. It killed a child's father and stole his mother, leaving him lost in the darkness. No other child, and no other adult, should ever suffer the same. It is a truth more real and obvious than any other. Even as a child I knew the power of that truth, if only dimly, and even as a child I decided to act on my terrible knowledge. If only vaguely.

At first I simply wanted to strike back, to "beat up the bad

guy" and stop him from ever being bad again. And so I began
with physical training, lifting heavy weights and running end-
less miles, stoking my young body's strength even as I built its
stamina, always chasing a dark figure through imagined shadows. The goal was simple—to overtake the man with the gun, to
corner him, and deal with him. Harshly.

I learned and practiced all the martial arts, using my inherited wealth to hire the best trainers available, doubling their
fees when they agreed to drive me hard. I learned calisthenics,
acrobatics, gymnastics, honing my reflexes, acquiring every skill
the human form can master. I grew fast and hard in a body
beyond my years.

But it was all physical, as Alfred Pennyworth pointed out
to me. As my late parents' butler, Alfred helped me lay them to
rest. And then, when they were under the ground, he became
my guardian and best friend, nagging constantly and sometimes
caustically, never letting me neglect my schoolwork, always
keeping my obsession in check. I often resented Alfred for it,
but I knew he was right and so I loved him, too, even through
the red and black haze of that alley. Without him I probably
would have spun all the way out of control, never to find my
way back, or any way back. With him, I remained driven but
disciplined, anchored to vital reality through his sternness and
arch humor, my soul tempered by his firm kindness and steadfast humanity.

As a youth, I owed much to Alfred, perhaps everything,
and as a man my debt is no less.

At some point, prompted by one of Alfred's mordant
observations, I came to understand that I was literally remaking
myself. I'd known it all along, of course, but never before so
clearly or consciously. It came with the shock of epiphany, the
wonder of revelation. I was preparing my body for that which I
had been unable to do at the most crucial time in my parents'
lives and in my life too. They were gone now. Haunting my

memory, they could do nothing more. But I was still here, still above the ground, and in their memory I had to act.

To do so I was forging my body into an instrument that could preserve life by warding off death. By stopping murder.

Alfred made me see the process for what it was, and his insight also revealed its flaw. Before I could beat up the bad guy, I realized, it was necessary to learn who he was. The shadows through which I chased were merely remembered or only imagined, the real trail long cold. There was no way to corner the bad guy with speed and strength alone. I had to identify him, track him, pursue him, and ultimately locate him.

Detection was the key. Without it, no amount of physical prowess would get me anywhere. And so I began to train my mind just as hard as I worked my body—and well beyond the Alfred-nagged bounds of schoolwork. If solving the crime was the only way to stop the criminal, I vowed, then I would explore and master every possible path to solution. I would learn basic detective methods as well as the specialized techniques of forensic deduction, and I would learn them all. Cold.

The extent of my commitment, exposing the depth of my obsession, astonished even me as I embarked on a program of rigorous research. Everything was connected, I quickly discovered, nothing too far afield. I studied every conceivable aspect of criminology, pathology, and profiling, all the cross-discipline applications of every useful area of knowledge imaginable— anatomy, odontology, acoustics, chemistry, entomology, physics, ballistics, serology, toxicology, geology, psychology, molecular biology, fingerprinting, DNA typing, anthropology, even archeology and more, each and every one of the many separate but interrelated sciences of forensic discipline.

At first I understood the word "forensic" only intuitively and by context, learning its actual meaning through the brief history lesson of an ancient crime—the conspiracy murder of Julius Caesar by twenty-three Roman senators. Were all twenty-three to strike a blow, the senators reasoned, no individual among them could be held guilty. But the physician Antistius decided to prove them wrong. By examining the scene of the crime and its best evidence—Caesar's corpse with its twenty-three separate stab wounds, detailing their different depths, directions, and degrees of force—Antistius exposed the conspiracy and proved all twenty-three senators guilty. His postmortem analysis was delivered in testimony to the Roman Forum, hence the word forensic, Latin for "before the forum."

I have never forgotten this ancient exercise in forensics, and never will. Even now its lesson is clear. Only by analyzing the crime can it be understood. Only by understanding a murder can it be solved. And only by solving it can its perpetrator be identified and brought to justice, and future crimes thereby prevented.

Each night in my city, lives are cut short, souls smothered, futures denied. Each night in Gotham, innocent people fall prey to those guilty of murder. Like Antistius, I have decided that I cannot let such deeds stand. I have determined that something must be done, some form of action taken.

And tonight, sitting here in the study, looking back on all my long preparations, I knew I was finally ready. The training and learning will never end, my mind and body dedicated to processes that are by nature ongoing. Maintaining peak physical ability and conditioning is crucial, as is remaining abreast of cutting-edge forensic developments, if not ahead of them. The time had come to use that which I have acquired, deployed by that which I have become. Confident that both are now enough, I was finally ready to dare the darkness and face its demons.

But how?

It was the same question I have so often pondered in recent weeks. Lacking a definitive answer, I knew only that I must operate on the same level as the demons, on equal terms and somehow in secrecy, stealing their edge to counter their power. I had to become something beyond a policeman, transcending a detective, superior to a manhunter. I had to become all of the above, and more. Something new and previously unknown.

But what?

And right then I received the answer, literally crashing through the window into my thoughts. Stunned or crazed, the black bat jerked and swooped through the study's bright light—the sign and the inspiration I needed, the one element missing from my bold and radical scheme. Its recognition was charged with both shock and thrill. This, I instantly knew, was the face and the form of the new entity I must become. A creature of the night, but serving light rather than darkness, preying not on death but on killers.

Stripped of the power stolen from shadows, criminals tend to be superstitious and cowardly. Just as tonight's intruding bat shocked and frightened me, so will its image frighten them. I will steal and rule the night, terrifying its killers deep within their own darkness.

And so the lone lost bat has given me a great gift, the shape of my future, showing me the sure way forward. There is even a cavern, a vast and secret space, hidden directly under this manor on the hill. Just as Bruce Wayne's face will be masked with the fierce visage of a bat, so will the Bat's cave remain masked by Bruce Wayne's wealth. And from this night forward, I will exploit both. Two starkly contrasting identities, light and dark, inhabiting two very different spaces: one mundane and out in the open, the other mysterious and underground; one identity concealed and secretly funded by the public persona of the other. So long as it is never suspected, the two entities never linked, their symbiosis will work.

The cave can be converted to a sanctuary, a base, and a crime lab equipped by Bruce Wayne with all the forensic tools required to identify murderers. And the Batman will then use those tools to pursue murderers and prevent them from killing again. Descending from the light of this manor, Bruce Wayne will transform into a dark and fearsome avenging angel. If my future resembles a form of madness, and surely it does, it will nevertheless be orchestrated by cool rationality and always driven by same.

In the name of my murdered parents, in memory of Thomas and Martha Wayne, and in honor of their tragically ended lives, I will use their inherited resources and do everything in my power to see that others need not share their fate. Born of horror and shaped by loss, I will become the darkest angel any night has ever held, hellbent on sparing others the same horror and loss.

Murder. There is no crime more foul. I despise its perpetrators. Using every means and method of detection, every forensic tool at my disposal, and every fiber of my physical being, I will solve murders and stop murderers.

Despite all my best efforts, I can never turn back the clock to make things right. But as the Batman, soon to enter Gotham's dark quarters and deep shadows, I can and will prevent future wrongs by opposing death every night for the rest of my forever-altered life.

That is the vow I will bring to my parents' graves, the same vow I will take to my own.

Every Contact
Leaves a Trace

24

Casefile #0017
Year One, Month Three, Day Seventeen

From the Private Files of the Batman

IN 1910, the French criminologist Dr. Edmond Locard observed that every criminal brings something to his crime scene and also takes something away, either inadvertently or by deliberate theft. Some of that which is brought to the crime scene is left behind as trace evidence—clothing fibers, fallen or pulled hair, shed or scraped flakes of skin, deposited skin oil, grit, powder, fingerprints, bullet casings, a fallen button or discarded cigarette butt, soil from a shoe or simply the shoe's print, saliva or semen, even a bite mark. Excluding obvious valuables or trophies, that which a criminal takes away may include a victim's speck of blood or strand of hair. Locard further argued that each and every bit of trace evidence offers a clue to its source, if not a direct route to the precise identity of criminal or victim, and Locard was right.

Yet by its nature, much trace evidence is easily overlooked if not literally invisible to the naked eye. Furthermore, evidence initially missed is forever lost, whether swept away or otherwise removed from the scene, deteriorated over time, or contaminated by subsequent contact. The search for it, then, must be painstaking and conducted as quickly as possible, and everything found must be preserved as relevant until proven otherwise and eliminated.

Locard's elegantly logical maxim forms the cornerstone of modern criminal investigation, which is pursued through the forensic harvesting, analysis, identification, and matching of such trace evidence from both sources, victim and suspect, crime scene and arrest scene. And the "related suspect scene," meaning home, hideout, workplace, or vehicle, if and when actual arrest occurred elsewhere.

I have embarked on what I hope will be a long-term enterprise. Given its lifelong goal, I have not ventured far on my newly charted course. It is still fairly early in this ongoing mission undertaken by the Batman. Still, more than any other case thus far, this one—just completed—demonstrates the simple genius of Locard's famous premise.

It began when a keen mind was teased and troubled by vague suspicions. Due to the relatively young ages of the deceased, a string of heart attack deaths hinted at something beyond natural causes. In response, Gotham Police Commissioner James Gordon directed Homicide Detective Harvey Bullock to review the coroner's report and investigate the backgrounds of the deceased. When Bullock's preliminary findings brought the vague suspicions into sharper focus, Gordon decided to seek further assistance at an unlikely place and from an unorthodox source.

I was just south of the wharves, two hours into a disappointing night of nothing but a single inept mugger. Having just scaled the wall of a warehouse to survey the surrounding area from its roof, I saw the shaft of strong light slash the darkness, stabbing diagonally upward to project a distorted emblem onto low-scudding clouds. It was the image of a bat, rising from the main signal rather than the smaller portable one. I cast a weighted line from the roof's edge. When it wrapped around a street lamp's spar, I tugged the line tight and leaped into space, swinging from the warehouse toward the signal beacon's source, not a crime scene, but the high roof of police headquarters.

"Gordon."

He started with a grunt, turning from the roof's far parapet to face me. "There you are," he said. "Out of nowhere with no warning." Stepping to the large klieg beacon, he threw its switch to kill the signal. "As usual."

"Trouble?"

"Feels like," Gordon said, "but maybe not." He took a step away from the doused beacon. "A cop sometimes sees crime even where it's not."

"A good cop verifies."

"Which I've done," Gordon said, "as far as I can. Officially."

"But not as far as possible. Unofficially."

Gordon shrugged. We faced each other across the dark roof, twenty paces apart. I stood my ground in the gloom and waited.

So did Gordon, but with less patience. He finally shook his head, as if resigned to the reality of a human bat but still not accustomed to it, perhaps still intimidated by it. Then he told me about the recent spike in heart attack fatalities, followed by the gist of Bullock's report.

"Out of the seven deceased," he said, "four played on the same high school football team at the same time."

"Making them the same age at time of death."

Gordon nodded. "Just twenty-eight—far too young to die."

"Any other connections?"

"Just that all four lived and died in Gotham. And the other three served on the same Board of Directors for Gotham University."

"And these three were presumably older?"

"Forties and fifties."

"Making their heart attacks somewhat less suspicious."

"But with no history of heart problems," Gordon said, "still too young to die."

"Murder." The word sounded cold, harsh, obscene.

"Wish I knew." He was clearly troubled. "It's my job to find out."

"Time frame?"

"Roughly five weeks from first death to seventh."

"Did the high school football players attend Gotham University?"

"None of the four."

"And no other links between them and the university regents?"

"All were male, and all resided in the Gotham area," Gordon said. "That's it, at least on the surface."

"Time to dig deeper."

Gordon turned away, reaching for something beyond the signal beacon. His hand came back with a thin file folder. "Detective Bullock's report," he said, "along with the death certificates."

Neither of us moved. "No full autopsies?"

"Just routine toxicology. Different doctor in each case, each facing an unusually young heart attack, but all of them unaware of the other deaths."

"So they all signed off on natural causes."

"They may have paused a bit, but in the end there was no real reason to suspect anything else. People do drop dead, occasionally even young people. The only truly suspicious element is the number of deaths and their concentration in time and place."

"Plus they were all heart failures." The wind stiffened, stirring my cloak. It billowed to the side, then snapped behind me. "If they were also murders, they may share the same modus operandi." I looked out over the darkness between the city's lights, wondering how many killers the shadows held and if I would soon face a new one.

"If we're right to suspect the worst," Gordon said, "I'd bet it's definitely the same M.O. But damned if I know what it could be."

"The most recent death?"

"Three days ago." He paused. "Scratch that. Three *nights* ago."

"Either way, sifting the scenes at this point might not turn up much."

"Probably not. But I could find some pretext to have each of the premises vacated for an hour or two. Arrange a look. Given enough notice, that is."

I held my distance and so did the police commissioner. We'd come to an agreement and an arrangement, two under-standings discussed only once, both of them unofficial and secret. We would work closely but never get close. If I became careless, I could not and would not expect Gordon to pick up the pieces.

He was still holding the file folder, searching my mask, waiting but already knowing. It would be an investigation prompted by odds and nothing else, no witnesses, no evidence, no confession. But there was a fair chance that murders had been committed. Evidence might exist, just waiting to be found. Any good cop would need no more than that, and the commissioner knew I needed even less.

"I'll look into it. Let you know."

Gordon nodded. The wind had died. Not wanting to approach me, he let the file folder drop to the roof at his feet, then briskly angled from the darkened signal toward the stair-well kiosk, perhaps headed home but probably back to his office for more work. When he was gone, I crossed the roof to the file folder and picked it up.

At the workstation in the cave (with Alfred's prepared sandwich untouched and shoved to the side), I read Bullock's brief report and compared the seven death certifications. As Gordon had warned, they were the simple standard forms used for death by natural causes. Several of the physicians were evidently puzzled and somewhat troubled, going out of their way to append notations of medical history. No heart defects, no prior indications of coronary thrombosis or occlusion, cholesterol levels within acceptable range. The doctors were claiming cardiac arrest while seeing no reason for hearts to seize.

Toxicology results were all essentially negative. Slightly elevated blood alcohol in two of the seven but nothing beyond a few beers or glasses of wine. No drugs or any other foreign substances, at least none of those routinely detected. Rare or elusive poisons remained a possibility.

In five of the seven certifications, gross facial features were noted, grimaces suggesting abrupt shock. Hardly unusual when the onset of chest pain is both acute and sudden. But still. . . .

I closed the folder and gazed off deep into the cave. Formations of merged stalactites and stalagmites framed the rustlings of unseen bats in the blackness beyond my light. I listened and wondered.

What did those dead faces actually express? Was it simply pain? Or was there some fear as well? Were the victims somehow *scared* to death?

I harvested the first scene that night, with no need to alert Gordon. It was the apartment where a former football player had lived and died alone, not yet subleased. Next of kin had been contacted but had not yet come, which meant the man's apartment remained uncleaned, his furniture and belongings still *in situ*. Of all seven death scenes, this one was therefore the least contaminated and would hold the most evidence.

Sliding the sprung window high, I immediately reached for the nose-rebreather in my belt. The body had been found near the coffee table between couch and television, but only after several days, and the smell of death lingered thickly. With the breathing filter in place, I gently punched out the screen and slipped through the window.

Just inside, I stood in the darkness to get its feel, letting my eyes adjust, cinching my gloves tighter, wondering if murder had been committed in this room. I moved cautiously forward, touching no switches, using only a halogen penlight held low.

Ten feet from the couch and coffee table, I went down on hands and knees to address the carpet before stepping closer. Inch by inch, holding the light in my teeth, I retrieved dust, lint, fuzz, crumbs, tiny bits of glittering grit, a small fragment of what appeared to be dried plant stem, and many dead flies— everything visible. Each find was sealed in its own small zip-top glassine bag, labeled with the coordinates of a rough mental grid. After each arm's length of carpet, I switched to the high-power hand vacuum. After some thirty minutes, with the carpet picked and suctioned clean, it was safe to stand and move freely.

I took everything from the coffee table—magazines, ashtray, ashes, butts, remote control, coasters, beer can, keys, and more dead flies—bagging each separately and tagging each bag. Then I used a magnifying lens and tweezers to extract hairs from the couch fabric, along with a few sample fibers and every other fiber that looked foreign.

Next came the widened search, outward from the couch to comb the rest of the apartment, inspecting drawers, cabinets, cupboards, shelves. The refrigerator was almost empty, as was the medicine chest. I found little of interest and bagged only a few items, knowing they were almost certainly irrelevant but wishing to overlook nothing.

Given the nature of death, whether induced by murder or natural causes, I did not expect to find any of the dead man's blood. And yet if murder had occurred, it may have been preceded by a struggle. Since the dead man's body bore no wounds or bruising, any such struggle would have been slight, but there was still a remote chance that some of the *perpetrator's* blood had been left at the scene. Although the normal penlight showed nothing, the presence of blood is not always visible in small traces or when scrubbed away. Just to be thorough, I sprayed Luminol, which reacts with even tiny amounts of hemoglobin, then subjected the sprayed areas to a separate ultraviolet penlight. Struggle or not, nothing was revealed.

Finally, I dusted every likely surface in the apartment, working methodically through the two rooms plus kitchenette and bath. It took more than two hours. As always, most of what the dust revealed consisted of worthless smudges. I ignored them. Also as always, most of the good prints, hand and finger, were only partials. I concentrated on those with at least five identifier points, carefully lifting each print with cellophane tape, then transferring the tape onto sheets of cardstock.

Then I gathered the meager harvest, killed my small light, and left. Closing the sprung window behind me, I bagged the contaminated rebreather. The cool air was a relief from the lingering aura of death. Breathing deeply, I unhitched my line from the fire escape rail and swung off through the night, feeling alive and quickened.

After notifying Gordon the next day, I visited the other six vacated scenes early that night and the next. With every scene long since cleaned, contaminated, or both, the pickings were even slimmer. I took what little I found.

Alfred attended me in the cave's well-lit workstation area, arraying the bagged samples across the large lab bench. He organized them into seven groups, one for each death scene.

"No luck with the prints, sir?"

Finished at the computer, I crossed toward the lab bench. "None."

Every identifiable fingerprint was either matched to the deceased or remained unknown, with no matched prints common to two or more scenes. Many or all of the unknowns were no doubt innocent, left by family members or visitors whose prints were not on file. If murder had been committed, and if the killer had been careless enough to leave a print or prints at one (but not two or more) of the scenes, that killer had never been arrested by any law enforcement organization sharing its fingerprint files with any data bank, local or international. Nor did the cave's mainframe database match the prints to anyone ever fingerprinted for any reason.

I reached the lab bench just as Alfred stepped back and turned to face me. As usual, his arrangement was neat and precise, his timing uncanny.

"I think you shall find everything in order, sir." In his crisply formal British mode, he was all business and ready to perform. "I assume we shall be examining strictly Q samples at this stage?"

"Right. We're looking for matches between the scenes, not to a perpetrator. Every item here is a Q, no Ks."

Forensic samples collected from potentially criminal evidence are "questioned," or Q, samples because their source is unknown. They must be analyzed, and preferably identified. Eventually and ideally, they will be held to direct comparison with "known," or K, samples, which are corresponding reference samples, fully identified. If the Q sample of an unknown fiber harvested from a crime scene can be matched to the K sample of a carpet in a suspect's home, the link establishes evidentiary value. Sufficient linkage between multiple Q and K samples adds up to probative value, which can lead to the suspect's conviction in a criminal trial. Because such evidence is circumstantial, the number and degree of linkages required for conviction can vary from one jury to another, the critical threshold always being "reasonable doubt." If the carpet in question is a common type found in many homes, then a matching crime scene fiber proves little or nothing. The more Q and K links, therefore, the better, each link adding weight to a growing chain of evidence. At some point, the accumulated weight becomes enough to haul even circumstantial evidence across the threshold of doubt. In cases resting on few matches between Q and K samples, the degree of each linkage must be extraordinary in the minds of the jurors and virtually impossible to explain away—as in precise matches between Q and K samples of DNA, essentially unique to each individual walking the earth.

"Ready when you are, sir."

I nodded. "We'll start with fibers."

Alfred extended the magnifying glass, a German lens manufactured to exacting standards by Zeiss, widely recognized as the best in the world. I took it and laid it within the area of strongest light, then reached for the first of the fiber samples. Because Alfred was familiar with my methods, I knew it would be in the first glassine bag of the first and largest of the seven groupings, the first scene harvested. All other fiber samples would be similarly placed first within their respective groups. I took them all from their separate bags for comparison against one another.

Among the many dozens of fiber samples, eleven shared the same brownish beige color and looked similar under the magnifying lens. This fact was significant because the eleven samples had been collected from three separate death scenes, two of the football players and one of the university regents. One of the three scenes, moreover, was the first harvested, the one not yet cleaned and least contaminated. And nine of the eleven similar fibers came from this one scene, with only one from each of the other two scenes.

I isolated three fibers, one from each scene. "Grossly similar, Alfred."

"And because commonality is always suspicious," he said, "shall we chamber the speeding bullet?"

I nodded. The "speeding bullet" of forensic investigation is side-by-side microscopic comparison. The term is not mine and I have never cared for it. From childhood on, I have never cared for guns or bullets in any context.

Alfred tweezed the three fibers one by one from the bench surface onto the microscope slide, carefully arranging them side by side. When he had them just so, he straightened and stepped back, still holding the tweezers ready.

I leaned to the eyepiece and tweaked the focus until the three images resolved to sharp clarity. Fairly smooth to the naked eye, they had actually been rough under the magnifying lens. Now, hugely magnified, they appeared shaggy, and all to the same extravagant degree. All three fibers, then, seemed to match.

"Looks good," I said, "but I want to compare cross-sections." Still peering through the microscope, I held out my right palm and felt the tweezers placed onto it.

Fiber cross-sections assume a variety of shapes—round, delta, trilobal, oval, and wrinkly. I used the tweezers to turn the fibers, one by one, for end-on views, readjusting focus each time.

"The same, Alfred." All three fibers were irregular or wrinkly in cross-section. "I'm guessing the fabric of origin was something rough, hardly a satin negligee."

"Shall we eliminate all doubt, sir, with the infrared?"

"Yes."

We moved over to the infrared spectrometer, where analysis revealed refractive indices and birefringence values all falling within the same hyper-narrow range.

"It's cinched, Alfred. These fibers originated from the same source, present at three of the death scenes. Three at a minimum; possibly all seven."

"And if we cannot yet *determine* that source," Alfred said, pulling pad and pen from his breast pocket, "perhaps we can at least identify its nature."

After he jotted the spectrometry values, I took them to the mainframe for input. Within minutes, the computer nailed a perfect match to a virtual sample stored in its data bank.

Alfred's eyebrows lifted as he scanned the monitor. "Sackcloth, sir? And according to your input notation, an 'unusual type' of sackcloth?"

I was equally puzzled. If the fibers had fallen from some sort of burglar's bag, why were all of the deaths routinely judged natural, with no indications of forced entry or any other kind of intrusion? Why were no valuables reported missing? And if there was some other explanation for the presence of sackcloth in the immediate vicinities of at least three suspicious deaths, why couldn't I imagine what that explanation might be?

"Undeniably sackcloth, Alfred. And however unusual, we'd better get used to it."

"My mind is already and once again serene," Alfred said. "As you well know, sir, I do love a mystery."

We returned to the lab bench and its array of glassine bags. The rest of the day was spent sifting and examining the remainder of the collected residue—bits of soil and clumps of dust, particles of grit, the sole fragment of plant matter, a tiny piece of plastic apparently snapped from the cap of a pen, dead flies, hairs from dozens of different sources, many of which would match the seven deceased men as well as some I hoped would eventually match their killer. But nothing beyond the fibers that seemed significant or worthy of exhaustive analysis. Not yet.

I did notice that the dead flies seemed too small, too young. It nagged at me, but I didn't know what to make of it.

At some point, Alfred went up the rock-carved steps into the manor and returned with two trays of hot food. As usual, the meal was superb and we ate in silence, both knowing the sackcloth fibers held some sort of answer, large or small. Until that answer could be guessed or known, however, there was nothing to say.

Alfred slid his cuff to check the time. "Approaching night-fall, sir."

"And darkness. I know."

We culled some of the trace evidence for probable disposal, although it would be separately retained until the case was closed. The rest was rebagged, reorganized, and filed away in seven separate side-by-side drawers set into the cavern's rock wall. At this point, there was little more I could do about the sackcloth deaths, nothing beyond briefly visiting one high school and one university. Including driving time, both would consume no more than an hour of darkness.

And yet Gotham is a large city, its predators many and always active. The late autumn's long night would hold no shortage of other work.

I nodded to Alfred and he reached for the dark cloak and attached cowl draped over its usual chair. Stepping behind me with his usual crisp comportment, he lifted the cowl high, letting the cloak mantle my shoulders. I reached up to pull the cowl down over my head, cinching its mask tightly to my face. Then I left the cave dressed for the night and its shadows.

Five hours after dawn, I awoke from a deep sleep in the manor's second floor master bedroom and headed straight down the stairs. Crossing the great hall, I called out before reaching the grandfather clock, telling Alfred I would take breakfast down in the cave. Then I released the hidden catch and swung the grandfather clock open on its concealed hinges. Passing through the secret entrance, I pulled the clock back into place and descended rock-carved steps winding down into cool cavern gloom.

At this point, with the sackcloth fibers linking two of the high school football players to one of the university board directors, I was convinced that Gordon's gut suspicions were justified. At least three, and probably all seven, of the deceased were victims. Murders had been committed, targeting two apparently unrelated groups. Of that much I had no doubt, and yet I still lacked real proof. Moreover, nothing yet pointed to any perpetrator. The victims were linked only to one another, not to their killer.

Although the means of murder would prove important, I strongly sensed that motive would prove to be the key. And motive might be revealed through greater understanding of the victims, by learning how and why seven different men all qualified as suitable targets for the same killer.

I threw the switch at the bottom of the rock steps and strode through stalagmite shadows toward the workstation's bright light.

When a killer selects his prey purely by physical type—all young white women, for example, all slim and all with long dark hair—the victims can be complete strangers, making their killings simultaneously connected yet random. This is what makes a serial killer more difficult to identify than a multiple murderer motivated by personal passion, personal gain, or personal revenge. Victims of the latter killer—all family members, for example, or all co-workers—share a commonality cutting across different physical types. In this case, with two different groups of victim types, former football players and current university regents, the crimes suggested personal motive derived from personal acquaintance or association. I was hunting a multiple murderer, then, not a serial killer. And the two groups of victims, as different as they were, presumably shared a single unknown commonality.

Last night's borrowed and copied records waited at the workstation where I'd left them at dawn. Hoping to find a further link between the two victim groups, something stronger than sackcloth fibers, I compared high school enrollment records from the appropriate time frame against a list of current Gotham University faculty, staff, and employees.

Several names turned up, each a suspect to be checked.

The most intriguing name was Dr. Jonathan Crane, a professor of psychology at Gotham University who'd been hired just a few years prior. Crane had attended the same high school at the same time as the four dead football players, and had now been employed for several years at the same university governed by the three dead regents. I found little in the computer about Crane and no criminal record. This proved only that he had never been arrested, however, not necessarily that he was innocent. And it fit with the computer's lack of prints matching those lifted from the scenes. Every killer starts somewhere, and something may have recently triggered Crane.

Then again, the killer might be someone else entirely, either a known criminal wearing gloves or someone else not yet arrested and never printed. Someone utterly unknown, who might as well be a ghost.

Both alive and identified, Professor Crane was my only lead and best bet. Should he prove innocent, he need never know he'd been suspected of anything.

After paving the way through Gordon—via Detective Harvey Bullock's discreet but official visit to campus security—I penetrated Crane's university office shortly after midnight. His bookshelves held a mix of titles, primarily texts on psychology with an extensive subcategory on the nature and examination of phobias and fear in general. Isolated in their own smaller section were a number of chemistry reference works.

Crane's desk drawers were locked. After picking them open, I found one side drawer filled with an eccentric jumble of small human skulls, the kind of plastic gimcrack novelties sold in dime stores and gumball machines. There were dozens of them, several with keychain eyelets and several that glowed when I switched off the light. In the bottom right drawer, under a pile of ungraded papers, there was a well-thumbed vintage edition of Washington Irving's *The Legend of Sleepy Hollow*, the only work of fiction in the office. At the time, it meant little.

The file cabinet held correspondence, back issues of academic newsletters and journals covering both psychology and chemistry, drafts of articles written by Crane, voluminous notes, and copies of Crane's course lectures. One was entitled, "The Psychology of Fear," another, "The Mind-Body Connection in Autonomous Fear Response," and a third, "Triggers of Terror." The article drafts had similarly suggestive titles, some lurid: "The Sum of Every Fear," "Assailing the Flayed Psyche," "Fear is Everything," "Bulging Eye and Beating Heart," "Panika Plus." I took them all and left the building.

Across campus, I penetrated the university's darkened administration offices to secure Crane's academic transcripts and employment records. Holding the penlight in my teeth, I used the office copy machine to make duplicates of both, along with copies of Crane's course lectures and article drafts. Then, after returning the transcripts and records to Crane's file, I left the administration building and slipped back to Crane's office.

Once the originals of the lectures and articles were replaced in the file cabinet where I'd found them, I took a last look around the small office. Its most salient feature was a stuffed crow perch-mounted to the wall opposite the professor's desk. When I sat in Crane's chair, the dead bird seemed to stare directly at me, shrinking back in wild wingspread terror.

Back in the cave by dawn, I put off sleep to go over Crane's academic transcripts and employment records. I also skimmed the copies of his lectures and articles.

With double majors in psychology and chemistry, Crane had been hired by the university to lecture on psychology while also granted private use of a small chem lab to pursue experiments in his "first love." Once again I wished the standard and cursory toxicology tests had been more thorough, wondering what strange alchemy a man like Crane might secretly brew.

Finished with the papers, I went to the equipment locker to retrieve the "Snifter," a vapor detector more formally known as the Portable J-W Aromatic Hydrocarbon Indicator. A device of breakthrough technology to begin with, this one—the only one of its kind—had been tweaked and enhanced by my best people at WayneTech Corporation, then condensed to a package weighing no more than five pounds. Deeper in the cave, I opened the trunk of the sleek black car parked at the mouth of the camouflaged tunnel exit. First wrapping it in foam padding, I then secured the customized Snifter inside the trunk, ready for future use.

Then, I mounted the rock steps toward the manor, nearly certain I'd found a human predator if not the proof required to halt his predations. For dark reasons of his own, apparently murderous reasons, Professor Jonathan Crane was obsessed with fear and its effects on both the mind and the body. From the beginning, faced with seven fatal heart attacks, I had wondered if seven grown men could have been literally scared to death.

Now I would have bet Bruce Wayne's bed and all its nightmares that they had.

Crouched in the shadow of a large air duct on the cafeteria rooftop, opposite the university's psychology wing, I wondered if the professor often worked so late after hours. When the light in his office window finally darkened an hour before midnight,

I took the minibinoculars from my belt and trained them on the doorway. And when the man himself emerged into the night, my mind instantly leaped to the book in his bottom drawer.

Extremely tall and stick-thin, little more than a skinbound skeleton lost in ill-fitting clothes, Jonathan Crane was the gawky and bespectacled spitting image of Washington Irving's Ichabod Crane. The identical last name and similar physique, combined with the presence of the book, transcended coincidence. For obvious reasons, real-life Jonathan identified with fictional Ichabod, at least up to a point.

But unlike tormented Ichabod, scared nearly to death by a swaggering bully disguised as headless horseman hurling jack-o-lantern head, this Crane was all confidence, meek in no way. I watched him move off across the deserted campus in a jaunty long-legged stride. At one point, he even hopped high to bizarrely click his heels, utterly unafraid of the dark and unafraid, it seemed, of anything. Yet if guilty, how could this freakishly frail and bookishly unassuming specimen induce fatal heart attacks in his victims? They were all mature men, four of them burly veterans of a violent sport. It made no sense.

I dropped from the roof and followed Crane to an apartment building just off campus. When a light came on, it marked the next place to search, first on the list for the following night, before Crane got home.

I never reached Crane's place the next night, however, detoured by another signal. This time it was the smaller portable beacon, not from the roof of police headquarters but from a crime scene. I swerved the car onto a side street and headed for the light.

Gordon waited in shadows a half-block down from strung yellow tape and spinning lights. It was the freshest scene yet, although the victim—another football jock from Crane's high school—had lain undiscovered next to his bed for at least forty-eight hours. Having alerted all hospitals to report any heart attack fatality under the age of forty-five, Gordon was notified and had immediately secured the scene less than an hour earlier. He told me he would hold his people back to give me another hour alone. I nodded, took the Snifter from the trunk, and headed up the block for the back entrance.

Inside, on the floor near the dead man's bed, were dozens of dead flies and a number of the same sackcloth fibers. I tweezed and bagged only one of each. There were also several bits of dried plant stems. Again I took just one.

Then, expecting little after two days, I activated the Snifter and slowly moved it up and down near the bed. It bleeped. I checked the LED readout. It indicated trace amounts of a lingering vapor, detected and captured but not identified in its data bank.

Whatever the vapor might be, it was something unknown or new, possibly unique. If it had been manufactured in a chem-lab at Gotham University, it meant I had found Jonathan Crane's trail a day or two late. Feeling strange unsettled, I left with my finds.

Back in the cave, Alfred helped me use stationary and mobile phase chromatography and electrophoresis to separate the trace vapor's constituent compounds. Even though this secret account is intended for few future eyes, the compounds will here remain unidentified by name.

"Nothing toxic," Alfred said, "and nothing known to induce heart attack."

"Nothing *individually* toxic."

"Indeed, sir. If the vapor is relevant, and one must presume it is, then it is relevant only in its mixed form of separately harmless compounds."

I looked up from the data, gazing into cavern gloom. "The Snifter captured only a minute amount, measured in molecules, so little as to be useless . . . "

Alfred's head snapped around. "Sir, you are not contemplating—"

" . . . and yet we've identified its constituents and their proportions."

"You *are*, sir, aren't you?"

"We have almost none of the vapor but all of its formula."

"You're actually contemplating it."

"We can replicate the mixture in a larger amount."

Alfred shot his cuffs to stiffly cross his arms. "You are, in fact, utterly *hellbent* on it."

"We can create a usable dose of whatever the gas may be."

"Hellbent on a willfully dangerous course of madness."

"This is serious, Alfred."

"As serious," he sniffed, "as a heart attack."

"Men have been murdered, as if they were items crossed off a list, and the list may be longer. The vapor *must* be tested."

"On a guinea pig," Alfred said.

"On a human, Alfred. On a man as large as a football player."

Alfred stared for a long beat, his gray eyes hard. "A human guinea pig, who may well seize up in cardiac arrest before my disapproving eyes."

"In which case I suggest you keep your eyes attentive, with a spike of adrenaline at hand."

Alfred looked away, gravely shaking his head but protesting no further. Never one to squander time on lost causes, he knew he had already pressed the issue to its limit.

I held the sealed flask high, slowly turning it against the light to study the greenish gas seething inside. It was still unnamed, unidentified even in the mainframe's huge data bank, its effects precisely unknown but presumably deadly, at least in sufficient quantity. Acting as my own guinea pig, I had no intention of taking a significant dose. I wanted only the slightest taste of this substance, the briefest and mildest experience possible, just enough to confirm its suspected effect. Still, what I was about to do was indeed willfully and extremely dangerous. Were other lives not in danger, it would even qualify as madness. Alfred was right. And yet, he knew, so was I. If this had to be done and done quickly, someone had to do it now.

He stood nearby, hazmat mask strapped over nose and mouth. If I went down, he would remain standing, ready to do everything possible to resurrect me. Cradled in a bed of gauze on the workbench next to him, a hypodermic was loaded with pure adrenaline. Should the worst occur, it would have to be punched directly into my stilled heart.

"Now, Alfred."

He nodded.

I carefully unstoppered the flask, just enough to release a single tendril of its gas, twisting upward like the faint ghost of a green snake. My head flinched back instinctively. I forced myself to lean forward for the barest whiff, and again my head jerked back. Since the gas was apparently odorless, I was not sure I'd inhaled any of it. Then my mind reeled and I knew the unknown substance was stunningly potent. I remembered the slightly strange feeling I'd had as I'd left the most recent crime scene. This was the same sensation multiplied tenfold, enough to make my vision instantly blur.

"Sir?" Muffled by the hazmat mask, Alfred's voice was distorted. Still, I knew it should not sound nearly this strange, as if coming from some distant, dreamy place deep under a thick ocean. "Master Bruce!"

"Yes?"

"The flask, sir! You're holding it open! Inhaling too much!"

His words startled me. "Right."

I sealed the flask and set it down with excruciating care, aware that my fingers were already trembling, my palms already slick.

"Bad, Alfred." I tried to look at him but must have turned in the wrong direction, finding only darkness. "Very bad."

"I'm ready, sir. I'm watching. I'm here."

But I was suddenly alone, Alfred gone and forgotten. There was no one but me inside my body and my body was all wrong, an alien cage trapping me inside a too-tight space stuffed with everything bad. I heard a rushing roar, sudden and deafening. A fierce suction filled my ears and I wobbled as it tried to pull my head inside out. I took a dizzy step back, desperate to be well clear of the flask's sealed contents, and a bomb blew up inside my rib cage. It slammed my heart and pumped my pulse, making my vision strobe forward and back. I felt wildly anxious and hyperaware. My blurred vision sharpened to brittle clarity. The light became far too bright, the cavern darkness too deeply black. My chest pounded harder, faster. I could see every molecule of the air before me, every molecule throbbing and heavy with menace. My parents were gone and danger lurked all around, ready to attack at the first moment I did not anticipate it. I think I spun around but could not be certain at the time. Control was gone, its secret key out of reach. I wanted to run out of my skin and leave my body behind where I could come back with some weapon to beat and crush it.

Then the worst was about to happen and I knew it with the most awful certainty I'd ever known. They were coming for me and I was helpless against their overwhelming power, hopeless against their enraged swarm of black wings beating blackness.

Bats. The cave was filled with the things. They ruled this place and they all hated me for taking their fearsome face and form. I was the thief who had stolen their dark essence, usurped their primal power. But who was I to think I could become one of them? I was nothing, nothing but a helpless child lost and screaming in the dark.

I strained my eyes and there they were way up high, effortlessly dodging jagged spikes stretching down from the ceiling. But how could that be? Why did spikes stretch from the ceiling, and what kind of spikes grew upside down? *Stalactites.* I'd forgotten. I was in the cave and they were up there everywhere, spikes of heavy rock dangling down. There might even be a stalactite ready to snap free and plunge toward my head, its sharp point poised to puncture my skull, to spear cold stone all the way down through my body. It could happen at any moment, and I decided to find the overhead spike before it fell, but the bats suddenly wouldn't let me.

They jittered and fluttered past, little black things in the air swooping faster and morphing larger, coming out of the darkness right at me, straight for my eyes. I raised my arms to beat them back or shield my face. They grew ever greater, streaking close, and then there was only one to be seen, a single monster filling my entire field of vision, gigantic and hideous, a huge flapping thing that wanted to kill me. I staggered back, went down, and it was on me, all over me, sharp talons digging into my shoulders, shaking me as if I were a loose dead doll, mouth gaping to reveal fangs trying to bite my face off and chew into my skull. It loomed closer until my eyes filled with its darkness.

"Sir! It's just me! It's Alfred! You passed out, Master Bruce, but you're *safe* now! You must have hyperventilated. Do you understand?"

"Alfred?" The monster began to transform again.

"Your pupils are extremely dilated, sir. You were hallucinating."

"It's you?" The terrifying face dissolved and faded.

"Your pulse is still racing, sir. Do you need—"

"No." Alfred was returning, his face leaning close into mine, peering hard, growing clearer. "No need, Alfred. It's wearing off. Heartbeat slowing. I can feel it. I'm coming back. Let me up."

Drenched in cold sweat, I let Alfred check my pulse every few minutes for a half-hour while I regulated my breathing. He'd set up a large fan to blow the air directly past us, then removed his hazmat mask. Now he brought a glass of water, waited while I drank, and again pressed two fingers to the side of my neck.

"Still decreasing," he said. "Nearly back within normal range."

"I know. My mind's almost clear now. But it was . . . terrifying."

He gave me a look. "Indeed." Now that I was out of the woods, he let his voice match his expression. "One hopes someone is proud of himself."

"Not proud," I said, "satisfied. We now know what the previously unknown vapor is capable of."

Alfred turned sardonic. "And we know it," he said, "most intimately."

I looked over at the greenish haze filling the stoppered flask. "An extremely potent but undocumented equivalent of hallucinogen and hyper-amphetamine." The tremor was almost gone from my fingers, although not quite. "With severe physiological side effects."

"To say the least."

"Arrythmia, Alfred, irregular and racing heartbeat, although not brought on by an actual amphetamine. Instead, it's a combination of adenosine inhibitor and adrenaline activator. Adenosine and adrenaline both occur in natural body chemistry, their levels unchecked in routine toxicology tests. And because the inhibitor is a synthetic equivalent of highly concentrated caffeine, it was missed, too." I pointed to the flask. "It's an ultimate form of 'fear gas,' Alfred, a hell's brew of separately harmless ingredients adding up to sheer terror." I paused. "And yet, it's not the whole answer. Maybe it could prove fatal to someone with a bad heart, maybe one or more of the regents, but not to all the younger football players. As much as I inhaled, as hard and fast as it made my heart pound, it did not kill me."

"Surely more than close enough, sir. And even though I was wearing a mask, it certainly scared *me* half to death."

"And *you*, in turn, scared me."

"Forgive me, sir, but I was merely attempting to—"

"Time to alert Police Commissioner Gordon, Alfred. The gas may not be lethal in itself, but it's at least *part* of Jonathan Crane's murder weapon."

The rest of the day passed quickly through distorted time. Now that the fear gas formula was known, I tested several of the dead flies collected at different death scenes. The results were positive for the previously unknown gas, less than fatal to a human in normal health but apparently toxic to flies. If so, it explained why the flies seemed too small. They may have died prematurely rather than naturally. In any case, evidence of the gas in the flies further confirmed the presence of the gas at the scenes.

But the gas, I remained convinced, could not explain the whole story. I had left the flask unstoppered for long moments, inhaled far too much of its odorless contents, probably more than any of the victims, and it was still not sufficient to kill me. The gas was certainly a component of Jonathan Crane's M.O., even a partial murder weapon, but it had not killed the victims, not in itself and on its own. So what had? What was missing?

There was no evidence of forced entry at any of the scenes, and the bodies of the victims showed no evidence of violence, nothing but heart failure. Heart failure set up by the gas but brought on by something more.

The worst and most terrifying moments of my own experience came when Alfred rushed to my aid. With the gas already inducing hallucination, I perceived him as a horrific monster. And what if he had not been my best friend? What if *someone else* had rushed at me like that, not hoping to aid me but actively *menacing* me?

Was that the missing element and the final key? It was certainly Professor Jonathan Crane's abiding obsession, fear itself.

But in what form?

Gordon's forensic team rushed to Gotham University, securing the small chem lab reserved for Crane's use. Knowing what to look for, they quickly identified trace amounts of the same constituent compounds making up the "fear gas." Combined with the other evidence, it was enough to justify an immediate arrest warrant.

Crane himself, however, was not in his university office, nor did he show up for the day's lecture.

Another team of techs, in the company of arresting officers, swooped down on Crane's apartment. It was vacant. Crane had bolted, apparently spooked by the presence of strangers on campus. The first team of techs had been as circumspect as possible, but they and their portable-lab vans were hardly invisible.

Meanwhile, three more former football players had been located. Two claimed no memory of Jonathan Crane, but Homicide Detective Bullock suspected they were lying. And the third ex-jock had come clean, admitting that he recalled Crane as the "number one geek" in high school. He and some of his fellow jocks, he further confessed, had subjected Crane to merciless ridicule and even physical hazing. While this proved nothing, I knew that school shootings had resulted from such bullying and wondered if it was a possible motive for Crane.

A more concrete motive turned up when Crane's name was brought up to the surviving university regents. They revealed that the psychology professor had been put on notice for unorthodox and unprofessional conduct, including the impromptu use of unwitting students in so-called "fear" experiments. One alleged incident had Crane stepping away from his lectern to pull a gun without warning. Aiming the weapon at each student in turn, he reportedly urged the other students to "keenly observe the reactions of stark fear." The gun, ultimately revealed to be a fake and incapable of causing harm, had nevertheless terrified everyone in the lecture hall. Crane had tried to laugh the whole thing off.

Called before the Board of Regents to explain himself, he attributed his actions to "an innovative demonstration of the subject under discussion." Dressed down in no uncertain terms, including the threat to permanently cancel his tenure, he was told that any similar incident of "operating outside the box" would suffice for dismissal.

Although Crane made statements of "unequivocal contrition," the regents suspected it was feigned. One said he "seemed to simmer with barely suppressed rage." But while the entire board braced for future difficulties, no one dreamed murder might occur. And when their three fellow regents died in quick succession, the survivors were "saddened and even disconcerted" but only mildly suspicious. "Such things," one surviving regent said, "do tend to come in threes." Had the deceased regents been younger—as young as the football players, for example—connections might have been made. One regent, in fact, claimed he *did* think of Crane but immediately dismissed the notion as "wildly paranoid" without mentioning it to anyone.

As for the former football players, they had largely drifted out of contact with one another, only one of them being aware that others had prematurely expired.

Although I still lacked proof, I now had little doubt of Jonathan Crane's guilt, his possible motive linking two otherwise unrelated victim types. Bearing a similar grudge against both types, he apparently killed regents and football players alike for the same reason of simple revenge, and he killed them all the same way, somehow stopping their hearts with induced fear.

With Gordon's forensic technicians sifting and probing every inch of Crane's abandoned apartment, I saw no reason to interrupt them, particularly not in daylight. If the place held any evidence to further corroborate Crane's guilt, Gordon's people would find it.

From my own more urgent perspective, it was an exercise in bolting the door long after the beast had gone. Evidence against a perpetrator meant nothing if the perpetrator was not found and brought to trial.

The surviving regents were placed under police protection, as was every former football player still in the Gotham area. But what if Jonathan Crane's motive extended to potential victims belonging to neither group, victims of a third type? Others against whom he bore a similar grudge and craved identical revenge? Others unknown.

It was imperative that the beast be brought to ground—and swiftly, before he killed again.

So I went back to the cave's forensic drawing board and remained there throughout the rest of the day, still shaky but regaining composure by the hour. With Alfred attending, I reexamined my own harvest of evidence, combing everything for some trail to the killer. We found it revealed in the bits of plant stem retrieved from two separate crime scenes.

A comparison of photomicrographs reduced to the cellular level matched the stems. They were both common straw of the same type. Chromatography and treatment with chemical reagents further detected and identified a trace amount of kerosene, absorbed by one piece of straw but not the other.

Finally, I turned my attention to minute traces of soil adhering to both bits of straw. Analysis of the two samples yielded the same composition for both. Compared against area soil samples stored in the mainframe's data bank, the composition was consistent with several nearby locations. One was a farm area across the bridge and some ten miles to the south, on the outskirts of the greater Gotham area. It was also very near the early childhood home of Jonathan Crane.

Night had just fallen, and all effects of the greenish gas had apparently passed. I was leaving the cave by car, clad as the Batman, aware of a mildly lingering headache but otherwise fully recovered.

"Godspeed," Alfred said, "and do take care, sir."

I jammed the shift and punched the gas. Tires shrieked and smoked, and the black car roared up the tunnel.

Crane's childhood home had been razed and replaced by a convenience store. With hope dashed at a dead end, I almost turned back for the city. Then I saw nothing but darkness stretching beyond the all-night store's parking lot, a large tract of fallow farmland not yet developed. Dead cornstalks, years old, rustled and rattled through the moonlit field. Once rising straight and green in orderly rows, the dark stalks now etched a chaos of crisscrossing slants, bent or broken by wind and snow, crushed by scavengers, decayed and sagging under the weight of their own death.

I remembered the crow in Crane's university office, stuffed and mounted in theatrically posed terror. A cornfield, straw, and a scared crow.

Cutting the headlights, I cruised slowly along the field's edge, grateful for the large harvest moon as I scanned through gaps in the roadside trees. A half-mile from the convenience store, the dark shape of a small structure was barely visible among the dead cornstalks, maybe fifty yards back from the road. I killed the engine and rolled off the verge down into the field, just far enough to hide the car in the corn.

With all systems locked down, I emerged from the car to stand amidst the dense dry stalks, listening and even sniffing. Hoarse caws from the distance again reminded me of the dead crow in Crane's office. I thought I smelled a faint whiff of kerosene but it passed immediately, either taken by the shifting breeze or nothing but wishful imagination. When the breeze stiffened, there was nothing but a long rush of dead leaves.

I parted the stalks and moved in the direction of the structure seen from the road.

It was an old shack, once used to store farm implements but now weatherbeaten and long abandoned, at least until recently. Its windows were tar-papered on the inside, but a fine slit of light glowed through a single peeling seam. It appeared too yellow for reflected moonlight, but I wondered if a film of grime on the black-backed pane could distort color. Moving closer to eliminate any such trick of the eye, brushing a minimum of cornstalks, I broke their fringe into the overgrown clearing in which the shack sagged. From a more acute angle, the crack of light showed brighter and even more yellow, undeniable and unmistakable. And then there was more.

Soft sounds, scuffings and clinkings, came from within. My heart quickened, but not from fear, as I circled the shack to find its door. Kicking hard, I went through the splintering door fast and found him inside.

I was right. Dressed in ragged straw-stuffed tatters, a *living scarecrow* spun to face me through a mask of rough sackcloth, bizarre and grotesque in the dim yellow light of kerosene lanterns. Time froze as we faced each other, Bat and Scarecrow both in momentary shock, both standing utterly still. He wore a black broad-brimmed hat with his head cocked to the side, burlap tunic belted with coarse rope. With his arms outstretched, he could have been mounted on a staked cross-pole.

The professor of psychology was clearly insane.

Just beyond him, on a warped wooden shelf between the kerosene lamps, a gas-fueled bunsen burner heated a flask, the reaction turning its bubbling liquid contents into gas. Next to the burner were racked test tubes and more beakers, several connected by distillation coils. The rough shelf had been converted to a makeshift chemistry lab, confirming everything. Transformed to a living scarecrow, Jonathan Crane was preparing to take further prey, bent on scaring yet another victim to death. First with his fear gas, then with his own garishly menacing disguise.

A much newer shelf, mounted too close to the floor, ran the entire length of the shack's side wall. Carefully spaced along it were more than a dozen stuffed animals. Dead center, flanked by life-scale human skulls, a plush teddy bear slouched with one button eye missing. Casting heavy shadows, the yellow-lit creatures seemed sinister.

The spell broke when the Scarecrow abruptly whirled away. Quickly snatching something from the shelf behind him, he then spun back with upraised hand cocked at the frayed brim of his hat. The hand held something round, glowing yellow-green in the kerosene light. I recognized the object just before it left his hand. It was another skull, this one miniature and much like the plastic novelties jammed in the drawer of Crane's office desk.

My left arm swept up, pivoting at the elbow, to ward off the hurled skull. Unlike those in his desk, this skull was not plastic but thin glass. It shattered easily against my forearm, releasing a small cloud of greenish vapor. The gas swept past my face, wreathed my head. On reflex, the breath caught in my throat.

Assuming I would be rapidly overwhelmed by terror, my hammering heart ready to seize and stop, the Scarecrow shrieked like a banshee and feinted forward with arms waving wildly.

I settled into a slight crouch without flinching. Then I smiled, inhaling deeply, breathing freely, making certain he noticed.

He seemed confused. The gas had never failed him before, and yet I would not scare. Trapped in the small shack, facing someone who would not flee or even back off, he slowly realized he would have to fight his way out.

"You don't scare me," he snarled. "You *can't* scare me. No bully can, not anymore. I've learned things, trained my mind *and* my body. Two hours a day on kicks alone. Now *I'm* the Master of Fear, and I know how to fight back. No one will *ever* beat me up again."

When he suddenly leaped forward, I braced to meet the attack.

With a fighting style best described as awkwardly graceful, the Scarecrow became a swift frenzy of long arms and legs lashing like flails, bits of straw flying from the cuffs of ragged tunic and trousers. He kept it up full-bore, shrieking and howling, kicking and slashing, for a full minute before the reality of the situation began to sink in. Then his onslaught faltered. Clearly, he didn't understand how I could resist or why his every blow was blocked, didn't know I had entered his shack with a nose rebreather already in place.

Finally, he broke his attack and took a long step back to study me. Then he returned to a tactic that had never failed him before, lunging forward with a barked shout muffled through his weird mask. I stood my ground.

He took another step back, even more uncertain. "You're not *afraid?*" His voice betrayed a slight quaver. "Not at *all?*"

I dropped my own voice a full register. "What's to fear, Crane? A straw man like you?"

"You think you're so smart, don't you?" Rising toward panic, his voice actually broke. "You think you know who I *am.*"

"It's finished, Crane. Give it up."

I sensed the strange figure's next moves would spring from desperation. Prepared for anything, I centered on his chest and neck, peripherally focused on his arms. Still, his strike came almost without warning, left leg pistoned high through a thrust-kick followed by a right roundhouse punch. I stepped to the side, narrowly evading both, then swatted the back of the black hat's brim and snatched the sackcloth hood-mask from his head. I squeezed the mask and felt its own built-in rebreather.

Crane twisted around, his naked face wild. I tossed the mask aside. "There's still gas in this shack, Crane. You can't hold your breath forever."

It was a bluff, played in the hope of forestalling further violence. With the door hanging shattered on its hinges, the gas had almost certainly dissipated into the night. Based on my own experience, whatever lingered and whatever he breathed would exert only minimal effect. In any case, I sensed the terror contorting his face was his alone, a fear he'd felt ever since childhood, always striking from within. It may have been imposed by outside factors, but it was a fear born of psychology, not chemistry.

He made a strangled sound between growl and gargle. "*You can't do this!*"

And he lashed out one more time, whipping a high sweep kick at my head. I chopped his leg and he spun around, staggering three steps before crashing to the hard-earth floor. He did not get up, nor did he even attempt to rise. He just sat there as the fight left him like air from a burst balloon. Then his shoulders slumped and shook in soundless sobs. I had never seen a transformation so extreme or more pathetic. After a time he found his voice and lost his mind, raving in hysteria, at times glancing up at me with quick birdlike darts of his head but mostly screaming and babbling at the stuffed toys arranged along the wall.

Much of what he said was beyond understanding. He repeatedly cursed me as "a bully just like all the others," wishing me "just as dead as them." In rage, he accused me of being "a night demon" trying to frighten him. In terror, he insisted that he could never be scared. And in abject defeat, he mewled that it was not fair, that he had conquered every insecurity to become "the Master of Fear." He vowed to use all his "powers of terror" to strike me dead where I stood and to "kill every other bully, too."

Not wanting to make it worse, I simply blocked the doorway and kept my distance, letting the storm rage, waiting him out. He stammered incoherently about his childhood, apparently reliving flashes of its worst moments, shrinking from the "horrors" of his mother and from black birds flapping at his face to make him "run like a craven coward." He said or shrieked many other things too, most of them unintelligible, all of them either fearful or bitterly hateful.

Finally he lapsed into a kind of catatonia, dead eyes staring at nothing. He seemed unaware of my presence, perhaps unaware of his own existence, completely docile. Using plastic zip-cuffs, I bound his roughly gloved hands behind his back and hoisted him to his feet. Then I dragged him from the shack and into stalk-striped moonlight through the field of dead corn. Although he whimpered all the way to the waiting car, he said nothing more.

Neither of us frightened a single crow.

It all came out over the course of the next three months as Crane underwent questioning by a series of defense and prosecution psychiatrists. Terrorized and terrified through his childhood, the young Jonathan Crane became obsessed with vengeance. And he fixated on "righteous" vengeance, determined to fight fire with fire, doing unto others what they had done to him. The study of fear became his life's work, with the ultimate goal of mastering that fear through a combination of chemistry and psychology, then exploiting it to his own murderous ends.

He succeeded seven times before murder was even suspected, and eight times before I could stop him.

The few loose ends were simply tied. Several of the victims had lived alone. These, Crane said, were "the easy ones." Forced to stake out the homes of the others, in one case "watching every night for weeks," he waited until "the wife and kids went out shopping or off to the movies," making his move only when certain the victim was home alone.

There were no signs of break-in at any of the scenes because entry was never forced. Because Crane's vengeance was always personal, he was known to every victim. They may have been surprised to find him on their doorsteps, especially late at night and in some cases after years since seeing him last, but they all opened their doors nevertheless.

Once inside and without warning, Crane released his unique Fear Gas. Then, while his unsuspecting victims were overcome, he transformed to his bizarre scarecrow guise simply by holding his breath long enough to remove his overcoat and pull on his sackcloth mask with its built-in breathing filter. To his distressed victims, already confused and beginning to hallucinate, the change may well have seemed supernatural.

The Scarecrow then menaced them any way he could, often brandishing a small hand-scythe, taunting them in cruel tones, lunging at them with near-miss slashes, darkening the room and flashing light in their eyes, chasing them. By now their pulses were racing, hearts beating dangerously fast. Crane refused to reveal precisely what the Scarecrow may have snarled or whispered, what psychologies he may have employed, but he did say he played on each victim's "greatest fear." And he kept at it until their pounding hearts finally gave out and they dropped dead.

Using his gas to first alter their perceptions and hammer their hearts, the Scarecrow then literally scared his paranoid, hallucinating victims to death. It was, he said, "the poetic justice of fear-induced vengeance."

Then he simply pulled on his long overcoat, removed his mask and hat, stuffed them in the overcoat's pockets, and calmly left the scenes. If anyone saw him, they saw nothing stranger than a "normal" man.

Finally, just yesterday, Professor Jonathan Crane was judged incompetent to stand trial on charges of multiple murder. Speaking as the Scarecrow and threatening to "kill every bully in the courtroom," he was committed to maximum security incarceration within Arkham's Asylum for the Criminally Insane.

Case closed.

Bagged and
Tagged

Excerpt From Bruce Wayne's Diary

ALFRED keeps bugging me about the "crucial and critical importance of the learned mind," always telling me I should work out less and study more. Well, last week his nagging finally got to me. I've started cracking the books, all right, but I haven't exactly been doing homework. And I haven't been bored either. Not hardly.

In fact, I can't think of anything more exciting than what's in these library books about forensic techniques. When they do it right, these guys are astounding. Just finished a long description of the standard—or actually the ideal—procedures for evidence collection. Incredible. And since Alfred says writing things down always helps to remember them . . .

The first thing good forensic techs do is secure and quarantine their scene, the sooner the better, using that official yellow crime scene tape to keep everyone else out. There's nothing they can do about the regular cops who got there first, responding to an emergency call or whatever, because that damage is already done. But the forensic guys always want to prevent any more contamination. People tromping through the scene can really do a number. If they don't destroy actual evidence, they leave their own traces behind, confusing the issue. Even careful forensic techs can do damage themselves, which is why they always try to minimize contamination every way they can.

First, they put on gloves, the real thin latex ones used by doctors so they can still feel the scalpel. Next come plastic bootie slip-ons, sometimes even facemasks and head coverings. If you need to identify some criminal from nothing but a hair or a fingerprint or a shoeprint left at the scene, you don't want to waste time identifying yourself. So only when the techs are fully ready like that do they "cautiously invade" the crime scene.

Once they're inside the scene (which can be outside, of course, like in an alley or wherever), they take pictures from every angle and distance, including the best possible master shot with closeups of every detail. Then they mark everything important—like blood spots or bullet casings—with chalk circles or little numbered prop cards. And then they photograph the whole scene all over again.

After that, they use the same kind of "grid approach" as archaeologists at a dig site. Sometimes they actually use sticks and string to divide the area into a bunch of squares labeled first on a rough diagram and later on an actual photograph. This way they can note exactly where every little thing was found, even a tiny bit of fuzz, right down to the square inch.

And the way techs find things is pretty much on their hands and knees with a magnifying lens and tweezers and swabs with little plastic evidence capsules and baggies. After they take everything they can see, they use brushes (coarse or fine, depending on the situation) to turn up even more. Then, they use a hand vacuum to suck up whatever's left that they can't see. Later in the lab, they empty the vacuum and put the contents on microscope slides. One case was actually solved by a single speck of unusual grit tied to identical particles found in the murder suspect's home. Nothing is too small to be important, which is something worth remembering.

Then the techs dust for fingerprints, which are patterns of sweat almost always invisible until the print dust clings to them. They also make plaster casts of footprints and tireprints to hopefully match some suspect's shoes or car. If they suspect violence was committed in a certain spot but can't see any evidence of it, they might spray stuff called Luminol on the floor or wall. When they shine an ultraviolet light on this Luminol—if there's been a chemical reaction—they can then see the spatters and splashes of invisible scrubbed-away blood. (Out, damned spot!) It's like techno-magic.

But the most important thing before leaving the scene is making sure that every "harvested" item and speck of potential evidence is separately "bagged and tagged." In other words, isolated and identified. This prevents one piece of evidence from contaminating another. It also establishes and preserves a "proper chain of custody," and the only proper chain is one that never breaks. If the chain does break, the evidence becomes worthless and gets thrown out of court. You have to prove the evidence has remained in secure custody through all the testing phases every step of the way. If it's been anywhere else for any length of time, there's no way to know if it was accidentally contaminated or deliberately tampered with, sometimes even switched with completely different phony evidence. Even a cop can be a criminal, and frame-ups do happen.

Once the crime scene has been picked clean with everything bagged and tagged, the investigation has barely begun. In the case of murder, it shifts to two different places, the lab and the morgue.

In the lab the techs go over everything they harvested—fibers, dirt, hairs, blood, bullets, whatever—and they go over it every way they can. They examine and analyze everything with microscopes, chemicals, and high-tech machines. If they have swabs of blood, they type it. If they have blood or saliva or semen or tissue, they do DNA analysis. If they have fingerprints, they compare them with their files or run them through a computer, looking for matches with known criminals. If they have bullets, they do ballistics, hoping to match the bullets to whatever gun fired them. Finding the murder weapon in a suspect's possession is almost always a lock.

And then the techs carefully preserve everything, keeping that vital chain of custody tight and unbroken. They never know. Any or everything might be needed in a future trial.

Meanwhile, in the morgue, the forensic harvesting of evidence continues with examination and analysis of the victim's actual body. This is done by a qualified medical examiner, also called a coroner, in the form of a postmortem ("after death") autopsy, or "necropsy." It's gut-wrenching—both mentally and physically—but the best autopsy explores everything. The whole body is completely opened up and taken apart.

But first the medical examiner takes photographs and X-rays, and more and more these days CAT scans too. Then comes an overall visual inspection, noting all obvious wounds and bruises. After that the coroner really gets down to business with an inch by inch examination of the outer skin, looking for needle marks or anything else out of the ordinary, even between the toes. Then it goes deeper, into the flesh and bones, with wounds probed, described, and diagrammed. If there are any bullets, they're found and removed. And then so are all the internal organs, which are measured, weighed, and dissected. Samples of everything are taken and preserved, even sliced cross-sections of the brain. Later tests are done on blood, tissue, and the contents of stomach, liver, bladder, bowels, you name it. These results can reveal the presence of alcohol, drugs, or poison. Using the average digestion time, stomach and intestine contents can even nail the time of death, or at least how long after his or her last meal a person died. Finally, it goes all the way down to microscopic examination of the preserved organ samples. The more we learn about how the body works, the more an M.E. sees through his microscope, and the more he can deduce about the time and manner of death.

So a dead body can tell a lot about what's been done to it, sometimes even who did it. This is why the corpse itself is always considered "the best evidence" in any case of murder.

Reading that, it hit me that "bagged and tagged" actually links both things together, the evidence harvested from a scene to identify a murderer *and* the murderer's victim, who has been turned into a body-bagged and toe-tagged corpse.

Kind of creepy but true, and it makes me mad. It almost makes me hate. I'm just glad Alfred handled the official identification of my parents' bodies. I was in a bad way that night, real bad, and I don't think I could have taken it, seeing Mom and Dad again so soon, bagged and tagged in the morgue with holes in them and all their life gone.

In my opinion, their autopsies were a lot less than perfect. If I didn't know it then, I do now. And the forensics guys in that alley weren't so hot either. Their procedures were less than standard and nowhere near ideal. The whole investigation, if you ask me, was weak. Forget the guy was never caught, he was never even identified. He's still unknown, still out there, maybe still free.

Bagged and tagged, evidence and death. It all comes down to that, two very different things described the same way. Somehow I'm going to use one against the other. I really mean it. I'm going to use bagged and tagged evidence to prevent the bagging and tagging of dead bodies.

So thanks, Alfred. Thanks for making me crack the books. And while I'm at it, thanks for everything else, too.

Tools of
the Trade

Excerpt From Bruce Wayne's Diary

AS the only child and sole heir of Thomas and Martha Wayne, I stand to receive even more than this awesome manor on the hill. Mom and Dad also left me an incredible amount of money. It's being held in a trust for now, administered by Alfred and the lawyer, but it all comes to me when I come of age.

Nothing's definite yet, but Alfie and I have already discussed a few ways to use and invest this legacy of mine. The biggest ideas won't happen until I'm older, but eventually I'd like to set up some sort of charity foundation for the victims of crime and poverty.

No one wants to be tougher on criminals, especially murderers, but it seems to me you can't arrest your way out of crime. If the point is to prevent victims, then the logical way to do it is by preventing criminals. And if poverty creates a lot of criminals, then any war on crime should also be a war on poverty. Not that this would solve everything—let's face it, rich people steal and kill, too—but it ought to help.

When I mentioned such a foundation, Alfred got all choked up and misty-eyed. He tried to stiffen his upper lip again by lifting his head and tugging the tips of his vest, but then he said something like, "I should consider that a superb expenditure, Master Bruce, one eminently worthy of your late parents' honor and memory."

(Which made *my* eyes go all misty.)

On the other hand, I also want to keep the money coming in, even build the inheritance larger, if only so there's more funding for the foundation. But there are also more practical reasons to invest in some kind of profitable enterprise. First, we need to keep this stately old manor up and running while giving Bruce Wayne something legitimate to do that can double as a cover story for what I *really* want to do, most likely in secret. Given that, it seems to me that a profitable business for the public Bruce Wayne could also advance any future personal activities. Since these activities will focus on detecting, solving, and stopping crimes (although *exactly* how I still don't know), I'm thinking I should set up some kind of research and development corporation dedicated to new forensic devices and technologies. Even things like a tougher-but-lighter form of bulletproof Kevlar outfit for cops and other crime-fighters.

A name like "WayneTech" would work.

In the meantime, until my own dream corporation brainstorms new wonders or improvements to existing technologies, here's a wish list of things I'll need to launch my future secret scheme—otherwise known as Ways to Start Spending My Fortune:

Optical microscope: Twin optics for the "speeding bullet" of forensic analysis, namely the side-by-side comparison of fibers, hairs, particles, plant spores, and other trace evidence. As useful as it is, however, the optical microscope is limited by the wavelengths of visible light magnified up to only 2,000 times. Which is actually a lot, but . . .

Electron microscope: This instrument enhances magnification from 2000 X all the way to an incredible *one million* X by transmitting a beam of subatomic electrons through whatever sample is under examination. Electrons are particles which also behave like waves, and their wavelength is much shorter than visible light—which, in a way, lets you see that which can't be seen.

Chemistry lab: The works, and I mean everything. Beakers, test tubes, retorts, distillate and precipitate equipment, bunsen burners, full array of specific chemical reagents, coil tubes, evaporator, incubator, centrifuge, everything from the ancient alchemy basics to the futuristic gizmos of molecular biochemistry.

Neutron activation analyzer: This determines the proportion of constituent elements in a substance by measuring their gamma rays as emitted after neutron bombardment. This baby is expensive—and as impressive as it sounds, it's coming under fire by lawyers and scientists alike. Maybe more and deeper research before springing the big bucks? (Fittingly enough for a guy whose last name is Pennyworth, Alfred always says: "Nurse every penny wisely, and never suffer a fool's loss.")

Spectroscope: To identify a substance, normal spectrometry (or spectroscopy) requires the destruction of some of your sample but usually only a very small part of it. When the sample is heated by laser beam or carbon arc, wavelengths of light are emitted and focused through a prism to create a spectrum unique to the sample substance being analyzed. Infrared spectroscopy adds infrared radiation to determine the class of synthetic compounds.

Microspectrophotometer: For performing a form of spectroscopy involving only microscopic samples, especially tiny chips of paint pigments.

Mass spectrometer: This is for testing chemicals and compounds in quantities too small (although not necessarily microscopic) for conventional chemical analysis. The minute sample is identified by its mass as determined via its path through a magnetic field after being ionized by electron bombardment. Different masses create different tracks through the magnetic field, and each track is keyed to a certain substance.

Chromatography equipment: Important in toxicology, this device is one of the best ways to detect poisons and narcotics. Basically, chromatography is an "elegant" means of separating and then identifying individual chemical compounds from a mixture, including a victim's blood, urine, and stomach contents. This is done in several ways. Gas chromatography uses a tube loosely packed with special solid granules, and flowing through this tube is a nonreactive or "carrier" gas such as nitrogen. When a test sample is vaporized into its own gas and injected into the tube, every chemical present in the gas will be "carried" through the tube at a different speed. The speed of a chemical is timed by a sensor at the tube's exit, and different chemicals are then identified by their speeds. In HPLC (for High Performance Liquid Chromatography), a liquid is substituted for gas in the carrier phase. Thin-Layer Chromatography (TLC) also depends on differences in the movement speeds of different chemicals. But here the samples are applied in liquid form to a specially coated glass plate. Then an organic solvent soaks up from the base of the plate, separating the sample's component chemicals and pushing them up the plate at different speeds.

Electrophoresis equipment: This process does the same thing as chromatography—separates and identifies the different chemicals in a mixture—and does it pretty much on the same principle. But here an electric current applied to the sample induces migration (or stimulates movement) of the sample's molecules. The rate of this migration movement differs according to the different weights of different molecules, and the weight is then used to identify what the molecules are made of.

Luminol: Spray this reagent around a crime scene and then shine ultraviolent light on it to make invisible scrubbed-away blood become visible.

Ultraviolet "flashlight": For shining on the above, as well as other uses.

Electrostatic lifter: A special mat charged with static electricity for lifting and capturing certain pattern evidence, such as a shoeprint left in dust.

Gel lifter: A thick sheet of sticky stuff for capturing pattern evidence left in (or by) something other than dust, like shoeprints of tracked-in mud.

DFO: A chemical to make latent fingerprints become visible—and actually glow—under laser or special blue-green light.

Ninhydrin: A chemical reagant that makes certain latent prints visible by turning them purple.

Lifter tape: For removing visible prints from the surfaces they were left on. (Just about any clear adhesive tape will do, but check to see if there's a "best" kind.)

Microtome: A special device sort of like a wood plane, for shaving extremely thin slices of tissue sample needed for microscope examination.

Forensic lab light: Pretty much a "superlamp" in every way, this is a special source of high-intensity light with built-in filters for ultraviolet and infrared. Other filters project a single-color (any color) light to screen out those parts of a busy pattern that are the same color.

Hand vacuum: Small in size, huge in power, for sucking up trace evidence—dust, dirt, fibers, hairs, mica particulates, flecks and flakes of anything and everything, all the small stuff.

Metal detector: A high-grade version of the kind used by coin hunters at the beach. For finding anything metallic (like shell casings) hidden under dirt or leaves or whatever.

Thermal imager: This instrument employs infrared technology to detect and display lingering heat, including the heat from a body no longer present. If used quickly enough (before normal cooling time has expired), this can reveal the positions occupied by perpetrator and/or victim, objects they have held or touched, and so on, as if their "ghosts" have remained behind to betray them.

Vapor analyzer: Also called a hydrocarbon detector. It draws in an air sample and feeds it to a hydrogen flame. A hotter flame indicates the presence of a hydrocarbon fuel, and therefore a fire accelerant. (But it seems to me you could probably combine this with built-in chromatography and/or spectroscopy devices to analyze and identify just about any gas present in the air. Maybe a project for the future WayneTech corporation to tackle?)

Polygraph: Commonly known as a lie detector, but not admissible as evidence because it does not really detect lies. All it does is measure the autonomous physical functions of a suspect under interrogation—sweating, pulse, and breathing—to reveal stress. And just as good liars can lie without getting stressed, some people can get nervous or emotional about telling the truth. So there are good reasons for not allowing polygraph results in court. But they can still help—if only as guidelines for harder investigation.

Fingerprint database: A lifted print is worthless if you can't compare it against the prints of suspects and criminals previously guilty of similar crimes. The bigger the fingerprint file, the better. (Somehow I'll have to get hold of the police database. Better yet, the fingerprint files of every law enforcement organization on Earth.)

Voiceprint analyzer: A device that translates a human voice (on a surveillance tape, for example) into something like an electronic graph. This can be used to recognize and identify the speaker, sometimes even when the voice is muffled or disguised. But only, of course, if you have the actual speaker or a voiceprint database for reference comparison.

Voiceprint database: See above.

Ballistics database: Guns get sold and stolen all the time, so a record of the "ballistic fingerprint" they leave on a bullet is vital. And when a criminal holds on to his gun, he'll probably use it again. Matching the bullets from a fresh crime scene to the bullets from a previous crime (solved or unsolved) proves the two crimes were committed with the same gun if not by the same criminal. And if the bullets can be linked to their gun, tracing that gun may help find its user.

DNA database: This is really looking ahead with almost no use right now because there's pretty much no such thing as a DNA database. Yet. But every criminologist agrees that this will become more and more important as future DNA research and techniques improve. DNA makeup can identify an individual human being even more precisely than his or her fingerprints.

Computer: They're getting better all the time, and I'll need the best. The biggest and the fastest, souped-up state of the art all the way and updated all the time. A lot of this list's earlier items (like spectroscopy and chromatography equipment) require or work best with a computer hookup. Plus a computer that can store and sort through all the various databases will save *lots* of time.

Already quite a list and no doubt only the beginning. The idea is to put together a world-class crime lab with all the best tools available, and I'm still learning about new ones all the time. Not only that, but the future will bring innovations nobody's even thinking about yet. Again, I may even hire people to come up with some of them. No way I'll let anything stop me, not at this point. The final goal is too important.

In June, I wanted to die. Now it's July. If I can stay focused and get through this, something big will come out of it in the end.

I swear. In the name of my parents, in their memory and using the gift of their legacy, I'll never rest until I find a way to do something about what happened to them.

Red of Fang
and Claw

Casefile #0009
Year One, Month Two, Day Five

From the Private Files of the Batman

B RIEF notes on subdued perp Joshua Thigpen, delivered into custody of Homicide Detective Rene Montoya. Related forensic samples and documentation follows.

1) Tentative match between suspect Thigpen's dental records and bite-marks on right breast of victim, Thigpen's late girlfriend. (Further odontology work—full casting of Thigpen's teeth—recommended to establish perfect bite match.)

2) Traces of skin and powder were scraped from beneath Thigpen's fingernails. Powder matched sample taken from victim's face. DNA signature of skin from suspect's fingernails compared against victim's tissue sample will eliminate all doubt.

3) Murder of primal passion, wounds inflicted by "fang" and "claw."

Life savagely wasted. Crime simply solved. Case closed.

Note: My immersion in forensic science has changed the way I look at crime scenes, collected evidence, and the harvesting of "invisible" clues. Thigpen's arrest and certain forthcoming conviction for murder did not need the help of a living instrument of fear and vengeance. Rather, it was the Batman's knowledge of forensics that identified and led to the arrest of the perpetrator. My hope is that a significant number of cases may be solved in this manner. My expectation, however, is that the more brutal side of the Batman will also be needed as I continue my dedicated campaign against those who would take innocent lives. When it comes to that, I will be ready.

Spiral
Striations

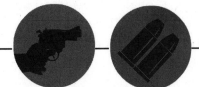

Excerpt From Bruce Wayne's Diary

GUNS give cowards an easy way to kill. If I could possibly avoid it, I wouldn't read or learn or even think about guns. I hate the things. I wish they'd all vaporize right now, burning every hand holding them.

But that's not going to happen. Guns are multiplying, not disappearing, zillions of them all over the world, up to a hundred thousand in Gotham alone. And because guns are what cowardly killers use more than anything else, I *will* keep reading about them. I'll learn everything I can about guns, and I'll use the knowledge every way possible. Guns are the enemy, and knowing the enemy is half the battle.

End of rant, time for business.

The forensic techs who deal with guns are often called the ballistics department, but most of them don't like the name. *Ballistics* actually describes the flight paths of projectiles, meaning missiles or bullets projected or shot from a gun. But determining flight paths is only a small part of what gun techs do, and a lot of times they don't even bother with it. The flight path is usually obvious and mostly irrelevant anyway, because it rarely helps to nail the perpetrator. So gun techs prefer to have their department called firearms identification—which is not the only thing they do, but it's a lot more accurate than *ballistics*.

Probably the most important thing they do is match bullets to guns. If you can prove that the bullet taken out of a murder victim's body was fired by a prime suspect's gun—and no other gun in existence—you've gone a long way toward solving the crime and obtaining conviction. And the way you can do this is by analyzing the "ballistic fingerprint" etched into every bullet fired by any gun.

The inside of a gun barrel is not smooth metal. It's actually rough with flaws and bumps and barbs. In a process called rifling, the main irregularities are deliberately made during the gun's manufacture. These are spiral grooves that make a fired bullet spin through the barrel because a spinning missile is more stable and will reach its target on a truer flight path. Luckily for the firearms techs, rifling grooves are at least slightly different for every gun barrel ever made, even two barrels rifled in a row. That's because the process uses a metal brush whose bristles cut the tiny grooves even as the bristles are dislodged or bent or worn down. The very act of rifling a barrel changes the brush doing the rifling, and that changes the spacing of the grooves inside each barrel, creating an interior pattern "as unique as a fingerprint."

This ballistic fingerprint gets transferred from the barrel onto any bullet fired through it. Tiny barbs along the barrel grooves actually scratch the bullet as they make it spin. These rifling mark scratches are also called spiral striations because they're diagonally wrapped around and down the length of the bullet, like a barber pole or a candy cane (except with more than one stripe).

The overall pattern of these side-by-side spiral scratches is what forms the ballistic fingerprint of "lands" and "grooves." The grooves are the actual scratches carved into the bullet, whereas the lands are the higher, untouched surfaces between the grooves. So you take a microscope photograph of your crime scene bullet, and its unique pattern of lands and grooves serves as your reference for future testing. Any bullet recovered from another crime scene, for example, can be compared to your reference. If there's a match, you know the bullet was fired by the same gun. And if the two crimes are similar, they were probably committed by the same criminal. If the crimes are extremely different, it's possible the gun has been sold or stolen and is now in the hands of a different criminal.

In any case, once you have a "fingerprinted" bullet, you can test and compare a suspected gun of the same caliber. If you get such a gun, you load it with the same type of ammunition and fire a bullet into either water, gel, or cotton batting. Then you compare *this* bullet's land-and-groove pattern against the reference of the actual crime scene bullet. If the patterns don't match *precisely*, you've got the wrong gun. And if they do match, you've found your murder weapon. And maybe (probably) your killer—the person you took the gun from.

Bottom line: Matching the inner surface of a gun barrel to the outer surface of a bullet links the two. Such a match proves that the bullet spun through the barrel of that gun and no other gun on Earth.

When this technique of "ballistics comparison" was demonstrated in his courtroom in 1902, the famous Judge Oliver Wendell Holmes said: "I see no other way in which the jury could have learned so intelligently how a gun barrel would have marked a lead bullet fired through it." Amen to that, Ollie.

Ballistics comparison is obviously complicated when a retrieved bullet has been squash-distorted or fragmented by impact. But even a surprisingly small fragment can contain enough of the overall pattern to make identification possible. Especially since lands and grooves are not the only markings used to match a gun and its ammunition.

Less conclusive but still fairly precise are indentations on spent and ejected cartridge casings (rather than on the actual bullets), marks that are virtually unique to a particular gun's firing pin and ejector mechanism.

Then there's also the "knurled cannelure," a circumferential groove impressed around a bullet or cartridge case by the loading mechanism, and at least slightly different for every gun.

A perfect match for lands and grooves is really all that's needed, but adding these other marks gives you a real lock. Because no one wants to send an innocent person to prison, juries need to have their doubts completely eliminated by hard evidence adding up to proof. The more evidence you can show them, the more you'll erase their doubts.

On the other hand, some forensic tests seem to go too far with exaggerated claims that can backfire. One of them is neutron activation analysis, a process that supposedly determines the atomic composition of a given bullet and then links it to other bullets from the "same manufacture batch"—like those in a partially used box of ammunition found in a suspect's possession. But discrepancies in research tests pose a big challenge to neutron activation. It seems there can be a bigger difference in composition between two sample pieces of the *same bullet* than there is between one bullet and another. So although the test is still used by some law enforcement agencies and prosecutors, it seems pretty much discredited to me.

Completely discredited and almost never used these days is the once-common paraffin test to determine if an individual has recently fired a gun. Waxy paraffin was used to lift residue from a suspect's hand or hands—and cheek, in the case of a crime committed with a rifle. The lifted residue was then analyzed for the presence of nitrates found in every gun's primer explosive. Problem is, these same nitrates are also present in newspaper ink, cosmetics, cigarettes, agricultural products, and even urine. (*Note to self*: Never smoke while reading the news in the john—and always wash your hands!)

So the abandoned paraffin test has been replaced by the newer P-GSR (Primer GunShot Residues) process. Here a common swab lifts residue from hand or cheek, and an atomic absorption spectrophotometer analyzes the residue for barium, lead, and antimony—also present in primer explosive but far less common in other, innocent substances.

If a bullet has completely transited its victim and is never recovered, then you can look to the victim's entrance wound for some help. Here the firearms identification techs team up with the forensic pathologist (or medical examiner) to find not a whole lot between them. The exit wound tells you almost nothing, and even the entrance wound gives you little more than the bullet's probable caliber.

A spinning bullet leaves its rifled barrel at a velocity exceeding 1,500 feet per second, creating a minor "tail wag" much like the wobble of even the fastest spinning top. For this reason, even the "neatest"—or most circular—entrance wound in human flesh will be slightly larger than the caliber of the bullet that caused it, although far smaller than the typically "star-burst" exit wound. And if the traveling bullet "tumbles" completely out of control, its entrance wound will be a large irregular laceration from which you can't really estimate caliber—and with an exit wound that's a truly ugly mess of flesh, bone, and blood.

A gunshot is nothing more nor less than a violent explosion slamming a hot piece of metal into soft flesh. And to me, that makes the gun humanity's all-time worst invention. A knife doesn't have to stab a heart, not when it can also cut bread. And a hammer works just as well building a house as it does crushing a skull. But other than maiming or killing, what else can a gun do? It has no constructive purpose whatsoever. Guns were invented to gush blood, period.

I hate the cold dark heavy things, and I hate the cowards who use them. The two together are death, and stopping death is the only thing I want to live for.

Blowback

Casefile #0139
Year Two, Month One, Day Twenty-Three

From the Private Files of the Batman

MORE careful than the common murderer, professional assassins are typically more difficult to
incriminate on the basis of circumstantial evidence. The caution they tend to exercise in their "profession," however, is
informed by personal experience rather than esoteric principles
of physics. Herewith, brief notes on the case just concluded,
wherein such principles shaped one hitman's downfall.

When a major figure in Gotham's underworld found himself
under felony indictment, murderer-for-hire Albert Runcible was
contracted to eliminate the key prosecution witness. Shot once
through the head at close range, witness became victim, leaving
the upcoming trial in jeopardy.

Murder occurred in the victim's bed, its commission cold-
blooded and methodical. A pillow pressed over the victim's face
was used to muffle the sound of the gun, thereby silencing the
witness with a nearly noiseless shot.

Passing through the pillow to enter the victim's head,
the bullet had then exited to embed in the mattress. It was
dug out and removed from the scene by the murderer. Thus
convinced that no weapon could be tied to the crime by ballistics comparison or anything else, Runcible disposed of the

bullet but retained his gun. If and when professional confidence transforms to arrogance, however, it can also become a fatal mistake.

Runcible was already suspected in a string of contract killings linked to the man under indictment as well as to other organized crime elements. But mere suspicion is never enough, and no case could be convincingly made against Runcible. The previous murders remained unsolved, and this murder looked to be no different.

Until I saw the pillow and remembered the phenomenon of "blowback."

As he had several times in the past, Police Commissioner James Gordon ordered Runcible's arrest on suspicion of murder with a warrant to search his premises. According to arresting officer Harvey Bullock, Runcible was "all cocky cooperation." Recently employed as a bodyguard, he freely produced his handgun along with the permit covering it. Yes, it had been recently fired, he admitted, but only on the target range. And while Runcible also surrendered a box of ammunition, the gun itself was the only thing I needed.

The assassin was obviously correct in assuming he had nothing to fear from the science of ballistics. With no bullet in evidence, there was no pattern of lands and grooves available for comparison with the rifling of his gun's barrel.

Runcible was wrong, however, to assume that his weapon could not be tied to the crime scene in any way. Rather than a bullet that had come out of the gun, the link would be something found *inside* the gun's barrel.

When a firearm is discharged, the resulting rapid expansion of high-pressure gases sucks outside material—if only dust in the air—into the gun's barrel. Even as the bullet is blown out, in other words, other matter is "blown back" in the bullet's wake and into the gun.

After Gordon gave me Runcible's gun, I extracted minute fragments from the interior of its barrel. Confirming what I hoped to find, gross microscopic examination showed the material to be tiny bits of *feather*. Mass spectrometry further established them as the *same type* of feather—eider down—as found in the sound-muffling bullet-holed pillow left at the murder scene. And finally, DNA typing conclusively linked the gun barrel's feather bits to more than a dozen of the pillow feathers, all sharing identical genetic markers. Feather bits and pillow feathers had come from the *same individual bird*, to the exclusion of all other birds on Earth.

With Albert Runcible's goose thus cooked, he was offered a reduced plea, albeit one still carrying a life sentence. And on advice of counsel, he agreed to cooperate. Having eliminated the prosecution's best chance for conviction in the original trial, the assassin will now take his victim's place on the witness stand. Runcible will, in fact, exert a different form of blowback by testifying against the very crime boss who hired him, now charged with an additional felony count.

One crime thus became the motive for another, and murder turned one case into two, both now closed.

Cause of Death

Casefile #0021
Year One, Month Four, Day Two

From the Journal of Alfred Pennyworth

I can only hope the master does not object to my presumption in recounting his most recent case. His own private accounts are the inspiration, of course, although I hardly wish to steal his thunder. Still and all, given this dreadful Joker business currently terrorizing the city, the master's preoccupation spares little time for anything else, let alone reliving a lesser case now closed, whereas my own time is less restricted.

Whether in brief notes or longer narrative, and whether eventually shared in sanitized form with others or forever confined to the master's private review, I see enormous value in the documentation of each of his intriguing and informative cases. Given the urgent pursuit now underway, previous knowledge risks loss. And since I have already been invited to contribute my own insights, if not wholly new accounts, I shall here stretch the invitation and endeavor to record the salient details of a curious mystery solved by rather ingenious means.

The body, that of a man in his early fifties, attired in T-shirt and shorts, was recovered from the southern shore of Gotham Bay. The immediate questions were obvious, and clearly posed a choice mystery. Did this represent an accidental drowning? Had the man deliberately committed suicide? Was he perhaps murdered by forced drowning? Or was this the retrieval of disposed remains following murder by other means?

When Gotham Medical Examiner Mortimer Gunt's findings proved inconclusive, the master was secretly accorded full access to the autopsy report along with appropriate samples from the deceased. Together in the cavern chill, we hunkered down to examine the material until I for one saw no way to improve on M.E. Gunt's performance. Not so the master.

He immediately focused on the recovered cadaver's advanced degree of adipocere, this being body fat transformed into a waxy grayish substance often described as soaplike, although to my eyes it appears distinctly unclean. Nevertheless, provided environmental conditions are known, the degree of a body's decomposition can indicate its approximate length of death. If at any unknown point the cadaver has been moved from one locale to another with differing conditions of heat, light, moisture, or any number of other factors, then all bets are off.

This, then, prompted new questions. How long had the man been dead? How long had his body been in the water? And were the answers one and the same? The degree of body fat deterioration, as measured by the amount of adipocere, might provide some clues. Or so the master reasoned, warning me, however, of certain complications specific to this situation.

Prolonged immersion in water, fresh or saline, retards the human body's "normal" decomposition while simultaneously accelerating the transformation of fat to adipocere, presenting a rather sticky wicket right off the bat. In this case, length of death assessed by degree of immersion adipocere had already been correlated with the dates of missing persons reports, of which only two were relevant. Using the two sets of dental records, Gunt confirmed the deceased as one of the persons reported missing, a businessman who had failed to return from a fishing outing. The body, Gunt therefore reasoned, had been immersed since the date of the missing persons report and therefore more or less since death. The master concurred, proceeding on the nearly certain hypothesis that the businessman met his end either on or actually under the water of Gotham Bay.

But again: Was this a case of drowning or dumping? Moreover, was the death accident, suicide, or murder?

Water in the lungs proved nothing either way, yet it was at this stage that the master first trumped M.E. Gunt. Microscopic examination of water extracted from the lungs revealed the presence of diatoms, these being tiny algae-like organisms of remarkable geometric structure. No surprise, because diatoms are present in all bodies of water hosting normal biosystems. Indeed, other than the fact that the bay is not yet thoroughly polluted, this finding also proved nothing. There was, however, a way to determine if the extracted water had been inhaled while the man was alive, meaning he had drowned, or had simply entered his lungs after death, meaning he had expired from some other and thus far unknown cause.

Using acid to dissolve a sample of the man's heart tissue (although other internal organs would have sufficed), we then microscopically examined the dissolved tissue. The same diatoms were present, proving the body's autonomous functions were still in play when water entered its lungs. Only through inhalation could the diatoms be thus absorbed and migrate into the man's internal organs.

This was unequivocal proof of drowning rather than mere dumping. The nature of the drowning, however, still remained in question. Was it suicide or accidental? Or even murder by drowning, had the man been forcibly held underwater until he could no longer suspend his breath. The latter would be extremely difficult to determine and likely impossible to prove. The master, in any case, considered murder by such means improbable on the face of it. Indeed, employing the principle of Occam's Razor, he cut straight to the matter's heart, as it were: The least complicated solution is most likely to prevail.

That left us with uncomplicated drowning, either accidental or suicidal. It also marked that inevitable point when the master always, if only temporarily, lays Occam's Razor off to the side. He is simply unwilling to write off any death as innocent until the slightest chance of foul play has been conclusively eliminated.

We therefore fell back on more traditional detective methods, seeking any possible motive and every possible suspect. And quite quickly, we learned that the deceased's business partner stood to gain from the premature death in two ways: as primary insurance beneficiary and by inheriting full ownership of the previously shared business. At the master's request, Police Commissioner James Gordon dispatched two of his detectives to interview the partner, who had in fact filed the original missing persons report. Queried about the day of the fatal fishing outing, the man could provide no alibi. Claiming he took the day off, just as his late associate had, he further claimed to have spent the entire day "relaxing alone at home." Fishing, he said, was not his "thing."

Aha. Given the partner's inability to account for his whereabouts on the day in question, we now had a logical suspect with indisputable motive and possible opportunity.

The information served to galvanize the master, sending us immediately back to the forensic evidence and more precisely to a deeper analysis of the diatoms present in the lung water as compared to those present in the dissolved organ tissue. There will always be more "free" diatoms than absorbed ones, more teeming in the lung contents than embedded in any tissue. Furthermore, values for a normal ratio between the two are known. In this case, a pronounced discrepancy in proportions suggested the man had drowned while unconscious—while barely breathing, in fact, rather than surrendering to swift, deep inhalation.

This, of course, might indicate foul play preceding immersion, although it was still possible that the man simply passed out and fell into the water.

Confronted with negative toxicology results, we effectively ruled out inebriation and poisoning, whereas Gunt's necropsy had further eliminated cardiac arrest.

Murder unfortunately looked better and better. And yet murder by forcible drowning was still difficult to accept. Had death occurred in a bathtub, the odds would have been considerably reduced, but this was out in open water somewhere on or near Gotham Bay. The drowning, then, was most likely precipitated by attempted murder of other means. In other words, drowning constituted the murder's final stage but not its beginning, and therefore less than the full story.

M.E. Gunt had discovered no evidence of blunt trauma or indeed any other antemortem wounds, nor could the master discern any such indications in the autopsy photographs and X-rays. No broken bones, no telltale lacerations or piercings, no obvious bruising. The fish, however, had not been idle. And while exclusively postmortem, their feeding only complicated our dilemma.

Nevertheless, with shooting, stabbing, beating, and poisoning all effectively ruled out by the evidence, the list of likely murder methods was significantly shortened. Ranked next in a virtual tie were strangulation and suffocation, one or the other resulting in loss of consciousness followed by immersion of the body while rendered helpless but still alive. In the absence of ligature marks on the neck, garroting was conclusively eliminated. Also absent was any evidence that the trachea had been crushed, nor had Gunt found any of the bruising typically inflicted by squeezing fingers or gouging thumbs, although the work of the fish left room for doubt. But only marginal doubt, resting on rather farfetched coincidence. (Would fish nibble *only* bruised flesh? Or, in any case, *all* of the bruised flesh?)

Strangulation moved down the list, letting suffocation rise to the top. And with no indications of obstruction in the man's air passages, there was no reason to assume he had choked on a portion of the sandwich found barely digested in his stomach contents. More likely, the master concluded, he had been smothered by a pillow or blanket, perhaps a wadded shirt or jacket. And such suffocation had likely been initiated without warning, possibly while the man slept or drowsed on a fishing boat after taking his lunch.

In any case, a well-known phenomenon is induced by suffocation and strangulation alike. This is known as petechiae, ruptures of tiny blood vessels in the eyelids and surrounding tissue. But here again, we were stymied. Any presence of eyelid or cheek petechiae had been thoroughly obscured by advanced adipocere formation in the fatty facial tissue, if not entirely removed by the avid appetites of marine creatures.

Although we had gone well beyond the work of the medical examiner, it was at this moment, quite candidly, that I was prepared to throw my own hands up. It was precisely the point when the master proved he will never cease to take me aback. He alerted Commissioner Gordon with a message that was to be relayed to the medical examiner before the body left the morgue.

The message, more or less, amounted to this: *Look to the mouth, and the dead man will tell his tale.*

Following this advice, Coroner Gunt easily discerned ruptured blood vessels where fish cannot reach, deep inside the mouth. Furthermore, with less fat layered in the hard palate than in soft facial tissue, and therefore less susceptibility to adipocere formation, the interior petechiae was readily evident. And immediately photographed as key exhibits for criminal trial.

Fanning out along the marina to check all boat rental establishments, Commissioner Gordon's detectives located the floating scene of the crime (leased through the dead man's credit card) within a single afternoon. Fingerprints lifted from the rented boat included seven matching the deceased and more than a dozen matching his business partner. Who, had he been more criminally astute, would have sunk the boat and swum to shore.

Subsequent arrest and interrogation, presumably less genteel than the initial interview, led to the surviving partner's full confession, thereby netting an "amateur" criminal who very nearly accomplished the perfect crime. Indeed, were it not for improbably detailed knowledge of both adipocere and petechiae, the man would likely have gotten away with murder.

I can only wonder how the master possesses such arcane details, as well as where and when he found the time to acquire them. In any event, as the master himself is wont to say, and as I will here echo . . .

Case closed.

The Joker and
the Profiler

Casefile #0023
Year One, Month Four, Day Five

Annotated Transcript of Police Interrogation

MORE than ever, I am now convinced that the "behavioral science of psychological profiling" is vastly overrated and overvalued, as demonstrated by the following verbatim exchange between police profiler and true madman.

Developed by the FBI at Quantico, profiling has achieved a mythical status it does not deserve. While of limited use in some cases and under certain circumstances, the process is almost entirely speculative, little more than educated fortune-telling and similarly based on statistical smoke and mirrors. But the myth dies hard. Volumes are written about the "stunningly accurate" predictions about unknown serial killers, including their natures, habits, and even future actions, but such accurate profiles are actually quite rare. Far more common are all-wet predictions hung out to dry with little notice and no mention.

Moreover, even the most "successful" profile tends to be heavily weighted with vague and essentially useless probability ("likely a white male in his 20s or 30s" who "probably owns or has access to a vehicle" and who "feels comfortable operating in the area"), as well as rife with the jaw-droppingly obvious ("probably afflicted with antiscocial tendencies" who "feels no remorse for his criminal acts" and who "will likely commit such acts again in the future"), while utterly lacking any meaningful specificity. The most thoroughly detailed profile typi-

cally narrows the list of possible suspects to mere millions. Such so-called analysis, in fact, tells us no more than what is clearly seen on the face of it.

I am not alone in my skepticism. Aware that perpetrators are almost always caught by more conventional means, most street cops simply ignore profile bulletins. Some laugh at them. Pop-culture fiction and true-crime bestsellers aside, even other FBI agents view profiling as a "misuse of vital resources" better devoted to the hard forensic sciences. One described the celebrity status of fellow agents in the Behavioral Division as "a sick joke."

When the "serial killer" in question is actually a multiple murderer like the Joker, with a mindset as unpredictably bizarre as his, any interrogation inevitably offers as much profile contrasting as comparing. The Joker may well be unique. And yet, as the very definition of "homicidal maniac," he surely shares certain traits and modes of behavior with other deranged killers. While it is still early in the Batman's career, I have yet to encounter a more dangerous individual and cannot imagine I ever will. Understanding his mind and learning from his example is therefore crucial. And even a misguided interrogation contains valuable insights, if only in the Joker's responses to obtuse or irrelevant questions.

Hence the following transcript, with profiler's name redacted and appropriate notes interpolated, although I do not myself pretend to have all the answers or fully understand the twisted evil of this nightmare clown.

Profiler: State your name for the record, please.

Joker: I'd rather tattoo it on your forehead. Etched by hand, with a blunt dirty needle dipped in dayglo acid. [*Laughter*] Yowtch, that stings!

Profiler: Your name, please. We can't begin this talk without it.

Joker: Then shut up.

Profiler: Your *name*.

Joker: Call me Pagliacchi. [*Giggling*] But hold the drama and kill the tears.

Profiler: All right, we'll let it go for now. You've waived your right to counsel and consented to this interview, is that correct? You have no objection talking?

Joker: I'd rather act than talk, but these restraints . . . [*Prolonged shrieking, howling, violent thrashing*] . . . well, they are rather restraining, aren't they?

Profiler: Any further such outbursts, I must warn you, will not be tolerated.

Joker: And they'll be stopped how? By restraining me? [*Laughter*]

Profiler: Can you tell me what happened to your face? Why it's so white?

Joker: I confess, I'm a night owl. The sunshine bores the daylights out of me.

Profiler: We're discussing something more severe than the lack of a tan. And it seems to affect all of your skin, not just your face.

Joker: Wanna verify, big boy? [*Wild giggles*]

Profiler: Just answer the question, if you will.

Joker: Chalk it up to a bleach job involving a tumble incident and a vat of chemicals. Here's me: Whoops, sploosh, yahh! [*Insane laughter*]

This was the truth but apparently dismissed by the profiler, given the sarcastic tone of his voice on the tape.

Profiler: And I suppose that's also the explanation for your, uh, peculiar facial contortion?

Joker: What peculiar facial contortion would that be?

Profiler: The rictus . . . the exaggerated grin. It seems to be frozen in place.

It is, suggesting permanent nerve damage. It may be that his skin has been more than bleached. It may have been seared, and I wonder if the Joker exists in a state of chronic pain.

Joker: I'd like to think the chipper smile suits me. Happy is he whose work is his pleasure.

Profiler: Work?

Joker: You don't think slaughtering in mass quantities is easy, do you?

Profiler: So taking lives makes you happy? Makes you smile?

Joker: We've already established I need no catalyst for the built-in toothy mirth look. [*Chuckles*]

Profiler: Let's talk about your mother . . .

Joker: So after I killed her, I left her for dead, so what? It's not like I ate her, tempting sweetmeat though she be. [*Maniacal laughter*]

This, like so many of his other responses, was a lie, or at least his idea of a joke. Apparently believed by the profiler, however, it led to some five minutes of dead-end questioning, here omitted along with a brief and meaningless discussion of the Joker's father. Both subjects are potentially valuable avenues, but only if explored by a more skilled interrogator.

Profiler: How do you feel when you kill?

Joker: Amused and fulfilled, like shooting mimes on a moonlit beach. Long walks on moonlit beaches, by the way, are some of my favorite things, along with puppy dogs with broken necks and hot fudge sundaes laced with strychnine. And before you ask, my favorite color is purple.

Profiler: So you're amused by the act of murder?

Joker: Like shooting bluefish in a shallow barrel. Or loud mimes on an empty beach. [*Laughter*] And don't forget fulfilled.

Profiler: Do you feel the need to kill? A compulsion?

Joker: Actually, a passing whim'll do.

Also apparently true, but in the Joker's mind, there may be little or no difference between compulsion and whim. Just as he hides behind the "mask" of his leering white face, a façade of twisted humor may conceal much deeper and darker urges. Like a jack-in-the-box, his violence springs forth in the guise of a garish clown. And because the dark box containing his violence is a psyche impossible to recognize or understand, its explosion is always unexpected. But unlike a jack-in-the-box—which first shocks and then draws laughter as relief—the Joker craves laughter first, then kills it with shocks of horror.

Profiler: You've been charged with murdering nine people . . .

Joker: Is that all?

Profiler: . . . and wounding seven more.

Joker: Gotta get out on that shooting range, sharpen the old aim. [*Laughter*] Pretty bad when they're still squirming after the fifth shot, but pass the ammo anyway.

Profiler: The people you killed or injured shared little in common. Different physical types, different ages, weights, races, both genders, and all were strangers. How did you select your victims?

Joker: Other than all having transparent windows, that's the standing issue, isn't it?

Profiler: Standing?

Joker: If they can stand, they can fall. I ask nothing more of future meat. [*Insane cackling*] With freshness thus assured, what hunter could resist?

Profiler: Then you're a hunter? You think of yourself as a predator?

Here the questioner again falls into a rhetorical trap, as he does repeatedly, demonstrating his ability to see only what he's looking for. He may as well be the Joker's straight man. Time and again, instead of objectively assessing his subject, he tries to fit the Joker into the familiar pattern of previous profiles, as if seeking some master key to unlock the pathology of every killer. But despite any and all similarities, every killer is unique. And in the case of the Joker, that truism is taken to an almost surreal extreme.

Joker: I think of myself as the clown prince of merry mayhem and murderous mirth, the scary trickster who makes you shriek. So what's your excuse?

Profiler: Your complete lack of remorse and empathy is noted. In fact, it's a given. Do you think you feel superior to other people?

Joker: Feeling *is* thinking, a waste of time, and killing time is always more productive.

Profiler: But is that why you're able to kill people? Because they seem inferior to you, not really people at all, more like animals? Just prey?

Joker: I ain't about to get religion at this point, bub, so just pray yourself.

Profiler: If you could drop the act for a minute, just between you and me, I want to ask you a serious question.

The modern jester persona may well be a pose, but the Joker's dementia is not an act. He is fully and genuinely insane.

Joker: I don't do serious.

Profiler: Would you describe yourself as a narcissistic personality?

Joker: I get the best cell in Arkham, don't I?

Profiler: To which you'll soon return. So how do you feel about that?

Joker: I could use the break. [*Soft laugh*] At least for a while, and then comes the other kind of break.

Profiler: How did you feel about being apprehended for the second time?

Joker: He cheated! [*Shrieking*] I don't know how, but he always cheats!

Here the Joker becomes enraged, his previous tone of lunatic clowning instantly gone.

Profiler: You're talking about Detective Bullock?

Joker: You know damn well who I'm talking about! Gordon's secret weapon—and they call *me* batty!

Profiler: If you're referring to this so-called "Bat-man," you're the third one to do so in the last month. And it's no joke, in my opinion. In fact, I sense a fascinating sociological phenomenon here, one with real momentum. Do you think the entire underworld could be in the grip of some strange mass hysteria?

Joker: You got that right, but nobody's laughing. I can't even get the boyos to crack a smile these days. They're all too afraid of their own shadows. I'll probably have to cut out his heart and serve it up on a platter before the good times roll again.

Profiler: You're *not* joking. You actually believe in this Bat-man, don't you? Even you.

Joker: A swift kick to the head works wonders in the convert department.

Profiler: But "a gargoyle coming to life"—a giant bat swooping down out the night sky? Surely that's just a myth, a figment of criminal imagination.

Joker: Looked upward lately?

Profiler: You're right, that bat image beamed into the clouds probably started the whole thing. But that's just some advertising gimmick. Or maybe the newspapers are behind it, looking to build circulation by concocting better stories.

Joker: And maybe the coppers are behind it. [*Sly disgust*] Maybe Gordon.

Profiler: If so, wouldn't it make more sense to see the light—maybe I shouldn't say this—as just a ploy on the part of the police department, some form of psychological warfare?

Joker: More like his logo, an upside-down spotlight cueing the main attraction, the big Bat's act.

Profiler: And yet the record here is clear. You were arrested by Homicide Detective Harvey Bullock.

Joker: That clumsy oaf couldn't arrest his own fetid breath! Bats *gave* me to the Bull! He turned me over to the cops, but he cheated!

Profiler: All right, how did he cheat?

Joker: You tell me and we'll both know! There's no way he should have found me so soon! [*Snarling*] You said it yourself, I only bagged nine, a lousy single night's work! I was barely setting up for Shooting Gallery Two, letting the next night fall and watching the lights come on in all the faraway windows, showing my longshot targets all around, and then he crashes down through the roof like hell busting loose before I can score my first shot! So you tell me how his boots found the right roof because I don't know! It's like he's in league with the darkness!

Or in this case with light, and more specifically the finely focused beam of a laser used to determine bullet trajectory.

The entire murder spree had taken less than three hours, from half-past nine to shortly after midnight, with all victims shot by high-powered rifle through their closed windows. Since the recovered rounds were all the same make and caliber, they were almost certainly fired through the same weapon, making ballistics comparison a formality that could wait. Finding and stopping the shooter was more pressing.

The victims were scattered, their punctured windows ranged near and far, and located on upper floors as well as lower. The bullet holes held the answer, and much can be gauged by the naked eye alone, including a shot's approximate angle, after closely examining the characteristics of a single hole through a single window. The beam from a portable laser projected from within the room, outward through the hole and along that angle, then traces the bullet's probable trajectory with a fair degree of accuracy. Such a laser beam, if not stopped by a building or some other obstacle, can reach all the way across the city. The beam, in fact, becomes an illuminated ghost of the bullet's passage, with the shooter's position located at some point along the beam, most likely its end.

Furthermore, a beam aligned through the window hole from a second fixed reference point—the bullet's terminus deeper in the room—traces the trajectory with perfect precision. Final impact with a victim, however, will yield only an approximation of the bullet's terminus, the victim having fallen or slumped.

These sniper shootings, fortunately, were committed from a considerable distance, with one or more misses preceding the fatal or wound-

ing shot at a number of the scenes. This meant that each missed shot left a second fixed reference point, a final impact in wall, ceiling, floor, or furniture. A laser beam projected from the bullet's final impact through its window entry hole would thus point straight to the shooter's position.

After selecting and visiting two scenes with missed shots and multiple holes in glass, wood, and plaster, I needed no further confirmation. Every beam projected from the first two sites lined up perfectly, converging on the same location from multiple angles and two different directions. And with every beam stopped by the same structure, they revealed the sniper's firing position with pinpoint precision, and the position revealed the sniper's identity. The killing spree bullets had been fired from the storage attic of the funhouse in Gotham's abandoned amusement park, where the Joker had indulged his latest idea of fun.

Profiler: Listen to yourself. "In league with the darkness." You're describing the bogeyman.

Joker: I told you, I'm describing someone a lot more batty than me. Who else could have stopped me? Why am I shackled in here instead of out plugging more windows?

Profiler: Good police work. Detective Bullock's report mentions a portable laser used to—

Joker: Don't make me laugh. [*Venomously*]

Profiler: All right, however it went down, you were arrested and here we are. Trying to get to the bottom of what happened *before* you were arrested. Can you just give me a sense of why you did it?

Joker: Surely you jest.

Profiler: But how did you come up with the idea? Was it something you planned for a long time or did it come on suddenly? Was it spontaneous? And what was the point of it? Were you trying to terrorize the city? Was it political in some way? Ideological? Or would you say you're simply consumed with unreasoning hatred for just about anyone and everyone, driven by urges having no other outlet?

Joker: All of the above, except most of it.

Profiler: Would you say your urges have certain triggers?

Joker: No, but my guns certainly do.

Profiler: And why do you use guns? Because they fill you with a sense of power?

Joker: Because they fill meat with holes. [*Insane laughter*]

Profiler: That's the best you can come up with? The best explanation for your appalling actions? A sick joke?

Joker: If you're so smart, trump me, baby.

The only predictable aspect of the Joker's criminally insane psyche is its inherent unpredictability. Given the chance, he will kill and kill again, but how, why, when, and whom he will kill cannot be anticipated. His reasons and methods are not random but are so quixotic and impulsive they may as well be. The overriding insight provided by this profiling attempt, therefore, is that the Joker cannot be profiled.

Profiler: I'm just trying to understand you. What you've done is wrong and this is the second time you've done it. Abhorrent multiple murder. Think about that, about all the truly despicable things you've done, all the heartache you've caused. And believe me when I say we want to help you stop, but you have to make *some* sense, okay? You have to toss me a bone here and we're running out of time. Now, before you're remanded back to Arkham as an incurable sociopath, isn't there anything important you'd like to say?

Joker: Nice tie, great shade of cop blue. Want me to tighten it until your face matches? Maybe pull your tongue out and staple it to—

Profiler: All right, the interview's over. I give up.

And I never will. Case closed—but only for now. Note to self: Explore improvements to Arkham security.

Telltale Tattoo

Casefile #0039
Year One, Month Six, Day Three

From the Private Files of the Batman

GUNPOWDER "tattooing" refers to the stippled marks of partially burned propellant soot driven into human skin shot at close range. Obliquely related to (but not at all the same as) ballistics evidence, such tattooing has just decoded the truth behind a carefully orchestrated public execution.

Quite simply, when a victim is shot at close range, the entrance wound will be surrounded by a "tattooed" pattern of burned powder blown from the gun barrel in its bullet's wake.

The pattern and extent of such a powder tattoo can thus be assessed to gauge the range and angle of the shot fired, although only within limited parameters. Because tattooing cannot occur when the gun barrel is pressed directly to the victim's skin or clothing, nor when the gun is fired from a distance greater than the ejected powder can travel, these parameters extend between a fraction of an inch to approximately ten feet.

When the actual murder weapon is unavailable, simple analysis of the fatal bullet will reveal the weapon's caliber and general type. A similar weapon can then be used to replicate the victim's gunshot tattoo on pigskin or some other substitute for human skin. Test firings from graduated distances, using tiny increments, followed by comparisons of the resulting tattoos, will then establish the distance between murder weapon and murder victim virtually to the inch.

(A related technique applies only to crimes committed with certain types of shotguns, wherein the "scatter pattern" of discharged pellets is used to establish shooting distance. The tighter and smaller the scatter pattern is, the closer the shotgun had to be—with more widely dispersed patterns indicating progressively greater ranges.)

In the case at hand, the murder weapon was a 9-mm handgun. The victim was a wealthy drug lord murdered in public on an uptown street with his bodyguard at his side.

Distant witnesses described a single gunshot from a speeding drive-by car. Closer witnesses said there may have been two shots, "almost on top of each other." The failed bodyguard, claiming familiarity with gunshots, attributed the discrepancy to "the echo of a single shot."

When police arrived at the scene, they found the victim already dead at the feet of his unarmed bodyguard. Eighteen witnesses gave statements, with all agreeing that no one other than the bodyguard was within twenty feet of the victim at the time of the shot or shots.

Coroner Gunt's autopsy description of the victim's gunshot tattoo, therefore, raised immediate suspicion. I asked permission to pursue the matter, and Police Commissioner Gordon granted the request.

Hating the feel of the 9-mm weapon in my hands, I conducted a standard series of test firings here in the cavern. (The echoes in this vast vaulted space were long and loud, and every reverberation pulsed with bad memories.) The resulting test tattoo that best matched the victim's tattoo was produced at a distance of some five inches—or, more precisely, no less than four inches and no more than six.

Since parked cars blocked the curb, any shot originating from the drive-by car was fired from a distance of at least fifteen feet. This strongly suggested, then, that the murderer could only be the falsely testifying bodyguard himself, moonlighting as a hired assassin. His 9-mm murder weapon was apparently removed from the scene by an accomplice in the aftermath of confusion and before the police arrived.

Because of the seeming circumstances and witness statements about the drive-by car, however, the investigating detectives did not think to conduct a P-GSR test on the bodyguard. In other words, they forever forfeited their opportunity to discover primer gunshot residue on the man's hands, proving he had recently fired a gun, whether armed or not when the police arrived.

This test should and must be routine. Gordon agrees, assuring it will be standard procedure, effective immediately.

With the damage done in this case, Gordon could only place the bodyguard under surveillance. When he began spending cash beyond the means of any bodyguard, we were virtually certain he was guilty of a contract killing. And yet there was still no real proof.

Gordon assigned an undercover officer to the tavern frequented by the bodyguard. It took more than a month, but the officer gradually ingratiated himself. And when the drunken bodyguard ultimately admitted to "scoring large for capping a guy," the undercover officer was wearing a wire. Gordon now had what amounted to a confession in the man's own slurred words, although we did not yet know the identities of his accomplices or who had hired them.

Confronted with the tavern tape and the powder tattoo evidence, fortunately, the bodyguard decided life in prison was preferable to the death penalty. In return for judicial consideration, he admitted that the drive-by shot—fired harmlessly high—served as a combined diversion and alibi staged by his second accomplice. The distant false shot, in other words, covered up the bodyguard's certain-death close shot.

The bodyguard/assassin further revealed the identities of both accomplices, one of whom still held the murder weapon in his possession. All three then gave up one more name. They had been hired by the dead man's son, whose greed and excessive lifestyle were deemed more important than his wealthy father's life.

With the son's delivery to Gordon some two hours ago, the case now awaits multiple trials and is closed at this end.

Two Much
Evidence

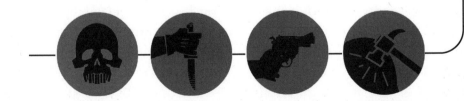

Casefile #0102
Year One, Month Eleven, Day Twelve

From the Private Files of the Batman

EVIDENCE properly analyzed opens a window on the past. A skilled detective can look back through time to "see" the event that created the evidence. Yet this view and vision is a work of the imagination, a mere reconstruction of the most likely past as shaped by informed logic and whose probative value must rank lower than that of an eyewitness account. Not that deduction and extrapolation cannot approximate a bygone event. It often can and sometimes does. But it is always a probability inferred from the residue of reality, never reality itself.

A man with a crushed skull is found at a new home construction site. If a hammer is also found, it may be evidence. But of what? Was the hammer used to crush the skull, build the house, or both? If fingerprints are found on the hammer, they may be further evidence. But of whom? Murderer, builder, or both? If the dead man himself was a builder, the prints could well match the victim. The murder weapon may have been a different hammer removed from the scene or may not be a hammer at all. The skull, after all, could have been crushed by anything from a baseball bat to a fireplace poker, although it would be unwise to assume that the murderer is a major league ballplayer or the owner of the nearest house with a chimney.

The harvesting of evidence, then, must be a process of blindly collecting cold facts. Subsequent examination and correlation of these initially unrelated facts can then form theoretical assumptions and eventually a coherent hypothesis. The "weight" accrued by any body of evidence derives from its volume of individual facts and their cumulative significance.

This always presumes, of course, an accurate assemblage of facts and their correct interpretation—neither of which should *ever* be presumed. In and of themselves, facts do not necessarily add up to the truth. Furthermore, even when properly correlated and correctly understood, facts can deceive.

Each bit of evidence, each separate fact, is nothing but one piece of a puzzle with many other pieces missing. While a complete picture of any unwitnessed crime is seldom if ever assembled, sufficient integration of available evidence can put enough pieces together to create a partial picture. And if enough of the picture is revealed, it may suggest where its missing pieces can be found, thereby completing the solution. Or at least the most likely solution.

Back to the dead man at the construction site. His crushed skull is itself evidence, and the very best evidence. If its wounds are consistent with those inflicted by a hammer, then everything changes. And everything changes drastically if blood, hairs, and brain matter are found stuck to the business end of the hammer. Should prints on the hammer match those of a previous murderer bearing a grudge against the deceased, any puzzle pieces still missing immediately assume less importance as an extremely likely picture not only emerges but leaps into sharp focus.

In certain rare cases, however, the most likely explanation should be the least trusted. This is a large truth often overlooked in the detail-obsessed science of forensics, yet it lies at the very heart of the matter. It is also a lesson, once learned, that must never be forgotten.

Six months ago, a Gotham district judge was found shot and stabbed to death in his home. Rich with trace evidence, the crime scene indicated either a sloppy criminal or a scrupulous forensics investigator. Perhaps both.

I was not directly involved in the case, at least not until its very end, and collected none of the evidence. Through the auspices of Police Commissioner James Gordon, however, I did follow the progress, although not in any great detail. At the time it seemed quickly open and shut, with one clue after another adding up to a classic textbook incrimination of the most likely suspect. This was one Immanuel Stubbens, an ex-convict paroled only weeks earlier from Blackgate Penitentiary, to which he had been twice sentenced by the murdered Judge Innskeep.

Given the wealth of crime scene evidence pointing to Stubbens, as well as a clear revenge motive, his alibi was discounted. Resting on the word of a woman who claimed she spent the night with Stubbens, the alibi could not be disproved, but neither would it likely survive cross-examination. The case was all but closed, awaiting only the formality of a trial in which the burden of proof would be easily borne.

When Stubbens fled arrest, however, I was called in. After tracking down the ex-con, I turned him over to Gordon.

Stubbens vehemently denied his guilt, but the guilty have good cause to deny what they have done. In this case—assembled by Gordon's best forensics investigator, Jordan Rankin—the volume and weight of the evidence was overwhelming, every scrap of it pointing to Stubbens's guilt and the guilt of no other person on Earth. Rankin was willing to stake his reputation on it, and the district attorney bought it all. As did Gordon, the best cop I've ever known.

And that, finally, is what bothered me, the absolute certainty and lack of any doubt whatsoever. That and one other thing—the look in the cornered man's eye as the Batman descended on him. There was the usual fear and disbelief, of course, but the two were mingled with a third quality I do not often see. A strange gleam of wildly shattered dismay, perhaps at the prospect of returning to prison. Or perhaps not.

"Too good, sir?"

"Exactly, Alfred."

We rarely discussed dark matters up in the manor, but I was having breakfast at three in the afternoon before sleeping the rest of the day, after rising from the cave where I had pored over casefile documents since dawn.

"And I take it this would be in reference to the *same* murdered judge discussed in the past?" Moving to the kitchen counter, he set a bowl of cubed melon to the left of the plate on which a perfect omelette steamed. "Innskeep, I believe, was his name?"

"The same judge, Alfred." I took my stool at the counter and started on the omelette. "And the *only* murdered judge, thankfully, in quite some time."

He gave me a sidelong glance with upraised eyebrow as his voice turned arch. "I only ask, sir, because I thought I understood you to say that the case against the judge's killer is *too* good."

"Far too good to be true." The same could have been said for the omelette. It had been a long night and now the better part of a long day as well. I was famished. "So much so that I'm now prepared to call it the case against his alleged killer."

Alfred took up a sponge to wipe down the stove. "I see," he said, and when he looked back over his shoulder there was a faint twinkle in his gray eyes. "Alleged killer. And yet, as of a fortnight past, I could swear the news identified one Immanuel Stubbens as a *convicted* killer. With a rather extensive prior criminal record, as I recall."

The toast was barely browned, warm but still soft. "A man can be less than innocent, Alfred, but still victimized."

"The perpetrator as victim?"

"Of miscarried justice, in which case he was guilty of prior crimes but not the perpetrator of this one."

"You intrigue me, sir." He rinsed and squeezed his sponge, then laid it to dry and turned to face me. "You also exasperate."

"I'm starved. And eating."

Turning down his shirtsleeves, Alfred buttoned the cuffs and leaned back against the opposite counter. Then, arms crossed and impeccably serene, he simply waited.

When the eggs were finished I began forking chunks of melon. "I suppose your patience has earned its reward."

"One should hope, Master Bruce."

"There's something wrong with the Stubbens case. I've just finished going over all of it, original police reports, forensics results, autopsy materials, district attorney's brief, news accounts, and full transcript of the trial. It's taken me two weeks."

"Since the conviction."

"Precisely since then. I sensed something in Stubbens six months ago, when I took him down. It made me uncomfortable, but I dismissed it at the time. Gordon believed the man was guilty as sin, and I had other cases to pursue. But two weeks ago the verdict reminded me of my uneasy feeling. Now that I've reviewed the entire case, I'm convinced my gut was right. On the face of it, Jordan Rankin and the D.A. did good work. They put together an excellent case. I'm sure they'd like it to be a model for every case. Not a single loose end, with every detail perfectly wrapped and neatly tied."

"As it should be, sir, if they've gotten it right."

"No, Alfred, there's always something missing, some detail that refuses to fit, something never explained because the only explanation is never discovered or fully understood. There's nothing like that here. Everything fits, and every fit is suspiciously perfect."

"Such as?"

"Judge Innskeep's murder occurred after forced entry. The back door was jimmied, and the gouge marks in the jamb perfectly matched the same make of crowbar used by Stubbens in a previous burglary for which he was sent to Blackgate by the same Judge Innskeep. But that particular crowbar had been confiscated as evidence—and could hardly be used seven years later."

Alfred's shoulders lifted in the slightest of shrugs. "Yet if Stubbens planned a return to his old ways following release from prison, sir, might not his first step be the purchase of a favored tool?"

"I checked. The Ergodyne Tool Company went out of business three years ago, and that make of crowbar is now scarce. In any case, while Stubbens always followed the same M.O., there's no reason to think he had a favorite tool. The doorjamb marks matched only his last crime and none of his earlier break-ins, in which several different jimmies were used." I finished the melon and laid down my fork.

Alfred immediately stepped forward to clear the dishes. "And this information was introduced at trial, sir?"

"No. I had to dig back into older records, Stubbens's earlier trial. But more than that, why was the judge murdered in his bed?"

Alfred paused halfway to the sink with dishes in hand. "Sir?"

"The house is not large, and there was nothing wrong with Innskeep's hearing. Why didn't the loud break-in wake him up?"

Clearly intrigued and barely aware of his actions, Alfred set the dishes in the sink, turned on the tap, and again rolled his sleeves up. "Did he, perhaps, take sleeping tablets?"

"I checked Gunt's autopsy report. Toxicology results were negative."

"Then might he not have been a naturally sound sleeper?"

"Maybe." I got up, crossed to the kitchen window, and looked out over the grounds. "And maybe every other suspicious detail has its own separate innocent explanation. But when does the string of coincidence finally snap?"

"What else, sir, do you find suspicious?"

The trees had grown while I was not looking. I remembered them as they were when I was a child, when everything beautiful had frozen and ceased to exist. "Judge Innskeep was shot *and* stabbed. Why both? If Stubbens entered with a gun, why resort to a knife?"

"I thought that Stubbens, unlike the typical criminal, was known to have employed a knife as well as a firearm in his past. It was one of the strongest points against the man."

"One of the strongest used to convict him, Alfred, but the point was flawed."

"How so?" The tap went silent, dishes done.

"As a youth, Stubbens committed only a single armed robbery, and that was with an unloaded junk gun. The experience apparently shook him badly, and he never used any type of gun again. In fact, while he's undeniably a thief, there's no evidence that he's violent, let alone a killer."

"Excepting the judge's murder."

"Yes." I remembered my mother walking under those trees, smaller trees, and I saw my father out there, too, the tossed ball arcing from his hand, both of them so alive and so young, like me now, but never to grow any older.

"And excepting too, sir, the incident with the knife."

"That was years later, when he stabbed someone in a barroom brawl. But the knife was pulled by the other man, the one who was stabbed. According to the witnesses, Stubbens took it away from his attacker and used it only in self-defense. Almost accidentally, they said." I turned from the window to watch Alfred dry my plate. With just the two of us, he rarely bothered using the dishwasher. "And those are the only two times on record when Stubbens used either weapon, let alone gun and knife during the same crime. In fact, the rest of his rap sheet is nothing but break-ins, all unarmed burglaries."

"Yet as you always say, sir, there is a first time for everything, including murder. Besides, there was more substantial evidence linking Stubbens to the judge's house. Shoeprints outside the back door, I believe."

"But not matched to any pair of actual shoes. Merely size eleven, same as Stubbens, along with a million other men in Gotham."

Finished with the dishes, Alfred turned down his sleeves and buttoned them just as he had shortly before, every move briskly precise. "The news mentioned a number of . . . I believe they were called incriminating idiosyncracies."

"Yes. A meal prepared and eaten, apparently by the perpetrator, dishes left on the table. Drawers pulled from desk and dresser, emptied one by one and stacked on the floor in a certain odd arrangement. The television left blaring, tuned to the same channel Stubbens had left on at several prior scenes. According to the judge's housekeeper, only two types of valuables were taken, cash and jewelry, compatible with Stubbens but hardly unique to his M.O. Plenty of burglars take nothing but cash and jewelry."

"Still," Alfred said, "each fact is another straw added to the camel's back." He had already begun seeing it my way and was merely playing devil's advocate at this point, drawing out my thoughts to help me focus on the specifics of the crime.

"Too many straws, Alfred, one for nearly every detail known about Stubbens. It's as if everything the man ever did in all of his previous crimes had been compiled on a master list to be repeated here in a single scene."

"Thereby cracking the spine of the case through overload."

"Exactly. The signal to noise ratio is severely out of kilter."

"And when there is too much signal without sufficient noise?" Alfred was plainly prompting me now, forcing the issue.

"Then some or all of the signal is actually noise in disguise."

I turned back to the window and we both remained silent for a long moment.

"False evidence," Alfred finally said, "and a great deal of it."

"Deliberately planted evidence, Alfred, its very abundance part of the crime. The entire scene was methodically salted with false clues." The sun had dipped near the horizon now, backlighting my parents, making their ghosts glow. "It was staged by the actual murderer, still at large."

Alfred quietly joined me at the window. "It appears some pruning may be in order."

I nodded. "The actual evidence weeded from the false."

"I meant the trees, sir."

"And I know what you meant, but let the branches grow." I was suddenly weary as well as exhausted, saddened by green beauty fading toward twilight. "Every miscarriage of justice, Alfred, is automatically doubled. The conviction of an innocent man leaves the guilty one free."

"And yet with the case officially closed, sir, what do you presume to do?"

"Reopen it, Alfred. Unofficially. Find the real truth behind the apparent truth."

"And your thoughts on the actual perpetrator?"

"Someone well versed in crime scenes." With no more than two hours of daylight remaining, I turned from the window toward the kitchen door and Bruce Wayne's bed waiting upstairs. "Someone knowledgeable about evidence and its impact."

Two nights later, I met Gordon on his roof, aware there was no good way to shake him badly. I didn't even try to soften it.

"What can you tell me about Jordan Rankin?"

"A good man, hard worker, my best forensics investigator." Gordon paused, then saw I wanted more. "Typical tech mentality, I suppose, focused on detail and procedure, all business and by the book. Long on data, maybe short on imagination."

"Is he hotheaded?"

Gordon hesitated. "Not especially," he said, "or at least no more than any cop." He pressed the bridge of his eyeglasses, as if to give me a better look. "Why?"

"I've been going through transcripts of the trials in which Rankin testified as a witness for the prosecution."

"Part of his job," Gordon said. "Gather the evidence, then help the D.A. walk the jury through it."

"There was a case with a heated exchange from the witness stand. Rankin was badgered by defense counsel trying to break him down, pick apart the evidence against the defendant. The lawyer impugned Rankin's integrity and competence, implied he had tampered with serology tests and was lying under oath about falsified results."

"Happens all the time."

"And Rankin should have known better than to fall for it. Instead, he took the bait. The transcript indicates it turned into a shouting match. Rankin kept it up even after the judge gaveled a halt."

Gordon looked uncertain. "I recall the incident."

"Rankin's anger then turned against the judge, who cited him for contempt."

Gordon was uncomfortable now, not sure where this was headed. "And I reprimanded him personally."

"Was his reputation damaged?"

"Not as an investigator, but as a witness, yes, at least for a while. He's been better since, always in full control on the stand."

"Was his job in danger?"

Now Gordon was clearly troubled. "The District Attorney was furious at the time, and I—"

"Threatened to fire Rankin because you had to."

"Yes."

"Because you can't tolerate a conviction being blown like that."

"Not by someone whose job is to *make* the case." Gordon's voice was harder, more impatient.

"You put Rankin on notice, put his job on the line, because you had no choice. It was forced on you by Rankin's contempt of court citation, issued by the late Judge Innskeep."

Gordon's eyes flashed. "The judge in that case was Innskeep?"

"I'm here about his murder, Commissioner. Stubbens is innocent."

"Like hell." He was in denial.

"Stubbens was a thief and perhaps still is, but he's not a killer."

"Everything pointed to him and to him alone—motive, opportunity, M.O."

"Not if the M.O. was staged. Not if Stubbens was framed precisely because he *had* a motive and framed at a time right after his release from prison, when he had the opportunity."

Gordon faltered but wouldn't quit. "I don't know why you're doing this, but I say you're wrong. I say Rankin's a good man. I know him. You don't. The case he made against Stubbens couldn't have been better."

"The case is dirty, and someone tainted it. Someone with inside knowledge about Stubbens and access to old evidence. Someone who could manufacture new evidence to match. False evidence. An expert in forensics, Commissioner. A bad cop."

Gordon shook his head. "No way."

"I checked the lock on the back door. It's scratched, but not by a key. It was picked before the murder. The initial entry was quiet, the door jimmied after the fact, probably on the way out after all the other evidence had been planted by the same man who later gathered it. Judge Innskeep's actual killer."

Gordon shook his head again, harder now. "I don't buy it," he said. "I can't buy it. Not Rankin."

"I visited his place last night." The cloak parted and fell away as I lifted the crowbar for Gordon to see. "This was in the back of Rankin's closet. No prints, but with a small chip of wood adhering to the tip. Consistent with the wood of Judge Innskeep's back door." I paused, letting Gordon stare at the crowbar, letting him take it all in. "I suggest checking your evidence inventory, seven years back."

Gordon was shaken even more severely than I'd anticipated. He did not speak for a long time, shattered by proof he could not deny. "All right," he finally said, "but you've done enough. Rankin is family." He reached out slowly to take the crowbar from my hand. "I'll go to him myself."

I turned for the shadows, knowing I would never forget the stricken look on Gordon's face.

Jordan Rankin proclaimed his innocence as vehemently as Immanuel Stubbens had earlier proclaimed his. Unlike Stubbens, however, Rankin did not flee arrest. Somehow and some way, he assured Gordon, he would vindicate himself at trial.

Still, given the new evidence and a similar motive of revenge, the case looked to be closed for a second time.

It was not.

"*Still* too good, sir?"

We were down in the cave, preparing the optical microscope to compare and photograph two locks removed from separate doors at my request.

"The crowbar in the closet, Alfred."

"That would be the crowbar incriminating Jordan Rankin beyond every shadow of any doubt."

"Were it not too good to be true."

He looked up from his microscope adjustments. "Unless the peculiar acoustics of this cavern produce an echo of remarkable delay, sir, I do believe you are repeating yourself."

"The process is repeating, with the original crime still unsolved, the case still not closed. Stubbens and Rankin are *both* innocent."

"Inasmuch as the Rankin angle thrusts us onto a new path, I trust you are willing, sir, to help me negotiate its turns." He returned his attention to the microscope but continued speaking. "Arguing that Stubbens is innocent, you convincingly deconstructed a host of planted evidence, therefore concluding the man was most likely framed by someone experienced in forensics. Key to the framing was the evidence of the jimmied door, gouge marks matching a crowbar used by Stubbens in a prior break-in. This proved to be the very same crowbar record-ed into police inventory, yet missing from same without expla-nation. As a police forensics investigator, Jordan Rankin had access to that evidence inventory and possessed the requisite experience to frame Stubbens. Rankin was furthermore found—by you—to possess the missing crowbar."

"Circumstantial evidence highly suggestive of guilt. And yet, as with the evidence pointing to Stubbens, possibly proving nothing." I remembered Gordon's belief in a good man's inno-cence, and the look on his face as damning evidence shattered his faith. "Rankin is a good tech, an expert who knows exactly what an unaltered crime scene looks like, the kinds of genuine evidence it contains and what kinds of false evidence would be accepted as plausible. Were he to stage a scene, I doubt it would resemble the judge's house, overloaded with nothing but perfect clues. Rankin operates on facts and cold hard logic. He may well lack the imagination to depart from the only reality he knows."

"One wonders, then, why he was so willing to accept such an unrealistic scene as unequivocal proof of Stubbens's guilt."

"That I don't know. Maybe a blind spot from the same lack of imagination, an obsession with details, an inability to see the forest for the trees. Maybe he simply saw what he was looking for, evidence to identify a suspect. Step by step, he found what he needed. And clue by individual clue, he discov-ered further confirmation. But he never stepped back to look at the whole, just its pieces one by one. Maybe he was distracted by other pending cases, pressed for time. Maybe he was tired or lazy and took the easy way out. But in any event, he simply accepted what he found as a rare perfect scene and he used it to build the rare perfect case. In an ideal sense, it was exactly how every case should be. Neatly wrapped."

"And the revenge motive detected in that trial transcript? Rankin's outburst from the witness box, drawing Judge Innskeep's contempt as well as a reprimand from the commissioner?"

Alfred had finished raising and recalibrating the microscope to accommodate the two removed locks. I laid them on the lab bench within his reach.

"All cops are stressed, Alfred, even forensic techs. Everything they do must be done meticulously. The evidence they develop must be above reproach and impeachment, then used to construct a complex scenario often amounting to a house of cards. One mistake, a single flaw in procedure, can undo everything. Under pressure like that, constant pressure, it's not surprising that Rankin's temper flared in a tense situation. The contempt citation *could* have motivated revenge, but it's far less compelling than the revenge motive attributed to Stubbens, who was twice sent to prison by the judge. Rankin was merely slapped on the wrist. And if Stubbens did not murder Innskeep, it's even less convincing that Rankin did."

Alfred lifted one of the locks and carefully positioned it on the mount. "Yet you *were* convinced, sir, were you not?"

"Not after reflection. In fact, I'm annoyed that I fell so easily into the same trap that snared Rankin and nearly convicted Stubbens. Now I'm convinced of the opposite. Rankin did not remove that crowbar from evidence storage, nor did he stash it in the back of his own closet."

"But since someone did hide it there, you suspect the crowbar was *also* planted evidence? Making the closet another staged scene for a second frame-up in which the apparent framer was himself framed." He reached for the second lock.

"Or just another layer of the same frame-up, a deeper level of staging. But yes, I'm already certain of it. Now I need proof."

"Speaking of which, sir, I believe you'll find the microscope ready." He straightened and stepped aside, giving me room. "I assume one of these locks is from Judge Innskeep's back door, and the other is—"

"From Jordan Rankin's front door." I sat at the bench and leaned to the eyepiece, fine-tuning the focus until seemingly smooth metal assumed unexpected texture.

I'd already found evidence suggesting the judge's house had been invaded by stealth rather than by force. It was a slight mark at the edge of the back door's keyhole, a fine scratch made not by a fumbling key but incised by a lockpick. Barely perceptible to the naked eye, it was identified only with a magnifying lens. Now, seen through the microscope, the scratch was revealed in astonishing detail, looking much like a rugged ravine observed by helicopter, a huge gash filled with many smaller fissures. Each of these was an identifying characteristic, and together they were as unique as the lands and grooves of ballistics. One interior incision stood out in particular, deeper than those flanking it and therefore serving as an ideal marker.

The lock on Jordan Rankin's front door was also scratched, and also not by a key. Through the microscope, the scratch was a similarly rugged ravine of the same width if not filled with an identical pattern of smaller features. I found the deepest interior groove, not in the same place as in the first scratch but flanked by a pattern of shallower grooves more than sufficient for comparison. The scratch was different but the same.

I turned from the microscope to the computer monitor. Displaying the two digitally captured views side by side and ready for printout, it confirmed that the two deep marker grooves were identical, as were both patterns of shallower flanking incisions. The smaller marks within both scratches, then, had been incised by the same microscopic barbs of metal projecting from the tip of the same instrument. It had been slightly turned from one scratch to the other, but both had been scored by the same lockpick.

"The two match, Alfred."

"Perfectly, I should say."

"Send it to Gordon, and print one out for me."

Alfred sat at the computer and first clicked print. "You were correct, sir. Both doors were circumvented by the same tool and therefore almost certainly by the same man, presumably the actual murderer." He shifted to the keypad, transmitting the comparison photomicrograph to Gordon's computer. "But who picked both locks to frame two innocent men?"

"Only one possibility, Alfred." I checked the printout for quality. "Someone who once balanced the scales of justice but who now tips them." The print was acceptable, eliminating all doubt. "Former District Attorney Harvey Dent."

"My thought precisely, sir." Alfred hit send and turned his chair to look up at me. "Two scratched locks, two staged scenes, two frame-ups, two innocent men, two murder weapons, even two means of entry, lockpick and crowbar." His keen eyes gleamed with excitement. "All obviously matching Dent's obsessive M.O. It *must* be Two-Face."

Former Gotham District Attorney Harvey Dent was now a fugitive from justice. I had spent a solid week trying to track him down after his escape from Arkham Asylum five months previously, and had intermittently pursued other leads for several more weeks. Every effort, however, led to a brick-walled dead end, as if the man were a ghost suddenly evaporated. And although I had hardly forgotten Dent, I did assume he was no longer in Gotham. A bad mistake, and now there was hell to pay.

Not so long ago, Dent and I had regularly cooperated through a secret arrangement brokered and overseen by Commissioner Gordon and now sustained with the current district attorney. But Harvey Dent had been Gotham's D.A. when the Batman began his career—providing evidence, identifying suspects, subduing perpetrators—and more than a few of Dent's convictions were obtained with my assistance. Until a single incident changed everything, dissolving the partnership instantly and forever.

Dent was prosecuting a notorious organized crime boss on multiple felony charges. Brilliantly conducted, the trial neared its end with the outcome in little doubt. Facing a long stretch in

Blackgate Penitentiary, and with nothing to lose, Boss Maroni decided to testify on his own behalf. It was a disaster. Every effort by the defense attorney to rehabilitate his client was absurd, and Maroni succeeded only in revealing himself for the arrogant thug he was. The jury was said to be visibly repulsed. When Dent rose to drive the final nail on cross-examination, however, he was unaware that someone had smuggled a vial of acid to the defendant.

The exchange grew heated and may well have been a trap. Scenting blood, Dent leaned aggressively into the witness stand, snarling and even shouting at Maroni. That's when the crime boss made his move, one hand sweeping up and around to dash the uncorked acid into his accuser's face. Dent spun away, howling in agony, hands clutching one side of his face. Those in the courtroom actually saw smoke rising from between his fingers even as they fused to his face.

When ER doctors later pried the hands away, they found a grotesque mask of corroded flesh. One side of Dent's face was literally melted, some of it vaporized and missing, the rest hideously scarred. And just as the district attorney himself was permanently changed, so was our relationship. Former allies would soon become fresh foes.

If every individual is a mix of good and evil, few of us are evenly balanced, most tipped heavily one way or the other. In the case of Harvey Dent, acid and shock and pain seemed to equalize and split the two sides of his nature and identity—light and dark, good and evil—into opposing extremes. He became obsessed with duality, doubles, halves, the number two in general. What he now saw in the mirror—his face starkly divided, one profile still smooth and normal, the other ravaged and deformed—mirrored his similarly altered and divided soul.

While there are reasons to suspect that Harvey Dent had long harbored extreme criminal tendencies, even before half his face was ruined, he had never acted on them, choosing to keep his dark side in firm check through sheer effort of will. It was the acid that tipped the scale from sanity to madness, and the acid melted more than flesh. It seared through his conscience and burned deep into his soul to free the evil locked within. As horrific as Dent's face looked, his schism was far more than skin-deep and more internal than external. Crimefighter transformed into criminal as a cool rationalist surrendered to the raging fires of a madman.

Shortly before his first crime spree, either while he was still in the hospital or immediately after his release, Dent abandoned rational thought and rejected calm deliberation. Now calling himself "Two-Face," he let the flip of a coin dictate every major decision and guide every major move. It was a trick coin with double heads, no tails, both sides identical except one face was pristine, the other disfigured with a deeply scarred X. If the coin landed with the normal head up, Dent's "good" side prevailed. He tended to act judiciously, at least for a madman or at least somewhat resembling the normal district attorney he had been. Should the coin show its damaged face, however, then Dent's dark side lunged fully to the fore. The inevitable result was unrestrained violence, including callous murder, for which he refused to accept any responsibility. Instead, he insisted, he merely imposed "impartial verdicts" rendered to him.

As fate or chance would have it, when Dent first flipped his trick coin, it landed scarred side up. Two-Face ran amok, in the end killing six people, three cops as well as three members of Maroni's crime family. Each and every murder somehow related to the number two. His coin may or may not have spared others subjected to "judgment."

After I tracked Dent down and turned him over to Gordon and the new D.A., he was found unfit for trial and remanded to Arkham Asylum for the Criminally Insane. The sentence was imposed by Judge Innskeep on the basis of forensic evidence gathered by Jordan Rankin.

Then Two-Face escaped, after which his coin had landed scarred side up at least twice, once for Innskeep and again for Rankin. The double "verdict" freed the former district attorney to act again, fully versed in all the ways evidence is deposited and gathered at a crime scene, then used to establish guilt and obtain conviction.

Gotham is talking about me now, criminals and cops alike, but the talk is vague and often whispered, the Batman little more than an urban myth. Many still deny my existence and always will, just as they should and just as I prefer. Fear understood is fear without power.

After Gordon arranged Jordan Rankin's release, I met both men on the roof, looming from the shadows barely enough to be seen. Rankin gasped and stepped back.

Gordon put his hand against the tech's back. "I warned you, but he's on our side."

"Sure doesn't look it." Rankin was a little man gone paunchy and bald. He had moved from college straight into the lab, skipping the street and never walking a beat. While he now held his ground, he still wanted off the roof. "But he sure looks real."

"He's one of us," Gordon said. "Working undercover."

"Yeah, but he . . . he's like some kind of—"

"Just talk to the man, Rankin. He won't bite."

"Not so sure about that." It was meant as a joke, but the whites of Rankin's eyes were clearly evident.

Gordon shifted his attention to me. "You wanted to talk about Harvey Dent."

"We need proof, Commissioner, but I'm certain it was him. The double nature of the crime and its aftermath points to Two-Face every step of the way."

Gordon seemed to frown from the gloom. "I ordered an inventory of the evidence from cases worked by Dent when he was still D.A. Turns out more than a few items are unaccountably missing, including a kit of burglary picks. Whoever took the other items, let's hope they were just souvenirs."

"Aside from the lockpick," Rankin said, "you're probably right. Missing evidence is hardly rare, at least not after trial. Check with any big department. Cops make great thieves."

"I don't care about other departments." Gordon's voice turned grim. "I'll be instituting changes in this one, tightening the chain of custody right down the line. Pretrial and forever after."

The night was wasting. I brought us back on track. "There were three victims here and Dent bore a grudge against two of them, the judge who sent him to Arkham, and—"

"Me," Rankin said. "The one who built the case against him."

"Yes. As for the third victim, although Dent's office prosecuted Immanuel Stubbens on burglary charges, Dent himself did not handle the case and I can find no reason to suspect personal animosity. In fact, I think he chose to frame Stubbens simply because he fit certain needs."

"Dent's deranged M.O.," Gordon said.

"Exactly, Commissioner. Stubbens was a plausible patsy whose history permitted indulgence of the mania for all things two. Innskeep had twice sentenced Stubbens, whose rap sheet included two offenses involving two different weapons, gun and knife. This gave Dent the crime's most important double aspect, the murder of Judge Innskeep by both shooting *and* stabbing."

"That," Rankin said, "really should have bothered me more than I let it."

"Dent punished his first victim directly, by murder, and his second victim indirectly, by framing him *for* the murder. And because Dent wanted to accomplish it with a *double* framing, he deliberately made the first frame-up obvious, almost transparent, knowing we would see right through the staging to the second frame-up."

Rankin lowered his head and looked away, his soft voice rueful. "Speak for yourself."

"In the end, Two-Face achieved his dual goals by first doubly murdering the judge and then incriminating the investigator with a frame-up times two. The complex orchestration of the whole thing, all the trouble he took and the extent of the madness underlying it, is almost head-spinning."

"And gives new meaning," Gordon said, "to the word *premeditated*."

"So we were wrong twice," Rankin said, "but at least we got one thing right in both cases. The motive. It really was revenge."

"And he no doubt wants more of the same. His list of potential victims may include everyone who ever slighted or offended him in any way, possibly every cop and every criminal he's ever known." I looked out past the roof at the dark city dotted with lights. "And he's still out there, maybe tossing his coin right now. We have to find him and stop him. We have to prove his guilt and take him down. Now."

Rankin looked at me, almost directly into my mask, for the first time. "How?"

"The same way it's always done. With evidence."

"Everything I gathered pointed to Stubbens and nowhere else," Rankin said, "and your evidence pointed to me."

"I exposed the truth of my evidence by looking deeper and harder. We have to do the same with yours."

"Except it's been done and done to death," he said. "There's nothing more there. I went over everything a dozen times a dozen different ways. And the commissioner tells me you went over it again yourself."

"Only what you cultivated as prosecution exhibits in court. I want to know what you held back, Rankin."

He stiffened as if struck. "Are you saying I would—"

"No one's accusing you of official misconduct. I just want to know about anything, *anything at all*, harvested from that scene that was not tied to Immanuel Stubbens."

"Oh." He softened. "You mean the usual irrelevant stuff."

"*Seemingly* irrelevant, but preferably *unusual*."

He seemed to gaze upward, taking stock and mentally sifting through it. "Can't really think of anything," he finally said.
"Just the typical residue, the kind of material that's always
unexplained and most likely innocent anyway. Hairs, fibers,
fuzz, and so on. But fibers would help only after he's caught,
when we can compare his clothing. They won't help us find
him."

"Something else, something subtle from a prime site where
the killer's presence is unquestioned. Either just outside or just
inside the back door, or next to the bed where the judge was
shot and stabbed. Something Dent deposited but too small for
him to notice, even too tiny to see."

"Well, as I say, just the usual dust and whatnot, skin
flakes, particles of reddish grit . . . "

"I want the red grit. Tonight. Now"

Rankin had analyzed the particles, finding them to be ground
glass. Red glass. In the end, however, he had been baffled by the
grit and dismissed it as evidence from an unknown source with
no apparent value, possibly incriminating Stubbens but just as
possibly tracked into the house by the judge himself.

In the cave, Alfred helped repeat and confirm Rankin's
tests. Structure was easily established through the electron
microscope. Because the forensic notes indicated failure with
conventional chemical analysis, the samples being too small, we
went straight to mass spectrometry just as Rankin had done.
Here we identified the compounds present in the glass—proportions of silica, limestone, soda ash, and other trace elements—by
their mass as determined by passage through a magnetic field
after electron bombardment. The values for each bit of grit
matched those for every other bit, just as Rankin had found.
Structure and composition were identical for all particles, then,
as were the concentrations of coloring and decoloring agents
present in each particle. The grit had all come from the same
shattered pane of red glass, made from melted sand, limestone,

soda ash, and metallic oxides used for color. Of the latter, the primary dye proved to be derived from a highly refined form of copper, and it was here that Rankin's analysis ended.

Alfred and I extended the process by researching the history of stained glass from its origins to the present, the processes used in its creation and the centers of its manufacture. At some point in the Middle Ages, an ancient glass-making technique first developed by the Egyptians, and again by the later Romans, was developed in Venice for the third time. It resulted in a form of red stained glass highly prized for its uniquely luminous and extremely vivid quality owing to a mysterious substance sometimes called *orachulum*.

European alchemists had rediscovered and experimented with orachulum, heating and reducing copper to a state from which they extracted a rich red powder. The powder itself was then apparently heated in a series of extended intervals until an "alchemy of transmutation" was achieved to produce the orachulum. No one knows what the Egyptians or Romans called the technique, but the alchemists claimed it required secret knowledge of the *Spiritus Mundi*, or "breath of the universe." And it was an alchemist who suggested its combination with glass, melting orachulum into a liquid state that could then be "mixed and fused" with melted sand. The ruby color of the resulting glass was said to fall somewhere between crimson and scarlet, somehow transcending both. Sunlight streaming through such glass produced "a redness richer than blood."

More art than science, this laborious medieval European process had long been simplified and superseded by modern methods. For the past three hundred years, at a minimum, red stained glass has been easier to manufacture but markedly less brilliant. Easier on the hands but duller to the eyes, it no longer glows.

"The red grit is old, Alfred."

"Likely older than Gotham, sir."

"And yet somehow present in Gotham. Somewhere in or near the city, these particles were embedded in the soles of Harvey Dent's shoes, then scuffed off inside the judge's home. If we can trace the grit to its source, locate a single pane of shattered stained glass, we'll know where Dent has walked. And if we're lucky, it'll be his current stomping grounds."

Medieval European alchemists had found other uses for their mysterious orachulum, but a quick check turned up no modern application. Besides, given the context, any other use was irrelevant. Our samples were in the form of grit and the grit's nature was undeniable. Silica. Sand melted and cooled to create a common substance with strange properties, a solid behaving in certain ways like a liquid. Glass. It was the grit's only possible source, glass stained vividly red with a secret ingredient unused for centuries.

Shifting focus to municipal records of Gotham cathedrals, I nailed the answer within an hour.

"Got it, Alfred. Saint Michael's in the old North Quarter, one of the city's oldest surviving cathedrals. Abandoned for years and recently condemned. Scheduled for deconsecration and demolition."

Alfred looked over my shoulder at the monitor. "But as old as it is in Gotham terms, sir, it's still far too new for our parameters. Indeed, even the earliest Gotham cathedral was built more than a century after the use of this orachulum became a lost art for the third time."

"Look closer." I scrolled the passage to center it on the monitor. "Here."

Like its Gothic design and many of its actual stones, Saint Michael's stained glass windows had been imported from a medieval Venetian cathedral of the same name, damaged by an earthquake and similarly condemned to demolition more than two hundred years ago.

"It would seem, sir, that you have struck the jackpot."

If so, the stained glass would not be rescued and salvaged a second time. If I was right, at least one brilliant red pane had already been smashed.

"The cloak, Alfred. There's still enough darkness to find out."

But I already knew the answer. The cathedral was located on Second Street.

Much of the old North Quarter had fallen into decay, and Saint Michael's Cathedral was no exception. I was surprised it had not been demolished long ago, but glad to see the process had begun with chunks of broken brick hurled from the razed lot across the street. On the sidewalk under one shattered window, in the light of a sodium streetlight, scattered grit brightly glittered, most of it red.

The boarded-up front door looked secure but had been breached, the nails on one side pried loose and bent down. Inside, the church was a vast trashed darkness of dust and litter. My light picked out an old mattress, cheap wine bottles, crack vials and candles, burned down and hardly votive. I checked the basement and found the same kind of ruin, the same evidence of recent use. But not by the faithful. Just vandals and squatters and junkies, kids escaping their homes and older types with no homes to escape. And no sign of Dent.

Back outside, I bagged several red particles from the side-walk and left before the sun could rise.

Compared in the cave, the new particles perfectly matched the old. Dent was not haunting the church, but he had passed it. If luck held, he would be found nearby, no doubt somewhere on that street.

The next night I whirled and whipped a weighted line high. When the Batarang caught fast to the spire, I scaled the old cathedral wall that had been imported stone by stone from even

older walls in Italy. Because the steeply sloped slate roof afford-
ed only one ideal vantage point, I slipped into the belfry with a
grim smile and hunkered down to watch and wait.

After a three-night stakeout, I was ready to give up shortly
into the fourth night. Although it was a near certainty that Harvey
Dent had walked this street, walked the sidewalk just below and
just before murdering Judge Innskeep, he might not do so again
for another week, another month, perhaps never again. I felt helpless and useless knowing he walked elsewhere at that very
moment, perhaps en route to his next victim. It was a sobering
realization, urgent enough to make me consider a change in tactics, perhaps abandoning the belfry for a widened search.

Just as I was about to do so, I hit the jackpot a second
time. It was all sound at first, heard before seen, footsteps from
the darkness up the street, growing louder, coming closer. Then
a figure broke into the pool of sodium light, a man with his
head hunched into the upturned collar of his trench coat, all
alone on the deserted street but nevertheless concealing one
side of his face. I watched him stride briskly past the cathedral,
under the broken window, over the scattered stained glass grit,
and I recognized his gait. I'd seen this man walk across the roof
of police headquarters more than a dozen times, approaching
empty-handed, departing with evidence in hand. The only difference was his head, held high and straight back then, ducked
and canted now.

I left the belfry, slid to the ground, and shadowed Harvey
Dent down the dark street. He was a wanted fugitive, and that
alone would have sent him back to Arkham, but I didn't want
to take him on the street. I wanted the justice he'd abandoned
and perverted, justice for the murder of Judge Innskeep. I wanted the crime solved. Proof. I wanted the stolen kit of lockpicks,
rug or clothing fibers that might be tied to other bits of
Rankin's "irrelevant" evidence, anything and everything to be
found in Dent's new hideout.

It was not far, little more than a block down Second Street. I stopped in a doorway to watch Dent enter a shabby two-story walk-up. Light came through one of two windows above the first floor pawn shop. I slipped forward, found finger-holds in the brick, and climbed for the dark window next to the bright one. I reached it in a matter of seconds.

The window stuck at several points as I raised it, but did not creak, letting me enter the gloom without a sound. Enough light spilled through the doorway from the other room to see that this one was fastidiously kept, the bed crisply made, everything in order, not so much as a pin out of place. Looking through the doorway, however, I saw the other room filled with utter chaos, a mess almost as bad as the trashed cathedral. Like his face and his psyche, Dent's new hideout was starkly divided into two areas of extreme contrast. And like the judge's house, like Jordan Rankin's closet, the hideout was another deliberately staged scene, but here the staging had been managed by Two-Face rather than Dent, dictated by madman rather than rationalist.

While the man himself was not visible, I could hear the sounds of his activity just around the doorway. It was impossible to tell what he was doing—moving papers, rooting through things in search of something else—but he sounded preoccupied. I crept for the doorway, for the light's revealed chaos, and for its deranged master.

Dent waited with a sawed-off double-barreled shotgun held in one hand, leveled at my mask, his other hand pawing through old newspapers heaped on a battered table. The sounds had been a lulling lure.

"The Bat," he said. "Finally."

I stood just through the doorway, ready to go either way, forward or back, watching his hand on the shotgun.

"You've been waiting for me?"

"For a long time." The shotgun remained steady on my eyes, its two barrels identical circles filled with black. Beyond, the two sides of the face at the shotgun's other end could not have been more different. "A long, long time."

"How long? Since the church up the street or from the very beginning? Did you sense me tailing you or was the judge just the first of two planned victims, a set-up for my murder?"

"Both," he said. "And don't confuse executions with murders."

"You need help, Dent."

He turned his head halfway away, showing the acid-burned profile. "*Dent's not here*," he snarled through the side of his mouth, through lips ragged and ruined.

"But Dent *is* here, Two-Face, if you want him to be." I kept my voice soft but firm. "You can choose to put the shotgun down."

"*We choose nothing*." The voice was a grating growl, as if the acid had eaten all the way into his vocal cords. "And *you* choose nothing." He reached into the trenchcoat's left pocket with his free hand, withdrawing his trick coin or another just like it, a replacement for the original booked into evidence. Holding the coin between thumb and forefinger, he turned it to show both sides, both heads, one pristine and the other scarred. "This and only this will decide—as judge *and* jury."

"That's not how it should be, Two-Face, not how it was when we worked together."

"Before you betrayed us," he said, again referring to himself in the plural.

"Us? I thought you said Dent wasn't here."

"He's here and you know it. Sometimes you can even see him—we're stuck together like glue—but Dent's not in control and you'll get no mercy from him or from us."

"I'm not asking for mercy. I just want to avoid—"

"*Shut up!*"

He flipped the coin. It spun high through the air, almost nicked the ceiling, then arced down to smack the floor, where it bounced twice before landing scarred side up between us.

"Guilty as charged," Dent said. It was difficult to tell, but his hideous face seemed to gloat. "Does the defendant wish to say any last words before sentence is imposed?"

"I reject the verdict, Harvey, as a travesty of justice and a mockery of your past."

"Harvey's past is gone, just like Dent himself." The one eye facing me, larger than the other, bulged and leered from its shriveled setting of scarred flesh. "There's only *us* now, only *our* future, and it's redressing the past."

I watched his finger crossing the double triggers, knowing both might be jerked at any moment. "Give it up, Harvey. It's not redress, not when you weight the coin to land that way. It's not justice when you tip the scales."

"Our verdict is impartial, its judgment final, the punishment capital." His voice had turned so cold it was almost calm, but I saw his finger start to squeeze. One way or the other, he had to be stopped. I decided not to jump back. Slow or fast, I would go only forward.

"Enough, Harvey. This is your last chance."

"*Our* last chance?" He almost laughed, but his finger froze on the triggers.

"To discredit your coin and do the right thing. To stop hiding behind a rigged jury manipulated by a corrupt judge."

"Look who's talking. You're the one who sent us to that hellhole called Arkham. On the basis of what? The testimony of some shrink who wouldn't know his—"

"Who saw that you're not thinking straight, Harvey. Look around at these two rooms. Look at how you're living, and think about how you're killing."

The bulging eye blazed with madness and rage. "*We told you to shut up!*" His arm straightened and stiffened, thrusting the twin barrels closer.

I kicked the table up and over even as his finger twitched on the shotgun's triggers. Newspapers flew in a wild flurry as the two barrels flashed with a double boom. I had already ducked forward and down. Both blasts went high, a foot above my head. When I rose into his split face, even the normal side was twisted, wild with shock. I swatted the shotgun across the room with a backhand chop. Then I hit him low with a right and high with a left, both shots hooked hard and deep into his body, abdomen and solar plexus.

He doubled over without air and caved to his knees, already out. I stepped aside and let him fall on his faces.

Harvey Dent was returned to his Arkham cell that night.

Three nights later I met with Gordon and Rankin on the roof for an update. The news was good. With Immanuel Stubbens still vowing to stay clean, Gordon had helped him get a job doing what he knew best. As a locksmith. And although Harvey Dent would probably not stand trial for it, the murder of Judge Innskeep was considered solved.

I told Alfred when I returned to the cave at dawn.

"And the proof, sir, is conclusive?"

"There was plenty to harvest from that hideout, including three different kinds of fibers tying Dent to the Innskeep murder scene."

"Then Jordan Rankin has ultimately redeemed himself."

I nodded. "Case closed, Alfred. Yet again."

"Third time is ever the charm." He took the cape and cowl, draped it carefully over the workstation chair, and shot his cuffs by way of adopting a formal air. "And your solution of a confounding double whammy, sir, can only be deemed impressive. Times two."

We walked side by side to the rock-carved stairs leading up to the manor.

Finger Furrows

Excerpt From Bruce Wayne's Diary

MORE good stuff from the library, especially on what one book calls "patterns of papillary ridges unique to each individual." Otherwise known as fingerprints.

But even better than that is what the pioneering Scots criminologist Dr. Henry Faulds said in 1879 about his theory of dactylography: "There can be no doubt as to the advantage of having a nature-copy of the forever unchangeable finger furrows of important criminals." You can say that again, Doctor, because probably no one else will.

And not long after that, also in Britain, Sir Edward Henry became the father of modern fingerprinting as a forensic science. Then, in 1892, the science really came of age when anthropologist Sir Francis Galton developed the first detailed system of print classification. Galton broke all fingerprints down into the eight basic types still used today:

Plain arch
Tented arch
Loop
Central pocket loop
Double loop
Turned double loop
Plain whorl
Accidental
And two more were added later:
Ulnar loop
Radial loop

Every person on Earth has fingerprints fitting into one of these ten types. Back when all prints were kept on card files, finding a match could take a long time, up to days in a big city even with a crew of five or ten detectives comparing a single print. Narrowing the search by tossing out nine of the ten categories eliminated ninety percent of the possibles and ninety percent of the work. Or actually not, because some fingerprint types are more common than others, but having to look through the files of only one category was still a big advance that cut down the work.

Right now just about every major law enforcement department is putting all its prints into computers programmed with "data file recognition," and it won't be long before print matching shifts from tedious man-hours of eyestrain to minutes or less by the computer.

The only fingerprints that are actually visible at a crime scene are those that have been impressed in blood, soot, or some pliable surface. These were the first prints ever noticed way back when, of course, the ones that gave birth to the science, but they're also really rare.

All other fingerprints—most of them by far—are "latent" because they're left on normal surfaces by nothing but tiny amounts of invisible sweat. They can't be seen with the naked eye, but they're definitely there and they stay there pretty much forever. Unless they're removed or destroyed anyway by later cleaning or smudging with overlapping prints. (Always quarantine and preserve the scene. Never contaminate.)

Latent fingerprints have even been lifted from objects left in ancient tombs. If King Tut's police force had kept a file of sample prints for matching, we could actually identify people dead for thousands of years. (What's the statute of limitations on tomb robbing?)

To lift and compare invisible prints, first you have to make them visible, and latent prints are revealed in a number of ways. The most common one is by "dusting" likely surfaces, which means the opposite of normal dusting, not wiping the surfaces clean but sprinkling dust *onto* the surfaces. The dust is actually an extremely fine powder that sticks to the invisible sweat deposited by anyone without gloves touching anything, and it reveals the papillary ridge marks of that person's finger-tips. Sometimes a special metallic powder is used, and then a magnet lifts away all the particles *between* the ridges because those particles are not sticking to any sweat.

Then you press transparent adhesive tape onto the remaining dust pattern and literally lift the revealed print right off the surface. What you're actually lifting is the ridge-stuck powder, obviously, but it's identical to the fingerprint. And once you press the tape onto a file card or whatever, you've safely preserved the powder pattern. It becomes a permanent record of a fingerprint left by someone at the crime scene, maybe left before the crime was committed, maybe even left by the victim, or maybe innocent for other reasons but possibly matched to some known criminal whose prints are on file back at the police station.

If you're dusting a brightly colored surface—or one with a busy pattern on it—you can use a special fluorescent powder. This looks pretty much the same as normal powder until you shine high-intensity longwave ultraviolet light on it to make the obscured print stand out from the surface color or pattern like a sore thumb . . . or finger.

Latent prints can also show up under certain laser beams.

It's fairly rare but not impossible for fingerprints to be left on human skin, so even the surface of a murder victim should be checked. But unlike other latent prints, these don't last forever. In fact, they "evaporate" very quickly. Instead of normal tape, a special high-gloss paper called Kromecote is used to lift prints from skin. But this can only be done within two hours of deposit, so the forensic tech must reach the scene and get down to work fast.

In a way, fingerprints left by a criminal are like the ghosts of his crime. They prove the criminal's presence at the scene, establish what he touched, and can even show what he did, sometimes including how the crime was committed. The best fingerprints are obviously ones lifted from a murder weapon— or, if it's theft, from a cracked safe or picked lock.

But one way or another, fingerprints tell the tale. And if you can't catch a crook red-handed, sometimes you can nail him, ink-fingered, later.

A Puzzle of 206 Pieces

Casefile #0105
Year One, Month Eleven, Day Twenty

From the Private Files of the Batman

THERE is no statute of limitations for murder. Each and every life is sacred, and it matters not why or when it was cruelly stolen. Whether committed yesterday or fifty years in the past, murder cannot be allowed to stand, nor can its perpetrator remain anonymous and free. That way lies hell.

Punishment is not even the issue, not in the face of a more profound and pragmatic imperative. To protect the innocent, the guilty must be apprehended. Others *must* be spared the horrific fate suffered by Bruce Wayne's parents and the trauma endured by their orphaned son.

Two murders transformed innocence into obsession, forever dimming a child's eyes by instilling the dark vision of an avenging angel. And the Batman's ongoing mission must ever pursue a single overriding principle, simply stated but fiercely upheld.

Murder cannot be tolerated, nor left unsolved.

It began with the delayed discovery of mortal remains reduced to the 206 component bones of the human skeleton. Found in a forest preserve across the river, some scattered over an area of some ten acres, every last bone was miraculously recovered after an intensive three-day search by police as well as more than seventy volunteers. Splashed large in the media, collection of the "mystery bones" teased both sides of human nature, lurid fascination as well as wistful empathy. The entire city seemed to find something intimately sad and ultimately vulnerable about this unknown individual deconstructed to so many naked pieces.

No one knew whose life had left these bones in the forest, nor how long ago that person had died. The basic nature of his or her death, however, seemed in little doubt. With two-thirds of the bones unearthed from a shallow grave after the other third had somehow reached the surface, one to be sniffed by a walked dog, any death by natural causes was extremely unlikely. Damage to a number of the bones—fractured skull, crushed hyoid, chipped ribs, and more—further suggested the violence of foul play. But was the damage antemortem, and therefore evidence of wounds inflicted by a murderer, or merely caused by postmortem scavengers and/or environmental conditions? The answer was probably both, some damage caused by a murderer and some by scavengers, but which was which? To eliminate all doubt, the pieces first had to be put together and only then sorted out.

Enter the science of forensic anthropology, in the person of Dr. Sabra Temple.

"I had René Montoya run a check on her," Gordon said. "And she's good." He threw the switch to douse the rooftop signal, then turned to face me through the gloom. "In fact, this Sabra Temple is one of the best in the country, definitely world class, with honors and citations from anthropology societies and law enforcement agencies alike."

"And now she's here."

"Hired her just last month," Gordon said. "This will be her first big case in Gotham, her first true murder mystery." The wind gusted across the roof, making Gordon hunch into the turned-up collar of his trenchcoat, dig his hands deeper into their pockets.

The cloak flared at my back. "And maybe an old mystery."

Gordon nodded. "Cold trail. Could be frigid."

"Which is why time is wasting, Commissioner." The wind blew even harder, pelting grit against the mask.

"I know you're anxious," he said. "Hell, you always are. And I know you're a one-man crime lab too, but this one could be special. And I am paying the woman, or at least the taxpayers are. I think this one requires certain expertise."

"Expert or not, Commissioner, I want to read those bones."

"Didn't say you couldn't." The wind shifted and Gordon ducked his head. "Damn roof." He waited for the wind to settle, then looked back at me. "Maybe we should stop meeting like this, but I'm not trying to shut you out."

"When?"

"Dr. Temple has agreed to do it after hours." He took his left hand out of his pocket, checked his watch. "Starting in ten minutes. And she's agreed to let you attend and observe, even contribute."

"Is that wise?"

"I've briefed her. Braced her." He shrugged. "As much as possible, anyway, for something like you."

Although her back was turned when I entered the lab, I could see that Dr. Sabra Temple was a slender woman with dark hair just short of her shoulders and a relaxed but engaged bearing. She stood at one of a dozen odor hoods arrayed across the far wall, each filled with bones. Her hands were inside the hood, slowly turning a vertebra this way and that. Slightly bent at the waist, she peered down through the transparent cowl at the small piece of spine.

I made a sound to let her know she was not alone. She turned and then flinched, but recovered quickly, only momentarily startled by the after-hours visitor to her lab. "Good evening," she said. "Ready to start?"

"Whenever you are, Dr. Temple."

Her strong features formed a strange look, even flirted with something approaching a smile. "If we're going to work together," she said, "you can call me Sabra, I guess." She turned back to the odor hood. "Wasn't much in the way of clinging tissue, but the last remnants are gone now, the bones boiled clean."

"You preserved samples?"

"As much as I could," she said, "but as I say, there wasn't much to preserve. Minute traces, complete skeletonization, no visible flesh or ligament. DNA probably won't help us anyway, not with an almost zero chance that the individual was previously typed."

"That's true. But anything that *can* be preserved—"

"*Should* be preserved," she finished. Her age was difficult to judge, seeming to shift with her mood, younger when she smiled, older when serious. Splitting the difference put her somewhere in the mid-forties. "I agree. Right now, however, I'm interested in assembling the bigger picture."

"Putting the puzzle together."

"Right." She gathered five or six vertabrae in her hands, withdrew them from the odor hood, and moved across the lab to a long table. There she carefully aligned the bones in proper sequence under bright fluorescent light. "Won't take long. At this point, I could do it in my sleep." She went to a different hood for more of the thoracic vertabrae, darting quick glances back at me, a spectacle too rare to process in a single look. I sensed she might become unnerved, even in the bright light, and used small talk to dispel fear.

"How did you become a forensic anthropologist, Dr. Temple?"

"Sabra," she said, "and I guess you could call it an accidental detour." When the spine was fully assembled, she retrieved ribs from yet another odor hood. "I thought I wanted to become a museum curator." She began arranging the ribs in relation to the vertabrae, her movements both quick and careful. "At least until I read a book about the Smithsonian Institution."

"One of the world's finest museums, yet it put you off your planned career?"

"No, no, it wasn't like that." She continued speaking as she moved back and forth between table and hoods, gradually assembling the body puzzle of 206 pieces. "I was just out of high school, still a kid, although a kid in her last summer, when a chapter in that book opened my eyes to a different career, that's all." She looked at me again, this time without averting her eyes so quickly, still disconcerted but increasingly more comfortable with my presence. "Back in the 1930s, the FBI put together its first crime lab in Washington."

"I know."

"As you should," she said, "if you're really the 'crack criminologist' Commissioner Gordon says you are." She placed the long bones of one arm on the table, twisting radius and ulna on a slight downward angle from the humerus. "Anyway, human remains are the best evidence in any murder, but only if you know how to interpret the evidence. Which the FBI agents did not, at least not until they realized there was a whole crew of world-class bone detectives right across the street in the Smithsonian's Gothic towers. Thanks to the efforts of the zoology and archaeology departments, in fact, the museum's anthropologists were curators of one of the world's largest collections of skeletons, representing virtually every known species, extinct or extant. These people knew bones like no one else's business, and they could see things in skeletons invisible to everyone else. At first, the FBI tapped the anthropologists simply to distinguish human remains from animal bones."

"Sometimes easy to be fooled. Especially by a bear."

"Exactly." She brought a handful of finger bones to the table and bent over them, carefully juxtaposing proximal, middle, and distal phalanges. "But it was immediately clear that the Smithsonian people could do a lot more than weed out the bears. They could examine genuine human remains to determine gender, age, race, and more. Sometimes amazing things, and sometimes from a single bone. The FBI couldn't believe their luck, and forensic anthropology was born."

"Which made you change career plans."

"As soon as I read that chapter in the book, yes." On the table, the puzzle was taking familiar shape, individual bones loosely but carefully arranged into a growing picture of death's ultimate form, slowly but surely adding up to a human skeleton. "Until then, I never even knew such a career existed. But paying honor to the dead, solving the mysteries of their bones, doing something about the violence perpetrated on them . . . well, much as I still love museums, all those other possibilities seemed like a way to make more of a difference. A real life and death difference, I mean." She gave a light shrug on her way back to the odor hoods. "So I was able to change my major just in time."

"And no regrets?"

"Sometimes it's lonely," she admitted. "But then again, not really. In a strange way, I'm never alone, always with someone. And just because they're dead doesn't mean they can't talk to me. Sometimes, in fact, I could swear their bones actually whisper, telling me secrets no one else knows." She looked up from the table, a metatarsus poised in her hand. "Or does that sound too weird?"

"No." With the ice broken and her fear gone, there was no need for further small talk. I watched and waited while she finished her work.

Placed just behind its detached mandible above atlas and axis at the top of the cervical spine, the skull came last, its rear area cracked and collapsed with multiple defects. Some of the detached skull fragments had already been arranged to the side, others never retrieved. Dr. Temple stepped back to survey the completed puzzle, a fully assembled but slightly exploded skeleton. "Done," she said. "And this is rare, you know. There's a lot of damage, some of it major, but every bone is here, either intact or represented by a sizable fragment."

"Gordon's people are good, and the volunteers helped. They excavated and sifted the entire area."

"Yes," she said. "I supervised the dig. Now how do you want to proceed? Clue by clue head to toe, or the way I usually do it?"

"Your way."

"Well, first I sex the skeleton . . ."

"Female."

"Right. Greater pelvic breadth than in a male specimen, plus wider subpubic angle. Clearly a woman."

"Race is European?"

"Yes."

"Height?"

"You seem to know my usual procedure." She reached for a tape measure.

"It's the accepted sequencing, the one that makes most sense."

She nodded. "I've already estimated five-five to five-seven, just extrapolating from the long bones." Now she tipped the skull on its side and measured the entire skeleton, pate to heel, then reached for a notepad. "Got to subtract my usual figure for the gaps I leave between bones, give or take a little for ligaments and cartilage." She scribbled quickly and looked up. "The final report may be more precise, but right now it comes out on the nose, roughly five-six."

"Age at time of death?"

She lifted one of the thighbones. "At birth, the skeleton actually has two-hundred-eight component bones rather than two-oh-six." She pointed to the lower tip of the thighbone. "That's because the epiphysis—between the end of the femur and the knee—begins as a separate element. Then it gradually enlarges, changes shape, and ultimately unites with the femur by the end of growth, temporarily leaving a fusion scar that quickly fades and cannot be discerned in the adult femur. Here the epiphysis in each leg has fully attached to the femur and there's no visible scar, indicating this individual lived past the end of growth to die as an adult."

"Older than eighteen to twenty."

"Yes, but not much. Overall bone density is pretty much peak." She replaced the femur and swept her hand along the skeleton as a whole. "And from examinination of wear and tear on the other joints and spine, as well as the condition of the teeth, I've calculated an age from twenty-five to no more than thirty. Far too young to die."

"Anyone who is murdered, Dr. Temple, is too young to die."

She stared at me, at first taken aback by the tone of my voice, but then in agreement with its sentiment. "My mother was . . . murdered," she said, and she seemed simultaneously older and younger, as if lost in conflicting emotions, suddenly drained even as she cocked her head in the attitude of a bewildered child. "When I was in high school."

"Before you read your book on the Smithsonian."

"Less than a year before that." She seemed quietly dazed, another survivor who had endured the same tragedy and felt the same pain.

"I'm sorry." I wanted to say more than that, wanted to tell her about my own loss, but forced myself to hold back. It would have been too easy to give too much away, and the mask must never slip. At risk of seeming cold, I indicated the bones on the table. "So it adds up to a female European approximately twenty-five to thirty years of age, five-five to five-seven in height. What else do you see?"

She broke her gaze slowly, as if emerging from a trance, to refocus on the skeleton. "Other teeth features and bone conditions, including the healing of a childhood leg fracture, further indicate a good diet, excellent dental and medical care, and a fairly sedentary lifestyle. In other words, a young woman of relative privilege rather than deprivation. Her life was short, but it was not hard."

"Before we get to the wounds, can you tell me anything else? From the bones themselves, not from their damage."

She fingered a loose strand of hair behind her ear. "In the case of this skeleton, not much, I'm afraid. Sometimes you get lucky with real Sherlock stuff. Bumps, calcified ridges, nicks, specific wear or noncongenital deformities, all these things can tell a lot. A transversed crooked spine, for example, is characteristic of a longtime postman slinging his heavy mailbag over the same shoulder day in and day out. A certain notch in the thumb suggests a tailor. There's even a type of bone wear called milkmaid's elbow. These days, of course, people are less likely to perform the same physical tasks through their entire lives, especially city people. Plus there's more automation, machines bearing the brunt bones once did. In any case, there's nothing occupation specific in these bones." She paused to frown, as if stumped. "But if I had to guess, I'd say this woman was either a neat-freak or devoutly religious."

"Why?"

"The patella." She pointed to the bones of one knee joint, then the other. "And the tibia, both of them. This wear here, and the pronounced buildup here—especially for someone her age—suggests she either prayed a lot, and I mean for hours, or scrubbed every inch of her floor on a routine basis. She certainly spent time doing something on her knees, far more than the average person."

I thought about it. "Anything else?"

"Not unless you're ready to analyze evident trauma."

"All right."

She drew a breath and began speaking quickly. "I told you the leg fracture was antemortem, fully healed. And I assume you're not interested in postmortem damage induced by scavengers and exposure to the elements, although I could tell you what animal gnawed which bone just from the teethmarks."

"I doubt it will prove relevant."

"If you change your mind, it'll all be in my report."

"Then for now, just the damage causing or contributing to death."

"Which still leaves a lot." Now her voice slowed and fell, still professional but softened to a more somber tone. "An unusual amount, in fact, and it's varied." She lifted the skull, delicately tracing its cracks and defects. "First, we have these skull fractures in the occipital and right parietal regions, multiple and overlapping."

"Not from falling, then."

"No, the victim was struck three times to the head, with differing degrees of force, the locations and angles suggesting attack from behind by a right-handed person wielding a blunt object and swinging downward. Ruling out a giant, I'd say it happened while she was seated and slumped to her left."

"Not kneeling?"

"Not unless her attacker was the opposite of a giant, extremely short, and definitely not while she was on her hands *and* knees. The angles are wrong for that. She was on a lower plane, but aside from the slump, her upper torso and head were essentially upright. Because we have radial cracks from one fracture overlapping into another—here, and here, too—we can determine the sequence of the blows. The first was fairly hard but tentative compared to the more forceful second blow, and the third was hardest of all."

I saw it happening in my mind and banished the image. "Escalating violence, but not what you meant by varied."

"No." She gently replaced the skull, then lifted a small U-shaped bone just below it. "Crushed hyoid, typical of choking."

"Usually by gouging thumbs."

"Yes." She moved down the table to indicate the bones of both hands and the left forearm. "And here. Multiple chips and scoring to the carpus, metacarpus, radius, and ulna, all inflicted by the same sharp instrument."

"Characteristic of defensive wounds, sustained while attempting to ward off slashings and thrustings."

Dr. Temple nodded. "Failed attempts." She pointed to the skeleton's ribs and sternum. "More chipping, nicking, and scoring here. Multiple stabbings of the torso, any one or combination of which could have caused death but probably didn't."

"Also from a right-handed assailant?"

"Yes, wounds inflicted from the front this time and while the victim was standing, although I'd say they made her sit down. And slump toward her left."

"Your estimate of the attacker's height?"

"Somewhere in the range of two or three inches taller, but shorter than six feet. Best I can do with no overhand stabs to gauge a better range. Assuming a single murderer, and based on the *victim's* height combined with the height of the average straight-backed chair, I'd put the killer right about five-eleven."

"Straight-backed because a stuffed easy chair tends to have a higher back?"

"Right, complicating any blunt instrument assault from the rear."

"And you do assume a single murderer?"

"I can't swear to it, obviously, but yes. Maybe I can't imagine three different attackers taking turns—choking, stabbing, clubbing. Or maybe it's just what I feel from the bones, feel in my own bones."

"And that's all the relevant damage?" I could see it was.

"That's plenty," she said. "It's brutal, savage."

"But possibly incompetent."

"I think you're right, another reason I can accept a single murderer with three different M.O.s."

"Put it together, Dr. Temple. How do you see it going down?"

"Although the weapons cannot yet be precisely determined, not until I run tests, the gross defects suggest a baseball bat or similar blunt instrument, kitchen knife, and human hands. All of which shapes up as a particularly messy, violent, and botched killing which was hardly the work of a professional hitman." She gazed at the ordered bones. "But certainly not an accidental killing, and probably not a murder of spontaneous passion either."

"You think it was premeditated?"

She waved a hand. "Well, not necessarily that either, at least not in the customary sense. But if not, if it *was* sparked by a flash of rage, it certainly didn't stop there. And if it was premeditated, it went terribly wrong. Either way, all indications point to deliberate murder by persistent amateur. Incompetent, as you say, but extremely determined."

"Likely scenario?"

"Blunt trauma to the head, preceded by unsuccessful strangulation and then stabbing. The head blows were fatal but unnecessary because the victim eventually would have bled to death from the multiple stabbings."

"So the final blows, in your opinion, indicate panic or impatience on the part of the killer."

She nodded. "Further evidence of a hellbent amateur, determined to kill but not good at it. How do you see it?"

"The same way. Because of the force of the head blows and your height estimate, the assailant was likely a male."

"I agree."

"It was probably domestic."

"Statistically solid," she said. "Absent evidence to the contrary, the spouse always ranks first for suspicion."

"The victim was approached in the kitchen, and frontal choking came first. Perhaps there was an argument, perhaps it was premeditated. The killer grabbed the victim's throat and squeezed hard enough to crush the hyoid bone but not long enough to induce death. The victim no doubt struggled, perhaps broke free. Finding strangulation more difficult than he'd anticipated, the killer then grabbed a kitchen knife. Whether it was inflicted with cool deliberation or in sustained rage, the stabbing and slashing came second, but all we can say with certainty is that the killer was not an accomplished knife-fighter. He managed to get past the victim's defenses, past her hands and arms to reach her torso, but not quickly and not easily. And still the victim did not fall. Unless a major artery is severed, it takes time to bleed out, and it makes a mess. If the killer felt no panic when snatching up the knife, he surely did when dropping it. He wanted death to be instantaneous, wanted this thing to be over, and two separate close-quarters attempts had already failed. His hands were probably bloody, the knife slippery. He needed to finish the job and finish it fast, but he wanted no more intimacy. He wanted less contact, more distance. Had there been a gun in the house, he would have gone for it. Instead, he thought about the baseball bat in the closet or some similar blunt instrument elsewhere in the house, and he went off for that. In the meantime, bleeding profusely, surely dying and losing strength fast, the victim staggered across the kitchen. When the killer returned with his new weapon, he found her collapsed on a straight-backed kitchen chair and struck the head blows from behind, finally causing death."

"Works for me," she said. "Something very close to that, anyway. Nothing more I can add."

"But you can, Dr. Temple." I fixed my eyes on her, knowing she would not like what came next. "And it's what I need most of all."

She took a step back, showing one palm. "Don't even ask me to—"

"I have to ask because I need to know. When did the murder occur?"

Her expression hardened. "Look," she said, "I realize that's the question. If we knew when the victim was killed, we might learn who she was, and if we knew her identity, we could start looking for her killer. But we *don't* know when she was killed, and I can't tell you."

"You can give me your professional opinion. Your best estimate."

She shook her head. "If there's one thing bone detectives have learned *not* to do, that's it. There are too many variables, and we've been wrong too many times." She turned to the skeleton laid out on the long table. "All I can say with any certainty is that these remains have existed long enough for the putrefaction of flesh and ligament to be complete." It was all she wanted to say, but I wanted more and waited for it. She frowned and went on. "I'm serious. That's it. This woman has been dead long enough to become nothing but bones, and long enough for her bones to become fully disarticulated, but not long enough for them to become dust. That's all we can know and the best I can do, all any forensic anthropologist could say with confidence."

"I'm not asking for precision."

"And you won't get it, not from these or any other bones, not from me."

I raised one gauntleted hand, swept it slowly down the skeleton's length. "Please, Dr. Temple, how long has this person been dead? Just give me a range."

She was irritated now, almost angry, not at all intimidated by the bizarre guise of her interrogator. "Anywhere from eight months," she said, "to eighty years."

"I need better than that."

"And I'm telling you I can't *do* better than that."

"Try. Even if it's just a gut feeling. You said the bones whisper. I want you to listen to them. Tell me what they're saying, Dr. Temple, what they're trying to tell you."

She stared at my mask for a long time. "All right," she finally said, "but it won't be anything more than a wild guess." Then she drew a deep breath and turned back to the silent witness, the only remains of an unknown life and the grisly handiwork of an unknown killer. Slowly, lightly, she ran her fingers over one bone and then another. "All right," she repeated. "Given the environmental conditions present in that area of the forest preserve, average temperature and moisture and so on, we have a bare minimum of, say, ten months for complete skeletonization. But then there's the shallow burial." Her hands still caressed the bones, absently now, as she thought it through. "Even a foot of dirt cover can double the time required for skeletonization. But acidic soil speeds the subsequent disintegration of bone. Low pH accelerates the chemical reactions transforming the bone mineral hydroxyapatite to crumbly calcium salts and phosphorus. The degree of such transformation in this case is slight, barely begun, but that's offset by the fact that the soil was not particularly acidic. Moving us on to other factors. Lack of surface greasiness indicates considerable degradation of the interior fatty marrow. These bones are hardly dust, but they are dry. That takes time. Then there's the difference in bleaching. Some of these bones, the ones most bleached and most damaged by causes other than murder, apparently reached the surface quite some time ago, no doubt dug up by early scavengers. Then there's the overall degree of flaking and cracking to consider . . ."

"Just feel it, Dr. Temple. Blurt it out."

She withdrew her hands from the bare bones, turned away from the complex armature of life consigned to death. "He did it thirty-five years ago, give or take a decade. Now go find the bastard if he's still around." She remained silent until her hard eyes softened. "And thank you."

"For?"

"For letting me guess." She paused. "And for calling me Dr. Temple."

Sabra Temple's wild guess was wrong, just as she'd warned, although she did save me thirty-four years worth of digging, from last year all the way to thirty-five years back. And while she could have been wrong the other way, making the bones more recent, I'd sensed her estimate was conservative. It took me a week of searching through fourteen further years of records before I was able to give the bones a name.

Combing each year's unsolved missing persons reports, I pulled every female Caucasian of the victim's approximate age and approximate height. When dental records were available for a hit, I compared them against the skull's remaining teeth. Whenever I could find medical records, I looked for documentation of a fracture in the right leg during childhood. And when nothing matched the skeleton, I kept looking for the dead woman in the lists of women missing, year by year deeper into the past, in the end finding twenty-eight hits through fourteen years of records. Twenty were eliminated, leaving eight possibles with no medical or dental records on file. And then I found her.

As wrong as Sabra Temple was about the year of death, she hit the nail on the head with a different deduction and the only clue I needed. It was the twenty-ninth hit and—with no identifying records—the ninth possible. The case remained open, the missing woman never found, no final report ever written. But the investigating officer's original notes were in the file, scraps of information gleaned from interviews with family members, friends, and acquaintances.

One hastily scribbled note was crossed out, as if a dead end not worth exploring, when in fact it was the answer. The notation read: *avid gardener.*

Reported missing forty-nine years ago by her husband of seven years, the young woman's name was Sarah Asquith. Seeding, weeding, planting, pruning, she was an avid gardener who had spent a lot of time on her knees, working soil, cultivating life. Then she had been murdered, nearly a half-century ago, her brutalized body left to decompose in its shallow grave across the river.

Sarah Asquith's husband was still living and living well in the affluent Riverside area. As sole beneficiary of a two million dollar life insurance policy, he had taken early retirement when his missing wife was declared legally dead four decades ago.

I made noise on the roof of his mansion, the side overlooking its rear garden, bought by Sarah Asquith's death but never worked by her hands. The back light came on and the porch door slowly opened. Out shuffled a stooped and wizened figure more than eighty years old, approaching death himself and soon to become his own puzzle of 206 pieces.

"Asquith."

The old man started and looked up as I dropped down. Billowing into vast dark wings, the cloak swirled and settled as I landed on the porch with the garden at my back. Rising slowly from my crouch, I faced and towered over Robert Asquith.

"I'm here about Sarah."

"S-Sarah?" His hands and head trembled violently, either in fear or from degenerative disease, wide eyes yellow and rheumy in the porch light.

"You reported her missing. She's been found."

Asquith stood as if petrified, shocked by my appearance but not my words. I could see it in his eyes. Discovery of the "mystery bones" had been big news, but no mystery to this man. He had been married to the victim, knew how she had died, where she had been buried, who she was. And he had followed the news in fear, too old and infirm to do anything but hope no one else would learn what he knew, hope his wife's bones could never be identified.

"Who . . . wh-who are you?"

"Sarah was horribly murdered, Asquith." I waited. "By you."

He did not deny it, even now thinking only of himself. "Please," he said. "I . . . I don't have much time. Let me have what little is left."

"You've already had far more than you gave your wife, not one more minute of her remaining time." Feeling troubled and even strangely moved, I forced myself to remain grim. "Did she beg for *her* life as you're begging for yours?"

The trembling grew worse, his eyes wider, wilder. "I . . . I didn't mean to—"

"Rob her of everything when you took her life? You're lying, Asquith. What you meant to do—its damage inflicted by *three separate means*—is forever etched into her bones. You strangled her, you stabbed her, and you clubbed her to death. Then you rid yourself of her mortal body as if it were trash, denying its proper burial."

"I'm sorry, but it was so long ago . . . " He quivered and sobbed, broken and pathetic. "And I'm not the same. You can see I'm dying, can't you? It won't be long now. Why can't you just let it happen? At this point, what harm can it possibly—"

"You've already inflicted the ultimate harm. And instead of showing remorse, you chose to live a lie funded by blood money. You collected the insurance to finance forty-nine years of luxury and silence."

His voice quavered as it rose to a shrill plea. "But I swear, I'll never do it again!"

"It's too late, Asquith. A bell rung cannot be unrung."

I reached to the digital recorder attached to my belt and turned it off.

After giving the recording to Police Commisioner Gordon, I notified Dr. Sabra Temple. Both thanked me.

Asquith was arrested and charged with Murder One. He may or may not live to see trial and face judgment.

Following a memorial service attended by a handful of surviving mourners, Sarah Asquith's bones were returned to the earth in a private burial funded by the Wayne Foundation.

Case closed.

Written in Blood

174

Excerpt From Bruce Wayne's Diary

GIVEN how small blood vessels are, the average human body contains a lot more of the red stuff than I would have guessed—ten pints in constant flux as long as the heart continues to beat. The study of these ten precious pints is called serology.

We all need antibodies in our immune systems to fight infection and disease, and the production of these antibodies is stimulated by antigens teeming in the blood. Serology uses these antigens as markers to define the different blood types. More precisely, the four main blood groups are classified by the presence or absence of two specific antigens:

Group A = antigen A present, antigen B absent
Group B = antigen B, but no antigen A
Group O = antigens A and B both absent
Group AB = antigens A and B both present

Using these markers, twenty different blood-grouping systems are now available to serologists.

Blood at any crime scene is always a red flag. Even when victim and perpetrator are both absent, any blood left behind is proof that violence has been committed and that death may have occurred. The blood itself is therefore crucial evidence that must be harvested, preserved, and analyzed.

If a murder victim struggled enough, chances are that the killer was scratched and may have deposited a blood drop or two at the scene. It's important, then, to collect and type all the blood found. Any blood not matched to the victim probably came from the perpetrator and can be used to identify the perpetrator. If it matches sample blood drawn from a prime suspect, case cleanly closed. But it can go the other way, too. If the *victim's* blood is tied to a suspect (found on his clothing, for example, or in his car), case also closed.

The forensic collection of blood is therefore vital and must be carefully done. The usual way is with a swab kit. This is like a little plastic test tube with a medically sterile swab in it. (If it's not sterile, any blood it collects can be contaminated, ruining just about every possible test.) The swab is nothing but a thin wooden stick with cotton on its tip. You take it out of the tube and use the cotton end to dab or wipe the stain, soaking up or "swabbing" the blood. Then you push the swab back into the tube, snap off the end of the wooden stick, seal the tube with a cap, label it, and take it to the lab for your basic serology tests. These can be followed—and increasingly will be in the future—by even more precise DNA typing.

Blood contains both white cells and red cells. The nucleus of a white blood cell is required for DNA "fingerprinting." Because red blood cells have no nuclei, they're useless in DNA analysis. Luckily, every drop of blood should have both types of cells.

To determine whether any suspicious stain is or contains blood, the Kastle-Meyer test is probably the most reliable. What the K-M test does is reveal the presence or absence of the blood enzyme peroxidase. Here a portion of the suspect stain, often fully dried, is extracted with damp filter paper, which is then treated with a mixture of phenophtalein and hydrogen peroxide. A resulting pink coloration of the filter paper indicates presence of the peroxidase enzyme and therefore blood.

Not everything that bleeds, of course, is human, so a precipitin test is used to reveal the antibodies in the blood. These are then compared to a range of serums representing animal species.

The results of these tests and a whole battery of similar ones can tell a lot. A serologist can distinguish between human and animal blood, determine human gender from the differences in male and female blood, and statistically narrow the blood's individual owner to a few people out of every thousand. (Again, DNA blood work does even better, narrowing the bleeder all the way down to one person out of millions.)

So that covers the *content* of the blood, but its *shape* is important too. (Alfred is forever griping about "style over substance" and "form over content," but the criticism flunks here.) There's even a forensic subscience called drip-pattern analysis. By careful examination of crime scene spatter sizes, shapes, and patterns, it's possible to deduce how the blood got where it is and even certain facts about who put it there.

A perfectly circular "splash" spatter on a floor, for example, means the blood drop fell straight down, and that means the bleeder was not moving. The diameter of the splash, along with the details of its "collar" pattern, can reveal what height the blood fell from. (The larger the splash, the farther the blood fell.) This can then be used to estimate the bleeder's own height, whether missing victim or unknown perpetrator. Any blood falling from a point below a certain height probably came from a bleeding hand or arm, whereas anything from above that height probably dropped from a bleeding face.

An oval or elongated splash on a given surface means it was hit by blood traveling on an angle, which can be calculated. Length of elongation indicates the flying blood's velocity.

Wall spatters are usually in the classic "exclamation mark" pattern, a segmented stripe of shorter and longer sections. This provides a "drip direction" indicating where and how the flying blood originated. Combined with other available bloodstains and the victim's likely positioning, wall spatters can establish whether the perpetrator is right or left handed—even when the victim has been removed and wounds cannot be examined.

The severing of a major artery (while the heart is still beating) results in a "geysering" or "jetting" of the released blood. These spatters and stains are truly huge and horrific, and they almost always indicate the use of a sharp instrument. Wounds inflicted by gunshot or blunt force can also produce tremendous blood loss but almost never create the "jetting" pattern.

Bottom line: Since violent crime often spills blood, details of the crime are written in blood. Careful study of that blood, reading it to see whatever picture it paints, can solve the crime and close the case.

A Very
Available Weapon

Casefile #0109
Year One, Month Eleven, Day Twenty-Nine

From the Private Files of the Batman

EXCEPTING those fires ignited by pyromaniacs for the sheer hell of it, the motive behind arson is almost always ill-gotten monetary gain. When a business starts to fail, for example, its premises may be worth more than its potential. And if the property is insured for that worth, acquiring the insurance premium becomes lucrative, provided fire as deliberate act can be passed off as accident.

But arson can also be a secondary crime committed to obscure an immediately prior primary crime. Indeed, arson is often used to disguise murder as accidental death, or simply to destroy all evidence of the murder, including its victim or at least the victim's identity. (Teeth, however, can survive the hottest of fires, even a blaze reducing other bones to ash, and metal fillings in those teeth can reveal the victim's identity.)

While arson is rarely the actual *means* of murder, fire has been used to kill. Firebombs and Molotov cocktails are obvious examples, although not the only ones. People themselves have been set ablaze, as have their beds, their homes, their cars. Noting that most things can be made to burn, a British firefighter further observed that "flame is a very available weapon."

In some cases, including this one, arson's motive can be monetary without involving the scam of insurance recovery.

And in all cases of arson, again including this one, murder can be an unintended consequence. This can never constitute an acceptable excuse. When a person is killed—as so-called "collateral damage" or not—that person is forever dead. The killer or killers must be hunted and taken down.

For obvious reasons and by its very nature, however, the crime of arson is especially difficult to solve. The fire itself is likely to destroy evidence of its origin. Unlike any other crime, arson therefore involves three separate and fully independent investigations.

The first is conducted by fire department arson investigators—to establish the cause of the fire and determine that it was, in fact, a crime of arson. Then the police department launches its own investigation—to identify and apprehend the criminal or criminals responsible. Third and final is the private insurance investigation—to discover some reason, any reason, to avoid paying the premium on an accidental fire that was actually deliberate.

In this case, the image of the Bat, projected by bright light into dark sky, signaled the start of a rare *fourth* investigation. Mine.

"Three fires," Commissioner Gordon told me, "all suspicious. Nine investigations, all ongoing, none getting anywhere."

"Geographically concentrated?"

"Not really." He stood by the darkened beacon, hands deep in his pockets with a fat folder tucked under one arm. "All on the South Side, but still encompassing a large area."

"Then what makes these fires suspicious?"

"First," he said, "every fire is suspect until proven accidental. Right now with these three, we've got nothing but timing and loose links, all of which could be coincidence but none of which I'm willing to let slide."

"Because coincidence itself is suspicious. What's the timing, Commissioner?"

"All three fires happened within the last month."

"That's out of the ordinary?"

Gordon frowned. "Maybe not," he admitted. "Fire Department says they'd expect anywhere from one to six or seven like this in that time frame. All things being equal, that is."

"Which is not the case due to the links."

"Loose links, but yes. All three were fast fires of roughly the same intensity. All three broke out between midnight and two. All three destroyed a small retail business in a commercial area rather than a home in a residential area or a larger structure anywhere else. None of the stores was in financial trouble. All three fires remain unsolved, when innocent accidental fires are normally solved quickly. And all three scenes, according to a number of different investigators, just *feel* wrong. 'Typically sinister vibes' is how one put it. Not much, I grant you, but maybe adding up to more given the time frame."

"All small businesses but not a common owner?"

"No," Gordon said, "nothing that easy. Different kinds of businesses, all doing well but otherwise unrelated. And like I said, scattered across the South Side."

"Forensic details?"

"All in here," Gordon said, taking the folder from under his arm. "What there is so far, anyway. Even the private investigators from the insurance companies are cooperating, not that they've turned up much to share."

"Any deaths in the fires?"

He blinked. "Is that a requirement?" And blinked again before poking the bridge of his eyeglasses. I wondered if the glasses were loose or if it was a tic brought on by stress or agitation.

"I despise all crime, Commissioner, but I prefer concentrating on those committed with violence."

He seemed to deflate. "No deaths resulting from the fires, maybe no violence involved at all." Then he ramped back up.

"On the other hand, lack of death could be nothing but luck. All three fires occurred late, but the flames moved fast. Had anyone been present, I'm told they probably would have burned." He paused. "Besides, I thought you said avenging murder is not the point. You want to prevent—"

"I'll look into it, Commissioner."

He gave a soft grunt, his usual way of expressing gratitude, and extended the fat folder of nine ongoing investigations.

I went through the folder at dawn in the cave. It was fat with reports and tests, but as Gordon warned, light on useful findings. Still, I found at least one further cause for suspicion. Frustratingly inconclusive, it was nevertheless based on hard forensic detail and related to the reported colors of flame and smoke at one of the fires.

Such colors, considered together, are clues pointing to the nature of the substances producing them. Blue flame coupled with black smoke, for example, indicates burning acetone. Yellow/white flame with gray/white smoke points to benzene. Pale yellow/white flame with brown/black smoke is produced by burning naphtha, whereas white flame with white smoke comes from phosphorus. And so on, through a long list of accelerants.

In all three of these fires, the reported flames were yellow/red. Fires one and three, however, lacked reliable smoke color. Darkness was a problem, and by the time there was enough light on the scene to assess color, any initiating substance may have burned off, leaving smoke colored by nothing but the buildings and their contents. And yellow/red flame on its own is almost meaningless because it can indicate any number of burning substances, including paper and wood.

The suspicion came from fire two, which had occurred in a well-lit area with solidly reported flame *and* smoke color—yellow/red coupled with gray/brown. This combination pointed to either burning fabrics or burning lacquer thinner. If flame and smoke were colored by the latter, then the lacquer thinner had almost certainly been used as an accelerant. It would explain the speed of the fire and clearly establish arson.

But then enter the frustration factor. Fire two had consumed a furniture store literally stuffed with fabrics.

I closed the file and trudged for the rock-carved stairs. Sleep until nightfall would be followed by my normal rounds. Then, sometime after midnight when the fires had originally occurred, and with no one else around, I would visit the suspicious scene of fire two.

Bound in yellow crime scene tape, it was little more than a blackened shell, much of its second floor open to the night air with roof and wall sections collapsed or burned away. From certain angles, it was barely recognizable as a building. I hid the car in a nearby alley, took out the arson kit, and slipped into the charred and ragged shambles of the former storefront furniture showroom. Even though the fire had occurred some two weeks earlier, its acrid odor was still pungent.

Sweeping the jumbled ruins, my light found little to do that had not already been done by three teams of previous investigators. Like them, I sensed that this was a crime scene, but it was also a scene reduced to ash and slag, with much or all of its evidence gone up in smoke. The firefighters had inflicted their own unavoidable damage, drenching and scouring everything the blaze had not consumed. First seared and then soaked, the entire place had been ravaged by two opposing elements, leaving little but the wreckage of stasis between the two. From reading the investigation reports, I'd known my own arson kit would be largely redundant. Now that I was on site, picking through the devastation wrought by fire and water, I feared the kit might see no use at all. Not unless I got lucky. . . .

A fire's point of origin is called the "seat" of the blaze. Because flame burns upward, the lowest point of damage is likely where the seat will be found. I ignored what remained of the upper floor, moving deeper through the ground level.

The seat of any fire is usually marked by a heavy concentration of ash, and multiple ash concentrations multiple seats of origin—are clear indications that the fire was deliberately set. Again, because multiple accidents rarely occur simultaneously, coincidence is inherently suspicious.

I found only one heavy concentration of ash, proving nothing either way, at the lowest point of damage. From reconstructions in the three investigation reports, all based on interviews with the storeowner and employees, I knew that this was a rear storage area where several large sofas had been stacked one atop another. Almost certainly the fire's seat of origin, its heavy ash concentration was thus easily explained. And yet there had been no wiring, faulty or otherwise, directly under or above the couches. So why did the fire start here? Had an employee leaned against the back of the couches, using them as a screen, while sneaking a smoke? Had fallen ash or a partially stubbed butt smoldered for hours before fully igniting the fabric shortly after midnight? Or had an after-hours intruder seen the stacked sofas as an obvious target to be doused with highly combustible lacquer thinner?

Owner and employees had all denied taking a cigarette break inside the store. But a careless smoker responsible for such a fire could hardly be trusted to confess. Therefore, like the three teams before me, I saw no way to proceed any further, nothing more to sample or analyze. The fire seemed to dead-end at its start.

Then, right before my eyes, the needed luck suddenly dawned on me. The fire had broken out here, in the rear storage area rather than out in the storefront's carpeted showroom. The floor here was bare, with cracks between its boards.

And fire requires oxygen.

I knelt at the fringe of ash concentration, focusing my light directly into a thin slit between two floorboards. The luck held. Deep in the crack, where it had soaked but failed to ignite due to lack of oxygen, there was a small amount of residue rather than ash. I opened the kit, pried up one floorboard, and swabbed a sample of the unburned residue. I also crumbled off a sample piece of charred wood from the floorboard itself. And then, knowing the two samples might be enough, I left the burned ruins.

In the cavern crime lab, Alfred looked up from his gas chromatography analysis. "Jackpot, sir. The residue harvested from the floor seam tests out as lacquer thinner."

I completed my own analysis at the same time. "And the same here, Alfred, absorbed into the charred wood of the board itself."

"Eliminating all doubt. Clearly, sir, you have detected your accelerant."

"And one that produces yellow-red flame with gray-brown smoke." I rose from the equipment bench to pace along the computer workstation. "A lot of fabric also went up in smoke, of course, but only *after* the ignition of lacquer thinner."

Doubt suddenly flickered across Alfred's face. "They did not manufacture furniture in that rear area?"

"Strictly retail sales."

"No refinishing, perhaps touchups to nicked tables or chairs?"

"None, Alfred. No used furniture, all brand-new, damaged goods returned to the manufacturer. No lacquer thinner or any other combustible stored on the premises."

"Then it would seem conclusive, sir. You are indeed dealing with a crime of arson."

"But one that's still a mystery, Alfred." I opened Gordon's thick folder to recheck the police report. "Here. Like the other two stores, the furniture showroom was profitable, its owner in no financial difficulty, making illegitimate insurance recovery an unlikely motive." I flipped deeper through the folder. "And here too. In their own separate report, the insurance company investigators were less commital, but even they seem to concur. No gambling debts uncovered, no expensive habits, and so on. The investigators are still digging for dirt, but thus far all three owners have been given clean bills of health, with no logical reason to damage their own livelihoods." I closed the folder and paced some more. "And a crime with no known motive points to no apparent perpetrator."

"Unless, sir, the fire itself *is* the motive."

"Let's hope not, Alfred. That's the worst-case scenario—utterly random crimes committed by someone with no connections to any of the scenes or people involved; a firebug who could be literally anyone."

"But perhaps someone with a prior history of arson."

"Gordon's people are all over it. Most of the area's known pyromaniacs are still serving time, only four released from prison and currently at large. All four have been under surveillance since the second fire. None of them lit the third."

Alfred shot his cuffs, crossed his arms, and stroked his chin. "Landing us, sir, squarely back on square one. Who *did* set these fires, and why?"

"Either you tell me, Alfred, or I'll have to find out."

Five nights later, on a rooftop across from an office supply store, I watched firefighters suppress another three-alarm blaze. And several hours after that, I followed the signal to the roof, unsurprised to find Gordon grim.

"Another fire," he said, "and another small business out of business."

"I know. I was there. Not particularly close to any of the previous scenes, but also on the South Side."

"The fire department team's still working it," Gordon said, "but they've already found multiple seats in this one, three separate points of origin on the ground floor."

I nodded. "It looked suspicious, and felt it even more so."

Gordon stared straight into my mask. "This time they also found two deaths." He waited, letting his unspoken point sink in. "The bodies reached the morgue an hour ago. Had to get him out of bed, but Coroner Gunt was waiting. Both victims are severely burned and locked in the 'pugilist posture,' according to his preliminary exam."

"Arms raised in front of the torso with fists clenched and knees drawn up, characteristic of death by fire."

"That's what Gunt just told me on the phone. He claims intense heat makes the muscles contract and stiffen."

"But only during the process of death. A corpse's muscles are incapable of contracting, which means we tag murder onto arson—with fire itself as the lethal weapon, rather than a secondary act obscuring murder by other means. No ID, I assume, on either victim?"

"Both burned beyond recognition." Gordon made a face. "Gunt actually had the gall to call them 'crispy critters,' believe it or not."

"No doubt earning harsh rebuke."

"His ears are still smoking."

"Care to wake anyone else up?"

"Such as?

"Two people. The business owner's dentist and Sabra Temple."

Even before forensics pathologist Sabra Temple used postmortem odontology to identify one of the two victims, my guess was confirmed by a panicked call to the police from the business owner's wife. Her husband had called to say he would be working late. She had waited up for him, increasingly worried. He had never worked so late before, not even when taking full stock inventory. Calls to the store would not go through. And then she'd heard news of the fire on the radio. Her husband, she knew, would not be coming home.

Now Sabra Temple made it official by matching the business owner's dental records and X-rays to the teeth of one of the victims. The other burned corpse remained unidentified, but I suspected it did not represent a victim at all. The owner had told his wife that he would be working both late and alone. If he had lied, then the other body could be anyone. But if he had really been working alone, then the other corpse could be that of the intruding arsonist. The two dead men, found in close proximity, may have been actual pugilists overcome by smoke and flames while locked in struggle.

Seeing my logic, at least in principle, Sabra Temple then accepted my request as more than the longshot it would otherwise seem. I asked her to compare the unidentified corpse's teeth against the prison dental records of recent ex-convicts, everyone released from Blackgate Penitentiary starting a month ago and extending back several further months. She agreed to begin as soon as the records could be obtained.

Meanwhile, Coroner Gunt had detected traces of a foreign substance present in the forehead, cheeks, and chin of the unidentified body but not the storeowner. Apparently something had fallen onto only one of the two dead or dying men, then burned and fused into the flesh of his melting face. The postmortem investigation was ongoing, with tests scheduled to determine the nature of the substance.

If I was correct to assume the arsonist had perished in his own last fire, then any future threat may well have been eliminated. But the question of motive persisted. If the dead man had been a pyromaniac, setting fires for the sheer hell of it, then why did he repeatedly select such uniformly similar targets? Like serial killing, pyromania is a crime of escalation. Because the craving for thrills can never be sated, each new fire tends to be bigger than the last. So why torch nothing but small businesses, all storefronts located in two- or three-floor structures and all resulting in such similar fires? Why not graduate to a chemical factory or some other site with more spectacular potential? The consistent focus of these crimes hinted at deliberate method rather than mere madness. And deliberate method, in turn, pointed to rational motive.

But it was not insurance scam, at least not in the usual sense. The beneficiary of every policy was the owner himself and/or his heirs, all of whom had more to lose than gain.

Of course, even if the motive did extend beyond twisted thrills to premeditated revenge or some ill-gotten gain, the fires still could have been the work of a single individual. And if the lone arsonist was now dead, then any future threat was still eliminated. Only the mystery of his past actions remained. Only the motive.

But revenge felt wrong. The four owners did not know one another, and nothing else tied them together, not even common membership in a small business association. Only one of the four, in fact, even belonged to such an organization. Revenge would therefore seem to demand a disgruntled customer bearing a deep grudge against four separate and unrelated stores. That such a customer would exact his revenge by methodically burning all four stores to the ground was not impossible, but surely extraordinary. Occam's Razor demanded a simpler, cleaner explanation. Which left only ill-gotten gain, its nature murky, unknown, and therefore a dead end.

Unless more than one perpetrator was involved.

Something about the crimes, in fact, felt both organized and unfinished. And if the arsons were indeed the work of more than one perpetrator, then their threat had not ended with the death of a single conspirator. Furthermore, the magnitude of the threat might be greater, and its predictability smaller, than the four actual arsons suggested. Small businesses would continue to be the targets, but I suspected the sample of four was too limited. Taverns, nightclubs, even restaurants might also be in jeopardy.

I told Gordon I wanted to maintain high vigil over the South Side during the danger hours of darkness from midnight until two in the morning. Then I sketched out a daylight plan for his detectives to pursue. He agreed to set them loose.

There were no more fires the next two nights, but basic legwork by homicide detectives Harvey Bullock and René Montoya uncovered a racket as old as organized crime itself. The motive actually was "insurance scam," although in warped form. It was the classic carrot and stick extortion of promise and threat.

Such a racket offers the carrot of promised "protection" from any and all harm that may threaten a business. Devastating fire, for example. Should such a fire occur as the result of arson, for which normal policies will not pay out, a very different kind of insurance is required. The offered carrot of protection comes with a price, of course, but is always less expensive than catastrophic loss of business, not to mention loss of life.

And should the carrot be rejected, the "insurance payment" not made, out comes the stick—the threat of the very fire against which there is no protection. Continued refusal to pay turns threat to reality. Word spreads through the business community. Fire happens, and "insurance" is needed. Extortion money is paid.

When the stick comes down too hard, when a deliberate fire has "accidental" consequences, the result can be death. Arson becomes homicide, with flame as the "very available" murder weapon.

I was right. The motive was ill-gotten gain, but the business owners were innocent. They were the victims of thugs, and we were dealing with multiple perpetrators.

"It's big," Gordon said, "and it's bad. Bullock and Montoya are convinced the whole South Side business community is running scared. A lot of them won't talk at all, and most deny paying protection money to anyone."

"Most, but not all."

"We have three owners talking, all telling the same story. But they have no idea who's behind the racket. They don't even know who they're paying the money to."

"No descriptions?"

"Nothing to describe," Gordon said, "because they never see a face. Just 'scary guys.' Collection goes down the same way in all three cases. Heavies appear at the rear service entrance, always unannounced and never on the same day of the week, two or three of them for intimidation. And always wearing cheap horror movie masks."

I looked out over the dark city, recalling the organized rampage of Roman Sionis. "Could be remnants of the Black Mask gang, Commissioner, resurfacing to run a new racket without their boss."

Gordon shrugged. "Or some other crew, anyone not wanting to be identified."

"I don't think so, not given the weird nature of these masks."

"You might have a point. Most mugs just pull a stocking over their heads or wear a bandana, maybe a ski mask."

"Exactly. And a dollar store horror mask does more than hide the wearer's face. It *transforms* the face into something different, turning the wearer into the Other. Such a mask secures anonymity, yes, but it also creates a new identity. And confers power."

According to his court-appointed psychologist, Roman Sionis harbored "deep-seated issues" with his father dating back to childhood. The conflict had driven him to set his family home ablaze, burning both parents to death. And with his own face badly seared, Sionis became further unhinged, determined to expand his revenge onto the world at large. But first, freed of his father and his past, he needed to become someone new, even as he needed to hide his horribly scarred face. He needed some way to transform himself, the new face of a mask.

Researching tribal beliefs common to ancient cultures worldwide, Sionis became fixated on the "primal power of the mask," obsessed with the mask's symbolic and totemic aspects. The mask of a lion, for example, allowed its wearer to absorb the lion's spirit, along with its fierceness and strength. The mask destroyed one identity by concealing it, even as the very means of concealment created a new identity. The mask simultaneously disguised and transformed, providing anonymity and protection even as it conferred mystery and power.

Insisting his previous identity was "burned dead," Sionis chose a new identity from its ashes. And so he was reborn behind a "face of death," a dark mask carved from the lid of his father's ebony coffin. Then, to support his new identity, Black Mask decided he needed a new "family," one in which *he* would serve as the "father."

A family in name alone and only in the sense of organized crime, the Black Mask gang was deliberately shaped according to the rituals and beliefs of a tribalistic secret society based on the transformative power of the mask. Each initiate into "the False Face Society of Gotham" was ceremonially awarded a new identity in the form of an intimidating mask. Few members of the gang actually shared their boss's beliefs or took his "mumbo-jumbo" seriously, but all enjoyed the power and ill-gotten gains derived from following him. And although they may have chosen a less garish style, all appreciated the logic of wearing masks while committing crimes.

Black Mask himself—Roman Sionis—was currently in prison, but a number of his gang members were still at large, leaderless and undisciplined, liable to engage in any number of criminal enterprises. And fire, they knew, played a large role in their boss's legend. It was also a powerful tool for extortion.

"It's them, Commissioner. It must be."

"All right," Gordon said. He was virtually convinced. "But either way, I don't see how it matters. Whoever's working it, this protection racket must be shattered, preferably before another fire kills anyone else."

"Agreed, but the Black Mask gang has already killed in other ways. With guns and garrotes, knives and clubs. Given the chance, they'll do it again. This is *our* chance to stop them, to break the False Face Society into pieces and sweep the mess away."

Gordon thought about it. "Just two or three would probably do, facing charges heavy enough. We might get them to plea bargain and give up the rest."

I nodded. "But to get those two or three to plead guilty and testify, first we have to nail them."

"With evidence of murder, not just extortion—hard evidence that'll stick but was probably destroyed in the fire."

"I have some ideas. One angle could be handled tonight—if you want to get Coroner Gunt out of bed again."

Gordon jabbed the bridge of his eyeglasses with a forefinger and smiled thinly. "I'd relish," he said, "nothing more."

Returning to the cavern from the morgue, I analyzed a sample of burned flesh from the unidentified corpse's face. As Gunt had noted, the residue of a foreign substance was melted into the flesh, but it had not come from something falling onto the burning man's face. It was a type of plastic commonly used in molded Halloween masks. The same type of disguise worn by the Black Mask gang.

Corroboration came the next day, when Sabra Temple matched the corpse's teeth to prison dental records. The dead man was an ex-con recently paroled after serving time in Blackgate on multiple charges of burglary and assault. He was also one of Black Mask's first initiates into Gotham's False Face Society.

What emerged was a reconstruction of the crime that had destroyed the office supply store. Retribution for refusing to pay extortion, the arson was also a warning to others contemplating similar refusal. The arsonist, an accomplished burglar, had penetrated the store after hours. After using an accelerant to prepare multiple seats for his fire, he was surprised while lighting them—literally caught in the act—by the storeowner who had been working late in his back room office. A struggle ensued. Both men were overcome by smoke and perished together in the flames, one wearing a dollar store fright mask that dissolved into his face. The bodies of both "pugilists" contorted into postures characteristic of death by fire. Three alarms sounded. The fire department arrived, too late for the accelerated blaze. And when it hit the news, a worried wife came to know horror.

Although three business owners had talked to Detectives Bullock and Montoya, only one was willing to cooperate further—a Korean woman who agreed to the installation of a wire under the counter of her modest dry-cleaning establishment. Gordon put a team in a battered van for daylight stakeout, while I took a nearby roof at nightfall. If it went down after dark, the play was mine.

They arrived at the shop's back door two hours after dark and one hour after closing time on the fourth night of surveillance. There were only two of them, arriving unannounced to pick up the week's insurance payment, both masked but both severely underestimating the shop's owner.

Wanting more than two as quickly as possible, I decided not to wait for plea bargains. Instead of taking them down on the spot when they emerged from the shop, I followed them some two miles to an old South Side brownstone. Emerging unmasked from their parked car, the two gangsters mounted the brownstone's steps. I slipped from the shadows and headed straight for the closing front door.

At least a dozen members of the Black Mask gang were still at large. I kicked down the door hoping for all of them but finding only seven, the two bagmen from the dry cleaner's shop plus five more, playing cards, eating takeout, watching a prizefight. All seven were barefaced and shocked, but I saw masks scattered on tables around the room.

When the first one moved, reaching for his gun, I kicked the television to the floor for additional shock effect, then slammed into the gunman before he could recover. The others put up less fight, several simply trying to flee.

After all seven were permanently down and securely trussed, I snipped a small piece from each of the scattered masks and left. Gordon's people were on their way and would handle the rest.

I returned to the crime lab under the manor and performed chemical analyses on the mask samples. Three separate samples proved to be the same type of plastic, precisely matching the residue embedded in the late arsonist's melted face tissue. Produced by the same manufacturer, the four masks had probably been purchased in the same store.

Delivering the samples and test results to the roof of police headquarters the next night, I found Gordon pleased.

"This'll be the clincher," he said, "although we probably have enough as it is."

"Confessions?"

"Incriminating evidence from the horse's mouth, all right, but hardly confessions."

"Voiceprints."

Gordon nodded, further pleased. "We strapped their masks on and made them talk. Two of the mask-muffled recordings perfectly matched voiceprints from the dry cleaner's surveillance wire."

"I could have told you who the two bagmen were."

"True," Gordon said, "but I doubt you'd care to do it in court." And his mustache lifted in a rare grin.

Both bagmen will plead guilty on reduced conspiracy and extortion charges, testifying against the others. They have also given up six additional names, against whom arrest warrants are now pending. And for whom I will begin searching tonight.

With Gotham's False Face Society thus unmasked, its members will soon join their "father" in Blackgate Penitentiary. Case closed.

Murdicide

From the Private Files of James Gordon

WHEN the first step is false, jumping to easy conclusions sets up a hard fall. Now that this department has very nearly gone off the cliff, it's wise to take a step back and use this case as a map to better chart the future.

It looked simple, so assumptions were made. Big mistake. We were wrong from the start, all of us, and every flaw that followed was based on that initial faulty assessment. Because of that, a killer nearly walked, something no police commissioner cares to admit and the cold fact prompting me tonight to write this unofficial report.

Sad truth is, suicide is less than rare in Gotham. For whatever reasons, citizens are driven to kill themselves in this city all the time. More of them, it seems, with each passing year. I don't like it, but I'm forced to accept it. As a cop, I'm no shrink—and I'm definitely the wrong cut for social services. My job is to keep this city safe for those citizens choosing to stick it out and slog onward through each new day. What I can't do is protect them from themselves.

Second sad truth. The above is way too defensive and nothing but an excuse. Fact is, after a recently divorced woman was found hanged to death in her home located in the Red Clay district, we did her a disservice and nearly dishonored her memory. The body was still suspended by an electrical extension cord looped around her neck, its other end tied off at the top railing of the second floor stairway. My forensics crew and

Medical Examiner Gunt all agreed on the same cause—asphyxiation due to self-strangulation. Death by her own hands.

And so it seemed to me, too. At first, anyway. Again, citizens do kill themselves, and all signs pointed to this woman being one of them. She had married early to her childhood sweetheart, the only boyfriend she'd ever had, and her train-wreck divorce had just been finalized. The kids were grown and gone. She lived alone, apparently too alone. People commit suicide for lesser reasons every day.

Excuses again. But maybe one saving grace, just barely. It was something in the death scene photos I couldn't put my finger on, something wrong in those pictures that I couldn't quite see. When it kept nagging the back of my mind, I decided to dig deeper by tapping the dark side, otherwise known as consulting my "Shadow Self." Pacing the roof and hashing things out has become a way of accessing a new frame of mind. It's helped before, and my Shadow Self immediately saw the photos with fresh eyes.

It was the odd position of the stool, neatly overturned almost directly under the hanging woman, definitely too close to her dangling feet. And as soon as this was pointed out, the whole scene suddenly seemed unnatural and appeared staged. If it had been kicked over out of the way by the woman hanging herself, the toppled stool should have come to rest farther away and probably at a different angle. More askew.

Then there was the hanging woman herself, who suddenly seemed too dressy, as if all dolled up to go out rather than check out. She even died with her shoes on. Or one shoe anyway, the other on the floor next to the toppled stool. Here again, the shoe was too close, right under the body's stockinged foot with no distance accounting for any "bounce factor."

While some suicides have, in fact, done the deed in their Sunday best, casual attire is far more typical. You even find underwear in the summer, housecoat and slippers in colder months.

None of this was conclusive proof, of course, but all added to the vague nagging I'd felt. It was certainly sufficient cause for the Shadow Self to dig even deeper.

Sure enough, when we went over Gunt's postmortem report again, my dark side found more serious discrepancies. The necropsy photos showed neck bruising and trachea damage feasibly consistent with hanging but more commonly found in asphyxiation by strangulation. The ligature mark, in fact, only seemed to match what should have been expected. The bruise line impressed into the neck was simultaneously too wide and too shallow for a thin extension cord—except in the front of the neck, where close-ups showed a ligature mark *within* a ligature mark, a second impression superimposed on the first. It was both deeper and narrower, exactly what an extension cord would make.

Then the Bat checked a posterior neck close-up. That there was a ligature mark in the back of the neck, he said, any mark at all, was the proof needed to reopen the case. He was right, and it was obvious in the death scene photos, dirrectly in front of my eyes the whole time. M.E. Gunt had never even queried forensics about the noose. He simply *assumed* a slip-knot, even though he found no knot impression anywhere around the neck.

Why ask? Citizens commit suicide in this city all the time.

But the truth was, this woman had been found hanging in a *fixed* noose that was not cinched tight, the cord pressing deeply into her throat but not even *touching* the back of her neck. And the triangular gap at the rear of the noose was fully evident in the death scene photos.

After cursing Gunt, I felt like a damned fool myself, embarrassed for not seeing any of this in the daylight. Worse, I actually felt guilty for needing the help of such a dark filter.

The original ruling on cause of death had been based on automatic assumption, not actual evidence. But this was clearly murder, and the killer had almost pulled it off.

I took my Shadow Self from the roof straight to the morgue. Adhesive tape applied to the ligature marks lifted a half-dozen fibers. And cross-section microscope analysis identified the fibers as fine silk. Electrical extension cord obviously contains no silk. No fibers of any other kind, for that matter.

Long story short, we learned the divorced and deceased woman had been anything but lonely. She had found a new boyfriend, in fact, with whom she'd had a dinner date the night of her death. A search of the boyfriend's closet found a necktie of fine Italian silk, perfectly matching the color and quality of the fibers lifted from his late lover's fatal ligature mark. The tie had encircled two different necks that night, far tighter around one of them.

Ruling of "death by suicide" has been revised to homicide by strangulation. After the killing, the death scene was poorly staged, with amateur homicide covered up as plausible suicide. The victim, in other words, had been framed for her own murder. And this department very nearly colluded with the sloppy killer.

Lesson learned, let's hope. Jumping to conclusions can be a sure ticket to a hard fall. Better to take every investigation step by step, with tiny steps all the way to the finish. Things are not always what they seem or how they appear. Sometimes they're something else, and sometimes they're two things. Like murder *and* suicide.

Murdicide.

So assume the worst, never the easy or obvious. Think darker and then act on it. Like the Shadow Self.

All the Way
to Bugs

Casefile #0073
Year One, Month Nine, Day Seven

From the Journal of Alfred Pennyworth

NIGHT has fallen and the Bat has gone, leaving me in charge of his cavern lair. And the night is rare, one of those in which I find my hands idle. There are no analyses to perform, no fingerprint or DNA checks to run, no outstanding database searches whatsoever. With dawn many hours ahead, I find every hour is mine to fill. But while such luxury is always welcome, it is also an opportunity to make myself useful. As young Bruce once said, "Even when there's nothing to do, Alfie, there's always something to do."

Indeed, and especially since my young charge came of age as the extraordinary Batman. And so I shall endeavor to fill this time by enriching the store of specialized information compiled in the master's files. Herewith, then, a catchall entry on human death and the creepy-crawly creatures attracted to it.

Of criminology's many diverse fields, surely none is more grue-some nor fascinating than that of forensic entomology, the study of insects correlated with "corpse ecology." These days, knowledge pertaining to this macabre science is largely harvest-ed from "the body farm," about which more anon.

But first a defining generalization: In the realm of forensic entomology, the length of insect life is used to gauge the length of human death. In this, of course, as in all forensic methodologies, the master has made himself an expert. Indeed, he has employed maggots to betray more than several murderers.

In any murder, the time of the victim's death can prove crucial to the apprehension of his or her killer. If a "postmortem clock" can be reliably established, for example, alibis can either be verified or demolished by virtue of being rendered irrelevant. In other words, if the time of death is proven to be earlier or later than the period of time encompassed by a suspect's alleged alibi (that is, if the victim was murdered when witnesses *cannot* vouch for the suspect's whereabouts), then the "alibi" is scarcely proof that the suspect could not be responsible for the foul play in question.

When a murdered body is quickly discovered, a medical examiner may determine time of death rather simply through one or more of the "triple time markers." First is body heat, or *algor mortis*, measured by a thermometer inserted into the brain, liver, or other organ. Second is muscle stiffness, or *rigor mortis*, assessed by touch. And third is lividity, or *livor mortis*, the degree of blood-settled pallor judged by simple observation. When enough time has passed for all three of these standard markers to have faded away, however, the investigator hoping to establish a postmortem clock must look elsewhere, and usually to forensic entomology.

Having researched and monitored this still nascent field in an effort to cull anything and everything useful to the master's ongoing endeavor, I have turned up several intriguing and illuminating sidelights that are worthy of recording.

While forensic entomology did not truly come into its own until the 1980s, its origins may well date all the way back to thirteenth century China. Indeed, as recorded in Sung Tzu's detective manual *Hsi Yuan Chi Lu* ("The Washing Away of

Wrongs"), basic knowledge of insects was employed to solve the mystery of a slashing murder some eight hundred years ago.

Returning from their fields to find the bloodied body of a fellow villager, Chinese farmers feared bandits might be lurking in the area, ready to strike again. After one look at the murdered body, however, the provincial death investigator immediately ruled out bandits.

"Robbers kill men only to take their valuables," he said. "This man's personal effects are still here, while his body bears many wounds more than fatal. If this is not a killing of hate, then what is?"

With every villager now a suspect, all were questioned in turn. Although the investigator discerned a possible motive, hard feelings toward the murdered man related to a debt, no confession was obtained.

Next, the villagers were ordered to produce their field sickles for examination, with the warning that any hidden sickle would be considered an admission of guilt. When some seventy to eighty blades were laid before him, the investigator saw that they were all much the same and that any one of them could have been the weapon used in the slashing murder.

Also noting that the hot day was swarming with flies, the investigator stood by the arrayed sickles and simply observed. Almost immediately, the flies gathered on one and only one of the blades, where they apparently feasted on invisible traces of blood. Furthermore, the imperfectly washed sickle belonged to the same villager who was owed money by the dead man. Accused of the crime, however, the villager continued to deny his guilt.

The investigator swept his hand along the row of sickles. "The other blades have no flies," he said, "but your sickle has killed a man, and so the flies gather."

Gasping at the significance of the fly-covered sickle, the other villagers then glared at its owner. Confronted by such proof, the murderer dropped to his knees, beat his head on the ground, and confessed in full.

Or so Sung Tzu wrote in his now ancient handbook for detectives.

Elegant in the scientific sense and involving a "study" of insects, the solution stands as the first recorded case of what could be called forensic entomology. Well done, even if no post-mortem clock had been established. But then, a long time would pass before such a concept was even conceivable.

Indeed, insects could hardly be used to gauge a corpse's length of death until science first overcame its long-standing theory of "spontaneous generation." This was apparently developed by Aristotle in fourth century B.C. Greece. Struck by the inexplicable appearance of insects "out of nowhere" (in a closed space, for example), Aristotle wrote: "Some bloodless creatures come into being not from a union of the sexes, but from decaying earth and excrements."

He was wrong, of course, although his logic endured for centuries, as later expressed by Rome's poet-scientist Lucretius:

With good reason the earth has gotten the name of mother
Since all things are produced out of the earth
And many living creatures, even now, spring out of the earth
Taking form by the rains and the heat of the sun.

It was not until 1651, in fact, that this theory of spontaneous generation suffered its first serious blow. Put forth by the English anatomist William Harvey, the revisionist alternative was controversial but spot on: Insects were not conjured from nothing, nor did they magically spring from dust or dirt. They developed from oviform or eggs, just like those laid by chickens, merely too small to be seen.

Seizing upon Harvey's notion in 1667, the Italian scientist-poet Francesco Redi conducted a series of experiments with pieces of covered and uncovered meat. The covered meat turned merely rank, whereas the uncovered meat attracted flies to become both rank and *maggoty*. And the maggots, in turn, eventually became more flies. This was proof that tiny eggs had been laid by the original flies while feeding on the meat. Death was the incubator of new life, which the incubator then nourished.

These observations prompted further studies on the life cycles of flies and other scavenging insects. And because a human corpse, already known as "worm food," is nothing but a large piece of meat, it was not difficult to correlate insect life cycles with the consumption and decomposition of dead people. The first postmortem clock had begun to tick.

A dead body attracts flies within moments to an hour. These first flies, entomologists now know, exude a pheromone scent that induces "oviposition frenzy," or an overwhelming urge to lay eggs. Over the next twelve hours, therefore, the swarming flies deposit a "creamy crust" over any and all soft, moist areas of the cadaver. This white paste is nothing more nor less than a film of minuscule eggs laid in open wounds, orifices, and eyes, everywhere freshly hatched maggots will be able to feed most easily. Depending on the particular species of fly, its eggs will hatch eight to fourteen hours later, the point at which maggot infestation begins. Again depending on the species, the larval maggot stage of development occupies an additional period of known time, further extending the postmortem clock with a remarkable degree of exactitude. The mere size of a maggot can be used to reliably measure time backward, virtually to the hour of its hatching.

If a body is found relatively soon, then, its time of death can be determined with near precision on the basis of flies and their maggots alone. Surprising accuracy can be achieved even for bodies found much later (and therefore subject to more advanced decomposition), simply by assessing the presence of maggot pupal cases to determine multiple larval generations. But flies and maggots are just the beginning, because the human cadaver endures ongoing predation by successive waves of other insect species. And they are nothing if not rapacious.

When this was first noted in 1878 by Jean-Pierre Megnin, a French veterinarian specializing in insect and arachnid parasites, the pioneering science of forensic entomology was truly born. Megnin, in fact, established the first start-to-finish time-line of death, detailing the effects of scavenging insects on a human cadaver from the very first flies all the way to the last bone-clinging bugs of fully skeletonized remains.

"We have been struck," the Frenchman wrote, "by the fact that the workers of death arrive at their table successively, and always in the same order." Armed with this preliminary obser-vation, Megnin then devised a meticulous calendar of what he called necrophilous ("dead-loving") insects, a timetable charting the progressive rise and fall of "the fauna of the tomb." Completed in 1894, Megnin's painstaking work was ignored and even denigrated by entomologists even as it was hailed by pathologists. The latter immediately recognized the value of Megnin's calendar as "death's own timepiece," clocking eight separate waves of insects and other arthropods, each successive-ly infesting and digesting a human cadaver left in the open. Devouring death down to the bone, each wave according to its own specialized tastes, the eight invasions define reliable inter-vals in the inevitable progression of mortality.

First come different species of common blow flies (or bot-tle flies) and their subsequent maggots, feeding and incubating and feeding again in soft tissues and open wounds.

Next are various species of flesh flies, these burrowing more deeply under the skin to launch the feast in earnest.

Then, beginning in the third month after death and end-ing after the eighth month, waves three through five consist of rove beetles and soldier flies, these being "secondary predators" feeding on the maggots of earlier flies, as well as scavenging cheese skippers and scuttle flies attracted by fermented proteins produced during the body's later stages of decomposition.

During months six through twelve, as the bodily fluids dis-appear, swarming mites move in to feed on the dry cadaver.

The seventh wave is comprised of various skin and hide beetles. These occupy the ravaged corpse during the second year after death, gnawing the dried-out skin until it is gone.

And finally, three years after death, clothes moths and spider beetles pick the bones completely clean.

Infestation by one or another species wave, therefore, serves as an obvious marker establishing length of death, the corpse furthermore bearing pupal cases and other evidence of preceding waves.

Megnin then produced a different and longer timetable for buried bodies, with each insect wave hampered by the grave's barrier of earth. Both charts and clocks, however, eventually reach the same result.

"In the end," Megnin wrote, "nothing rests next to the white bones but a sort of brown earth, finely granular, composed of insect pupal cases . . . and the excrement of successive generations of insects . . . Thus is accomplished the parable of the scripture: 'You are dust and unto dust you shall return.'"

Dust processed by the meek of the earth. By insects.

Ever since these initial studies, each new generation of forensic entomologists has driven the science onward, recalibrating the postmortem clock toward ever greater precision. The species included in Parisien Megnin's eight localized waves (and the intervals of his timing) have been altered and supplemented for different geographic and climatic conditions, even for the materials used in modern clothing.

Given knowledge of the geographic ranges for particular species, the presence (or evidence of past presence) of anomalous insects within a corpse can offer further valuable clues. Among other things, these clues may indicate postmortem relocation of the remains, the region from which the remains were moved, and even how long after death such relocation occurred. The latter determination is governed by the absence of same-region foreign species in successive waves, replaced by native species.

I still recall, for example, my initial doubts when the master once flatly announced: "The killer—or *someone*—moved the victim's body at least ninety miles northwest some nineteen days after death." In the end, the insects proved him right, shattering my skepticism from that moment onward.

And that Holmesian moment reminds me of a similar case. A corpse discovered in the Gotham area was nevertheless ridden with pupal cases foreign to Gotham. Equipped with this single clue, the master ultimately identified not only the body itself but her murderer as well.

First, he identified the pupal cases, which had been left behind by the maggots of hairy blow flies native to tropical regions. In North America, these particular hairy blow flies thrive nowhere other than the Florida Everglades. Immediately checking with the appropriate authorities in Florida, the master was then able to identify the remains as a missing woman who had lived near, and disappeared from, the Everglades area. The woman, then, had lived and died in Florida. That her dead body had been found in Gotham was obvious proof that it had been moved. Using a modernized and localized "Megnin eight-wave timeline," the master next analyzed the cadaver's other insect evidence to establish that the woman had been dead for approximately nine months, but that her body had been in the Gotham area for only three months. Ergo, it had been moved three months earlier, six months after the woman's death.

Suspects in the case included a Florida man who had dated the woman. Six months after her disappearance, the man had moved north and was now residing in Maine. Inspection of the man's credit card records revealed that he had purchased auto fuel in the Gotham area en route to Maine. At this point, although proof was still lacking, the case was effectively solved. Simple police work did the rest.

Having survived several rounds of questioning but aware that he remained a suspect in the open investigation, the murderer knew he was safe only until his victim's body was found.

At that point, he feared, DNA and other evidence taken from the dead body could tie him to the crime. His nerve finally gave out after six months, at which time he retrieved his victim from her shallow grave in the Everglades, put the insect-infested body in the boot of his auto, and drove north. Then, disposing of the body halfway between the scene of the murder and his new home, he stupidly used his credit card to purchase petrol in the same area. Not that it mattered nearly so much as other facts.

Indeed, forensic examination of his auto yielded traces of the victim's decomposing tissue in the boot, along with several dead maggots of the same hairy blow fly species. Case instantly closed.

The refinement of Jean-Pierre Megnin's original postmortem clock continues even now, most productively on the aforementioned modern "body farm." Scattered here and there across this country and others, these rather ghoulish tracts are constantly maintained and monitored by entomologists for the benefit of medical examiners and law enforcement agencies worldwide.

Much like "reverse crops," fresh cadavers donated to science are planted on and in these body farms to decay rather than flourish. Exposed to the varying elements of each farm's different climate and geographic region, the bodies are further subjected to a variety of conditions within each region—indoors and out; in dense woods and open field; in full sun, full shade, partial shade; fully and partially buried in every type of local soil; through a range of damp to dry environments; fully and semi-immersed in fresh and salt water; and so on through the full spectrum of "natural habitats." And then, whether naked, clothed, or wrapped in plastic, the planted cadavers quite simply serve as insect bait. Observations of each body—along with the behavior and progress of their scavengers—are recorded on a daily basis. This then provides a detailed reconstruction of the human form's deconstruction via consumption. If the work is excessively unpleasant, as I submit it certainly must be, its morbidity hardly renders it less valuable. Indeed, constantly updated and available for correlation with human remains found in the wild, body farm findings are now considered crucial to basic murder investigation.

With much still to learn, today's forensic entomologists continue fine-tuning Megnin's original postmortem clock for every conceivable situation, hoping to match any given reality to a comparable simulation. If every life is different, the same holds true for each death. Every detail may be vital because small variations can exert large effects.

As noted in an earlier entry, body fat's transformation to adipocere "normally" occurs over months, but insects (like water immersion) can drastically alter the process. In cases of full maggot infestation, for example, adipocere transformation is speeded to as little as three weeks. In the very act of nourishing themselves, moreover, insects and their larvae hasten the overall putrefaction of corpse tissue. Just as a cadaver will decay more rapidly in a tropical climate, the work of non-tropical insects can also create a deceptive appearance, making the degree of decomposition and length of death seem greater than is actually the case, at least prior to informed analysis of larval cycles and species waves. Even then, however, anomalies are not uncommon.

And yet every anomaly offers a clue to be explained and exploited. Were I Watson to the master's Sherlock, I might recount the demystification of one such anomalous clue in something perhaps called "The Case of the Inordinately Fat Maggot."

The remains of a gunshot victim were found in a wooded area of Gotham's Fairfield Park. From the extent of decomposition blackening the face and marbling the extremities, Coroner Mortimer Gunt could only say the man had been dead "some three days to several weeks." This, of course, hardly satisfied the master's exacting standards. And so, with nothing else to go on, he examined the preserved maggots extracted from the victim's face and bullet wounds.

They belonged to two species of common flies, bluebottles and sheep blow flies, both of which begin laying eggs within hours of settling on a body. The maggots fell within three distinct size classes, the largest class represented by but a single specimen. One and only one maggot was much larger than all the others.

The smallest maggots were obviously those most recently hatched, feeding for the shortest length of time, and therefore spawn of the latest arriving flies. Given the prevailing environmental conditions, these would have laid their eggs only up to the third day after death. At that point, the corpse would have become too rancid for the surprisingly fussy taste of both species.

Matched against data from a body farm, all the larger maggots—except for the one, the largest of all—proved to be seven days old. Adding ten to twelve hours for the incubation period, the victim would have been murdered seven and half days earlier, on the evening or night of the previous Tuesday. Except, that is, for the problem of the single anomalous specimen.

Too large by far to fit the other evidence, the maggot measured some 18 millimeters. According to the appropriate body farm data, a maggot of this size would have been three weeks old. But if the body had been dead that long, why had it not been found sooner? The wooded area was isolated, yes, but only for a *city park*. And where were all the large maggot's three-week-old brothers and sisters? Why was there only *one* of such prodigious size? Furthermore, where were the *two*-week-old maggots? What of the entire interval between? It made no sense.

Just then came news that the victim had been identified by Coroner Gunt and the police. It was a man last seen eight days before the discovery of his dead body, on the afternoon of the previous Tuesday. Again, seven and a half days seemed an ideal backdated time of death. If not for that one confoundingly huge maggot.

The master wondered if it had been an errant interloper, squirming onto the human remains after first fattening itself on the nearby carcass of a bird or squirrel. While he had never heard of such maggot migration, nor could he imagine it impossible provided the two dead bodies had lain in close proximity.

And so he ventured to the park for an examination of the scene. Searching well beyond the feasible range of any crawling maggot, just to be certain, he found no such carrion anywhere in that wooded area.

As is his wont when stumped, the master fell back on his principle of Occam's Razor, which posits that the simplest solution is also the most likely. This led to several conclusions. Despite its anomalous size, the maggot was only seven days old. *Because* of its anomalous size, which seemed to indicate it was *twenty-one* days old, it had somehow fed three times faster than normal. And feeding three times faster than normal, it had consumed three times as much nourishment as had all the other seven-day-old maggots.

All well and good, I agreed, but how to *explain* such conclusions?

"The litter," he said.

Litter?

"In the park, Alfred. I found no dead animals, but the police found plenty of litter. It's all catalogued in Jordan Rankin's preliminary forensics report. Crack vials, plastic packets, other paraphernalia. Clear evidence of drug use in those woods, perhaps drug dealing."

And . . . ?

He went straight to the vial in which the gargantuan maggot had been preserved. "And that's the answer," he said, checking the vial's label. "The maggot came from the deep naso area."

I heard no clap of thunder, nor did the proverbial lightbulb highlight my balding pate, and I'm sure my helpless shrug said as much.

"The maggot was dug from one of the man's nostrils, where it had eaten and burrowed deeply into the nasal passage."

But is that not, I asked, what maggots normally do? They eat and they burrow.

"But not that much in seven days, Alfred. Not unless the interior of the nostril was compromised before the maggot even began, not unless the nostril's normal tissue barriers were already broken down. Raw, soft, moist. Maybe even bleeding at the time of death."

And the victim, I asked, had not been struck to the nose?

"No struggle at all," he said. "The autopsy found no evidence of any blunt force violence, nothing but the three gunshot wounds to the back."

I had finally begun to see the light. Any nosebleed had resulted from a different cause.

The master nodded and immediately queried Gunt about toxicology results.

Nothing yet, came the answer over the phone.

And had the victim's nostrils been wet, the master asked, perhaps even bleeding at the time of his death?

Gunt said it was possible, but could or would not commit himself with confidence.

And so, with the victim's toxicology still pending, the master made do with that which was at hand. He dissected the overlarge maggot itself and then tested its tissue for the presence of cocaine. The result was positive. Before its own death and preservation, the fat maggot had been flying high and feeding easy inside the warm cocoon of a cocaine-abraded nostril.

From there, the rest was tedious but nevertheless elementary. With the master's guidance passed on through Commissioner Gordon, the police did most of the legwork, whereupon the Bat swooped down to bag the culprit. Boiled down to its essence, a reconstruction of the crime follows.

The victim had been a heavy cocaine user. He was also unemployed, long since sacked from his job due to erratic attendance. On the evening of Tuesday last, having snorted the last of his supply, and snorted his already ravaged nostrils further raw, he went out in desperate quest of more cocaine. This took him to his usual supplier, conducting clandestine business in the usual place. The place was isolated. The addicted victim was broke, no doubt hyper-agitated, presumably obnoxious. And the supplier, perhaps already in a foul mood, was armed. A perfect recipe for the disaster of murder.

In other words, seven and a half days prior to the discovery of his maggot-infested remains, the victim had gone to the park with no money and impossibly high hopes. After a heated verbal altercation, the man had been turned away and then shot in the back by his enraged cocaine supplier, who was already owed a large sum of money, who lacked an alibi for the maggot-measured evening in question, whose record included a prior arrest and conviction for dealing drugs in that same wooded vicinity of the park, whose fingerprints were all over its littered crack vials, and whose gun ballistically matched all three bullets extracted from his erstwhile customer's expired body.

The drug dealer had fled after the shooting, although not far enough, even as the flies had gathered to feed and breed.

Thereby closing the Case of the Overlarge Larva.

Dawn cracks, the night is done, and the Bat is due.

And so, Watson, Doyle, and most assuredly Pennyworth aside, leave it to the immortal bard to most eloquently offer the final word on mortality. From *Hamlet*:

> *We fat all creatures else to fat us, and we fat ourselves*
> *for maggots. Your fat king and your lean beggar is but*
> *variable service—two dishes, but to one table.*
> *That's the end.*

9000 Degrees at 18,000 Miles per Hour

From Bruce Wayne's Diary

NO doubt I'll be dealing mostly with guns, knives, and blunt instruments, but bombs kill, too. And if the bomb is big enough, it's a nightmare that kills lots of people all at once. So here are some things to remember about explosives and the forensic investigation of an explosion site, from the ground zero epicenter all the way outward to the edge of wreckage.

First, an explosive is *any substance or mixture of substances that is only temporarily stable.* Permanently stable substances simply do not blow up. But undoing the stability of a temporarily stable substance—either by inducing a chemical reaction or somehow applying heat—results in a sudden release of energy in the form of hot and rapidly expanding gas.

And we're talking *very* sudden, *extremely* hot, and *incredibly* rapid. An explosion's detonation (or shock) wave can reach 9,000 degrees Fahrenheit with a pressure as great as 1,200 tons per square inch traveling at 18,000 miles per hour. This kind of heat, energy, and speed obviously explains how and why a bomb wreaks the awesome damage and destruction it does.

Most explosives rely on the abrupt combination (or "clashing mixture") of carbon and oxygen. The more compact the sources of carbon and oxygen, the greater the force of the resulting explosion.

The "best" explosions (meaning the worst) are the ones that produce the maximum possible amount of gas while leaving the least possible amount of residual, or non-vaporized, solid. In other words, the "efficiency" of a bomb is judged by how much of its "solid" substance (which can include a volatile liquid such as nitroglycerin) is converted to explosive gas.

The most favored sources of oxygen are nitrates and chlorates, both readily available in fertilizers and weed killers. This explains the homemade "truck bombs" of choice, requiring nothing illegal and not much more than a trip to some garden supply store.

The site of an explosion makes for one mess of a crime scene. ("Hell on earth," some investigators call it.) Even so, aside from rescue efforts that always come first and sweep everything else aside, it's still important to isolate or quarantine the scene and preserve it from contamination as much as possible. In the case of a huge explosion, this is nearly impossible to do, so you just do your best.

Then simple observation and examination of the "debris distribution pattern" can establish the epicenter of the explosion, a "ground zero," which in most cases will be obvious. The epicenter is where the bomb was planted and where it went off, releasing its energy outward in all directions. This 360-degree rule holds true even for a specialized "directional" explosive device, which merely shields and deflects some of the outward force to channel most of it into a certain direction. And here the debris distribution pattern will obviously reveal the shockwave's main direction.

Working outward from the epicenter, taking distance measurements through the various stages of damage distribution, and assessing the weights of strewn materials, you can add everything up to calculate the precise force of the explosion. Also important to examine is the type and degree of damage inflicted to walls, support pillars, vehicles, anything and everything in the vicinity. The overall range of a bomb blast is defined by the outer limit of its damage, the point beyond which only billowing dust has traveled. The primary range terminates at the farthest pieces of hurled debris, whereas the full range extends all the way to the last windows shattered by the shockwave.

But the epicenter is always where you focus your search for major clues, namely any solid residues remaining from the bomb's detonation. If you get lucky, you might even find gross solids, things like fragments of wires, detonator caps, timing device components, maybe even pieces of the bomb's outer casing or the container that held the explosive material. And if you're really lucky, you just might be able to lift a fingerprint from one of these fragments.

But let's face it, a blown-up bomb tends to destroy its own evidence, just like a fire. So you have to look hard with specialized tools and equipment.

If you find any solid residue of the actual explosive substance itself, even a tiny amount of it, you harvest the trace residue just like any other forensic evidence, bagging and tagging it straight to the lab. Then you run standard tests to analyze and identify the residue, which in turn gives you the type of explosive device that left it behind. Such tests use specific chemical reagents, chromatography, and all the other usual methods.

But let's say your luck is bad and no solid residue is found or harvested at the ground zero epicenter. This is when you get fancy and try using portable vapor detectors and analyzers to identify any lingering gas. And if you know the gas, you can then work backward to determine what type of solid was vaporized to produce it. In other words, if you're quick enough and barring a stiff wind, you can actually conjure the bomb's identity right out of thin air. (Like Arthur C. Clarke said: "Any sufficiently advanced technology is indistinguishable from magic."

Always worst of all, just about unbearable if you ask me, is the victim recovery and identification. There's no easy or polite

way to say it. Explosion victims are often found in pieces, sometimes pieces so small that the only hope is DNA identification.
I don't know how the rescue workers and investigators do it,
but I really respect them.

So that's more or less the story on bombs. The things are
just as cowardly as guns, if not more so, plus they can kill and
maim more people in a lot less time. A split second, in fact.
Which means anyone who commits mass murder by time delay
or remote control is especially monstrous and must be stopped
with a screeching halt.

Even so, I really hope I never need any of this information
and never have to face the hellish wreckage of such a crime
scene. Not to mention its carnage.

I'm working hard on getting tougher, inside and out, but
I'm not there yet. Right now, looking at people blown to bits,
I'd probably scream.

The Best
Evidence

From the Private Files of the Batman

THE best evidence in any murder is always offered by the "silent witness" of the victim's corpse. In other words, dead men actually *do* tell tales, although their stories must be teased out, bit by bit and one layer at a time. Even then, the narrative proceeds only in fits and starts, and only in a foreign language of visual symbols. These hieroglyphics, etched into lifeless flesh and bone, must be decoded and interpreted by an expert variously described as: coroner, medical examiner, forensic pathologist, or autopsist. The duty of such an expert is to interrogate the silent witness, with all "questioning" posed through a rigorous scientific exploration of the corpse, its various conditions, and especially any and all damage sustained, external and internal. An autopsist, in other words, performs a postmortem examination of mortality's evident facts.

Also known as a necropsy, this autopsy involves the dissection and inspection of a dead body and its organs to determine the cause of its death in the greatest detail possible. Or so it may be stated in scientific terms.

In human terms, an autopsy is also an unavoidably gruesome business that intimately violates the dignity of a life whose sanctity has already been ravaged. It reduces a person's unique individuality to the anonymous structures and functions of shared biology. It rips out a person's heart and slices his or her brain into sections thinner than cold cuts. By its very nature, an autopsy precludes any respect for mortal remains. It is nothing less than the methodical disassembly of a human being's once-working parts, digging deep into the body's innermost chambers to remove its secrets one by one, until that which was once a person becomes nothing but an empty shell, a deconstructed carcass of cold meat.

And yet, as callous as it seems, it is the kindest and most caring thing one can do to any victim of murder. It analyzes and interprets the crime's best evidence to reveal the unjust cause of death, thereby affording the potential to redress the crime through identification and apprehension of its perpetrator.

In that sense, a thorough autopsy—the ultimate violation of a departed soul's abandoned body—can preclude the necessity for more of the same.

Whereas autopsy was once crucial to the study of disease, advances in the fields of biochemistry and molecular biology—as well as noninvasive technologies such as magnetic resonance imaging—have severely reduced the importance and frequency of the procedure. The medicolegal investigation of murder, then, remains the last bastion of forensic pathology. There is simply no better way of determining the cause of violent death than by examination of the vulnerable flesh sustaining that violence.

No one knew this better than pioneering forensic pathologist Sir Bernard Spilsbury, whose detailed autopsies—and whose perceptive inferences drawn from them—solved a series of difficult murders committed in Britain during the 1800s. Criminology's debt to Spilsbury, in fact, extends to forensics methods in general. Appalled by the sight of London police using their bare hands to gather the pieces of a murder victim's butchered flesh, Spilsbury helped Scotland Yard assemble the first standardized forensics kit. Known as the Murder Bag, it contained gloves, tape, and fingerprint powder, along with other vital tools. Still, it was Spilsbury's expert analysis of cadavers that obtained actual convictions and established the primacy of a thorough autopsy. Anyone reading this account in the future would do well to revisit the past. There is still much to be learned from a study of Spilsbury's original casefiles.

In the case at hand, as in those handled by Spilsbury, only by listening to the victim was her murder solved. Representing my first actual autopsy, as opposed to the mere study of others already on record, the experience just obtained will surely not be my last.

I learned of the murder, and received its preliminary case-file, from Police Commissioner James Gordon during last night's surreptitious meeting atop police headquarters. There is no doubt that Gordon now accepts and values my unofficial assistance. But just as clearly, he is still taken aback by its form. While he fully appreciates my appearance as a necessary disguise and even a "psychological edge," it still seems to unnerve him. And yet he will no doubt become gradually more comfortable with what he calls his "scary secret weapon." Last night, in fact, proved it. While we kept our usual distance on the roof, the breakthrough of a shared car ride occurred at meeting's end.

"A young woman," Gordon said, "badly mutilated. Ugly sight, tragic waste."

"Found where, Commissioner?"

"Her apartment, second floor of a two-flat. In her bed."

"Evidence of a break-in?"

"No, but the front door was unlocked."

"Making a stranger possible, but unlikely. Any suspects?"

"The usual."

"Spouse?"

"She was unmarried, still attending Gotham University, with a night job waitressing."

"Boyfriend? Fellow student? Restaurant patron?"

"Closer the first time, but she was dating three different men, all older. We've already interviewed the three, one of whom is almost certainly guilty."

"You think you know which one?"

"No, just going by the odds."

"Polygraphs?"

"After the first refused on advice of counsel, the other two followed suit." He frowned. "Which is their right."

"Alibis?"

"Nothing that couldn't be lies told by protective friends. In one case, by another girlfriend. Just 'hanging out,' watching the game on TV, romantic evening alone."

"Anything extramarital?"

"No, all three are single and living alone. They're not *that* much older than the victim. Just five, six years, old enough to be out of school rather than fellow students."

"If there are three, why not more? Why not a new pick-up?"

Gordon gestured at the air. "Unlikely, due to a witness. The landlord lives on the first floor, last one to see the victim alive other than her murderer. He was taking out the trash about half-past ten, saw her coming home from her waitress shift, even said hello. Says she was alone and seemed dog-tired."

"Time of death?"

"Based on lividity and extent of rigor mortis, no earlier than one AM, no later than four."

Lividity describes the skin's complexion as infused by blood. Normal lividity begins to fade when the heart ceases to function, with pallor increasing as the body's blood settles to the lowest possible point dictated by its position subjected to simple gravity. Rigor mortis is the stiffening of muscle tissue ensuing after death and increasing over time to a point of maximum stiffness, then decreasing over further time as the muscles begin to deteriorate. By assessing and combining the two conditions (in a body found relatively soon), an approximate time of death may be calculated.

"Between one and four, during which time the landlord heard nothing?"

"Says he's a sound sleeper, just like his wife. Plus the victim's mouth was still taped—along with her wrists—when she was found in the morning."

"By whom?"

"A friend. Girl she rides to campus with. No response to car horn or doorbell. But as I say, the door was unlocked. As soon as the friend opened it, she says she 'smelled something bad.' Didn't stop her from going up the stairs, though, fearing her friend might be sick. The odor led her straight to the bedroom." Gordon looked down, shaking his head. "She was in hysterics for hours, probably still in shock now. Definitely excluded."

"You said 'mutilated' . . . "

"Multiple knife wounds, dozens. Blood everywhere. Frenzy. Sexual assault. Murder of so-called passion." He made a face, angry and disgusted.

"Bringing us back to the three boyfriends. Do they admit to sexual activity?"

"None of them. Two said 'not yet'—smugly, no less—and the other seemed to be offended."

"Were they credible?"

The commissioner shrugged. "Hard to tell from the tapes. The voice-stress analyzer indicated all three may have been deceptive, or at least nervous. But about what? Two may have been bragging, the other acting."

I thought about it. "The first two made a double statement. They said there'd been no sex, but they also claimed it was only a matter of time. Either component could have been the lie."

"Exactly, and the third may have been less offended by the question than he put on. His response could have been a cover for not 'scoring,' not being 'manly' enough. Detectives Bullock and Montoya conducted the actual interviews. Said they couldn't tell from their faces either."

"All the blood belonged to the victim?"

"So far, yes, although they're not finished with all of it. Lab's still running tests."

"But no scratches or injuries on any of the three suspects?"

"Nothing visible."

"Anything in the victim's blood?"

"Clean so far. No alcohol, none of the common drugs."

"Her clothing?"

"She was naked. T-shirt and underwear on the bedroom floor."

"Blood distribution?"

"All in the bedroom and adjacent bath."

"None tracked or dripped anywhere else through the apartment?"

"Not a drop. The bedroom was left a mess—you can check the photos or the actual scene—but the bathroom was wiped clean."

"Oh?"

"No visible blood anywhere, just traces soaked into the grout between tiles. And more in the plumbing traps, sink, and tub."

"You're saying the killer took a shower before leaving the scene?"

"That's the way it looks. The bath also opens onto the hall. You can enter from the bedroom, but you don't have to go back through the bedroom to get out."

"So the perpetrator may have been naked when he murdered the victim, his clothes never inside the bloody bedroom."

"That's what we think, but it doesn't quite add up. Let's say they both undressed elsewhere in the apartment, most likely the living room. Then they retire to the bedroom, where the murder occurs. The killer enters the bathroom naked but covered in blood. He cleans up and exits through the hall door. Back in the living room, he gets dressed and then leaves. Seems the most likely scenario, easiest explanation for why he failed to deposit any blood elsewhere in the apartment . . . "

"Except none of the victim's clothing was found in the living room."

"How did you know that?"

"You said it didn't add up. Other than the T-shirt and underwear, where *were* the victim's clothes?"

"Waitress outfit in the laundry hamper, everything else either in her dresser or closet. She *could* have brought her clothes from the living room and dropped them into the hamper before the assault began, but it just feels wrong."

"I think it is wrong, Commissioner, and for additional reasons. If the killer entered the bedroom naked, where did he hide the tape used on the victim's mouth and wrists, not to mentioned his weapon?"

"Good catch," Gordon said. "Possibly behind his back, but that feels wrong too."

"Plus there's the minimum of ninety minutes between the time the victim got home and the time of her murder. The landlord said she seemed tired, making it unlikely she would have stayed in her waitress uniform for that length of time, perhaps equally unlikely that she would have changed into another outfit. I think she was wearing nothing but the T-shirt and underwear, dressed for bed when the killer arrived."

"Maybe *waiting* for him in bed." Gordon thought about it. "Makes sense, but there's still the problem with the murder weapon and the tape."

"What kind of tape was it?"

"Electrical. Black. The kind used to insulate wiring."

"Matched to a roll in the apartment?"

"No. Either brought to the scene, indicating premeditation, or taken *from* the scene, indicating who knows what."

"Foreign hairs recovered?"

Gordon nodded. "Quite a few, especially from the tub drain, matching a few from the bed."

"But no comparison hair samples from the suspects?"

"All three refused, just like the polygraph. As I said, one's almost certainly guilty, the other two spooked."

"Fibers and prints?"

"Plenty as usual, but all telling us nothing yet, waiting for a match with someone or something. But the fingerprints may be a dead end, because the killer was apparently careful. The bedroom light switch and both knobs on the front door, as well as the bathroom's hallway door, were all wiped clean. Any other prints matching the suspects could be explained by previous visits."

"Murder weapon?"

"Knife."

"Not left at the scene?"

Gordon shook his head. "No such luck."

"Anything else?"

"You have the reports," he said, "but they won't tell you much more. Not until the autopsy, anyway. This one's high-profile, certain to splash big in the news, the kind of autopsy always performed by Municipal Coroner Gunt himself. Or Chief Medical Examiner Gunt." Gordon made a face. "Two titles for one man."

"You disapprove?"

He shrugged. "Gunt's capable enough, I suppose, at least as a pathologist, although I have my doubts about his deductive abilities."

"By either title, the job demands a good doctor *and* a good detective."

"A rare combination and my point exactly." He seemed resigned but none too happy about it.

"Politics?"

"Let's just say that Mortimer Gunt has been the mayor's good friend and loyal supporter for more than a decade."

"Before the mayor *became* mayor."

"There's your answer." He stared directly into my mask, a view he seldom dares, perhaps afraid of what he might see. "And my reality." He held the stare, waiting.

I let it hang for a moment, hoping I understood him correctly. "And if I wanted to see this autopsy, Commissioner, with my own eyes?"

"I expected nothing less," he said, "and hoped for nothing more." He checked his wristwatch. "Gunt has agreed to perform his autopsy this evening, scheduled to commence in some twenty minutes." He looked back at me. "And Gunt has further agreed to accept the presence of an anonymous observer."

"How did you manage that?"

His smile was grim. "By threatening to request one of his deputy coroners."

"Are they any better?"

"As pathologists, definitely not, and probably not as detectives either."

"Sheer bluff, then."

He nodded. "But it worked. Gunt knows the game and knows he'd need more cause to go to war." He indicated the rooftop kiosk, accessing the stairwell to the station's rear entrance. "Ready for the morgue?"

I nodded back, and we left the roof together.

Part of the smell was familiar, the bad part encountered at any scene of death. But it was different too, heavily laced with antiseptic and other chemical odors. I tried to ignore the former, as I always do, this time by focusing on the latter rather than through sheer force of will.

Entering the morgue fully gowned and masked, I had no need for any other disguise. To Coroner Gunt, I was simply a pair of eyes, a mysterious observer whom he was forced to tolerate. Even had he known me, which he did not, there was no way he could recognize Bruce Wayne, nor could he know I was the Batman. Furthermore, according to Gordon, Gunt was one of those convinced that the Bat was mere myth and rumor. And so, other than the police commissioner's consultant or associate, I was no one as far as the coroner was concerned.

Nor did he seem to care. Even when Gordon and I first entered the chilled room, Gunt and his assistant barely looked up from their gleaming tray of prosection tools.

Given the sadness of her terminal vulnerability, I found it difficult to look at the dead woman on the stainless steel autopsy table, its side troughs waiting to drain her remaining fluids. Already sponged clean, her wounds were strangely rude and raw, made all the more shocking by their lack of blood. The sight would soon get worse, of course, but for now there was no need to dwell on it. Instead, I chose to look above and beyond the body, focusing on Coroner Gunt himself. A thin bald man of more than average height in his mid-fifties, he conveyed an air of professional experience, efficiently arranging his preferred array of instruments on their chest-high tray. From left to right, in roughly ascending size, were various scalpels and larger knives, followed by three different surgical scissors, the largest for snipping through tough sinews. Then, somewhat startling even though I knew from study that their use in autopsies was fairly common, a pair of gardening shears. In a separate row above these basic tools were a variety of clamps, prises, probes, two different electric bonesaws, suturing equipment, and a magnifying lens.

Satisfied that all was in order, Gunt snapped on a pair of surgical gloves and turned from his tray to the autopsy table. He looked down at the waiting body, glanced up only briefly at me, then settled his calm eyes on Gordon. "As you can see, I've removed the tape and turned it over to your forensics people. They just took it away. Even I could see several prints."

Gordon stiffened. "Fingerprints on the tape?"

"Possibly on both sides, but clearly visible to the naked eye on the gummy adhesive side. I don't think you could ask for better."

"Good news."

Gunt nodded. "Shall we begin, Commissioner, to look for more?"

Gordon nodded back. "We may ask questions during the procedure."

"That's fine," Gunt said. "I can edit the transcript." He nodded to his younger assistant, who activated the tape recorder. Gunt then checked the wall clock, cleared his throat, and began speaking for the record. "Ninth of November, seven-thirty-three PM. Necropsy conducted by Chief Medical Examiner Mortimer Gunt on subject Victoria Newsome, age twenty-one, female Caucasian, light brown hair, brown eyes, five-five in height, approximately one-hundred-thirty pounds. Apparently in normal health at time of death, subject is severely mutilated by sharp instrument, including the severing of major arteries. At this stage, evident cause of death is heart stoppage induced by rapid exsanguination."

In other words, the victim had bled to death.

"Commencing gross external examination of anterior surfaces." Moving to the bottom of the table, Gunt extended his hand to accept the magnifying lens from his assistant. The coroner then bent over his subject's left foot and used the lens to carefully inspect every bit of skin from toes to groin. "Slight bruising of the left thigh some six inches above the knee, already faded and likely sustained several days prior to death."

Gordon and I stepped back as Gunt came around the table to inspect the right foot and leg. He then shifted to the young woman's right hand. "Fingernails intact, scrapings already taken, but no indications of defensive struggle."

She had been cowed, no doubt terrified. Either that, or taken by complete surprise.

"Bruising of the right wrist, consistent with tape used to bind the subject and left on the body."

Moving back around the table, Gunt similarly inspected the left hand and arm, noting only the same wrist bruising. Then he returned to the groin.

"Vaginal bruising, consistent with antemortem sexual assault."

Victoria Newsome, then, was still alive when she was raped by her eventual murderer. I saw red and fought for control.

"Absence of semen suggests an incomplete act or the use of a condom."

"Which was not," Gordon said, "recovered from the scene."

Gunt merely shrugged and returned to his inspection, as if it were his duty to note the facts at hand, not correlate them with others. I decided Gordon's assessment was accurate. Good pathologist, but not much as a detective, at least not beyond his own medical findings.

Gunt slowly moved his magnifying lens up the torso, pausing here and there to stoop and peer more closely, carefully exploring every inch of the dead woman's skin around and up to the edges of her many wounds, but for now ignoring the wounds themselves. It took him more than five minutes to reach the throat.

"Bruising to the neck, with multiple finger impressions on the right side, single thumb mark on the left, consistent with forcible restraint rather than strangulation."

Gordon spoke. "The bruises were made by a left hand?"

"Yes," Gunt said, "likely while the right hand wielded the knife."

He continued up the face. "Absence of petechiae makes strangulation further unlikely."

Gunt set his lens back on the tray while his assistant lifted the body by both shoulders until its head hung freely above the table. The neck gash gaped and Gordon turned away. Gunt then reached into the dead woman's hair, his fingertips gently probing the top and back of her head. "Scalp intact and seemingly normal." He looked up at Gordon's back. "Shave the hair?"

"Your call," Gordon said.

Gunt continued his probing, then said, "I think not. Bumps and fractures would be obvious, and I would feel any significant bruising as well. This was all sharp instrument confined to the lower regions, no blunt trauma to the head."

Gunt and his assistant lowered the woman's head and shoulders and then rolled her entire body facedown on the table. Again taking up his lens, Gunt conducted a posterior inspection in the same manner, from toes to nape of the neck, even peering into each ear.

Finally finished, they turned the body over again. Gunt straightened and arched his back, rolling his head until his neck audibly cricked. "No needle marks," he announced, "consistent with the negative results of blood tests already conducted. Bringing us to an examination of the wounds." He looked to his assistant. "A total of thirty . . . ?"

"Thirty-seven," the assistant said.

"Thirty-seven wounds, confined to the torso with the single exception of a gash to the right neck, severing the carotid. Nothing inflicted to limbs, extremities, or face." He drew a deep breath.

And then, proceeding from lowest to uppermost, Gunt carefully examined, probed, and described each and every wound in detail, noting precise anatomical location, width, depth, and surrounding characteristics or lack of same.

Only when he was done did I finally speak. "Murder weapon?"

Apparently startled by my voice, Gunt fixed on my eyes above the surgical mask. "As you heard, maximum penetration was some five inches with a number of the wounds reaching that depth and several of those accompanied by collar bruises and abrasions made by the weapon's grip guard. The blade had a single sharp edge, not serrated, bluntly squared along its other edge. In my opinion, whatever their width or depth, all wounds were inflicted by the same sharp instrument, apparently a five-inch buck knife or its equivalent."

"And what do the angles tell you?"

Gunt looked back at the body on the table. "Excluding the relatively shallow carvings and etchings, a majority of the remaining and more forceful wounds resulted from overhand stabs, with a lesser number inflicted by underhand thrusts. In all those cases, they were dealt by someone of considerable strength more or less straddling the subject's thighs, likely an adult male and definitely right-handed, as surmised earlier."

I looked at Gordon. "Does that exclude any of the suspects?"

He shook his head. "No lefties among the three."

I turned back to Gunt. "What else can you determine from the wounds?"

He pointed to a single wound between the third and fourth ribs on the body's left side, one of maximum penetration surrounded by deep bruising. "This," he said, "was the first blow struck."

"How do you know?"

He swept his hand over the torso. "First of all, more than three-quarters of these wounds are *a priori* excluded."

I nodded. "Due to lack of ecchymosis."

Ecchymosis describes skin and flesh discoloration caused by extravasation—blood forced from its disrupted vessels into the surrounding tissue. If ecchymosis discoloring or bruising is present along a cut, or around a stab, it proves the wound was antemortem, sustained before death while the heart still pumped blood through the vessels. Cutting a corpse produces no ecchymosis. And much of this body's mutilation, lacking bruises, had therefore occurred after death.

"Right," Gunt said. "None of the postmortem wounds could be the first, eliminating more than three-quarters of what we see here. Of the remaining nine antemortem wounds, those edged with ecchymosis, this one to the left ribs was sufficient to cause death on its own, as was the slash-cut or slice to the neck, along with three of the other torso stabs. In other words, any one of these five wounds, given time, would have proven fatal. And not much time was required. After the first, only eight subsequent blows were struck while the subject was dying but not yet dead. That, however, is neither here nor there. The point is, this wound was first by virtue of hosting the greatest concentration of grime."

"Grime."

He nodded. "Not dirt, as in soil, but some other contaminant. My guess is some sort of carbon soot, but that's just through the magnifying lens. We'll need to swab a sample for analysis."

"Two samples."

Gunt stared at me, then at Gordon, who nodded. Gunt shrugged. "More than enough, I suppose."

"So you're saying the knife was dirty."

"I don't see any other way such foreign matter could have been forced into the wound."

"The blade was coated with grime or soot, driven into the body."

"Exactly, and progressively removed from the blade with each plunge into moist flesh." He paused. "There are traces of the same substance in five different wounds, all five with ecchymosis, all five antemortem. Furthermore, the traces decrease as the blade was gradually cleaned by the subject's repeatedly penetrated flesh. So we can establish the actual order of the first five blows, at least with reasonable certainty, starting with the wound containing the greatest amount of grime and ending with the one containing the least. This wound between these ribs contains the most grime by far. Ergo, it was the first blow struck, inflicted when the blade was most contaminated."

"It works." Again, the coroner was a much better detective when the clues derived from his area of expertise.

He turned to his assistant and indicated the five appropriate wounds. "Get as much of it as possible."

Using five separate swab kits, the deputy pathologist harvested the trace evidence, labeling four of the sealed containers and handing the fifth to Gordon.

"Now," Gunt said, "we'll commence the internal examination." He reached for the largest scalpel on his tray.

I braced myself, committed to observing every detail of what would follow.

Although I knew from study what to expect, much of the reality was difficult to endure. I was not looking at mere photographs in that morgue. This was an actual body, once a real person, dissected before my eyes. I heard the sounds of its tearing, smelled its released odors, even felt its moistness on my brow. It was terrible and profound, all the miracles and mechanics of life exposed through a raw exploration of death. While I could not control my mounting anger, nor dispel an inner outrage at seeing what a murderer had done to his innocent victim, I did manage to suppress its physical expression.

Standing next to me, Gordon flinched several times and even turned away at one point. It was hardly his first autopsy, but he was still not inured to its clinically grisly effect. I suspect he never will be.

None of it seemed to affect the coroner or his deputy in any way, both of them calmly methodical and emotionally detached. They had already done this many dozens of times, Gunt himself probably hundreds of times, perhaps thousands. It was their job, and this was the only way to do it. Clearly, I must become more like them, although never at the cost of losing anger or outrage.

Gunt dictated in his flat monotone as he went along, announcing each step of the procedure and the findings thereof, the voice-activated recorder omitting gaps of silence for smoother transcription. I detected no significant deviations from standard protocol. The autopsy was, in every respect, a textbook performance.

It began with the classic Y-shaped incision extending from both shoulders under the breasts to the bottom of the sternum in the midline, then straight down to the lower abdomen's juncture of both groins. After a short horizontal incision across the solar plexus and some additional undermining cuts, Gunt was ready to lay the body open. Standing at the head and firmly grasping the top flap of skin scored by the upper parts of the "Y," he peeled it up and over the shoulders, leaving it bunched like a scarf around the neck. Then, reaching into the seam of the lower vertical incision, he spread the other two flaps, peeling one to each side.

With the garden shears, he separated the chest plate, snipping through one rib after another all the way around the sternum. Then, gently digging his fingertips under the freed chest plate, he pried it out of the body with a soft suction sound.

The entire torso, chest cavity and abdominal cavity alike, was engorged with free-floating bloody fluids. As much as had been left in the bedroom, even more remained in the body. Both standing on the same side of the autopsy table, Gunt and his assistant tipped the subject until her fluids spilled out and drained down the troughs.

The body's interior was now revealed. Virtually every visible organ had sustained deeply traumatic punctures and/or lacerations.

Taking up a different scalpel, Gunt next removed the overlying intestinal tract by stripping the bowel from its attachments. The intestines had been fully severed at three different points, partially severed at seven more.

There were now two accepted ways to proceed. The Rokitansky method removed each organ one at a time for separate study, whherreas the *en masse* method removed groupings of

multiple organs, those of the chest in one group and the abdominal organs in another. Gunt preferred the second course,
explaining that it enabled a better examination of the function-
al relationships between organs, as well as a clearer determination of the disturbances to same.

First, he severed and ligated—tied off—all the great vessels
to neck, head, and arms. This permitted removal of the chest
organs as a unit. Transferred to a separate stainless steel dissection table, the grouping was first examined *in toto* and then separated into its constituent organs. During further individual
dissection and examination, Gunt dictated details pertaining to
the external and cut surfaces of each organ in turn, describing
its vascular structures, including arteries, lymphatics, fascial or
fibrous tissue, and nerves. After finishing with each organ, he
placed it on a scale to note its precise weight for the record.

His assistant then took each organ in turn to a large
microtome, slicing off and preserving thin sections for later
chemical stain and microscope analyses. Gunt indicated that
these tests would be *pro forma* and unlikely to reveal anything of
significance. Unstated was the fact that cause of death was
already obvious and could hardly be more so.

The neck organs were then examined *in situ*, with Gunt
detecting no abnormalities or any other contraindications dic-
tating their removal. The right carotid artery had been fully severed, he noted, repeating that this was sufficient to cause death
in and of itself.

Next, Gunt removed the contiguous grouping of abdominal organs and more or less duplicated what had already been
done with the chest organs. Based on the estimated median time
of death weighed against the contents of, and their progress
through, the subject's digestive tract, Victoria Newsome had
last eaten circa ten P.M., at or near the end of her restaurant
shift. The meal had consisted of a bread roll with barley soup
and coffee. For some reason, Gunt's flat announcement of this

mundane but humanizing fact hurt like a kick in the gut. But I suppressed my emotions; the necropsy was not over.

While further lab tests were still required, Gunt's gross examination of the abdominal organs, as with those of the chest, revealed no surprises.

Returning to the body, Gunt ignored its emptied torso to stand at the crown of its head. With yet another scalpel, he made an incision across the vertex of the scalp from left ear to right, sparing as much of the hair as possible for funeral purposes but unavoidably letting some fall. He then reflected both flaps of the split scalp, peeling them inside out front and back. With the subject's face now covered and her cranium exposed, Gunt accepted the circular bonesaw from his assistant. Its sound was harsh and too loud, amplified by all the hard surfaces of the morgue, and the whine turned worse when the saw bit into bone. Starting at what had just been the forehead hairline, Gunt cut all the way around the skull. Then, in silence, he removed its top.

After studying the exposed brain in position, Gunt freed all its attachments to carefully extract it for weighing and further examination. He found nothing remarkable.

At this point in some autopsies, the spinal cord may be removed, either from the front by sawing through the vertebrae or by making an incision in the back through which the vertebral arches can be removed. After inspecting the vertebrae *in situ*, and noting only several surface nicks incurred by thrusting blade, Gunt elected to do neither.

The procedure, then, was essentially complete. After the organs and skullcap were restored to the body and all incisions were sutured, the body would be released for its funeral with no visible evidence of the autopsy having occurred. Chemical, toxicological, and other analyses would then be performed on organ contents and sections. Pending the results of these tests, Gunt would incorporate his detailed findings with the overall

clinical picture to create a "pathological correlation," concluding the medicolegal record. Until then, we were left with a summary of his "provisional anatomical diagnoses."

No one expected any real discrepancies between the two.
Bluntly stated, the subject had been stabbed to death. More
tellingly, Victoria Newsome's life had been cut short by relent-
less violence inflicted with merciless cruelty.

In that sense, the internal dissection and examination
had proven almost unnecessary, conducted to exclude unexpected possibilities rather than in the expectation of finding
something new. No hidden trauma had been exposed, no internal disease, no indication of poisoning. Death had been caused
by the savage intrusion of a knife and that knife's intrusion
only. Gunt's gross external examination, including the probing
of obvious wounds, had already told me all I truly needed to
know.

But as disturbing as it was, the full autopsy was required
by law, and there was value in witnessing its every detail. Seeing
the murder's surface evidence, the knife's thirty-seven separate
entrances, was somehow not enough. I needed to comprehend
the full extent of each and every wound, what the knife had
done to the *inside* of this dead woman's body, the damage deeply
inflicted to the very core of her being.

There was further value, too, in watching the entire autopsy. I learned far more from this one actual procedure than a
whole raft of books could ever teach. Future murders will not be
so self-evident, and I feel prepared now for what future autopsies can and no doubt will reveal.

In the gloom of the morgue's rear parking area, again cloaked as
the Batman and with my own car hidden not far away, I needed
one final answer before leaving Gordon.

"Did Detectives Bullock and Montoya question the suspects about the front door?"

Gordon nodded. "All three claimed the woman would never leave it unlocked. One said she was 'paranoid' about living in the city."

"Did they have keys?"

"They denied it, but there's no real way to know. Besides, she knew all three and would have opened the door to any one of them."

"But then, presumably, she would have locked it immediately after entry."

As he does whenever given pause, Gordon pressed up on the bridge of his eyeglasses. "You're right. Suggesting the assault would have begun right then and there, before she could turn the lock."

"And yet there's no forensic evidence of any violence at or near the front door."

"No." He frowned. "Everything's in the bedroom. No blood or any other sign of a struggle elsewhere. The entire murder occurred in that one room. Maybe the knife was shown just inside the door, its threat enough to force her into the bedroom."

"Maybe."

"If it felt right, which it doesn't." He looked at me. "You're onto something?"

"Nothing definite, not yet. Just questions, things to check. Starting with the coroner's sample of grime."

Gordon reached under his trench coat into his trousers pocket. "Thirty-seven wounds," he said, extending the sealed swab-kit. "That's one hell of a taste to acquire, and if he gets hungry for more . . . "

"He won't, Commissioner. We won't give him the time." I took the swab kit and moved into cold shadows as Gordon trudged for his car.

Gunt's guess was correct. Analysis proved the swab sample was carbon in the form of soot. The dust of unburned coal.

I left the cave to visit the crime scene.

The rear door sprung easily and almost without sound. I slipped inside and used my light to find the stairs to the basement.

The roaring furnace was old, with a broad shovel propped against the wall to its left and a dark recessed area just beyond. Flicking my light into the darkness, I found a chute angled down from a ground-level window at the building's side gangway. Under the chute, fist-sized chunks of black filled the entire small room, knee-deep and slightly higher. The small recess was a coal bin.

Crouching at the furnace, I opened its bottom grate to fish out fallen ashes and still-glowing embers. Amidst this, along with small bits of charred coal, were other things not fully burned. I bagged several samples of the grate's contents, including ashes but avoiding embers.

Deeper in the basement, heaped atop a broad bench, was a haphazard collection of tools and various maintenance supplies. I leaned closer, holding my light at a sharp angle above the clutter. A fine layer of black soot covered everything.

I left the basement and crept up the back stairs to the second floor apartment, occupied until this morning by Victoria Newsome.

Already picked clean by Gordon's forensics team, the apartment would hold little or nothing to harvest. Nor did I even try, moving through the rooms simply to get a feel of the overall layout and to confirm what Gordon had told me. Everything was as he'd said.

I looked into the bedroom, appalled by the amount of blood, but did not enter, moving instead to the bathroom's hall door. Both towel racks, large and small, were bare. I left the apartment and the building as I'd entered, out the back doors.

Back in the cave, I quickly went through Gordon's casefile and then turned to the bagged evidence from the furnace. First, sifting through the ashes with a magnifying lens, and then using the optical microscope for closer inspection, I finished with complete spectroscopic and chromatography analyses, along with two separate Kastle-Meyer tests. By the end, I had nearly everything I needed and more than probable cause.

Among the furnace ash were small gobs of tarlike residue. Comparison testing would be required for certainty, but the substance was consistent with melted electrical tape.

Also in the ash were charred scraps of several different materials. One scrap was from a plaid workshirt, and one of the K-M tests revealed the presence of blood soaked into the material. Type AB, the same as Victoria Newsome's.

Another scrap was terrycloth, also soaked with blood, also AB. Both of the bathroom towel racks had been bare. The casefile's itemized evidence list included a hand towel but not a bath towel, indicating the latter had not been removed from the scene by the police. Instead, it had been taken to the basement by the killer, to be burned in the furnace.

Gordon was still in his office. I left the cave to meet him on the roof.

"We were wrong, Commissioner. The boyfriends are clear, all three of them."

"How do you know?"

"Because the true killer told the truth about his wife being a heavy sleeper."

Gordon cocked his head, as if in challenge or disbelief. "The landlord?"

"It's his duty to keep the furnace filled with coal. In case of emergency, he needs a master key for the upstairs apartment."

"But we ran a check on him. Nothing but some trouble as a juvenile. No real record."

"Even a killer like this has to start somewhere. He's still young, isn't he?"

Gordon nodded. "Late twenties. How did you know?"

"Because killers like this always start young. How did he come to own the property?"

"Inheritance. He went through a number of foster homes before he was finally adopted by an older couple. They both died within the same year, three or four years ago. No other kids, just their one adopted son."

"With a troubled past. This may have been his first time, Commissioner, but the murder was his. And by the way, he was at least partially clothed during it."

"Back up," Gordon said, "all the way to the beginning."

I told him about the evidence and used it to reconstruct the crime.

The landlord had probably told the truth about seeing and perhaps speaking to Victoria Newsome at ten-thirty, while he was taking out the trash and she was returning home from her waitress job. Whatever was said may have served as a trigger.

Then, after his wife had gone to bed, the landlord had stayed up thinking about the girl upstairs, perhaps brooding over the three different boyfriends he had noticed coming and going, perhaps resenting them.

At some time near or after midnight, the landlord had gone down to the basement, where he perhaps fed the furnace for the night, and then obtained a roll of electrical tape and a knife from his soot-covered workbench. At this point, if not earlier, his crime was premeditated.

He then went upstairs and used the master key to quietly enter his tenant's second floor apartment. Victoria Newsome was not merely dressed for bed when her killer arrived. She was already *in* bed, and probably sound asleep, when the landlord snuck into her bedroom.

Not yet undressed, still wearing a plaid workshirt and slacks, he took his victim by surprise, taping her mouth and holding her down before she could put up a fight, while she was still half-asleep and utterly confused. At this point, he probably turned on the bedside lamp to show his knife, forcing the helpless woman to remove her T-shirt and underwear, after which he taped her wrists.

The assault then occurred with the landlord still partially clothed and either using a condom (perhaps further indication of premeditation) or failing to complete the act. Then, whether he had planned to do so from the start or became enraged for some reason, he committed the murder in a frenzy, splashing himself and his clothing in the victim's blood.

Much of the damage, and the horror, occurred after Victoria Newsome's death. There is no way to know precisely how long it took. When he was done, the killer wiped the lamp switch, either with an unstained portion of sheet or his own clothing. Then, knowing he had touched nothing else other than weapon, skin, and bedding, he assumed the room was clean, overlooking the tape applied to his victim.

He then entered the bathroom, where he rinsed out his bloodstained clothing, showered, and used the bath towel to wipe down the tiles, thereby rubbing traces of blood into the grout. Rinsing the towel, he bundled it around his wet clothes, murder weapon, and roll of electrical tape. Handling the door-knobs with a flap of the towel bundle, he exited the bathroom by way of the hall.

In his underwear at most, he left the apartment through its front door, again using the towel to wipe both knobs. Although it was dark, there was still *some* chance of being seen. That he left the door unlocked may be an indication of panic. Or it may have been part of some hastily formed calculation to cast suspicion onto one of the victim's three suitors. The unlocked door, of course, ultimately proved irrelevant. Whether using a key or gaining admittance from the victim, any one of her boyfriends could have committed the murder, making all three likely suspects.

In any case, the real killer quickly returned to the base-ment furnace, where he burned his bundle of incriminating evidence. The roll of electrical tape melted into gobs of residue small enough to pass through the ash grate. Unburned scraps of towel and clothing also fell through, rinsed but not entirely blood-free.

The deed was now done and presumably—but sloppily—covered up. Returning to his own first-floor apartment, the killer slipped into bed with his heavily sleeping wife none the wiser.

Finally, I told Gordon, the unrecovered murder weapon had probably been hidden in the basement for later disposal off-premises. Perhaps first thing in the morning or perhaps not yet.

"And what," Gordon asked, "was his motive?"

"Unknown in its particulars but essentially the same as all sex killers. Repressed sociopathic tendencies. Simultaneous attraction and hatred toward his victim. A need to 'own' what he couldn't have. Narcissism and compulsion. A dead or undeveloped conscience, inability to empathize. All the usual traits, in general. As for the details, we don't know the full nature or extent of his relationship with the victim. It may have gone beyond landlord and tenant."

Gordon thought it over. "Give me time and I might find holes in what you've pieced together," he said, "but only small ones and right now it holds up, at least as probable cause for a warrant." He angled straight for the stairwell kiosk. "Which I'll shake out of the night judge now."

Homicide Detective Harvey Bullock approached the building with two uniformed officers and a battering ram in tow. They waited at the front steps while Detective René Montoya and two more uniforms went down the side gangway to the back door.

As promised, Gordon had rushed the warrant. It was just before dawn and still dark. I watched from the roof of the south adjacent building, also a two-flat, crouched behind the chimney of another coal-burning furnace.

When Bullock started up the front steps, I moved from the chimney to the roof's front edge. Leaning over, I watched Bullock stab the landlord's first-floor bell and immediately pound the door.

"Police! Open up!"

Waiting no more than a count of ten, Bullock stepped aside with a nod to the two uniforms. Hoisting their ram between them, they rushed forward and breached the door with their third smash. They dropped the ram and Bullock led the way as all three cops entered fast with weapons drawn.

Similar sounds then issued from the rear as Montoya's team bashed the back door and also entered.

Now coming from inside the apartment, the sounds were muffled and muted. A woman's voice yelped in shock and then confusion. Kicked doors banged and splintered. Cops barked and shouted, moving heavily, fast. The woman's voice turned shrill and angry. Cop voices fell to gruff rumbles. The sounds persisted too long, and no one emerged from the apartment. Even with front and rear both covered, something had gone wrong.

I moved along the roof for better vantage over the first-floor side windows but halted as I glimpsed movement on the opposite roof. It was the trapdoor access, starting to lever upward. Montoya's team had taken too long at the rear, giving the landlord time to reach the back stairs.

Returning to the chimney, I watched a beefy figure in white underwear squirm through the trapdoor into predawn gloom. He looked first north, then south, judging the best direction for flight. Then, with a running start across the roof, he bounded onto the low parapet and leaped across the gangway onto the next building. Choosing south and choosing wrong.

He landed hard and sprawled across the tar, then pushed himself up into a limping trot, heading either for the new roof's trapdoor or another leap onto a third roof. I surged up from behind the chimney, blocking both options, rising to my full height above the cause for my first autopsy. He stumbled to a frozen halt right before me.

"Who–?!"

I lowered my voice to its deepest and most menacing register. "Someone who's seen what you've done and seen it in infinite detail."

"I . . . I don't know what you're talking about." His own voice quavered higher. "Who are you? How did you get on this roof? What are you—"

"I'm here to see that you never do it again."

Even as he cringed away, I knew Victoria Newsome's terror had been far greater and it was impossible to hold back. I hit him. Just once, but hard.

The landlord fell again. This time, he did not get up.

I called down to Bullock and Montoya.

It is now three days later. The landlord has been arraigned and awaits trial without bail. His neighbors were all shocked. He always seemed like such a nice young man, they agreed. Quiet, maybe, but extremely personable and even charming. Such a nice smile, and always willing to help out. No one dreamed he could or would be capable of doing such a terrible thing. Not even his own wife, or so she said in the first interviews.

This is not uncommon with sexual predators, particularly those who become serial killers. They are able to repeat their crimes, to kill time and again, precisely because they are neither suspicious nor suspected. The most accomplished predators are those who do not seem likely to prey, the ones least obviously on the prowl. They show no sharpened fangs, nor do they foam at the mouth. Instead, they operate freely by appearing ordinary and seeming normal. If not disarming, they are at least anonymous.

At least on the surface. But the tendencies are there, deeply rooted and almost always planted in troubled childhoods. Further digging by Detective Bullock has already turned up the fact that additional juvenile offenses were expunged from the landlord's record. The others—shoplifting, petty theft, cruelty to animals—have become more significant with hindsight. And while the young man seemed to overcome his past, whether through genuine effort or pure cunning, it was merely suppressed and left to simmer.

In a sense, the landlord's wife has now become his second victim. The initial shock after her husband's arrest, it seems, was sheer denial. Just yesterday, she broke down and spoke more freely, saying she "should have known and prevented it," even blaming herself for the murder. Although refusing to discuss them in detail, she says "the signs were all there to see" in the ways her husband treated her, but she "just kept looking away."

There were other signs, too, between her husband and the tenant upstairs. Citing the area's housing shortage, she claims her husband could have "rented to anyone." Instead, when Victoria Newsome wanted but could not afford the upstairs flat, the rent was lowered. When the wife objected, she was told to shut up and mind her own business. A "clean tenant" was worth the loss of income.

The landlord even helped his clean tenant move in. After that, according to his wife, "he was always up there, supposedly fixing things," although she knew better. They fought about it, but "the fights only made him spend more time upstairs."

And then, the wife said, "something happened." Her husband suddenly turned cold toward Victoria Newsome and "started talking her down." Already jealous, the wife suspected a rebuffed advance or something even worse, the end of an actual affair. Whatever happened, the landlord now seemed to hate their upstairs tenant, although "the gleam was still in his eye whenever she came up the street."

After the murder, the wife suspected the worst but did not want to face or believe it. Her marriage, she said, was too sacred and "every marriage demands loyalty." Besides, the Newsome girl "slept around," and any one of her boyfriends could have killed her. The wife had "no proof" of her husband's guilt.

The district attorney does have proof.

Two other rolls of black electrical tape were excavated from the clutter on the landlord's basement workbench. Samples from both were subjected to burn tests. The resulting melted substance was then compared to the tarlike residue retrieved from the furnace ash. A chemically perfect match established all three rolls as products of the same manufacturer, probably from the same production batch, and likely purchased at the same time from the same outlet.

Further blood work established a genetic link between the victim and the bloodstains found on the charred scraps of clothing and terrycloth towel recovered from the furnace grate.

Seven hairs from the bathtub drain and three from the bed, two of the latter soaked with the victim's blood, were matched to the landlord.

Nine separate fingerprints were found on the adhesive sides of the tape removed from Victoria Newsome's mouth and wrists. All nine prints conclusively match the landlord. He and he alone applied the tape to his victim.

Finally, Coroner Gunt proved to be correct about the murder weapon. A five-inch buck knife, washed clean but now coated with an even thicker layer of soot, was recovered from the basement, hidden at the bottom of knee-high coal. Under the soot, and congealed between the knife's blade and guard, were traces of the victim's blood.

Postscript: Two more days have passed and the landlord has begun to talk in what amounts to a conditional confession. While admitting to the deed, he refuses to admit any guilt. Yes, he repeatedly stabbed Victoria Newsome. And yes, she died as a result of those stabbings. But, he insists, it was not his fault. She never should have "teased" him by "accepting his offer to lower the rent."

Besides, he says, he "didn't mean to kill her" and never even intended to stab her. The knife was "just a threat" to make her "deliver what was due." She "led him on," but never "came through." She "owed" him.

Did he put the lights on in the bedroom? Yes. Was his face covered? No, it was "important for her to see who it was." And if he hadn't planned to kill his tenant, how did he think he could get away with assaulting her? He doesn't know, he says; he "wasn't thinking at all." But did he really expect Victoria Newsome to remain silent? Yes, "if she knew what was good for her."

Then what happened to make him change his plans? Why *did* he stab her?

The landlord claims he still doesn't know. Something "came over" him, but it's "all a red haze." After the rape began, he says, it was "suddenly no fun" and he "couldn't finish it." When his victim "kept staring with those big eyes," it made him "mad." There was "just something about her," and he "hated it." Then, he says, "she must have made a wrong move," but he "can't really remember that part."

The next thing he knew, "the knife was in her and it was too late." He "couldn't believe it" and became enraged that she "made him do such a thing." When she began "thrashing and making sounds through the tape," he snapped and "just couldn't stop stabbing more and more." But it wasn't his fault. There was nothing else he could do, "no way to stop it," not after Victoria Newsome "made" him start.

Although it is not yet certain (and with further investigation of his past now pending), this was apparently the landlord's first killing. But he does fit the profile of the repeat sexual predator and may even represent a nascent serial killer. His lack of remorse and willingness to blame his victim are particularly disturbing. For such a sociopath, first blood can be instantly addictive. And if the first step is difficult, it charts a path increasingly easy to follow. Had the landlord gotten away with the murder of his tenant, he may well have gone on to kill again.

Now, that will not happen. Case closed.

My Brother
Esau

Excerpt From Bruce Wayne's Diary

AS far as forensic value goes, hairs blow fibers right out of the water. Both can be left at a crime scene (maybe by the criminal himself), but fibers will only tie back to a certain type of material or clothing. At best, by matching the degrees of wear and color fading you can argue that a retrieved fiber "probably" came from one particular shirt, for example, and "likely" no other shirt, not even one from the same manufacturing lot. But a hair had to fall from one person and one person only, and that hair contains its owner's unique DNA and no other DNA on Earth. In that sense, the hair is lot like a drop of blood—but a criminal is far more likely to drop a hair at the scene of his crime than he is to bleed on the spot.

Even if you match crime scene hair to suspect person, the hair doesn't necessarily prove its owner is guilty of the crime, but it does prove the person's presence where the crime was committed. How and when the hair got there—before, during, or after the crime—is always another matter. Like all forensic evidence, then, hair evidence is purely circumstantial. But the best circumstantial evidence can be just as powerful as direct eyewitness testimony, and sometimes even more damning.

If the hair is found not just at the scene of the crime, for example, but clenched in the murder victim's death-gripping hand . . . well, that's a juicy fact for any investigator (or jury) to chew on long and hard. Same thing if the hair is stuck in the victim's blood.

From top to bottom, the six different types of human hair shape up under the microscope like so:

Head hair: Generally circular in cross-section, often with split ends. Unless it exceeds the limits of other types, the hair's length means nothing.

Eyebrow and eyelash hair: Circular in cross-section but finer and smoother than head hair, with tapered ends. Here, length has obvious limits.

Beard and mustache hair: Stiffer and generally curlier (but not always), often triangular in cross-section. Length has little meaning.

Body hair: Oval or triangular in cross-section, generally curly. Length varies only slightly within upper limit.

Axillary or underarm hair: Oval in cross-section. Length varies within upper limit, which generally exceeds the limit for body hair.

Pubic hair: Usually springy, oval or triangular in cross-section, with female pubic hair generally shorter and coarser than male. Slight variation within maximum length.

Any one (or more) of these six types of hair can be deposited and later retrieved at a crime scene, although head or scalp hair is the type most commonly lost and found. This is because the average person sheds six head hairs per hour (even more for top-thinning types like Alfie), so even a crime scene abandoned in ten minutes will probably yield at least one hair dropped by the criminal.

Pubic hairs are most commonly harvested, obviously, as evidence in sex crimes. And because the absence of semen in sex crimes is more common than you'd think, for whatever reasons, the presence of pubic hairs becomes all the more important.

For outdoor crime scenes as well as indoor scenes where pets may have been kept, it's smart to weed out animal hairs from human ones before wasting a lot of time, effort, and money on DNA and other analysis. This is surprisingly easy to do, with no tests and nothing fancy or complicated required. All you need is the "Speeding Bullet" of direct microscope comparison, and the trained eye doesn't even need to compare. Simple examination of the suspect hair alone will do. That's because you can clearly see, at least under magnification, differences in the structure of animal hair, especially in its patterns of overlapping scales.

When the hair is definitely human, it can be used to determine its owner's racial type. African hair is generally curliest, whereas the hair of Asians is generally straightest. Barring the gray of age, Asian and African hair both tend to be black. European hair falls in the middle, ranging from straight to curly but usually somewhat wavy, and spanning the color spectrum from near-white blond to jet black but most often some shade of brown.

In addition to DNA, hair can contain other valuable evidence—especially if it's the hair of a completely decomposed victim. The stomach, intestines, liver, and other organs are normally the first places to look for evidence of poisoning. But even when a body's flesh and blood is long gone, its bones and hair remain available for testing. In the case of poisoning, the bones probably won't help, but the hair's keratin can retain traces of just about any poison almost forever.

This evidence, in fact, was used 140 years after the fact to solve the mystery of Napoleon Bonaparte's death. The presence of arsenic in his corpse's hair proved his death was probably murder—unless Napoleon somehow had the arsenic smuggled into his cell so he could poison himself. But this seems unlikely since the keratin arsenic distribution along the length of the hair shafts indicated the poison was "periodically administered"—probably laced in food—during Napoleon's imprisoned exile on the island of St. Helena. In other words, he ingested regular doses of arsenic through the four months of hair growth ending with his death. The former emperor himself said it loud and clear. "I am dying before my time, murdered by the English oligarchy and its hired assassins." Meaning his jailers—and so it would seem, according to the evidence found in his hair 140 years after he died. It doesn't take a Sherlock to figure it out. If you wanted to commit suicide by poisoning, would you really drag it out to four months of long, slow, painful death?

The only other possibility (beyond murder) is accidental poisoning, and this would demand the same accident happening every day for some 120 days in a row. That's a lot of arsenic—and even more coincidence—to swallow.

I say what the forensics investigators and most historians say: the hair itself says murder.

On the other hand, after another team of investigators exhumed the skeletonized remains of U.S. President Zachary Taylor—whose mysterious death was also a suspected case of poisoning—no proof or evidence was found. Similar analysis of Taylor's hair and fingernail keratin produced negative results, no poison detected, and his death remains a mystery. At least for now, but who knows what kinds of advances in forensics technology the future may bring.

The Bible says something like: "My brother Esau was a hairy man; I am a smooth man." But other than those afflicted with a rare condition called *alopecia* (complete absence of all six types of hair), no criminal is smooth enough to escape all the detection methods of hair analysis.

Let's hope, and let's make it even more hairy for them.

Cat Marks

Casefile #0116
Year One, Month Twelve, Day Sixteen

From the Journal of Alfred Pennyworth

THE master is reluctant to compose this account for reasons he denies but which I find rather transparent, if not amusing. Were the woman involved not a fugitive felon, the reasons might even be titillating.

She has come to be known as the Catwoman, apt enough for a female cat burglar conducting her activities in the guise of an anthropomorphic feline. This, of course, makes her something of a counterpart to Gotham's equally mysterious "Bat-man." Indeed, her bizarre costume may well have been inspired by the master's own, or at least rumors pertaining to same. It certainly shares dark similarities, although the differences are apparently pronounced and telling. And it is, I gather, actually tighter.

In any case, it strikes me that bat and cat similarly rule the night as nocturnal predators of extraordinary prowess. They also share its moonlit mystery and romance, whether they acknowledge the fact or not. In this case, one seems to playfully exult in it while the other merely scowls.

Or, as the master has said: "I'm a crime fighter, Alfred, and she's a criminal."

Indeed, but a most fascinating and alluring criminal. If not quite irresistible.

It can be said that the case at hand, just completed, began with two triggering incidents rather than one. The first incident was also the master's first encounter with the Catwoman, the first clash between two unlikely creatures of the night. The second incident, months later, was a particularly vicious murder committed during the course of a cat burglary.

Although the master is primarily determined to prevent murder whenever he can, and to bring murderers to heel whenever he cannot, this hardly prevents him from pursuing crimes of all types, even those falling fortunately short of life and death. It was only a matter of time, therefore, before an ongoing series of unsolved cat burglaries—seven of them at that point—attracted his notice.

From their common *modus operandi* alone, he was convinced that all seven burglaries represented the work of a single thief. All were post-midnight stealth penetrations of carefully selected and similar targets, penthouses, brownstones, and hotel suites occupied by women of known wealth. In every case, other items of obvious worth were ignored as the thief focused solely on jewelry—bracelets, necklaces, rings, and brooches of diamond and gold, sapphire and emerald, adornments sharing the complementary traits of beauty and value. And in every case, entry and escape were always clean, the losses unnoticed until morning. Alarms were defeated or circumvented. Windows or doors were quietly and efficiently breached. In some cases, safes and strongboxes were expertly cracked. And whether their owners were out for the night or blissfully asleep mere feet away, jewel collections were plucked of their prize contents as if by a ghost. It was highly unlikely, then, that two or more thieves of such specialized skill and impeccable taste would be active in the same place at the same time.

To make certain, however, the master requested my assistance in the cavern crime lab during his inspection of the evi-

dence documentation assembled by the police department's
chief forensic investigator Jordan Rankin. It did not take long
to discern irrefutable links between the seven crime scenes, as
Rankin himself had already done.

"The doorjamb and window casement gouge marks match,
sir. Same width and showing the same tiny flaw in the jimmy's
edge. Made by the same tool."

The master looked up from a number of microphotographs
arrayed side by side. "And the same scratches in the metal of
three different locks, including minute irregularities. All were
sprung by the same lockpick."

"We also have the same type of alligator clips used to
bridge wires in four different alarm systems."

The master nodded. "And snip marks made by the same
cutters."

"All adding up," I concluded, "to the same burglar. But no
fingerprints or hairs left at any of the scenes."

He shrugged. "Given the other evidence, all indicating a
high degree of skill and caution, I'd be surprised had the thief
not worn gloves."

"And a ski mask, perhaps?"

"Or a stocking pulled over his head, some type of hair covering." He leaned back, indicating the casefiles spread across the
workstation. "Rankin did a decent job with all seven scenes."

"As did the thief, sir, leaving traces which link each scene
to the others, but hardly to himself."

"Until we compare his tools once he's been caught."

"In these cases, sir, perhaps easier said than done."

"We'll see." Rising from the workstation, he strode
toward the rock stairs leading to the manor above. "Starting
tonight."

And so, whenever time permitted, the ensuing nights included a
round of likely targets not yet hit—homes containing jewel collections of value. Six of the seven known victims had been fea-

tured in the society pages, including photographs of their attendance at various galas and functions, temptingly adrip in glittering necklaces and the like. The master therefore focused on the residences of women similarly featured.

It was not until the fifth night, however, that his intermittent patrols paid a dividend. Seen from the distance of an opposite rooftop and therefore little more than a living shadow slipping across the terrace of an uptown penthouse, the furtive figure was nevertheless clearly and startlingly feminine.

I shall never forget the master's expression when he later commented, "Cat burglar indeed, Alfred, she was dressed literally like a cat." The skintight costume included gloves and a cat-eared head-cowl, he said, leaving little more than the woman's eyes and mouth exposed. Even now, I envision her sleek feline form limned against the moon, but then perhaps I have always been an incurable romantic. In this case, of course, the romance is decidedly second-hand and vicariously experienced. Nor, in truth, would I wish it otherwise. All thrills aside, rooftop acrobatics are hardly my cup of tea.

In any case, as is the master's usual daredevil wont, he deployed one of his lines to gain the purchase of a railing on the opposite building's fire escape. Then swinging across to a lower landing, he mounted the fire escape swiftly and silently, reaching the roof from below just before the woman reached the fire escape from above. Now they stood mask to mask at the edge of the rooftop terrace, both no doubt intrigued.

She wore a small kit bag slung over one shoulder with some five or six freshly stolen necklaces looped around her neck. Coiled around her other shoulder was something the master took to be a length of rope or line. It was not.

After a silent standoff in which each sized up the other, it was the Catwoman who first spoke. The master provided no quotes and very little that was specific, saying only that she invited him to "join her in the night."

This took me aback. "As her accomplice, sir?"

"Something like that." But he would reveal no further detail, merely that the woman continued to "taunt" him in a manner both playful and provocative. This was apparently intended as a form of bait—which, of course, was not taken.

At some point, still smiling and with no warning, the woman proved herself "extremely fast" and "extremely athletic," launching a high sweep-kick. The master rolled into an evasive maneuver designed to take him behind the woman. Even as he surged back to his feet, however, he found the woman spinning around with a dip of her shoulder to loose the kit bag—which she then slung at his face. He batted it harmlessly aside, by which time the woman now held something else at the ready. Taken from her other shoulder, it was not a "rope." It was a weapon, the type of lash called a cat-o-nine-tails.

Then, after whipping the master, she escaped into the night, trailing laughter in her wake.

Sensing that further detail would not be vouchsafed, I did not press for any. But presumably after licking his wounded pride, if not any actual wounds, the master retrieved the fallen kit bag and returned with it to the cave.

The bag was filled with a small assortment of high-quality burglar tools precisely matching the forensic evidence gathered at the seven crime scenes. We now had our cat burglar, as if there had been any doubt. And yet we had nothing at all, not so much as a hair from her head. Just her lasting impression, indelibly reflected in the master's eyes. He seemed simultaneously piqued and impressed. While I cannot say that he admired the woman, there was little doubt that he remained fascinated by their first encounter.

I have long worried about the master, even before he adopted the mantle and mask of the Bat, ever since he was a youth, in fact, all the way back to our terrible night of loss. And despite my growing confidence in his judgment and abilities, a confidence stronger with each passing day and which now verges on the unshakable, my worries are in some ways greater than ever. Nightly focused on his audacious mission, almost single-mindedly driven toward its inevitably unattainable goal, he has left himself no time whatsoever for frivolous pursuits and very little time for any normal social intercourse. But certain urges cannot be perpetually suppressed. By denying himself the healthy companionship of ordinary women, I wonder, might he not run the risk of falling prey to the tempting wiles of a criminal *femme fatale*?

On the one hand, I find that his obvious response to the Catwoman, however much he attempts to conceal it, is strangely reassuring. But on the other hand, it is more than slightly discomfitting.

Over the next several months, four additional burglaries were committed by the same thief—but none, as luck would have it, while the master was watching. Then, five nights past, he was summoned by signal to the roof of police headquarters.

Thanks to his surveillance belt-recorder, the following account of his meeting with Police Commissioner James Gordon is very nearly verbatim. I have done but a minimal amount of editing and have added very few comments of my own.

Commissioner Gordon spoke first. "Another jewel theft, and it finally escalated."

"To what?" The master seemed instantly on the alert, even suspicious.

"Murder. A nasty one, slashing and stabbing. The victim was a high society matron named Letitia Sternwell. Old money, long widowed. A helpless woman past sixty, living alone."

"No servants?"

"Two, but living in separate quarters on the floor below. A female cook and maid, and a male butler and driver. The cook found the body this morning when she went up to prepare breakfast. It's all in here, at least the prelim reports so far."

The master accepted the working casefile. "And you're linking this murder to the previous burglaries?"

"Look, I know you think you learned something on that roof, maybe even saw something in this Catwoman's eyes, but Gunt's rough time of death puts it within the same two-hour window after midnight. That's her favored shift. Rankin established that the same type of tool was used to gain entry. Her favored type of tool. And according to the two servants, nothing but jewelry was removed from the scene." The commissioner pauses. "Her favored swag."

"But you have nothing conclusive?"

"Not until we have the perp to match with the actual evidence, no, but common sense screams connections." Here, Commissioner Gordon's sigh is audible on the recording. "The victim profile is a perfect fit. Stolen goods are the same. Similar break-in evidence. The murder happened during a cat burglary committed in the same time frame as the previous cat burglaries, and we have a known cat burglar actively—"

"It wasn't her." The master's voice was flat, decisive.

"You haven't so much as opened that file yet, and you're already certain we have a second jewel thief in town."

"Was an alarm system defeated?"

"The victim lived in the rooftop penthouse of a tall building with lobby security."

"So all you really have is—"

"Look, no one wants to jump to conclusions here. We've all learned our lessons. But there's no chance of that happening in the first place. We already know the Catwoman is guilty of the prior burglaries. That alone is enough to take her down."

"And we will. Sooner or later she'll make a mistake and I'll be ready."

"Fine. And when it happens, I'm betting we tie her to *this* crime. That's all I'm saying."

"And all I'm saying is your bet runs the risk of overlooking another criminal—the true killer."

At this point there occurs a fairly long interval of what I take to be uncomfortable silence, during which I imagine the police commissioner trying to assess the master's motive for opposing him. Finally, the commissioner speaks. "The true killer. Who so far exists only in your mind. Rankin recovered no foreign prints or hairs, just like all the other scenes, nothing that doesn't match the victim or her two servants."

"Absence of evidence is never proof of guilt, Commissioner, and the Catwoman is not the first or only burglar to wear gloves and a head-mask."

"Don't lecture *me*." Clearly annoyed, the commissioner quickly softens, as if now attempting to reason with the master. "Look, you caught her red-handed yourself, the stolen loot dangling round her neck, even if the rest of her body got away."

"She took me by surprise." Here the master's voice is edged with a quality of defensiveness uncommon for him.

"I'm not blaming you. I'm just—"

"I didn't expect the whip. It came out of nowhere."

"And stung your eyes. You told me. By the time your vision cleared, she'd disappeared into the shadows. Fine, it happens. But the fact that she escaped hardly makes her innocent."

"Not of burglary, no, but it doesn't make her guilty of murder, either." The master has immediately regained control, his disguised voice once again deep and cold, almost grating. "The pattern held. There was no murder at that scene, no violence at all. The victim was not even home."

"And aside from that, the pattern holds here. Same M.O., similar break-in evidence."

"How similar?"

"The gouge marks are different, but don't forget she lost her old tools to you. They're in that kit bag stored in the evidence room right now. So she acquired new tools and she used them. Everything points to her."

"No. Only the evidence of burglary points to her, and only tenuously. The murder itself is this crime's most salient element, and that element does *not* point to the Catwoman. It actually violates the evidence of every previous scene. This was not the work of her hands."

"I don't get it. Why are you so sure?"

"Because she does it for fun, not blood. It's a game to her, a lark, some sort of moonlight fantasy, and violence plays no part in it. She operates strictly by stealth, always avoiding confrontation, avoiding any physical contact with her victim at all."

"She attacked *you*."

"Only when she was cornered, only to escape, and only after she tried to negotiate her way to freedom."

"And when she *couldn't* talk her way out of it, she attacked. You said it yourself—'like a hellcat.' So why are you so—"

"Trust me, Gordon. She didn't do it."

"Why not, dammit? How do you know she wasn't interrupted and cornered by Mrs. Sternwell? What the devil makes you so stubborn?"

There was, the master admits even now, no real answer, just his unswerving conviction. "Because I know, that's all."

By this point, the commissioner sounds thoroughly exasperated, and no one listening to the exchange could truly blame him. "So now you've added ESP to your arsenal of detective tools?"

"You weren't there, Commissioner. You didn't see her."

"Exactly—and by your own account, she's quite a sight. So maybe I'm the one in a position to remain objective, whereas you're not. Maybe you've been blinded by the package to the point where you can't see the bomb ticking inside."

The master loses his own patience, his voice a near growl. "You're wrong, Gordon. I haven't just seen her, I've seen *through* her."

"Maybe so," the commissioner said, "and maybe you're right. Then again, maybe you should look in the mirror."

"Meaning what?"

"To see if this hellcat has gotten her claws into you."

"That's uncalled for."

"So is your advocacy for a criminal."

"I'm not defending her. I'm just telling you she's a thief, not a killer."

"Telling me is not good enough." The commissioner's voice trails off, apparently as he turned away. "You'll have to prove it."

The recording contains nothing further, just the sound of fading footsteps. The meeting had concluded with their first fight. Over a woman.

"The M.O. may seem the same, but the forensic evidence is only superficially similar." We were in the cavern, at the workstation, the master having just finished his first review of the casefile. "Similar gouge marks in the casement, but the thief failed to spring the window. He gave up on his jimmy and resorted to smashing the glass."

"Which may have roused the victim from her sleep, sir, leading to the murder."

"Stick to what the evidence tells us."

"Very well. The entry was inept, unlike prior entries, and therefore uncharacteristic of the Catwoman's demonstrated skills."

"Exactly." He leafed through the file. "Plus we have Gunt's postmortem report describing stab and slash wounds almost certainly inflicted by a left-handed attacker."

"And the Catwoman, I take it, is right-handed?"

"When she cracks her whip, she is."

"I see. Intriguing, sir, but rather slight. Unless there's anything further in the reports?"

"Not much," he said, "other than the crime's probable solution."

This admittedly startled me, as he well knew it would. "Oh?"

"The killer shattered the window of the bedroom, the same room where the jewelry was kept, as well as the room in which the victim was murdered."

"Implying possible foreknowledge. How many windows were available overall?"

"The report doesn't say."

"But surely not so many as to stretch coincidence beyond its snapping point?"

"The point concerns shattering, Alfred, not snapping." He tapped the report before him. "The window shards fell where you'd expect, most of them inward and onto the floor under the broken window, with finer bits of the shattered glass traveling deeper into the room. Jordan Rankin found such particles embedded in the victim's nightgown."

"Glass particles from the window of the room in which she slept."

"Yes, but her bed was on the other side of the room. No particles in the sheets or spread."

"Telling us . . . what?" I pondered it. "She was neither asleep nor even in bed when the window shattered? She was ready for bed but still up and about? Or perhaps roused by something else, something prior to the sound of breaking glass?"

"More than that, Alfred. Her body was found on the floor between window and bed, with the same particles embedded in the carpet around her body—but not, I'm betting, *under* it. The report doesn't say, nor does it mention glass particles stuck in the nightgown's congealed blood as well as in its fibers, but I'm also betting they're there to be found. Which means the shattered glass fell *on her*, rather than the other way around."

"You're saying she was murdered *before* the window was smashed?"

"Exactly, with the break-in staged after the fact. That means actual entry was gained by some other means, of which there is no evidence. So whether the crime was premeditated murder or a burglary gone wrong, it was most likely committed by someone with a key."

"An inside job, therefore pointing to the servants?"

He nodded toward the casefile. "The murder weapon was a carving knife of a type consistent with the one missing from a cutlery set in the victim's kitchen. Making her servants definitely the most likely suspects."

"One of whom may be, dare I say it, a *copycat* burglar."

"So it would seem, Alfred, with the cook-maid representing the least likely of the two. The wound angles and depths suggest the generally greater height and strength of a male. Not to mention the fact that two different female cat burglars *would* stretch coincidence to its snapping point."

"Meaning the butler actually *did* do it?"

He smiled thinly. "It happens."

"Not, sir, in *my* circles."

"Calm down. Since we still lack proof, the honor of your profession remains intact." He lifted the scrambled phone and pressed its speed dial. "For now, although not for long."

When Commissioner Gordon answered at the other end, the master spoke in the lower register of the Batman. "Have Rankin check for glass particles in the nightgown blood. And a reinterview of Letitia Sternwell's male servant is in order—with special attention to whether the butler is left-handed."

I sniffed, too softly to be heard but with indignation nonetheless sincere. Some proof, I told myself.

But as ever, the master was well ahead of me, his sights already aligned on much more.

He returned with it just before the next dawn, which is to say the morning of this writing, even as I waited at the workstation. Fearing the freshly prepared breakfast tray would go cold, I brightened in response to the familiar roar echoing up the tunnel. But when the dark car screeched to a halt and the master disembarked, his purposeful stride told me he was focused on anything but eggs. No doubt I sighed.

"News, Alfred?"

"Much of it, sir, in a message left by the commissioner. It seems that glass particles are indeed stuck to the nightgown blood, proving the victim was struck down before her window was shattered. You were right. Furthermore, the woman's butler, I regret to say, is indeed left-handed."

"I know." Still briskly approaching the workstation, he extracted a glassine bag from a pouch on his belt. "And this should nail it."

"Evidence, sir? You've been to the scene of the crime?"

"Not quite." He swept past me, shedding his long black cloak and cowl—which I barely caught—as he followed a straight line for the optical microscope. "One floor down."

"The servants' quarters." I draped the cloak over its usual chair.

"The butler's bedroom closet, to be precise, in which every article of clothing was either recently cleaned or laundered." Having reached the counter, he tapped the small bag's contents onto a microscope slide. "But it didn't matter." He fixed the slide in place and peered into the eyepiece, carefully adjusting the microscope's focus. "This is just a small sample of what's still embedded in the fibers of one shirt hanging in that closet."

He peered through the microscope for a long moment, then turned to Jordan Rankin's evidence file. Withdrawing a certain photomicrograph, he studied it only briefly before looking up at me.

"Bad news, Alfred."

"The butler did it."

He nodded. "A butler betrayed by fine particles of the same glass Rankin found in the victim's nightgown."

Glass, the master then informed me, is only a "seeming solid." Despite its ubiquitous presence in everyday reality, glass is, in fact, a highly unusual substance—actually a liquid cooled below its (extremely high) point of solidification. Another way of putting it: The seeming solid exists in its "natural state" only when subjected to the heat of a fierce fire.

This makes glass somewhat similar to ice, albeit with a much higher conversion temperature than that of water, and gives the common substance some rather strange properties.

When a pane of glass is shattered inward, for example, only seventy percent of the fragments travel away from the force, with thirty percent traveling backward "the wrong way." This thirty percent includes particles fine enough to pass for "mist." Which, one must admit, conforms to a certain consistency of logic. If glass can be a "solid liquid," why not a "solid fog"?

But the point remains, any intruder breaching a window will always have bits of backward-leaping glass trapped in his or her clothing. Even when all visible fragments have been removed by careful plucking and picking, tiny particles will escape detection. Furthermore, because these tiny pieces of grit are caught in the clothing's weave, where they cling to its fibers, some (but far from all) will be dislodged by washing or dry cleaning. They will, in fact, remain trapped in the clothing indefinitely.

Forensic analysis of retrieved particles can serve to match or exclude them from other such particles, thus establishing a link to the glass of a particular shattered window.

If and when this is done, of course, the owner or wearer of the clothing is in deep trouble. There is only one explanation for the presence of the particles in his or her clothing. Quite simply, he or she stood in front of the window at the precise moment it shattered.

"But how did you know which shirt the butler wore?"

"I didn't." He began his usual habit of slow pacing, always thinking better on the move. "I simply kept the closet dark. Only one shirtfront glittered under the penlight."

"And where, might I ask, was the butler himself during all this?"

"In his bed right outside the closet, where he's probably still sleeping now." His expression darkened. "Far too peacefully for the conscience of a killer."

"Then that, I suppose, is that, and the honor of my venerable profession be damned."

He pointed to the microscope. "Linking these particles from the butler's shirt to identical particles in the victim's nightgown seals a convincing lock."

"And yet, sir, your evidence having been, shall we say, unofficially obtained, is it not impermissible in court?"

"There's a lot more where it came from. The nightgown particles alone—already in custody—prove entry was gained with a key. And that's sufficient cause to obtain a search warrant for the butler's quarters."

"Which in turn will obtain the shirt and the rest of its embedded particles through a normal chain of custody. Congratulations, sir. It seems you have solved the murder as well as one of the burglaries." I paused, wondering if I should bite my tongue. "If not the others."

He stopped in his tracks, turning to gaze off into the cavern depths so that his expression was impossible to read. "She was there too, Alfred."

I actually flinched. "The Catwoman?"

"The cat *burglar*."

"But she was present at the Sternwell murder scene?"

"Looking down on my ledge from a higher roof as I emerged from the butler's window." He seemed to replay it in his mind. "Almost as if she'd been waiting for me."

"And did she say anything?"

"Just four words. 'I didn't do it.'"

"To which you replied?"

"I told her I knew she didn't do it, that I even had proof, but that she was still guilty."

"And then?"

"She laughed—soft, throaty, mocking—and she left."

"Eluding capture once again, sir?"

"This is no common criminal, Alfred. She's extraordinary. Her leap was spectacular, from a high roof all the way across a service courtyard onto a more distant building."

Even now I wonder about what I chose to say next. Was it another example of my usual acerbic teasing (the master himself calls it "arch sarcasm"), or was I seeking justification for a seeming lapse? Offering him an opportunity to explain? In any case, whether blurted or calculated, it was said.

"And this was beyond the reach, sir, of your long arm of the law?"

He gave me a sharp look devoid of amusement. But knowing me all too well, neither was he irritated. His expression was simply flat. "I *could* have pursued her, but too late and only into darkness. She knows the advantage of shadows, Alfred. And I was more concerned with pursuing the killer, establishing *his* guilt."

"Which you've now done."

"Her time will come. Sooner or later, I'll take her down."

"Of that, sir, I have no doubt." Steadfast and resolute, I kept my upper lip stiffly braced against any hint of a smile.

Or, for that matter, a frown.

The remainder of the day has proved remarkably eventful. Some five hours ago, just before the master departed on his nightly rounds and just before I began this account, news from Police

Commissioner Gordon has essentially laid the matter to rest, at least insofar as we are concerned. From the master's tone of voice, little or no hard feelings remain, making the commissioner's news all the better. The gist follows.

An emergency search warrant secured the incriminating shirt, which Jordan Rankin has already used to confirm the Batman's findings. Also confiscated from the butler's quarters was a recently purchased jimmy, quickly matched to the failed gouges in the window casement. A flake of paint on the jimmy's edge furthermore matches the window paint.

This, combined with the previous evidence, justified the butler's immediate arrest. Now in police custody, he awaits arraignment on multiple charges, premeditated murder obviously the most serious.

While the stolen goods have yet to be recovered, a suspicious amount of cash was discovered on the premises. The jewelry (or perhaps just its component gems) was apparently pawned for considerably less than its worth, yet more than a butler typically earns in six months. The money, in any case, may well constitute the lesser of two motives. According to the female cook-cum-maid, her fellow servant had long despised their mutual employer, resenting his "shabby treatment" at Mrs. Sternwell's hands. News accounts of the unsolved and ongoing cat burglaries apparently heated this long simmering hatred beyond its boiling point. Until then, the butler no doubt knew, he would immediately become a prime suspect in any murder of the Sternwell woman. Killing her during a copycat burglary, however, would enable him to avoid suspicion as well as to profit through his "revenge."

Finally, the murder weapon has been retrieved from a Dumpster in the building's rear service area. Well aware that his fingerprints at the scene of the murder would prove nothing (and would, indeed, be expected), the butler did not wear gloves while doing his dark deed. And although he was careful to wipe the carving knife before concealing it in the Dumpster, he missed one partial print—containing enough points of identification to determine that it was impressed by his thumb. Were this the only evidence against him, a competent defense attorney could no doubt argue that the butler had merely carved the previous night's roast. Combined with the wealth of other evidence, however—the jimmy, the glass particles, the cash, the murder weapon's location, the cook-maid's testimony, as well as that from pawnshop clerk or clerks (when located, which is only a matter of canvassing time)—the murder weapon thumbprint will be nigh impossible to explain away.

Once again, then, the master has solved a seemingly insoluble mystery. He has done so this time, however, rather ironically if not disturbingly—apprehending one criminal by exculpating another.

Although the matter may well be rectified in the future, as the master strenuously insists, for now the Catwoman remains at large, slinking her way through Gotham's high shadows and tempting moonlight, apparently begging for dark sport. And even as this case is closed, I can only hope she attracts no one willing to play.

Residue of
Innocence

Casefile #0127
Year Two, Month One, Day Four

From the Private Files of the Batman

ANOTHER mistake has been made, this one caught too late and therefore the worst mistake of all.

If extreme actions are taken on the basis of circum-stantial evidence, actions affecting human life, that evidence must be compelling if not impeccable in its fundamental nature and verifiable quality. Furthermore, the word of any killer must always be held suspect until confirmed by unimpeachable proof. "Garbage in, garbage out" is a truism, but never an excuse. Relying on tainted evidence, even when it is not recognized as such, is unacceptable and cannot be tolerated. The following example illustrates the inherent danger better than any other case thus far on file.

When Emil Bauer was fired from his job at a small tool-and-die shop in South Gotham, his heated reaction included threats of revenge.

Three days after Bauer's dismissal, an explosion destroyed the tool and die shop. Three workers died instantly in the blast. Two more subsequently expired in the hospital emergency room. Seven additional employees survived various injuries, including loss of limbs.

Forensic investigation of the site harvested a residue of nitroglycerin at the explosion's epicenter, as well as fragments

of a glass bottle in which the unstable liquid had been introduced into the shop. Reconstruction of the crime concluded
that the bottle had been jerry-rigged to fall and explode when a
metal lathe's calibration was readjusted. The detonation, in
other words, was the result of a crude bomb, and the five resulting deaths therefore constituted murder.

As a "disgruntled former employee" who had angrily
vowed payback, Emil Bauer immediately qualified as a prime
suspect demanding investigation. And minute traces of nitroglycerin were indeed found on a counter in the man's apartment.

Bauer freely confessed to planting his bottle-bomb but
then surprised interrogators by giving up an unsuspected
accomplice. This was Nicholas Danoff, a fellow employee of the
tool-and-die shop. It was Danoff, according to Bauer, who
enabled the volatile nitroglycerin to be planted, staying after
hours the previous night to open the rear door for Bauer and
his bomb.

Danoff had failed to show up for work the next day, calling in sick less than an hour before the bottle fell from the back
of the lathe to claim five lives. To the original team of investigators, this fact was tellingly suspicious.

Through interviews with surviving employees, it was further learned that Danoff had on several occasions criticized the
company supervisor in addition to "griping about" a variety of
shop rules. This was deemed sufficient motive warranting further investigation.

An immigrant recently arrived from Europe, Nicholas
Danoff denied his guilt as best he could in broken English.
Bauer, he claimed, "makes jokes and troubles for my ways of the
talk." The two men had even "fighted," Danoff said, and he
would never help Bauer do anything, let alone "make the bombing."

Swab tests of Danoff's hands, however, proved positive for
residual traces of nitroglycerin. He was immediately arrested.

The two men were tried separately. Both were convicted.

When Nicholas Danoff's guilty verdict was announced, the man seemed confused. Then he clutched his left fist and seemed to snarl "either in shock or rage," as one reporter characterized the display. But cameras had been allowed in court, and the actual news footage suggested to me the third possibility of pain. Indeed, although I had not been involved in the case prior to that moment, the television coverage filled me with instant, sinking dread.

That night's covert penetration of Danoff's apartment confirmed my worst fear. It took less than a minute to find it in a bedside drawer, indisputable evidence of Nicholas Danoff's bad heart: Angina medication in the form of prescription tablets. Filled in its patented brand name, contrived to sound good in advertising despite being meaningless, the prescription label failed to identify its contents—inert nitroglycerin for easing pulmonary congestion. That the prescription bottle had not been bagged and tagged into evidence, let alone analyzed, was a glaring and unforgiveable oversight.

Despite all appearances, then, Nicholas Danoff was utterly innocent. Emil Bauer alone was guilty of cowardly multiple murder, committed with no assistance and no accomplice whatsoever.

It has now been learned—through belated examination of the guilty man's key ring—that Bauer had stolen a key to the shop's rear door, thereby gaining after-hours entrance on his own. (This incidentally explained a series of petty thefts occurring over the previous several months.) Furthermore, it was a dispute involving Danoff that had resulted in Bauer's dismissal, making Danoff the bombing's primary target. Actual illness, not feigned, spared Danoff from Bauer's fury, although only until Bauer improvised an alternative form of vengeance by falsely implicating the crime's target in its commission.

Circumstantial evidence literally depends on the circumstances in which it is discovered. Unless and until the details of those circumstances are adequately known and understood, the evidence itself can never be correctly interpreted.

Danoff had used his sick day, the day of the bombing, to visit a doctor. Complaining of sporadic aches in his chest and left arm, Danoff was diagnosed with mild angina. The bedside medication represented his first and only filled prescription. Due to his limited command of English, he was apparently unaware of its nature. Indeed, he seemed to completely forget about the prescription, never asking for any medication through the entire course of his wrongful trial. In any case, his defense attorney was completely unaware of the nitro pills.

Using the bedside phone, I conveyed the truth to Police Commissioner James Gordon on the spot. It was already too late. Nicholas Danoff, an innocent man, had just been found dead of congestive heart failure in his prison cell. Danoff's name will be posthumously cleared, the only form of justice now available, and the best conclusion possible.

Case tragically closed.

Cutting and
Culling

Casefile #0199
Year Two, Month Six, Day Nine

From the Private Files of the Batman

IT may be that killers cannot be evaluated by degree. Categorized, yes, but perhaps not "graded." All killers may be all bad, period. Still, if it is possible for certain murderers to be worse than others, then surely the worst are those who kill for "fun."

Serial killers. Twisted murderers who continue killing until they are stopped.

The first recovered victim had been dumped over the guardrail of the old palisades road, across the river and some thirty miles south of Gotham. Concealed by tall brush near the bottom of the steep hillside, the savaged body was discovered by teenagers apparently having a beer party. All five had been instantly scared sober.

On instructions from Police Commissioner Gordon, Chief Medical Examiner Mortimer Gunt performed an immediate after-hours autopsy. I attended in my usual anonymity of surgical cap, mask, and gown.

Withheld here, the victim's name was already known, her fully clothed body quickly identified by relatives who had filed a missing persons report nine days earlier. An attractive female

Caucasian, 28 years old, with a slim build and long brown hair, the victim had been stabbed to death. Gross external examination revealed no evidence of sexual assault while meticulous probing of each wound shaped a clear picture of the murder weapon.

Coroner Gunt set the maximum blade width at slightly less than one inch, with a single extremely sharp cutting edge, smooth rather than serrated and tapering to a slightly upcurved point. Deeply driven, the stabs had been inflicted with considerable force. All wounds were edged with ecchymosis, making them antemortem, although only one, the deepest, displayed any contact bruising. This had been dealt by the hand holding the knife rather than by a hilt or grip guard, which the weapon therefore did not possess. Although the precise blade length was difficult to determine, Gunt set it at approximately eight inches.

I pressed for an identification. "Carving knife?"

"Precisely," Gunt said. "A butcher knife."

In addition to the four separate stab wounds of deep penetration, any one of which would have caused death, there was a single vertical slit, roughly an inch long, lightly scored down the center of the victim's forehead. In that location, where the body's overlying tissue is at its thinnest, it would have been easy for any blade to reach bone. This wound, barely deeper than a scratch, did not. It had been inflicted with painstaking care by an instrument designed to cut much deeper. Gunt noted fine bruising around its edges, ecchymosis here too, caused by a heart still functioning and able to pump blood from severed vessels into the surrounding tissue.

I thought about it. "So the forehead wound was likely the final one inflicted, while the victim was still alive, but probably unconscious."

"Yes," Gunt agreed, "hardly during a struggle, and not even weak struggle, let alone panicked thrashing. The cut is too careful, too perfectly incised. Ecchymosis tells us the subject was still alive, but the cut's precision says just barely. It was inflicted while the subject was already bleeding out from the four deep stabs. Likely near death, certainly immobile."

I stared at the small slit parting the forehead skin, upright and aligned with the nose. It was the only wound that could not have caused death, yet it was unsettling in a way the four deep wounds were not. This made it significant, the kind of detail qualifying as a signifier, perhaps part of the killer's twisted M.O., even his "signature."

From the angles of the four deep wounds, Gunt established a right-handed perpetrator. In all four cases, the blade had penetrated with underhand sweeps rather than overhand stabs. Forceful, but probably not frenzied, nor even necessarily hurried. As deep as they were, then, the wounds seemed to represent evidence of cold calculation, deliberate viciousness rather than uncontrolled "passion." Cruelty rather than savagery.

Gunt offered no opinion on the perpetrator's height because he did not believe the victim had stood upright when sustaining the wounds, citing ligature bruising on her extremities, posterior wrists and forearms, and anterior ankles and shins.

"She was bound," he said. "Probably with common clothesline, one of the thinner gauges. I extracted a number of fibers from the ligature impressions. Forensics has them." He then indicated the victim's face, tracing bruise lines from the corners of her mouth across both cheeks. "Gagged as well. Knot bruise at nape of neck, under the hair."

I turned to Gordon. "But no line or gag was found with the body?"

He shook his head. "Apparently removed by the killer. Or at least by whoever dumped the body, presumably one and the same. The kids who found her say they kept their distance, never came close to touching the body. I believe them. Dressed like thugs, spooked like babies."

I turned back to Gunt. "Bound in a way that prevented her from standing erect."

"More than that," he said. "Bound in a way that suggests suspension. I may be more certain once we go inside."

He was. Immediately after opening the body, he focused on its exposed ribcage, ignoring the obvious knife penetrations to indicate several other points between different ribs. "See here? And here?"

I leaned forward to peer more closely. "Torn cartilage."

"Separated in several places," Gunt said, "and stretched where it's not torn. This entire ribcage was subjected to tremendous stress, and apparently for prolonged duration. Combining this evidence with the ligature bruising, I'd say the subject's back was severely arched, arms and legs pulled back and bound together over the small of her spine."

"Hog-tied."

"And hoisted up, probably by the same line used to bind the forearms and shins, to hang suspended facedown." Gunt's eyes were flat. "Which is buttressed by another factor. You noticed there was no need to drain the body. That's because it's virtually empty, almost completely exsanguinated."

"The victim was hung up to bleed out."

Gunt shrugged. "Whether that was the *purpose* of the suspension, I don't know, but that's what happened. The body *did* bleed out while suspended."

I tried to banish the mental image even as I concentrated on what it might imply, screening horror to focus on fact. "And if the victim was *stabbed* while suspended, it not only explains the wound angles, but also why all four penetrations were struck underhand."

"Hadn't gotten that far yet," Gunt admitted, "but yes. Even if the subject was suspended high enough for the perpetrator to stand comfortably under her, overhand stabs still would have been awkward to perform, certainly not natural."

Gunt found little more of relevance, using the extent of maggot and other insect infestation to estimate that the young woman had been dead for at least six days but no more than nine. Given the date of her disappearance, then, the evidence indicated a period of captivity which could have been as long as three days. Her empty stomach and bowels were not good signs.

When the autopsy concluded, I felt I had glimpsed the work of yet another demon freshly sprung from hell. Quite possibly the worst demon of all.

The forehead slit still haunted me out in the morgue's rear shadows. Gordon's face was drained and grim.

"Let's hope it's isolated," he said. "Just a one-off."

"We both know it's not, Commissioner."

He grunted, nodded. "A repeater."

"How many outstanding missing persons reports?"

"Seven in the last five weeks matching the victim's physical profile." He turned away, head lowered. "Down to six now. We brought only one family in, mother and stepfather, based on the clothing and photos. They confirmed our identification. It was awful, the one part of this job I never ace and never will. Dealing with the survivors, trying to comfort them when there's no hope left to give, nothing but the dead body of their loved one."

All cops try to hold it in. It's a requisite of the job, and Gordon seldom expressed his emotions so plainly. I remained silent for a long moment, then spoke softly. "We have to assume it'll get worse."

"I know." His own voice was even more muted. "Maybe seven times worse."

"I hope I'm wrong, Commissioner, but this one feels completely out of bounds. Especially vile, truly evil."

He turned back to me. "What are you getting at? Something I missed in there, something even Gunt didn't see?"

"I agree with his reasoning about underhand stabs, but I also think the killer *did* stand comfortably under her."

"Meaning?"

"I think he wanted to shower in her blood."

Gordon blinked and pressed the bridge of his eyeglasses, then turned away again. "I've already ordered an all-out search at first light, along that full stretch of palisades road. Divers too, for the river."

"Most you can do. At this point."

I left him standing in the gloom.

Hoping to do more while it was still dark and before the morning search began, I drove across the bridge and south along the river until the road climbed the palisades. It was deserted and dark, the only light from two half-moons, one hanging in the sky above the other reflected off the river below. The winding road hugged the escarpment roughly halfway up the palisades' full height. Using the Global Positioning System data from Gordon's preliminary report, I stopped just short and took the forensics kit from the car, then walked the final tenth of a mile.

With the passage of at least six days since the body had been dumped, finding anything useful would require luck, a certain measure of which was already in play.

It had rained off and on for the past week, leaving the road's shoulder still somewhat soft. I found and took casts of tire impressions left by three separate vehicles that had pulled off the road directly above the point where the dumped body had been found. At least one of the tire prints, possibly all three, could have been impressed by police or rescue vehicles earlier in the day. But if luck held, one of these tread casts might match a tire on the car from which the victim's body had been dumped.

And by morning, in any case, new impressions might obscure these three forever.

Before leaving the scene, I stepped to the guardrail and looked down the steep hillside of dense scrub and brush barely visible under the moonlight. A good three hundred feet of slope stretched down to the river, winding along the bank and out of sight for more than a mile. The area had already surrendered one corpse, and I wondered how many other horrible secrets it might hide even now.

Back in the cave, I photographed and stored the tire casts before going over Jordan Rankin's preliminary report. With much of the forensics team's analysis either ongoing or not yet even begun, and final results still pending, there was little hard evidence although a fair amount of promise. I circled one of the scheduled analyses, scrapings of soil from the treads of the victim's sneakers.

Beyond that, the report did little more than confirm my worst fear. The victim had been fully clothed when her body was found and fully clothed when she had been murdered. Defects in her blouse and slacks matched the four stab wound locations, with bloodstaining confined to those penetrated areas of the material. The clothing, in other words, was heavily stained without being fully saturated. According to Rankin, however, the front of the clothing was "finely misted" with tiny blood flecks spattered between the localized stains.

There were three inferences to be drawn. First, with actual rape already ruled out, a fully clothed victim argued against the crime being a sexual assault in any sense at all. Somehow this only made the murder more chilling.

Second, there was no longer any doubt that Gunt's reading of the ligature bruises and stressed ribcage had been correct. The clothing's blood evidence confirmed that the victim had been suspended face (and wounds) down, bleeding out from that position before being driven to and dumped from the palisades road.

And finally, the blood "misting" meant that I was right, too. The mist had come from below, splashing upward off the killer as he stood directly under the red rain of falling blood.

To his relief, Gordon learned the next day that one of the six missing women was alive and well. She had simply fled a troubled marriage, calling her husband from Oregon six days later. The husband had not bothered to cancel the missing persons report.

One dead, one alive, leaving five still missing.

Gordon jumped all over the news, hoping we'd both been wrong, that the murder was a single isolated event, that none of the others were dead, that all five had simply run away to new lives elsewhere. But he also told me his hopes were probably wishful thinking.

I knew he was right. It kept me awake all day, following the news.

On the roof that evening, Gordon was visibly shaken. The day's search had been hideously successful, with four more bodies recovered from the same half-mile stretch of brush below the palisades road and above the river but none from the water itself. And with four of the five missing women now found, Gordon's hopes were crushed to one, a single runaway failing to contact home. Either that or one further body still awaited discovery, perhaps washed farther downriver.

The entire area was now staked out from above, with plainclothes officers strung along the palisades ridge to maintain constant surveillance on the road below. The diversion of manpower and resources was almost certainly futile, however, because the first discovery had already made the morning news, followed by ongoing coverage of the day's ensuing search. Even if there was another body yet to dump, the killer's favored site was now the last place it would happen.

"Gunt's still doing the autopsies now," Gordon said, "but he's certain they were all killed by the same butcher knife."

"Wielded by the same serial killer, Commissioner, and we didn't need Gunt to tell us. The tight grouping of disposed bodies is enough. Consistent M.O. as well?"

"You were right." He hunched deeper into his trenchcoat. "This one's truly depraved, probably ritualistic. M.O.'s more than consistent. It's identical."

"Literally identical?"

"All bound and suspended in exactly the same way. All roughly the same physical type, all clothed, all drained of blood. All deeply stabbed with underhand thrusts, four times in every body, with—"

"A fifth wound to the forehead."

He nodded grimly. "The same shallow slit, straight up and down, clearly his calling card."

"More than that, Commissioner."

"Like what?"

"I don't know yet. Maybe an insight into his dementia, why he does it. What else from Gunt?"

"Not much yet, and nothing different. The bodies are in varying stages of decomposition, the oldest one dead for a month or more, probably the first woman reported missing. As far as Gunt can tell, they're kept alive in captivity some two to four days."

"Much evidence for Rankin's forensics team?"

"Plenty, but nothing compared to what's already been collected."

"These weren't the first." It was what I'd dreaded. "He didn't start in Gotham."

Gordon drew a deep breath. "After the third body was found this morning, I checked the FBI's VICAP (VIolent Crime and Apprehension Program) database. No real hits at first glance, so it looked like we were dealing with a brand-new homegrown perp. But I decided to dig deeper, weeded my way through the knife killings, found a few improbable but possible matches. They panned out."

"How many matches?"

"It's big," Gordon said, as if to brace me. "More than Bundy, more than Henry Lee Lucas, even more than the Green River Killer."

"Tell me."

He lowered his head, as if humbled and shaken by the magnitude evil can attain. "Looks like sixty-seven in four other cities, which means probably more. Another eight victim types are still missing from those four areas." Then, slowly, he lifted his eyes to meet mine. "The most prolific serial killer in the nation. And he moved to Gotham some five to seven weeks ago."

"Why five to seven?"

"The last murder in the previous city, Miami, occurred seven weeks ago."

"And the first Gotham victim was reported missing five weeks ago."

"Right."

"You spoke directly to the FBI?"

"Immediately, even before the last body was found this morning." He turned away, slowly pacing toward the rooftop signal beacon. "They're calling him 'the Butcher.' Sent their best casefiles, along with an overall summary of the other murders and a perpetrator profile worked up by their behavioral science unit. Arrived by special courier two hours ago." Reaching behind the beacon, he lifted a thick accordion file and paced back. He seemed exhausted and numb, almost dazed. "These copies are for you."

I took the accordion file and gave him three photos, one of each tread cast. "From the palisades road. Better check them out. One or more could be from your tires."

"I'll shoot them over to Rankin's people now." He pressed the bridge of his eyeglasses, then raked his graying hair. "Meanwhile, I've got a lot to do. Task force arrives from Quantico in the morning."

It was clear he did not relish the intrusion, but nor could he object to the FBI's help. Facing the worst threat to Gotham during his tenure as police commissioner, he was about to lose all control of it to federal agents notorious for their secrecy—not to mention a habit of treating local commanders as irrelevant nuisances.

Seeing no reason to wait for the FBI, I took their accordion file back to the cave. Filled with the usual vague generalities, the Behavioral Science Unit (BSU) profile was worth only a skim. I set it aside to review the overall task force summary with greater attention, then gave the actual casefiles the full concentration they deserved, highlighting promising details and making my own separate notes on all hard evidence of relevance.

Both revealing and disturbing, the summary confirmed my assumptions. The FBI had kept certain details tightly guarded secrets, even from their own VICAP database, including the signature forehead slit. This explained why Gordon and I were unaware of such a salient characteristic. Indeed, based on public knowledge, there was little reason to suspect that four separate murder clusters, committed in four different regions, might be the work of a single hand. Without access to such privileged FBI information, in fact, local police departments would struggle to see any connection.

There were legitimate reasons for this selective control of information, of course, but I wondered if good intentions outweighed potentially bad outcomes. In this case, Gordon had quickly detected possible matches in the VICAP's data, as incomplete as the details were. No time had been lost in Gotham. But what if the Butcher had taken his knife to some other city, one whose police department was run by someone less experienced than James Gordon, with a mind less keen and persistent?

In any case, the uncensored summary eliminated all doubt, cataloguing a long series of previous murders whose evidence clearly matched the Gotham victims. Before coming here, the killer had taken a devastating toll in Detroit, Chicago, Phoenix, and Miami, actively killing for declining periods of twelve to three months in each city before moving on to the next. The Butcher, then, was a "roving" serial killer, although not a drifter. He was someone who put down roots and then relocated for reasons of his own, either when he felt threatened by capture or when his preferred pickings grew slim. Perhaps when he simply felt restless or bored.

Of all the task force suspects, none had resided in all four areas at the appropriate times. The list was a dead end, hundreds of names long.

The only variations in M.O. occurred after the first seven murders, all in Detroit, where a total of sixteen victims had been found. After those first seven, there were two differences for all the rest. First, instead of being quickly killed, subsequent victims endured periods of captivity ranging from one to several days. Second, the scenes of their murders were unknown.

Everything else was the same, abduction followed by horror, terminating in murders consistent with each other as well as with the first seven. Antemortem bruises indicating facedown suspension. Five wounds, never more, never less, four deep penetrations of the anterior torso with one slight incision in the forehead. Fatal wounds all swept from below by a right-handed perpetrator, all administered by the same (or a similar) butcher knife. Victims suspended and exsanguinated. Bodies dumped in areas sufficiently remote to delay discovery for days, weeks, even months.

And with only one exception, every victim conformed to the same general physical type. Slender white females with long dark hair in their late 20s or early 30s, young but not girlish. They all disappeared in similar ways, called "eerie vanishings" in the FBI summary. One failed to return from jogging. Another left for work but never arrived. One went out to dinner after work, then left for home and "disappeared into thin air, car and all." Another was last seen in a shopping mall, her car abandoned in the parking lot. Still another vanished while walking her dog, the leash-trailing pet eventually returning home on its own. And so on. The women were prey, all snatched by a predator whose prowess seemed almost supernatural.

The sole exception to victim type was a 43-year-old heavyset male, killed in precisely the same way, including the key elements of hog-tied suspension and forehead slit. The only difference was an additional sixth wound of lacerated scalp and fractured skull in the right parietal region, caused by blunt trauma struck from the rear by a right-handed attacker. Unlike the female victims, then, the man had been rendered unconscious prior to his abduction. And given his weight, evidently dragged and bundled into a nearby car before disappearing into the night. I imagined either a laborious struggle (noticed by no one) or a killer possessing considerable strength.

Although it is unusual for a serial killer to claim victims of both genders, it is not as rare as the public assumes. In this case, the exception was the only killing with a transparent motive, either warning, taunt, or revenge, since the male victim was an FBI special agent charged with tracking the Butcher. Having worked late, he disappeared after leaving his Chicago Task Force office but before reaching his car. This was the last of the Chicago killings, followed by discovery of the first Phoenix victim three weeks later.

Hardly good news for Gordon. The Butcher had audaciously abducted and murdered a federal agent, making it personal for the Bureau ever since. And while a local cop like Gordon would be eager for the FBI's help, he might well be marginalized and left largely in the dark by them.

Their loss.

All the real juice resided in the actual casefiles, seven of them covering the first seven Detroit area murders and the Butcher's first known crimes. These were the best cases with the "best" victims, those who lived alone and had not been abducted and taken elsewhere, whose bodies were not dumped but found hog-tied and hanging in their invaded homes. The only ones left where they died, at the actual scenes of the crimes.

Normally, the coldest cases are also the least illuminating. Here the rule was not just broken; it was shattered. Duplicating the ensuing murders in virtually every detail, then, the Butcher's first seven atrocities were crucially different in one respect. Containing full investigations of the only Butcher crime scenes found thus far, the casefiles therefore documented the task force's richest harvests of evidence. Best of all, each file bulged with photographs.

They were horrific. All seven victims had been found hog-tied and suspended facedown above their own splashed blood. Gunt was right about the cord used, thin-gauge clothesline in every case, although from several different manufacturers. In two cases, the cord was secured over exposed beams. In four other cases, from chandelier or light fixture braces. One home, a tiny studio apartment, offered no easy way to suspend its tenant from the ceiling. Here the Butcher had improvised by resorting to the apartment's tallest piece of furniture. Hoisted over a hutch used to store linen and dishes, the body was suspended only four feet off the floor and resting against the hutch rather than freely hanging. While the victim exhibited the same five wounds, an adult male could not have inflicted them from directly below without kneeling or crouching. I wondered if the Butcher had felt sufficiently frustrated to change his M.O., although I sensed additional factors urging him to add kidnapping to murder.

The photos showed a tremendous welter of blood under each suspended body, always matched to the victim. Tracked from each welter, the same bloody footprints, made by the same pair of shoes, led straight to the door and out into the night. In every case, the bloody footprints were interspersed and flanked by elongated drips and splashes left by the killer moving with a normal-to-slow gait. Outside, the footprints and drip spatters faded to nothing several blocks from each scene. The killer, then, had not only stepped through his victims' blood, he had been covered with it, literally drenched and dripping as he left the scene.

I'd been right but still didn't know what to make of it. Was the Butcher using each victim's blood to wash away the sin of murder even as it was committed? Or was some other mania in play, some blood obsession that might never be fully understood? At this stage, there was no way to know.

Most important, however, each scene yielded smaller blood traces separate from the overall welters. These began as circular spatters, indicating blood droplets falling straight down some six to ten feet from the edge of each victim splash. The small spatters then elongated as they led *into* the overall splash. Or *under* the splash. In no case did these drips match the victim, instead matching one another across all seven scenes. The killer had therefore deposited small amounts of his own blood at each scene of the first seven crimes, initially bleeding from a remote stationary position and then while moving into place under his suspended victim.

Furthermore, it was possible that the killer himself had bled *first*, if only slightly, prior to making his victim fully bleed out.

And there was more. Although none of the dead women knew one another, the same foreign fingerprints had been lifted from their homes, proving the same hands had been active at all seven scenes, linked only by murder.

So the FBI Task Force had the killer's blood and his fingerprints. Hoping to match one or the other to an actual suspect, they had looked hard and everywhere but thus far in vain, with all databases negative on both fronts. Whoever the serial killer was, he had never been incarcerated, arrested, or finger-printed, or had his DNA filed anywhere at any time.

Finally, all seven casefiles contained evidence of break-in. Whatever his identity, the killer was likely a stranger rather than someone known by the victims and invited into their homes.

And there the entire matter rested, more or less, with the task force stuck in one rut after another, spinning its wheels in every one. Even with an abundance of physical evidence left in his wake, the perpetrator remained a ghost.

It was frustrating. Trapped in the cave with the night wast-ing, I felt anxious to prowl the darkness, to hunt the hunter before he claimed new prey. But like the FBI, I saw no trail to follow, no way out of the ruts.

I started going through the summary and seven casefiles again, rereading certain passages, taking more notes, making lists, roughing out diagrams and charts. Staring at the awful photos. Only when my neck suddenly ached did I realize it had been tensed for hours.

Alfred came down from the manor with coffee.

"Any way I may be of further assistance, sir?"

"I need enlarged maps of the five cities and surrounding vicinities, fifty miles out in all directions. After that, you can get up to speed with this FBI material."

"Very well, sir." He laid the tray within my reach and moved off to the master computer.

I spread seven photos across the workstation, closeups of a circular drip spatter from each scene, then reached for the coffee.

It was near dawn when I turned to the map blowups, using notes from the FBI summary to mark the homes and workplaces of all known victims along with the locations of their disposed bodies. It was a longshot, but I hoped to detect some pattern between hunting grounds and dump sites, pointers to areas deserving greater scrutiny, preferably ones the FBI had overlooked. But when I finished the first map of the Detroit area, nothing jumped out.

Moving on to the Chicago blowup, I decided to use Alfred as a sounding board while I marked the map, talking out whatever I'd gleaned from the files. Maybe a clue had lodged in my subconscious, some vague detail Alfred's conscious mind could help tease into the open.

"The same victim type, Alfred, with only one exception. Thin young white women with long dark hair. What does that suggest?"

Closing the summary report, Alfred responded immediately. "The killer is probably but not necessarily white himself. He operates selectively, certainly with premeditated deliberation, attempting to satisfy an obsession which can never be quelled."

"Nothing else?"

He frowned. "Well, at risk of tossing profiler darts in the dark, sir, perhaps the killer harbors a deep hatred for some woman of the same physical type from his past, someone by whom he feels wronged and whom he now repeatedly 'kills' by proxy."

"Or the physical type simply represents his ideal victim for some other reason."

"Psychosexual, sir?"

"Not necessarily. Or not solely."

"What else, then?"

"Expedience." Finishing the second map and again seeing no obvious pattern, I reached for the Phoenix area blowup. "Pragmatic selection of prey. Possessing less strength, a woman is more easily overcome."

Alfred nodded. "Especially a slender woman, although this hardly explains the common age and race, least of all the long dark hair."

"It may be a combination of pragmatic and psychological factors. But even a full understanding of them probably won't help at this point anyway."

"And have you found anything else, sir, that will?"

"The true mystery, Alfred. The killer's own blood, left at every one of the known crime scenes."

"Indicating defensive struggles?"

"Unlikely. No blood or tissue scraped from the fingernails of any victim."

"But surely some of them would have put up a fight?"

"Given a chance, yes. Somehow he prevents it."

"By drugging them?"

"Difficult to see how. After the seventh known murder, there are no further crime scenes, not yet. From that point on, the victims were all killed in unknown locations after being snatched right off the street."

"With little opportunity to administer a drug."

"Let alone wait for it to take effect."

Alfred crossed his arms, running scenarios through his mind, just as I'd already done. "And in the first seven cases," he said, "wherein the killer invaded the scenes, even a handkerchief soaked with chloroform would require *some* time to take effect, surely long enough for one victim to inflict a scratch. Indeed, such an assault would *provoke* instinctive struggle."

"Dead end, Alfred. If he uses a drug, it's either rare or undetectable. Other than a few hits for prescription medications, the toxicology reports are largely negative. About a dozen victims tested positive for alcohol, three for marijuana, one for cocaine."

"In all cases meaning little or nothing, since such substances were no doubt voluntarily ingested before the fact."

"And most of the victims were sober in any case. All of which implies he subdues his victims with abrupt and overwhelming force."

"After they've been lulled by trust?"

"Otherwise known as seduction. Maybe. Or psychology; some form of deceit. Either that or he takes them completely by surprise."

"Which explains the absence of blood or tissue under their fingernails but does nothing to dispel the mystery. If the victims didn't spill his blood, who did? What explains its presence? Self-inflicted wounds?"

"Not that I like it, Alfred, but that's how it looks. The blood evidence is the same across all seven scenes, a half-dozen to a dozen droplets, no spurts or splashes, all dripped from similarly minor wounds in every case." The third map was finished, still revealing no discernible pattern. "Commissioner Gordon senses an element of ritual. If he's right, and whatever its point, the ritual is all about bleeding."

"Blood sacrifices, sir?"

"Maybe, but not in the traditional sense. And beyond sacrifice, some private ritual in which the sacrificer himself also sheds blood. As if the killer feels a compulsion to bleed *with* his victim."

"Sharing her pain?"

"An extremely limited sharing."

"More's the pity."

"Take a look at the strangest aspect." I indicated the seven photos farther down the workstation. "The killer's blood drips. Tell me what you see."

Alfred leaned close to each photo in turn. "All circular splashes," he said, "rather than the elongated 'exclamation mark' made by flying blood."

I nodded. "Those are closeups of the first drip at each scene. Later drips are more stretched and oval."

"Yet the first ones did fall straight down, sir, another indication they did not result from a defensive struggle. Self-inflicted while the killer stood still."

"Did you compare the scale in each photo to the others?"

Again he peered at the photos. "Different sizes," he said. "Every drip splash has a different diameter, with a correspondingly different edge-pattern as well."

"Meaning each drop fell from a different height, Alfred. The FBI worked it out and I confirmed their figures. The largest splash was made by a drop falling from approximately forty-six inches, whereas the smallest fell from only fifteen inches above the floor, lower than knee height."

Alfred tapped his chin. "Flowing from open wounds, the blood ran down the killer's torso or limbs, finally separating and falling from different points on his body. Either that or the blood dripped from a blade held very still at a different height within each scene."

"Or the drops fell directly from different wounds located at different heights."

"And therefore wounds inflicted to different areas of the killer's anatomy."

"Right."

"And you find this, I take it, the most plausible answer?"

"Yes, because at all seven scenes the subsequent elongated splashes, made while the killer walked forward, fell from roughly the same height as the initial circular splashes."

"A telling clue, sir, but telling what?"

"You tell me, Alfred. I'm stuck with nothing but a ritual I don't understand and can't even imagine."

"But surely the key to the case?"

"One of *two* anomalous keys."

"The other being . . . ?"

"The fifth wound in every murder. The forehead slits." I showed him one of the death photos, watched his face change as he studied it. "They're all the same, each slightly more than an inch long, always vertical, always in the same location. What does it remind you of?"

He frowned. "I . . . I really can't say, sir. But something, I think."

"A third eye?"

"Yes, that's it." He rotated the photo ninety degrees. "A third eye turned on its side and barely open, sleepy looking, just above and between the other two eyes."

"Precisely where mystics have long claimed such an invisible eye resides."

"Yes," Alfred said, "the third eye governing 'second sight' or some sort of telepathic intuition. Superstitious belief in it, as I recall, dates all the way back to ancient cultures."

"More scientifically, it's on a direct line with the pineal body."

"Which is . . . ?"

"I looked it up, Alfred. 'A small glandlike body of uncertain function located in the brain.' What if the killer attributes second sight to this uncertain function?"

He thought about it. "Then the cuts may be a deliberate opening of the victim's third eye, an awakening of her inner sight, even as life leaves her two normal eyes."

"Good, but why? To what purpose?"

"The killer desires to be 'seen' by his victim even after she dies?"

"Or after she loses consciousness but continues to bleed out all over him."

Alfred pursued the thought. "Perhaps he wishes to be seen by her departing soul, remembered throughout eternity?"

"Keep going, Alfred. Blue-sky it as far as you can."

"He wishes to *impress* himself on the victim's departing soul, to 'merge' with the soul as it leaves this reality, to accompany it, venturing beyond life into death."

"A form of death wish."

"But only a safe one, sir, a vicarious journey to the hereafter while he remains alive and well in the here and now."

"The death wish of a coward."

"Indeed." His shoulders slumped. "All of which, however, brings us no closer to identifying the coward."

I wanted to encourage him. "Not yet, but it remains to be seen in the end." We were groping in the dark, grasping for straws, but it was the only way to strike sparks and provide light. "Never hurts to think outside the box, Alfred, but you're right not to place too much weight on it. That's what some of the profilers tend to do."

He nodded. "And in any event, sir, the forehead wounds may well signify something else entirely, something perhaps unfathomable to the killer himself, nothing but cruelty or dominance, sick marks demonstrating the killer's power over life and death. Graffiti etched in flesh."

It was true. "A way of 'signing his work,' thereby proving that each kill is his alone."

"Or the cuts may simply prolong the horror for purposes of sheer evil."

"And so on, Alfred, all the way to all of the above or none of it. The positioning of each final wound may be deliberate but nevertheless coincidental, having nothing to do with the pineal gland's 'third eye.'" There was no way to know, but I could not stop thinking about it. Even when I closed my eyes, I could still see the small shallow wounds, one in the morgue, the others in photographs, all the same. "Whatever its significance, all we know is that it's somehow profound to the killer." I opened my eyes and reached for the fourth map. "Sum it up, Alfred. General thoughts on everything."

"Very well, sir, although I've only reviewed the summary." He poured more coffee as he considered his thoughts. "Setting aside the usual new twists brought to bear by every serial killer, I should think this 'Butcher' is fairly typical. Other than the single male, apparently a brazen message directed to the FBI, all known victims are similar. Physically unimposing women. Like most serial killers, then, he functions as the consummate predator, culling the weak and vulnerable from each city's human herd. And like every predator, he cannot stop without ceasing to exist."

"But he did change."

"After the first seven murders, yes, one major change in tactics while everything else remained the same."

"Why?"

"Possibly as the result of nearly being caught or found out, although I sense this was not the case."

"Why not?"

"Because the difference between the first seven murders and all those that followed was less an actual *change* in the nature of the crimes than it was an escalation in their degree."

"How so?"

"The early murders were all of relatively short duration, committed soon after his invasion of each victim's residence. Certainly completed within the same night."

"And he wanted more."

"They always do, sir, do they not?"

"Definitely in quantity."

"And here, I think, in perversity as well. When the early murders failed to satisfy the killer, he sought to prolong the experience through a period of captivity. Intimacy on his terms rather than intrusion into his victim's home, a risky environment where time was critical and limited. And so, whether through force, ruse, or seduction, he began claiming his victims off the street, spiriting them off to a location of his choosing, his own turf as you Yanks say, a place prepared in advance."

"Where he is in full command and feels safe to take his time. I agree, Alfred. But also, such an escalation served to increase the victim pool. He's no longer restricted to single women living alone. Now he can prey on wife, mother, sister, daughter, roommate, literally anyone fitting his preferred type. They need be alone only briefly."

"Indeed, only long enough for him to secure their abduction."

"Anything more?"

"Merely the obvious, sir, and also a form of escalation. The interval between crimes has decreased at a fairly steady rate. In Gotham, his timetable has reached the rate of one victim per week on average, with less than that having passed between the two most recent murders, only four days. If each period of captivity is some two to three days, as it seems, then he is swift approaching a state of nonstop predation, making him the worst one yet. The escalation is precipitous. And time, sir, is of the essence."

"I know."

With the Miami map finished, I visualized the Gotham sites without aid. The five dumping sites were located some twenty to forty miles from the outskirts of each city. Other than that, no real pattern had emerged. No way out of the rut, no route to the killer.

Gordon called just after dawn.

"You were right," he said. "One of your tread casts matches the front left tire of the ambulance that took the first recovered body."

"But the other two casts are still alive?"

"Right. No matches with any of the squad cars or forensic vehicles sent to the scene. They all pulled off on the other side of the road, up against the palisades cliff."

"The casefiles are good, Commissioner. They don't seem sanitized, but the summary has no actual evidence. Can you ask the FBI for tire casts taken at the other dumping sites?"

"Already done. They thought they might have had matches from three of the other four cities but dismissed the evidence or at least put it on the back burner. The matches were all made by the same common brand of tire, Maximal Radial 309SB."

"Like one of my casts."

"And one of the two not from the ambulance, which is why I requested photos of any FBI casts. Cooperation with a local like me may not be one of their priorities, but Quantico claims I'll have the photos for comparison sometime this morning. Definitely before dark."

"After which, I'll see you on the roof."

Alfred came back down with a hot breakfast. I'd decided to forego another day of sleep, going over the summary, seven casefiles, notes, and maps one more time with the greatest concentration yet. As Alfred had noted, the Butcher would soon prey again. Until he did so, the only hope of finding him lay hidden somewhere right in front of me.

I hoped I wouldn't need any further evidence, not when its cost would be paid with yet another victim's life.

That night, I returned from police headquarters to compare the FBI's tire casts against mine. Gordon had already told me they appeared to match, and he was right. Tread depths decreased from earliest cast to latest, suggesting the FBI photos could depict the same tire showing progressive wear, and the sequence extended through the impression in the shoulder of the palisades road. My cast, the most recent, exhibited the shallowest tread depth of all. Given the tire's popularity, however, coincidence was still plausible.

Until it was ruled out by a tiny but telling feature, the kind of detail easily overlooked by strained eyes. And coffee or not, I had to squint through the magnifying lens to detect it.

Appearing in the earliest cast taken, at the Chicago area dumping site, it was a hairline crack, slightly curved, splitting one section of the tread pattern, the second band from the edge. Whatever the cause—bump, pothole, or manufacturing flaw—the rubber had slightly separated in this one region of the tire.

Focus and resolution in the FBI photographs varied from good to excellent. If the tiny defect could be discerned in one photo, it should be visible in the others. It was not. But while its presence would have established a significant connection, its absence meant nothing, because the other impressions could have been made by different wheels on the same vehicle. Furthermore, neither of the other two photos showed a full revolution of the tire. One cast, captured from a dried puddle, encompassed only nine inches of the tire's overall circumference. This could have been impressed by a different portion of the same tire while the tread defect was located somewhere up in the wheel hub.

Examining a photo of the cast I'd taken, I thought I saw the hairline crack but couldn't be certain. Hardly surprising. Even if this was in fact the same tire, it had been driven more than the equivalent of cross-country before reaching the Gotham area. And given a shallow crack in the first place, the resulting tread wear might be close to exceeding its depth.

Whatever its resolution, a photograph is always a substitute for the primary evidence, never its equal. I went to the evidence drawer set into the cavern's rock wall and took out the actual cast. Under strong light and through the magnifying lens, the hairline crack was definitely visible, in the same second band from the tire's edge. While it no longer spanned the band's full width, it did display precisely the same slight curve, disrupting precisely the same "ripple" detail in the tread design.

The evidence was unmistakable, providing a third way to identify the killer—through his fingerprints, his blood, and now his vehicle. More than solid, the case would serve a slam-dunk to any prosecutor. The only thing missing was someone to prosecute, the actual serial killer still at large. We had the cart but not yet the horse.

The Butcher still had to be found. And stopped.

I decided to first replicate the FBI timeline derived from their synthesis of known and suspected victims, and then extend it with the Gotham data. According to missing persons reports from the first four cities, there were thirteen additional women of the same physical type whose remains had not been recovered and might never be found. Although one or more of these potential victims could still turn up alive and well, the FBI included all thirteen in their analysis. I did the same, interpolating the disappearance times of the missing women with the forensically estimated dates of death for all recovered remains.

The resulting chart of likely if imperfect intervals between murders was disturbing confirmation of the task force findings
noted by Alfred. Early murders had occurred more or less at the
rate of one per month. Then, after a three month break between
the final Detroit killing and the first Chicago victim, the pace
had quickened alarmingly. And further accelerated through the
Phoenix and Miami murders.

By the time he reached Gotham, highly accomplished and
apparently feeling omnipotent, the Butcher was killing on a
weekly basis and apparently at will.

Gordon called just before midnight with the worst news possible.

"Husband reported his wife missing."

"And she matches the victim type?"

"Afraid so. At first he thought she was just working late,
but it turned out she never showed up today. We just found her
car, parked at a convenience store near her home, where she
stops for her morning drive coffee."

"What about the previous victims? Anything useful from
Coroner Gunt?"

"He's more or less finished with all the autopsies. Says one
of them died no more than two days ago. It was the body closest
to the first, the one found by the kids, and probably dumped
only hours earlier. Made Gunt revise his best guess on the period of captivity."

"To what?"

"It's bad," Gordon said. "No more than twenty-four to
thirty-six hours."

"Not much time."

"No."

I hung up and went back to work.

At best, the missing woman was living in terror, with the clock
fast counting down to her death. Frustrated and desperate, I went

back to the raw missing persons reports. But this time, instead of fixing on females, I eliminated them, all of them. Then, from the remaining males, I extracted those falling within the killer's likely age range, early 20s through early 40s, finding more than a hundred from the first four metro areas within the relevant time frames. Next, I winnowed the list to reports filed shortly after the last murder occurring in each city. This left eighteen names.

The long-shot logic was simple. Whoever the killer was, he had lived for a fairly extended period in each city before moving on to the next. I hoped he was also a man whose escalating blood mania had forced him to "drop out" of his previous life, at least in Detroit if not in the subsequent cities, leaving behind someone to report him missing.

Had the same man been reported missing in two or more of the cities, an obvious lead would beg pursuit. I scanned down the list of seventeen, hoping the same name appeared more than once. It did not.

I then focused on the four missing persons reports filed shortly after the final Detroit murder. If the killer had roots in any of the four previous killing fields, it was most likely they would have been planted in the first of them.

The most intriguing name was Anton Zsasz, a psychoanalyst with a practice in Grosse Point, outside of Detroit. Unmarried and with no family in the area, Zsasz had been reported missing by his receptionist when he vanished without explanation, without even canceling his appointments, some three days after the Butcher's last murder in Detroit.

I crosschecked the other fourteen reports. Although their names were different, a psychiatrist had been reported missing from all three of the other cities shortly after the final murder occurred in each. Because the FBI had focused solely on female missing persons reports, there were no photos of missing males. The written descriptions, however, roughly matched Zsasz with a single difference. The psychiatrist who disappeared from Miami, the last city prior to Gotham, was noted as bald.

I wondered if the Butcher had grown tired of washing his hair or if he had come to crave even closer contact with the hot blood gushing down on him.

A computer search on Anton Zsasz turned up several references to an article written by the man for a psychiatry journal. It was entitled "The Pleasure of Self-Cutting's Pain."

Using Alfred Pennyworth's credit card, I subscribed to the online version of the journal and immediately downloaded the archived article.

Recognizing it as the breakthrough I needed, I read the article fast.

It was an authoritative examination of the phenomenon known as slow-cutting self-mutilation, most often performed by young women suffering deficiences of self-esteem. Often associated with anorexia, bulimia, and other related disorders, these self-inflicted incisions are characteristically shallow and seldom pose serious physiological risk, although they are always deep enough to create blood flow. "Gently" and carefully performed, such slow-cutting initiates minimized pain quickly, which is paradoxically followed by a twisted form of pleasure due to triggered endorphins and other blood opiates created by natural body chemistry and released in reaction to trauma.

As for psychological implications, author Zsasz proposed that such "piggybacked" pain and pleasure implanted a "comforting affirmation of life" in those feeling "dead inside." Cutting and bleeding thus "thrilled the moribund psyche into vivid awareness, a clarity of being transcending all normal states of mind."

In this sense, Zsasz concluded, self-cutting was equivalent to "consumption of a potent and extremely addictive drug."

I drank more coffee, then paced and tried to think how I might obtain a list of all psychiatrists who had recently opened practice in Gotham, including a psychiatrist turned monster, to become the nation's worst serial killer. I came up with nothing. Phone books and registries would not include anyone arrived in Gotham no more than five to seven weeks ago. Application to some sort of municipal board was probably required, but finding the appropriate person at this time, so long after normal business hours, would be neither easy nor quick. And even if I reached and roused such a person, the necessary files would hardly be at hand in his or her home. Gordon could probably wake someone to fetch the names, but it would still consume precious time.

Alfred's words came back to me. Time was of the essence. The clock was ticking.

Escalating precipitously, the killer threatened to spiral out of control. His obsession was unquenchable now, his mind disintegrating, perhaps ready to explode. Even as he had claimed victims more and more often in each city, he had maintained his "normal practice" over shorter and shorter durations. If it continued, eventually nothing of the psychiatrist would remain. Only the madman, only the monstrous Butcher.

Taking a chance that escalation had attained its logical conclusion, I decided to abandon pursuit of newly arrived therapists, instead skipping straight to male missing persons reports filed in the Gotham area during the last seven weeks. Even if I was wrong, it would not take long.

I found a hit within minutes, a psychiatrist reported missing some four and a half weeks earlier. Dr. Lambert Nilho. It may have been wishful thinking, but the name rang falsely. Then the description nailed it. Like the missing Miami psychiatrist, Nilho was also bald.

Disappearing after a week of practice, before he had even hired a receptionist, Nilho had been reported missing by his only Gotham patient after she found his office deserted and could not reach him by phone over the next three days. The lease for Nilho's office listed a residential address, and the landlord of the apartment building had confirmed that his tenant was missing from those premises as well.

Nilho—née Zsasz, I was certain—had not only abandoned his practice almost before launching it, but had seemingly left town as well. Yet the killings had continued, had even escalated. Another woman had just been abducted on the heels of the last murder. The Butcher was still active in the Gotham area, and if he was now living elsewhere, somewhere unknown, his new home was probably also still in the area. It was likely the place where he now practiced his one and only profession, feeling safe to take his time. The same place where he had already killed at least five Gotham women, probably six, and where he might be holding a seventh even now.

The scene of the murders.

Able to maintain his façade of normalcy for only a week at this point, he had spun wildly out of control. "Escalation" was inadequate to describe his current activites and state of mind. He was now a full-time predator, able to do nothing but hunt and kill.

I had nothing that constituted proof, but neither did I have any doubt. It had to be him. The Butcher was Zsasz and Zsasz was Nilho, as well as the other three psychoanalysts missing from Chicago, Phoenix, and Miami. We had his fingerprints, his blood, his car. All I had to do was find the man before he washed himself in the stolen blood of another victim, and I had the address of his last known residence. It was on the nineteenth floor of a high-rise apartment building, in the Ravencrest area of Gotham.

And the clock was still ticking.

I went in through the high window without awakening the new tenants, then used night-vision lenses and infrared light to creep through their bedroom into the hall. Looking for an area subjected to the least amount of cleaning and vacuuming, I opened the coat closet near the front door and crouched amid its clutter. Moving boxes and boots, I used a penknife to pry residue from five different floorboard crevices.

After bagging the residue, I closed the closet, crept back down the hall, through the bedroom, and out the window. Then I cast a line and swung down into the night, heading back for the car and the cave's crime lab.

Once the usual fuzz, dust, and fibers had been separated, much of the unbagged floorboard residue proved to be common soil. Some of it could have fallen from the shoes of the new tenants, of course, but I hoped they were confirmed city dwellers more comfortable with sidewalks than earth. In any case, only weeks had passed. At least some of the soil could have been deposited by the previous tenant. By Nilho. By Zsasz. The Butcher.

Under microscopic examination, the first bit of soil exhibited the same clay-rich composition as the palisades area where at least five bodies had been dumped. Although Nilho-Zsasz had dropped out of sight prior to four of the five known local murders, abandoning his apartment and office alike, the clay suggested he had been in that closet, perhaps for the final time, after disposing of his first Gotham victim.

Finding residue linked to the killer was a hopeful sign without being helpful evidence. Not only did we already know about the palisades dumping site, but we also knew it was probably the last place the killer would ever again be found. (Although there was still a slight chance that Gordon's surveillance might pay off, since certain serial killers *have* been known to revisit their disposed victims. In this case, however, with the dumped bodies now removed from the scene, any hope depended on the killer having no exposure to the news.)

What I needed was evidence revealing where Zsasz was now, where he had gone after leaving his office and apartment. If I was right to assume the place served two purposes, somewhere to kill as well as live, it would have demanded careful selection. It required a location at least somewhat isolated, where Zsasz could feel safe committing atrocities and where he could take his time doing so with minimal risk of discovery.

Wherever this place might be, he had probably scouted it at least once before abandoning his apartment. And if Zsasz's new home was in fact the scene of all five or six Gotham murders, including the first one committed while he definitely resided in the Ravencrest apartment, then Locard's famous maxim would hold.

Every contact leaves a trace.

Evidence from the scene of the murders should have been deposited somewhere in the Ravencrest apartment. If any of that evidence remained, it would most likely be found in a place least cleaned and least contaminated. In a closet, under boxes and between floorboards.

I went back over the residue with a magnifying lens, tweezing out all the tiny clumps of clay. Much of what remained was a darkish loam associated with the clay, but there were several small clots of less friable, more powdery soil. Their color, too, was different, a lighter ocher. Peat. I placed one of these clots onto the microscope platform and tweezed it apart while peering through the eyepiece. It was embedded with tiny flakes of mica.

Aside from the first autopsy, I had not yet seen any of the primary evidence related to the Gotham victims, all of which was still being examined and analyzed by Gordon's chief forensics technician Jordan Rankin.

I called the man at once.

"Did you harvest soil from any of the victims? Shoes rather than clothing."

"From four of them, yes, the ones wearing textured soles, sneakers in three cases and those ankle-high urban hiking boots in the fourth. The other victim wore flat, smooth soles, with almost nothing to harvest other than embedded grit."

"Do any of the four samples match?"

"All four matched each other, but none match the palisades soil. The victims were dead before they got there. They never walked that ground."

"Describe the soil."

"In the reports—barely finished, by the way, before the feeb task force swooped down to snatch them—I believe I called it 'peat mixed with schist mica.' Either that or—"

I hung up, heart pounding.

Given the possible link between Nilho-Zsasz and four of the Gotham victims, I called up the computer database of area soil compositions. Mica-rich peat was characteristic of seven different areas widely scattered beyond and around Gotham. One of these areas, I hoped, held ground trod by the killer and his victims, including the most recently abducted woman with only hours to live. If she was not already dead.

But which one of the seven areas? There was no time to systematically search all of them, nor did I want to scare off the killer with simultaneous searches conducted by police squad cars. I needed some other way to pinpoint the quarry fast, then take him down by stealth. It was the missing woman's only hope.

My thoughts jumped to the marked-up maps. And one of them, the mental map of the Gotham area, finally surrendered a simple pattern. Only one of the seven mica-peat areas fell roughly along the line linking Gotham to the palisades road. South of the city on the far side of the river, it was roughly halfway between hunting and dumping grounds. Almost certainly hosting the scene of the murders, it was also an irregular area equivalent to some twenty square miles. Still too large and not good enough.

I called Gordon and told him everything, including what I needed.

The south riverside area encroached on the jurisdictions of two separate township police chiefs. Gordon said he would wake them before waking the FBI.

I felt light-headed as I drank more coffee and briefly paced the cave, mind buzzing on caffeine but hampered by lack of sleep. There was no way to further short-circuit normal procedure. I'd done all I could on my own, narrowed the possibilities as much as feasible. And the fuse was still lit, the clock still ticking.

I decided to leave the cave and hope for the best. Gordon's scrambled call, patched to the car, might provide further leads. In the meantime, I would start searching the area blind, twenty square miles in the dark.

Adrenaline countered exhaustion, leaving my grip steady on the wheel. Any jitters were internal, and my strength and senses actually seemed enhanced. The unlit river road was narrow and winding with enough hills and dips for a roller coaster. I pushed one-twenty on the straights, somehow anticipating each new curve before it loomed in the headlights. Locked in an altered state of supreme focus, I saw the night with perfect clarity.

A deer leaped from the darkness. I swerved just past the white tail and nearly off the road, then drove on without ever hitting the brake. The sign for Bedminster Township told me I was nearing the area of mica-peat soil.

Gordon's call came through.

"Just talked to the Bedminster police chief. There's a hunting cabin right off the river road down there, remote location well within your soil region."

"Rented by a newcomer to the area?"

"In the off-season, no less, and only days before the time Gunt set for the first Gotham murder."

"By Nilho-Zsasz, Commissioner."

"Locals see him in the grocery store, but other than that, the man keeps to himself and doesn't seem to work. Police chief says his car is almost always in the driveway, called him a hermit. Also says he's bald."

"It's him. Address?"

"Nine-three-two. Police chief says it's painted on the mailbox. Between his people and mine, we have six units converging on the cabin right now."

"Hold them back, Commissioner. I'm close. Give me a chance to save the woman."

Gordon hesitated.

I shot past a mailbox numbered nine-one-three. The cabin was just ahead. I realized I'd gone right past it that first night, after the autopsy and en route to making the palisades tire casts. "It's her best chance and you know it."

"All right," Gordon finally said, "but I can't hold them back for long. And I have to notify the FBI now."

"Or at least within the hour."

Trying not to think about the captive woman, her circumstances or state of mind, knowing only that she had to be saved, I cut the call and roared faster.

Leaving the car amid trees just off the road, I sprinted up the cabin's long driveway, staying on the grass fringe to avoid the crunch of gravel. The breeze was light, the moon dim behind an overcast sky.

Tree frogs made a constant thrum broken only by an owl, then the barking of a distant dog. There were no other sounds, none from the dark cabin or the car parked at its side. Was the Butcher asleep? If so, where was the woman?

I stepped carefully onto the gravel and crouched to shine my penlight on the car's left rear tire. It was the same common brand, Maximal Radial 309SB. The second tread band of one tire, I knew, would be still slightly nicked, linking the car to the palisades dumping site, but finding the telltale flaw could wait for Jordan Rankin's forensics team.

Starting to rise, I froze when a pale piece of gravel squirmed at the edge of my light. Then I saw another movement, and another, until the slowly scanned light revealed dozens of stirrings. It was not the gravel.

With the light, I traced the movements from the back wheel to the rear of the car. Squirming through the trunk seal, fat greasy maggots bounced off the rear bumper to hit the gravel curling and crawling.

Knowing it was already hopeless, I picked the lock anyway. Inside the trunk, I found life feeding on death, thousands of maggots infesting a single corpse. Everything flashed red as exhaustion combined with horror. A loud roar filled my ears and I wanted to scream. But only for a split second. Then my vision cleared and calm strength seeped back.

The clock stopped dead. I was too late to rescue the abducted woman, too late to do anything except prevent the next abduction. But there was no rush now, no need to crash the cabin. I could take the time to steel myself and do it carefully, make sure the killer was not spooked into flight, eliminate any chance of escape. End the Butcher's activities for good and forever.

I closed the trunk silently, without locking it, and turned to the dark cabin. The farthest window suddenly filled with light. I dropped down and waited, prepared to rush the door. Within moments, more light spilled from a nearer window. I stayed low and crept toward the room just lit.

The curtains were slightly parted at the bottom of the window. I knelt down and peered into the lit room. What I saw explained almost everything even as it made my skin crawl.

Anton Zsasz, the psychiatrist turned homicidal maniac, admired his nearly naked body in a full-length bedroom mirror. Wearing nothing but a loincloth wrapped in the fashion of a Hindu mystic, if not the infantile manner of a diaper, he turned this way and that, striking one flexed pose after another. And he smirked all the while, taking both pride and pleasure as his muscular physique bulged and rippled in the mirror.

I realized he was more than strong enough to seize and subdue slender females from behind, quickly pinning their arms and binding their wrists. Exerted with surprise and speed, in

fact, such strength would virtually preclude any defensive struggle, enabling him to abduct his victims without sustaining a
scratch. In that sense, his strength possessed genuine utility.
Yet it was also clear that he appreciated his sculpted body on a
purely aesthetic level. His shifting facial expressions, the bright
gleam in his eyes, left no doubt. He reveled in the pure look of
himself, in the sheer spectacle of muscles honed to perfection.

A surprising number of serial killers have been diagnosed
as sociopaths with narcissistic obsessions. The self is everything
to them, other individuals insignificant and victims less than
that, nothing but living meat waiting to be butchered. If
remorse is not an alien concept to the serial killer, it is certainly an alien emotion. They are incapable of feeling empathy,
even immune to the suffering they cause, existing solely to satisfy their own depraved cravings. Killing without a second
thought, they simply move on to kill again. Murder may be akin
to eating, something done as a matter of course and something
they cannot cease without ceasing to exist. With a soul dead to
true feeling, the narcissist fully and obsessively loves himself
even as he cares not at all for anyone or anything else.

Still facing the mirror, Zsasz shifted his stance from body
builder to martial artist. He executed a quick karate kata, left
twist-punch, right twist-punch, left thrust-kick. Then he stepped
back to do it again. And again. He was good, each move tight
and precise, pistoned with authority and power. I wondered if
he could be shocked or intimidated by my bat guise or anything
else. If not, taking him down would hardly be easy.

The repetitions broke sweat and his physique gleamed.
Still he continued, thinly smiling as he attacked his own mirror
image again and again. But as much as the strength of his muscles explained, it was the taut skin sheathing them that revealed
far more. And that had instantly turned my blood cold.

Taut skin scarred nearly everywhere, from neck to wrists
and ankles, every area of his torso, arms, and legs.

The scars had been made by inch-long cuts arranged in scattered groupings. There were even several groupings, less precise, etched into his back, everywhere except hands, feet, face, and bald head. Each grouping consisted of four side-by-side vertical cuts crossed by a fifth diagonal. Appalled by the sheer number of scars, I was spellbound by their significance.

Each cut, I realized, marked a different victim. The scars were scores, visual tallies of his victims, like notches in a gunslinger's Colt. Zsasz's entire body was a living record of the death he had dealt. Even worse, it was an ongoing count.

The scoring explained the blood spatters at the first seven murder scenes and, no doubt, at all the other scenes yet to be found. In each case, splash size and edge pattern varied because each drop of blood had fallen from the different height of a different cut, now healed to a different scar.

With one last thrust-kick, Zsasz suddenly stood immobile, his breathing still shallow and easy. Directly in front of the mirror now, his face drained of all expression. He stared at himself long and hard, taking cold measure of his vein-corded sinews, assessing all the scars in his slicked skin. Finally, he closed his eyes, then tipped his head back and up until it faced the ceiling. His right hand slowly rose to his chest. Then, with his fingertips barely touching, he traced the line of one short scar after another. Each touch was soft and lingering, the loving caress of a different victim each time, of himself every time.

A *memento mori* is some object, often a skull, which represents death and serves as a reminder of the inevitable end awaiting us all. Zsasz himself was a walking *memento mori*, his entire body a collective memory of many deaths, a written history of multiple murders, and every mirror enabled him to relive any death of his choosing. Reliving his past, now, gently reading the braille chronicle of his skin, he seemed lost in ecstasy.

I realized the cuts possessed a secondary significance. They were visible manifestations of the phenomenon described in the psychiatry journal article. Like the Scarecrow, Zsasz had written about his own disorder, disguising autobiography as learned treatise. And given his "dead soul," the pain and pleasure of Zsasz's slow self-cutting may well have provided the same "comforting affirmation of life" he theorized for others, typically young thin women.

And the scars may have conveyed even more significance, complex webs of meaning deliberately woven by an expert in all manner of psychic disorders.

The evidence was consistent at each of the first seven murder scenes. Spatters of his own blood led into the overall welter of his victim's blood. And from there, bloody footprints emerged in a different direction as he left the scene. This was proof that he cut himself before stabbing his victims. Bleeding was important to him, and it was important that he continued to bleed, if only slightly, while his victim completely bled out all over him.

Hinting at vampirism, it may have been enactment of an equally primal concept, that of usurping the power of one's enemy by consuming his heart. The simultaneous bleeding may have even been a way to claim a "trophy" or "token" of each kill, in this case a *living* trophy of death in the form of mingled blood. With each woman's blood permanently incorporated into Zsasz's own body, her death became part of his life, killer and victim forged together as blood siblings. With the scars to prove it.

First turning his knife on himself, Zsasz vicariously shared his victim's experience by "killing himself" just a little bit. It was the death wish suggested by Alfred. Many serial killers apparently harbor such a wish, although few to the point of actual death. More, as Alfred had said, is the pity. Any serial killer with a true death wish would spare the innocent and their survivors worlds of grief. Instead, Zsasz was inflicting his own "death by a thousand cuts," using his life to commit slow suicide through a long process of swift murder committed time and again.

The length of the scars suddenly struck me. Each was roughly an inch, with each group of four verticals tightly spaced so that even the fifth diagonal required only an inch to cross them. This dropped the puzzle's final piece, explaining each victim's fifth and final but nonfatal wound. The inch-long forehead slit, whether an "opening of the third eye" or not, served as a corresponding tally, a mate and a match for Zsasz's self-scoring of each kill.

I was too late to save his last victim, but time was still running out. Gordon would not hold back much longer. The safest and surest way to end the Butcher's spree would be to wait until Zsasz emerged from the cabin, then take him by surprise from behind just as he probably took his victims. But since he might not emerge until morning, I had to act now, had to find some way to penetrate the cabin with stealth. I decided to test the door. If it was locked, I would either pick it or try one of the other windows, then slip into the bedroom with at least some measure of surprise.

But even as I started to move away, Zsasz broke his trance and twisted from mirror to window. His right hand remained against his chest, as if pledging allegiance to past sin. He seemed to stare right at me, although it was impossible for him to see out through the lit room's window into darkness, let alone through the narrow curtain gap. I realized he was staring at something else, atop a dresser against the wall just below and to the left of the window. Then he stepped forward with a thin smile, fixed on that same point, eyes locked on something out of my sight. Wondering what it was and what he planned to do next, wanting to make sure he stayed in this room before I attempted to invade another, I held position.

He stopped just to the left of the window, only an arm's length through the wall, close enough to show which scars were faded and which were fresh. I saw one recent grouping of four upright cuts, not yet diagonally slashed, on his abdomen just above the loincloth. The fourth cut was barely healed, still scabbed. These, then, marked four Gotham victims.

His right hand finally slid from his chest and reached down out of view. I leaned to the right, mask pressed to the glass, but still couldn't see. The curtain slit was too narrow, the angle too extreme.

Zsasz seemed to hunch forward. His body shifted, then flinched and tensed still. I began to panic.

He stepped back fully into view, still hunched over, staring down at the sharp point of a butcher knife slowly cutting his abdomen, lightly scoring a red diagonal across the four freshest verticals. Most of the blood ran down the previous scars to soak his loincloth, but a single drop slid several inches along the knife blade before separating and falling straight down to splash a small perfect circle at his bare feet.

All around, the floor was spotted with older bloodstains.

Zsasz turned away, still holding the knife point pressed lightly to his own body, letting more blood run down the eight-inch blade to drip a trail of slightly elongated spatters as he crossed the bedroom. Toward the doorway to the next room, the one from whose window light had first spilled.

Bleeding was important to him, and it was important that he continued to bleed, if only slightly, while his victim completely bled out all over him.

Urgency, desperation, sleep deprivation, all had interfered with my thinking. But now full realization hit hard and all at once in a blinding flash. There were too many maggots on the gravel and in the trunk, too much scabbing on that fourth cut, with not enough time for either. The corpse in the trunk was an old body, the only one not yet found, not yet matched to the sole outstanding missing persons report, the one woman Gordon still hoped had merely run away. The only body Zsasz had been unable to dump, perhaps alerted by the team searching along the palisades road.

But if he had been scared away from the dumping site, he had not stopped his predation. Nor had the clock stopped ticking. The most recent victim had been abducted less than twenty-four hours ago. She was still alive, still held captive in the next room.

I surged up from the window, pulling the long, heavy Batarang from the back of my belt, and sprinted along the cabin.

The far window was also curtained and showed nothing inside. I took three steps back and launched myself forward, crashing through the glass and whipping the curtain aside before hitting the floor of the cabin's main room.

Zsasz was already through the doorway but still short of the woman suspended from the room's exposed crossbeam. I rolled across skittering glass and came up between the killer and his would-be victim.

The woman dangled utterly still, but there was no blood on the floor. Thinking she might be unconscious, I risked a quick glance and saw eyes wide with terror. Facedown in extreme contortion, she was probably spent from long struggle, no longer able to move. Some of her ribs, I knew from Gunt's autopsy, might be separated. Even dulled by shock, the pain would be severe. I wanted to free her at once. First I had to save her.

Already looking back at Zsasz, I spoke to the woman. "It's all right," I said. "Close your eyes."

If the killer seemed confused and uncertain, it was only for a second. Then he leered and rushed, butcher knife flinging blood as it swept high.

I used the Batarang to parry his downward slash. He followed with a kick, but I was already braced to block it with my shoulder. I kicked his chest while he was still off balance. He staggered back but kept his feet, still firmly grasping the knife.

I hurled the Batarang before he could recover, but his arm moved at the last second. The Batarang missed his wrist but smacked the knife, spinning it from his hand through the doorway behind him, back into the bedroom. The deflected Batarang bounced off the wall and clacked to the floor.

I started forward but held my ground when he squared his body into a familiar stance. He was about to unleash the same kata performed for the mirror, left twist-punch, right twist-punch, left thrust-kick. Knowing what to expect, I picked off all three strikes and countered with my own combination.

The first punch landed, left hook to the body, but he barely grunted as he slipped the second punch, a straight right to the jaw meant to drop him. Instead, it glanced off the top of his bald head and he stepped back barely fazed. I followed with a sweep-kick that missed completely as he leaped away to a nearby table. He snatched its lamp, brass-bottomed with a glass shade, and jerked the cord from the wall.

The room went nearly black, the only light now coming through the bedroom doorway. I heard the woman moan through her gag, then sensed Zsasz rushing forward and raised a forearm to shield my head. The lamp shattered just above my elbow, its shards pelting my mask. I slashed a flattened hand to chop his forearm. He dropped the broken lamp.

I stepped back, buying time for my eyes to adjust. Zsasz did not wait, barking a loud *ki* as he struck through the gloom. I felt the punch slam my throat, landing flush with full power. My vision blurred and another punch struck my forehead. I ducked down and rammed forward to smother the next blow, a kick to the ribs, then struck back at the dark form barely seen.

The punch missed a vital area, barely drawing a hiss from Zsasz as he countered immediately. The kick grazed the side of my cowl, followed by two more rapid-fire punches, both full and hard in my face. I twisted away and slipped free, needing time and distance to clear my head.

Zsasz was lashing out blindly and without pause, fighting with a speed nearly out of control. But while the frenzy would have been easily countered in full light, he had already dazed me in the gloom. I could not afford to take another solid blow, could not risk losing the fight, not while the woman still hung helpless in the dark. Letting Zsasz retrieve his butcher knife was not an option.

I felt air on my chin, driven by another kick just short, and dodged aside. Needing an edge fast, I angled toward the rectangle of light, trying to remember the unseen Batarang's position in relation to the bedroom doorway. Then, hearing Zsasz right behind, I dived into a long slide across the hardwood floor, outstretched arms spread wide. When the Batarang scuffed under my left shoulder, I dug it out and rolled to my feet. Zsasz pounded closer, coming fast.

I spun, slashing the Batarang at full arm's length. It hit Zsasz's skull hard. He yelped and I slashed backhand the other way, again cracking his head. A high kick whistled past my eyes and I slashed a third time. Another yelp as he jerked back. I used the respite to edge around, putting him between me and the rectangle of light.

When he was visible, I waited for his blind rush and smashed the Batarang across the bridge of his nose. He grabbed his face and screamed into his hands. I heard his blood spatter the floor.

It was working, light and the Batarang's greater reach giving me the advantage.

I closed to finish him. But then, whether he had suckered me or simply gone berserk, he exploded from pain into all-out rage, kicking the Batarang from my hand and then kicking the side of my head. I feinted back but moved forward, blocking his next punch and ducking the one after that. I kept driving forward until my forehead struck his chin, then dug a right hook deep into his stomach. He started to double over, but I jabbed his face back with a left and levered the right cross over and down from maximum distance. It spun him away and he hit the floor hard.

I could still see him, a dark bulk near the lit doorway. He started to rise, heaving himself to hands and knees. I kicked his gut as hard as I could. He collapsed and thrashed onto his back, right arm flailing into the doorway light. I stomped his hand and fell on him, straddling his chest and punching down into his face until I felt blood flying from my fist. I couldn't stop, punching long after his struggles halted. Then I groped for his ears, lifted his head, and bashed it back to the floor. He was out, utterly unmoving. I punched him three more times and rolled his dead weight facedown. Pulling one ankle and one wrist over the small of his back, I wrapped them with my line and cinched tight. Then I twisted his other wrist and ankle back, bound all four limbs together, cinched the line again, and tied it off.

Only then, breathing hard but feeling strong enough to toss a car, did I rise in the gloom and come to my senses. Never more alert on the animal level, I realized my mind and nerves had been stressed and strained to the breaking point. I'd come very close to snapping, losing everything to senseless rage. It shook me hard, until I remembered the woman.

I scanned my penlight until it found another lamp. When I switched it on, the woman's head twisted to face me, her eyes still wide.

There was no way to banish her trauma, but I tried to break through the fear. "It's over. You're safe now. Do you understand?"

She just stared.

"Forget how I look. I want to get you down, not hurt you. If you'll let me, I'll take you out of this place, away from here forever. Back to your home and your husband. All right?"

Finally, awkwardly, she nodded her head with a sound muffled by her gag. Without letting her see it, I took the small knife from its belt-pouch.

Then, standing under her and using one hand to arrest her fall, I sliced the thin-gauge clothesline with my other hand. After lowering her to the floor, I freed and soothed her as best I could. She said nothing when I removed the gag, seeming almost unaware of me, even unaware of herself. I tried to get her up to her feet, but her legs gave out immediately. Her eyes were still wide, her expression otherwise blank.

I massaged her wrists and told her to flex her hands. Her swollen fingers barely twitched. I rubbed her legs, but still she could not stand. Her entire body began to shake uncontrollably and her breathing quickened with a rhythmic whimper on each intake.

I left her on the floor and crossed to the bedroom doorway, checking Zsasz as I passed. He was still unconscious and would not be able to move even after he revived. I retrieved the fallen Batarang and tucked it back into my belt.

In the bedroom, I left the butcher knife on the floor, with Zsasz's fingerprints all over its grip, and pulled the blanket from his bed.

Then I wrapped the trembling woman and carried her outside to wait for the police.

She would probably never recover from the ordeal, not fully, but she was young and I knew she would get better. In time, entire days might pass unhaunted by the memory. It was the best I could give her.

Gravel crunched at the bottom of the driveway. Spinning lights flickered across Zsasz's car. I looked at its trunk and felt dead inside.

If Anton Zsasz had been killing the same woman over and over again, exacting proxy revenge on someone from his past as Alfred had proposed, he has not confirmed it thus far. Neither has he confessed to anything, in fact, nor discussed the crimes in any terms. When questioned, he rarely speaks at all. He simply smirks, slowly fingering his orange jumpsuit here and there, gently feeling different areas of his torso and limbs.

Likely destined for Arkham's Asylum for the Criminally Insane, he will perhaps begin talking there, psychiatrist to psychiatrist. He has a lot to explain, more to account for, and there is much to be learned from the darkness of his debased mind.

Wherever he is bound, whether to Arkham, Blackgate, or some other federal penitentiary, his journey will soon begin. He had been caught literally red-handed and his ongoing trial is unlikely to take much longer. Even though I can hardly testify in open court, the case is nevertheless open and shut. Its new evidence, all presented by Gordon's district attorney, none from the FBI, is overwhelming.

First is the right front tire from Zsasz's car, with its curved tread defect perfectly matching tire casts taken at several different dumping sites.

Then there is the corpse in the trunk of the car, forensically identified as the sole outstanding Gotham victim.

Blood traces also found in the trunk match at least twenty-nine previous victims from all five cities.

Soil samples from the shoes of the Gotham victims match the ground outside Zsasz's cabin.

Blade characteristics of the butcher knife found in Zsasz's bedroom precisely match every wound inflicted to numerous victims.

Prints lifted from the knife match Zsasz's fingers.

Zsasz's fingerprints also match those lifted from the first seven murder scenes in the Detroit area.

While Zsasz began shaving his head shortly after arriving in Miami, he is not naturally bald. Now growing out, his hair matches some of those harvested from the first seven scenes.

Fibers found at three of those scenes have been matched to shirts found in the cabin south of Gotham.

Bloody shoeprints leaving the Detroit murder scenes match a pair of shoes also found in the Gotham cabin. Blood soaked into their sole threads has been matched to the blood of four different Detroit victims.

Blood evidence harvested from the Detroit murder scenes, as well as from the Gotham cabin, has been genetically matched to Zsasz. The DNA evidence is conservatively assessed to have a statistical certainty of one in ten billion, at a time when six billion humans populate the earth.

Most damning of all is the testimony of the rescued woman. She seems to have the jury's full sympathy and is holding up remarkably well on the stand. If her voice quavers at times, it is always strong, even when she meets the defendant's piercing eyes.

Finally, of course, there is the living record of Zsasz's obsessive scorekeeping, a full confession written in hieroglyphic scars all over his own hide.

Case closed, putting an end to Anton Zsasz's unprecedented rampage of culling and cutting.

The Butcher is the most savage killer I have yet encountered, and almost certainly the worst I will ever hunt. Having done everything I could, as swiftly as possible, I still regret I could not stop Zsasz sooner.

The feeling is further incentive for my mission and good reason to renew my dedication to that mission's cause. It has only strengthened my determination to protect the innocent by apprehending every killer taking up gun, knife, or club. And to this end, I will employ all means at my disposal and every crime-fighting tool and technique available, from this moment through every dark night all the way to my own end.

Epilogue: Revealing the Hidden

From the Private Files of the Batman

IN Gotham, as elsewhere and everywhere, it will never end. Whatever its cause—poverty, madness, free will governed by flawed or corrupted human nature—the murders will not stop. Guilty criminals will continue to kill, and innocent victims will continue to die.

I can only prevent so much of it. Even as the Batman, I am just one man, whereas the demons are legion. Too many of them infest the darkness, and I cannot haunt its every shadow alone.

I've always known this, of course, even before giving dark wing to the secret mission. Nevertheless, I was determined to act, doing everything in my power to accomplish as much good as one man possibly can.

The decision was clearly made on a conscious level and carried out through sheer force of will, even as I instinctively knew all its dangers and suspected every risk of failure. Going it alone has not been easy, but I have managed to save lives. I have brought killers to heel and removed them from the street. Despite all the risks, I've done all I can and I have not failed. And yet, even more *could* be done. Help *would* help.

Alfred, of course, has proven invaluable. Without his efforts and assistance, any number of murderers might now remain at large. But Alfred must serve both of my personas, Bruce Wayne as well as the Batman, public face and secret mask. Given this double duty, then, performed at his age (as spry and vital as he is), Alfred must remain in place, more or less bound between the linked manor and cavern. In either location, I could ask for no one better. But beyond these two realms, however willing he may be, I can only ask so much of one man.

Which is the problem. In the manor, Alfred sustains the illusion of Bruce Wayne. In the cave, he helps the Batman prevent future murders. But it's in the field where another mind and extra hands might help to save more lives in the moment. I need help in the shadows, on the rooftops, at the fresh scenes of recent crimes, during the chase.

Looking back, I suspect that I have compiled these case-files with the prospect of such future help in mind, at least in the back of my mind, foreseeing the possibility of sharing whatever I've learned, both from early studies and later experience. That possibility has now unexpectedly arisen.

I have, in fact, been given the opportunity to affect a life, to mentor a protégé, perhaps train a new aide or even partner. He is someone whose present circumstance duplicates my own dark past. That past shaped my future.

He is still young, as young as I was, and he has just lost his parents to murder, as I lost mine. That he has been orphaned by such similar horror and tragedy is a coincidence that will shape his own future, one way or another, for good or ill. There is one key difference between us, however. He lacks an Alfred to fall back on, surely tipping the scale away from good.

And so Alfred and I have already initiated legal efforts to provide him with a new home as the ward of Bruce Wayne, if not the Batman.

He knows me as both, although he is not yet aware that the two are one and the same. He may never know it. If I decide to offer him certain choices, I will urge him toward nothing he does not choose.

Even with an entire police force at his disposal, Commissioner Gordon quickly recognized the value of unofficial and unorthodox assistance. Alone night after night in the darkness, I have finally come to this same recognition. And help is not the whole of it.

While I can never oppose murder nearly enough, I deal with death far too often, seeing too much darkness, not enough light. In that sense, I have already been helped by my future ward. He is good and decent, providing contrast and balance. As youth and life, he represents hope for the future, as well as all the other reasons I choose to risk everything in the shadows.

His mind is sharp and quick. Whatever he learns, he will learn it well.

He comes from the circus, already an accomplished acrobat. Even a daredevil.

His name is Dick Grayson.

Bibliography

Baden, Michael M. *Unnatural Death: Confessions of a Medical Examiner*. New York: Random House, 1989.

Evans, Colin. *The Casebook of Forensics Detection*. New York: John Wiley & Sons, Inc., 1996.

Ferllini, Roxana. *Silent Witness*. Buffalo, NY: Firefly Books, 2002.

Helpern, Milton. *Autopsy*. New York: St. Martin's Press, 1977.

Innes, Brian. *Bodies of Evidence*. Pleasantville, NY: Reader's Digest, 2000.

Lee, Dr. Henry C. *Cracking Cases*. Amherst, NY: Prometheus Books, 2002.

Lewis, Alfred Allan. *The Evidence Never Lies*. New York: Holt, Rinehart and Winston, 1984.

Maples, William R. *Dead Men Do Tell Tales*. New York: Doubleday, 1994.

Noguchi, Thomas T. *Coroner*. New York: Pocket Books, 1984.

Noguchi, Thomas T. *Coroner at Large*. New York: Pocket Books, 1986.

Owen, David. *Hidden Evidence*. Buffalo, NY: Firefly Books, 2000.

Platt, Richard. *Crime Scene*. New York: DK Books, 2003.

Sachs, Jessica Snyder. *Corpse*. Cambridge, MA: Perseus Publishing, 2001.

Smith, Sir Sydney. *Mostly Murder*. London: Grafton Books, 1984.

Ubelaker, Dr. Douglas and Henry Scammell. *Bones*. New York: HarperCollins Publishers, 1992.

Wecht, Cyril. *Cause of Death*. New York: Dutton, 1993.

Wecht, Cyril. *Grave Secrets*. New York: Dutton, 1996.

Weiss, Peter. "A Shot in the Light." *Science News*, January 11, 2003.

Wensley, Frederick Porter. *Forty Years of Scotland Yard*. Garden City, NY: Doubleday, Doran, & Company, Inc., 1933.